A BLINDING SHAFT OF PURE WHITE LIGHT FLASHED ABOVE THE VILLAGE

In the blink of an eye, the lead rocket exploded. The swiftness of this attack had barely registered in Tanya's consciousness, when the second cruise missile burst in a fiery cloud.

"Good heavens," her uncle whispered, "they've finally done it! For the first time ever, a surprise nuclear strike can be undertaken with little risk of a counterstrike. The entire balance of military power will be upset. World War Three is all but inevitable!"

Tanya shivered uncontrollably. She knew she would do whatever Lev asked to get knowledge of this momentous event to their contact in the West.

She could only pray it wasn't too late.

WHEN DUTY CALLS

BOOK YOUR PLACE ON OUR WEBSITE AND MAKE THE READING CONNECTION!

We've created a customized website just for our very special readers, where you can get the inside scoop on everything that's going on with Zebra, Pinnacle and Kensington books.

When you come online, you'll have the exciting opportunity to:

- View covers of upcoming books
- Read sample chapters
- Learn about our future publishing schedule (listed by publication month *and author*)
- Find out when your favorite authors will be visiting a city near you
- Search for and order backlist books from our online catalog
- Check out author bios and background information
- Send e-mail to your favorite authors
- Meet the Kensington staff online
- Join us in weekly chats with authors, readers and other guests
- Get writing guidelines
- AND MUCH MORE!

Visit our website at http://www.zebrabooks.com

WHEN DUTY CALLS

RICHARD P. HENRICK

Zebra Books
Kensington Publishing Corp.

http://www.zebrabooks.com

ZEBRA BOOKS are published by

Kensington Publishing Corp.
850 Third Avenue
New York, NY 10022

Zebra and the Z logo Reg. U.S. Pat. & TM Off.

Third Zebra Printing: June, 2000
10 9 8 7 6 5 4 3

Printed in the United States of America

"We shall have to man the majority of submarines with very young recruits. Youth is no shortcoming, when there is real manhood within. Youth is unencumbered, youth is healthy. But their training must be all the more thorough, and it is all the more important that the quality of human material recruited into the Navy be of the highest."

—Karl Donitz, Commander in Chief of the Greater German Reich's submarine forces, October 8, 1943.

"Now victory or defeat in war will depend on how the State will be able to reliably protect important objectives on their own territory from destruction by strikes from the air and out of space."

—Soviet Marshal of Aviation Georgi V. Zimin, Commandant of the Zhukov Military Command Academy of Air Defense, 1976.

"All of us are now approaching a point of no return at which a new stage of the arms race might begin, with unpredictable military and political consequences."

—Soviet Premier Mikhail S. Gorbachev, following the breakup of the Icelandic Summit, October 12, 1986.

CHAPTER ONE

The dawn broke cold and gray. Roused from his hard cot by the shrill cry of the bosun's pipe, Chief Helmut Keller stirred groggily. It took him several seconds to reorient himself.

His sleep had been sound and dreamless. This seemed almost always to be the case on those rare occasions when he slept on solid land. Keller was more accustomed to the rolling pitch of the open seas, and knew that he'd be returning to that all too soon.

Aware of the muted grumblings of his awakening shipmates, the twenty-three-year-old chief engineer sat up stiffly. The barracks were lit by a single kerosene lantern. In the dim illumination he could see his icy breath in front of his face. Even though he had been stationed there for three months now, he still found himself unable to adjust to the harsh Norwegian climate. Mornings were the worst. Heated by a pot-bellied, coal-burning stove that was allowed to go out at night, the barrack was at its most inhospitable at reveille. Because the structure housed twenty-three others, it was to Keller's advantage to be among the first to make use of the cramped head. With this in mind, he slid his legs off the mattress.

The bare concrete floor seemed as cold as the frozen permafrost that lay outside. After slipping on his boots, he yawned, scratched his thickly bearded chin, then rose, still clothed only in his stained longjohns. His fellow sailors were just peeping from their blankets as he silently shuffled off into the still-vacant bathroom.

A string of six bare lightbulbs hung from the head's ceiling. Helmut triggered the switch, and momentarily shielded his eyes from the harsh light that followed. With a wide yawn, he turned to relieve himself at the cracked, porcelain urinal. Once his bladder was emptied, he walked over to the sink.

The hot-water tap had never worked properly since they had arrived at the Norwegian base, yet he tried it anyway. The water pipes coughed alive, and spat forth their usual trickle of rust-colored, icy-cold liquid. Thankful for the luxury of lye soap, he scrubbed his hands, neck, and face. After washing out his mouth with a handful of water, he reached for one of the room's well-worn linen towels. It was while drying off his beard that he noticed a single gray hair protruding from the thick red mass that covered his right cheek. Peering intently into the mirror, Helmut grabbed the silver whisker at its base and yanked it loose. He studied it under the bare light, and shook his head in amazement. Here he was barely twenty-three years old, and already he was turning gray!

Helmut studied his reflection in the mirror that

was hung above the sink as if viewing it for the very first time. A full, fiery red beard tended to veil a rather plain face. His hair was the same color as his whiskers, and was cut in a short, spiky style.

Other than his unique hair color, the one other facial feature that separated him from most of his shipmates was the color of his eyes. Like crystal-blue pools, his pupils had an almost hypnotic look. His mother had always said that Helmut's eyes captured the color of the alpine sky itself. Helmut wasn't sure. He knew they were greatly admired by the ladies.

As he scanned his solid six-foot physique, he saw just a hint of alien fat around his midsection. What he needed was a good workout in the shipyards. That would get him back in shape quickly enough. Unfortunately, his present duty allowed for little physical conditioning. Submarines were sedentary environments. No wonder he felt like an old man.

Helmut yawned again. His thoughts were interrupted when another individual entered the room behind him. Visible in the mirror, this familiar skinny figure turned for the urinal. He yanked down his longjohns, noisily cleared his nose, and then spoke out.

"Well now, Herr Keller, you certainly are up with the chickens. Perhaps you miss the rolling pitch of the deck, or maybe it's the scent of diesel oil that you long for."

Helmut was used to the torpedo man's dry sense of humor. "You hit the nail right on the head, Hans. To those of us who are born with salt water in our veins, it's solid land that's alien."

9

"Then why don't you ask the Captain to allow you to sleep on board? I'm certain that he would be most accommodating," Hans Meyer quipped.

Helmut couldn't help but smile. "Next time, perhaps I'll take your advice, Herr Meyer. A fellow could get used to this soft life all too easily."

"Not a hard fish like you," retorted the torpedo man. Helmut turned to leave the bathroom. As the red-headed chief ducked out of the doorway, Hans Meyer's voice rose. "Don't forget to save me a bratwurst, Helmut!"

Chief Keller returned to his cot and dressed himself. Around him, several of the men were still stirring from beneath their blankets, while a silent, disheveled line of sailors had risen and was pointing itself toward the head. Glad that he had beaten them to it, Helmut made the final adjustments on his uniform, pulled on his greatcoat, fumbled for his muffler and gloves, and proceeded towards the barrack's sole exit.

Outside, the cold hit him with a breathtaking slap. Helmut pulled up the collar of his woolen coat in response. The Arctic dawn barely colored the desolate landscape. Hidden by thick fingers of grayish fog, the series of snow-covered hills that encircled the town were barely visible. Ever present was the ripe scent of the sea. A lonely gull cried from above, and Helmut began his way down the narrow, winding path that would take him to the mess hall. Careful to avoid the slick patches of ice that coated much of the walkway, he found his thoughts solely centered on his empty stomach. Only when he passed a group of local fishermen, busily working on their nets, did the direction of his thinking change.

How long had it been since he had been immersed in such an innocent, mindless task? Though it seemed like a lifetime ago, Helmut knew otherwise. Born in the coastal village of Bremerhaven, he had spent most of his boyhood learning the ways of the fishermen. This had been his family's occupation for generations past. Not one to break with tradition, he gratefully allowed his father to become his mentor. The youngster all too soon showed a natural talent for repairing their trawler's well-worn engines. By the age of thirteen, he could overhaul them all by himself.

Knowing little else but the sea and its ways, Helmut grew into manhood. It was in 1939 that his father was conscripted into the Navy. Before that, he had paid little attention to the rise of the Nazis and the vast changes they were bringing along with them. A year later, the notice arrived informing him that his father was missing in action somewhere in the North Sea. Helmut had little time to mourn, for his own conscription orders were soon served.

A wealth of new experience awaited him as he boarded the train for the ride to bootcamp at Kiel. This was his first trip outside of the village of his birth, and he looked at the passing countryside with awe. It didn't take long for the loss of his father to be forgotten. After an intensive four-week training period, he was sent to a nearby shipyard. His mechanical expertise was noted, and he was named a foreman in the Navy's fledgling U-boat construction program.

Helmut not only enjoyed his contact with the other men, but also derived great satisfaction from watching the fruits of his labor take to sea. For three busy years he was thus occupied, until new orders sent him packing for Saint-Nazaire, France.

The year 1943 saw the peak of the U-boat war in the North Atlantic. Helmut was to get a taste of the excitement firsthand, for his assignment was in the engine room of a war-going submarine. He had been there ever since.

A savage gust of icy wind smacked Helmut head on, and the twenty-three-year-old chief engineer pulled his collar tight, in a vain attempt to counter it. Well aware of the strange course of events that had led him to this godforsaken Norwegian valley, Helmut carefully traversed a particularly slippery portion of walkway, and entered the corrugated steel structure that housed the mess hall.

The relief was instantaneous. The interior of the mess hall was warm and smelled of frying meats and coffee. After hanging up his coat, he entered the dining room and found its dozen or so long tables occupied by a mere handful of fellow sailors. An intense-looking, blond-haired officer, who was sitting alone, caught Helmut's stare and motioned him over. The red-heated chief nodded in response and turned to hit the cafeteria-style serving line.

To satisfy his gnawing appetite, Helmut chose a bowl of oat porridge, a pair of hard-boiled eggs, a fat, white-skinned bratwurst sausage, some fried potatoes, a crusty chunk of caraway rye bread, and a piping hot mug of black tea. Careful not to upset the balance of his well-stacked tray, he made his way over to his blond-haired shipmate.

Karl Hirsacker was U-313's second in command. A grizzled veteran at the age of twenty-five, the bespectacled lieutenant was known for his quiet efficiency. A loner by instinct, he remained generally detached from the crew, preferring to keep his thoughts and emotions to himself whenever possible.

On their last patrol, a close miss by a British depth charge had sent a torrent of surging seawater into the U-boat's stern compartment. It was then that Helmut had found himself working side by side with the introverted officer, who proved to be as brave as he was resourceful. They had split a bottle of beer afterwards. Though few actual words were passed between them, the shared tragedy had provided grounds for a common understanding. That was why Helmut really wasn't surprised that Hirsacker had beckoned him to have breakfast at his side.

"Good morning, Herr Lieutenant," greeted the chief, as he set his tray down on the wooden-slat table. "It appears that we have quite an excellent choice this morning."

A single, half-filled bowl of porridge lay beside the lieutenant. Taking in the assortment of bowls and dishes that Helmut Keller was positioning before him, Hirsacker commented, "I'm glad to see that someone around here enjoys the local cooking. For my taste, it's much too heavy."

Helmut responded between mouthfuls of porridge. "Hearty's the word for it, sir. The way this damned climate saps all the heat from you, filling your belly is the only way to get even. I guess it's

13

just like feeding a furnace with coal in the wintertime. Run low on your supply and the entire house
will soon enough go cold."

After utilizing a crust of bread to sop up the last
remnants of hot cereal, Helmut went to work on his
eggs and potatoes. Watching him shovel in this food,
the lieutenant was somewhat repulsed.

"Oh, what I wouldn't give for a real croissant and
a decent cup of cafe au lait," Hirsacker mused
dreamily.

"Sounds like somebody still has France on his
mind," Helmut offered between bites of rye bread.
"To tell you the truth, that French cuisine was tasty
enough, but not too satisfying. I'll take a plump
sausage any day of the week. Now, this is food that
sticks with a man!"

Cutting into his bratwurst, Helmut savored the
rising steam like a true gourmet. Oblivious to the
juicy grease that was soon streaming down the sides
of his mouth and merging with his beard, the chief
devoured the sausage in less than a minute. He was
still thoughtfully chewing the last bite when he
swallowed a mouthful of tea. To insure that he didn't
leave anything behind, he then proceeded to mop up
his dish with the remnants of the rye bread. This was
followed by another sip of tea and a hearty burp.

"Ah, now that's eating!" observed the contented
chief. With his half-filled mug in hand, Helmut
momentarily caught the lieutenant's serious gaze of
inspection. Diverting his glance, the chief looked
down to the empty plates that sat before him.

"I really think that you should try eating more, sir.
It will make the cold that much more bearable."

"Thank you for your concern, Herr Keller," Hirsacker replied. "But I will manage. Besides, I dislike putting to sea on a full stomach."

"Then we're still proceeding as planned?" Helmut asked.

U-313's second in command waited almost a full minute before answering. "That we are, chief. Captain Eisenbach informs me that the final preparations remain right on schedule. We should be ready to set sail with the arrival of the morning tide."

A look of relief painted Helmut's face. "That's certainly good news. I was beginning to wonder if we'd ever get to sea again before the war's conclusion."

"What do you mean by that statement?" Hirsacker questioned sharply.

Ignoring the confused stare of his immediate superior, Helmut dared to fully express himself. "Come now, Herr Hirsacker. It's common knowledge that the end of the Reich is imminent. Allied troops have surrounded Berlin. It indeed appears that our esteemed Fuhrer has displayed his last miracle. Not even Admiral Donitz can save him now."

"Such talk is pure defeatism," the blond-haired lieutenant said angrily. "Besides, it's also mere speculation. I heard told a completely different story. At last report, the SS had launched a massive counterattack. Even the brave Americans were seen running."

Meeting the lieutenant's gaze straight on, Helmut merely shrugged his shoulders. "Perhaps that is true, but it still doesn't cover up the fact that the Reich is finished. Wake up, lieutenant, and quit deceiving yourself."

Blushing with anger, the senior officer strained to contain himself. "Your impertinence is noted, Herr Keller. Of all my shipmates, I had expected much better from you. Your confused babbling reeks of cowardice. In these dark days, the Reich deserves our total effort, now more than ever before. For as long as a single fighting unit still exists, Germany will continue its brave struggle. This includes U-313. Our sub will do its best to continue to fight to the very end, whatever the outcome."

"Please don't confuse my personal opinion with cowardice," Helmut said passionately. "It is my duty as a German soldier to obey the orders of my commanding officers. I will continue to do so without question. I just find it hard to fathom how effective our U-boat can be in this so-called final offensive with its load of torpedoes removed."

"Who told you such a thing?" shot back the red-faced officer.

Surprised at the torrent of emotion he had generated from the usually mild-mannered lieutenant, Helmut answered cautiously. "It would take a blind man not to notice the strange preparations currently taking place aboard our vessel. Scuttlebutt has it that the torpedo crew's last official task, before being ordered off the sub yesterday, was to remove the spare torpedoes. What way is that to fight a winning war?"

"Gossip is for old women, Herr Keller," Hirsacker countered. "You will be happy to know that U-313 currently carries a torpedo in each of her five available tubes. So you see, we do have some sting left after all."

"But why take off the other spares?"

The senior officer smiled. "Patience, chief. I have it right from the Captain's mouth that all of us will be fully briefed of our upcoming mission as soon as we hit the open sea." Looking down at his pocket watch, he added. "Do you think that you can wait another three hours?"

As he realized that Hirsacker most likely knew just as little as any other crew member, Helmut's face lightened. "Of course I can, Herr Lieutenant. Please pardon my impertinence."

"Your apology is duly noted, chief," returned the blond-haired second in command as he pushed back his chair and stood. "Now I must gather together the latest navigational charts. See you at the docks."

Nodding goodbye, Helmut Keller reflectively sipped his lukewarm tea. So intense had been the conversation that he only now realized that several other shipmates had entered the room and were well into their breakfasts. The chief belched up the taste of greasy sausage, and reflected on what had just happened.

He found himself surprised that he had divulged his knowledge of the torpedoes' removal. Hans Meyer had begged him to keep this to himself. What he didn't reveal was a report of an even stranger nature. Last night, when one of the men had tried to return to the sub to pick up a forgotten pipe, he had found himself abruptly turned away by an armed squadron of SS guards. Though he hadn't been allowed near the docks, he had managed to catch a brief glimpse of the flurry of activity taking place

17

there. He had been able to briefly view a line of covered transport trucks lit by a bank of powerful portable spotlights. Emptying their interiors of dozens of rectangular wooden crates had been a large number of laborers. The puzzled submariner could only assume that these crates were being loaded directly into the hold of U-313.

If this were indeed the case, what could they possibly contain? And why go on a patrol at all, with a load of only five torpedoes to attack with? Hopeful that he'd soon know the answers to these questions and much more, Helmut Keller rose to refill his mug.

U-313 was one of the newest submarines in the German fleet. The vessel, 220 feet long from its sharply edged bow to its tapered stern, was designed as the ultimate attack platform. Unlike previous classes of submarines that had had extremely limited underwater capabilities, U-313 was one of the first of its kind to be equipped with a snorkel. This novel device allowed the sub's various mechanical systems to "breathe," even while the hull rode beneath the ocean's surface. Two powerful diesel engines gave it a surface speed of well over eighteen knots. While it was submerged, a pair of battery-run motors was engaged. Though the resulting speed was significantly cut down in this mode, near-silent operations could be achieved.

From the exposed bridge of the vessel, Captain Gunther Eisenbach looked out over the black hull of his boat and watched his crew approach the docks.

No line of pretty, flower-carrying maidens or smartly suited political dignitaries greeted them at the pier. Only a solemn squad of armed SS troopers was visible. How different this was from their departures in France. At that time they had had the inspirational sounds of a military band to send them off. On this frigid morning, they only had the slap of the waves and the cries of the gulls for accompaniment.

Eisenbach took a deep draw on his cigar and scratched his scraggly salt-and-pepper beard. Dressed in a well-worn, gray leather jacket, he barely noticed when an icy gust of wind blew in from the northwest. His inner thoughts were totally focused on the strange mission he was about to undergo. Fresh from a briefing with Admiral Donitz's personal representative, the thirty-seven-year-old Captain knew just what was expected of him. As always, he would do his best to not let the admiral down.

As he watched the last of his men somberly approach U-313, Eisenbach contemplated how vastly different this mission would be from the dozen previous patrols he had completed. For the first time ever, he would not be on the offensive. Of course, that could be said of their previous series of patrols as well. During that time, they had not released a single torpedo. This wasn't for lack of targets. Since the Allied D-Day invasion, the North Atlantic had been bustling with convoys. The trick was getting within firing range.

For the last twelve months, the success of the U-boat effort had been steadily deteriorating. This was in vast contrast to the earlier days of the war, when the seas were theirs to do with as they pleased. Since then, new Allied tactics had abruptly turned the tide, and now it was the U-boat that was hunted.

Radar, sonar, and sophisticated radio-intercept methods were the tools the enemy was using to decimate the German submarine fleet. Eisenbach couldn't begin to count the numbers of seagoing acquaintances he had lost these last two years. Gone was the cocky confidence that had dominated earlier missions. In its place was the gnawing fear that the U-boat was nothing better than an iron coffin.

Command had recognized the reversal of their fortunes but was slow to react. Modern vessels such as the Type XII class boat he was presently in command of were too little, too late. Eisenbach could only hope that the so-called super-weapon that his superiors had hinted at would soon be available. Otherwise, Germany would be forced to capitulate.

A patter of footsteps echoed off the steel-latticed catwalk behind him, and the Captain pivoted. Standing there alertly was his blond-haired lieutenant.

"Permission to report, sir. All hands present and accounted for. Engine room ready, upper and lower decks cleared for departure."

"Very good, Herr Hirsacker," returned Gunther Eisenbach. "Send the men to their stations and see us out of the harbor. We have many miles to travel and must get underway at once."

A proud smile etched the lieutenant's face as he nodded and turned to do the Captain's bidding. Eisenbach looked up, and took a last look at the pier and the town beyond. Oblivious to the still-gusting winds, the line of SS troopers stood like robots. Behind them, a rugged group of fishermen approached their battered trawlers. The fog momentarily lifted, and he could clearly view the ridge of snow-covered hills that circled the city. Bleak and desolate, they somehow provided a home for a brave, industrious people who would exist long after the Germans had gone. Grunting in awareness, Gunther took a draw on his cigar and redirected his gaze as the sub's whistle cried out shrilly, once long and twice short. This was followed by the firm voice of the lieutenant.

"Let go aft! Haul in the stern line!'

Eisenbach watched as the mooring lines were pulled in and neatly coiled. Several seamen stood on the foredeck with boathooks in hand, to keep U-313's bow free from any obstacles as the final group of fenders were withdrawn.

Again the lieutenant called out firmly. "Hard aport! Starboard engine ahead one-third!"

Slowly, the boat surged away from the pier. Satisfied that Hirsacker was competent enough to get them safely to open waters, the Captain allowed him the honor of seeing them out into the open ocean. He would be relying on his junior lieutenant greatly during the long voyage that was to follow. Thus it was important that he continued to build his confidence whenever possible.

"Lookout party to the bridge!" Hirsacker ordered.

In response, three heavily bundled seamen, with binoculars in hand, emerged beside the Captain. Each man gave a salute and immediately took up his station. They wasted no time before scanning the horizon for any sign of danger.

Only a week ago, a U-boat had been attacked by an enemy bomber as it entered this very harbor. The men were well aware of this and took extra care to scan the gray skies above them. Confident in their diligence and young eyes, Eisenbach began mentally preparing the briefing he would soon share with the boat's officers.

Meanwhile, below deck, the rest of the sub's fifty-man complement busily went about their duties. Helmut Keller's first watch sent him to the control room. There he went about the tedious task of checking the vessel's all-important hydraulics systems.

The solidly built, red-headed chief found himself genuinely happy to be back at sea. Though it certainly had it discomforts, sub duty was the Navy's most elite assignment. Once one got used to the cramped quarters and all, each day offered a new challenge. They were completely self-reliant. If a vital system went down, they had to fix it using whatever means were available. All fuel, food, spare parts, and ammunition lay packed within their hull. Until their patrol was over, they would have to make do with what they presently carried.

Helmut was in the process of inspecting the pressure of the diving planes when an icy hand tapped him on the shoulder. Turning, the Chief set his eyes on the familiar skinny figure of Hans Meyer. It was evident that something serious was bothering him.

"What in the heavens is the matter, Herr Meyer? You look as if you've just had a run-in with the devil himself. Did the mess hall run out of bratwurst before you arrived this morning?"

"It's not that, chief," whispered Meyer. "I tell you, something strange is happening on this boat. You wouldn't believe what we're carrying in the forward torpedo room."

"I'll bet a month's pay that it has something to do with those crates Gustav saw being unloaded at the docks last night," Helmut guessed.

The torpedo man nodded. "That's just part of it. The bow compartment is so filled with those rectangular wooden containers that one can barely pass between them. They completely fill the torpedo storage compartment and extend well into the crew's sleeping area."

"Any idea as to what lies inside them?" quizzed the chief.

Hans Meyer sighed. "I was just preparing to see for myself, when I found myself forcefully pulled away. I turned, and saw a uniformed figure standing before me. A Jap! Now why do you suppose that we'd be taking along a Jap? And what right does this Nip have to manhandle me right in the midst of my own compartment?"

Before Helmut could attempt an answer, the hatch leading to the conning tower opened above them. The distinct odor of cigar smoke wafted downwards. Seconds later, the Captain could be seen, climbing down the iron rungs of the ladder. His cheeks were red and he slapped his hands together before setting his eyes on the two men who stood beside the diving controls.

"Good morning, Chief Keller, Herr Meyer. I hope I'm not disturbing something."

Helmut knew their Captain to be a straightforward officer and addressed him directly. "Not at all, Herr Captain. Hans was only telling me of the stranger he encountered in the forward compartment. Is it true that we're carrying a Jap on board?"

Without hesitation, the Captain answered, "Actually, there are two of them here. Don't look so surprised. After all, they are our allies. Next, you'll be wanting me to explain the nature of the cargo we're presently carrying. Though even *I* don't know what's inside those crates, if you'll join me in the petty officers' galley, I'll be explaining to the crew just where we're bound for. Does that satisfy your curiosity a bit?"

"Of course, sir," Helmut responded.

"Good," said the Captain. "Now please round up the others. I want to complete this briefing as soon as possible."

Without further comment, Captain Eisenbach turned toward the stern and disappeared out the rear hatchway. Before the chief could do likewise, he mulled over the foreboding words of Hans Meyer.

"It doesn't take much imagination to guess where we're headed, my friend. My gut tells me that the U-313 is bound for the Orient."

Helmut Keller was surprised to find that Japan was indeed their ultimate destination. The Captain's official briefing was concise and to the point. It had apparently been Admiral Donitz himself who had picked the U-313 for this mission. Loaded within their hold was a top-secret assortment of war materials. It was of the utmost importance that this freight reach the Far East quickly, for the very outcome of the war could hinge on the delivery. Gunther Eisenbach then went on to introduce their passengers.

The two trim figures who soon stood before them wore the uniforms of the Japanese Imperial Army. Both men were officers and had been studying in Germany, the personal guests of none other than Adolf Hitler.

The Captain told the crew to stay well clear of the precious cargo. The two Japanese were in charge of making certain that the crates remained intact. They were armed with Lugers, and authorized to shoot if they so desired.

As this warning was delivered, the deck began to pitch quite violently. It was evident they had finally entered the open ocean. Deciding to skip the normal test dive that usually took place at this point, the Captain ordered the men back to their stations. With practiced efficiency they went to their posts thinking about the call that was sending them to the other side of the planet.

Three days later, while U-313 was passing off the southern coast of Ireland, an incident occurred that impressed the crew with just how serious their mission was. Helmut Keller had just completed an exhausting twelve-hour stint in the engine room. A bearing in the number-two diesel had gone bad, and it had taken an entire day to repair. Coated with grease and oil, the chief was headed straight for his bunk when the deep-throated gong signaling battle stations sounded. Since his assigned station was in the control room, Helmut wasted no time crossing the series of narrow, equipment-packed passageways that led to the sub's nerve center. He arrived in time to see the bridge watch climbing down from the exposed sail. Their oilskins still bristling with seawater, the seamen, who were led by the Captain, went right to the hydroplanes.

It was Chief Keller's job as diving officer to insure that U-313 was ready to submerge. The order to stop the diesels had been conveyed to the engine room by a series of hand signals. Helmut could picture the engineers in action as they efficiently stopped the flow of diesel oil into the engines. At the same time, the exhaust and air intakes would be sealed. Then the energy stored in their batteries would be tapped to power the electric motors.

A pair of signals were flashed at the chief, and he called out to the Captain. "Ready to dive, sir!"

With his slicker still dripping water, Eisenbach shouted, "Flood vents!"

After repeating this order, Chief Keller made certain that the sailors responsible for this task did their job properly. As they hit the various valves, the compartment filled with the bellowing roar of venting air. This would make room for onrushing seawater that would fill the ballast tanks from below and drag them down.

At the same time, the hydroplane operators set the forward and after planes down. The bow dipped in response and a final wave crushed against the exposed bridge. Seconds later, a hushed silence signaled that they were safely under the ocean's surface.

"Proceed to periscope depth!" ordered the Captain, who only now stripped off his oilskin. As Eisenbach headed towards the periscope well, he added. "Sound man, do you hear anything up there?"

The sailor responsible for monitoring the listening devices implanted in the sub's hull answered from the tiny cubicle where he was seated. "I'm picking up various screw sounds, Captain! Sonic bearing two hundred fifty degrees."

Grunting in response, Eisenbach turned the periscope to 250 degrees, then pushed it slowly upwards. His back was still hunched forward as the lens broke the ocean's surface.

"Damn it to hell!" cursed the Captain, who intently peered out the eyepiece. "Of all the infernal times."

From the diving console, Helmut Keller heard this puzzling statement. He looked on as Lieutenant Hirsacker approached the Captain's side. Though the blond-haired officer spoke softly, his words were clearly heard throughout the compartment.

"What's the matter, Captain?"

Eisenbach studied the surrounding seas for another thirty seconds before backing away. "Take a glance for yourself, lieutenant. Just look at the size of that convoy!"

Karl Hirsacker bent down and placed his forehead against the eyepiece. It didn't take him long to spot the dozens of surface ships that had caught Eisenbach's attention.

"Why, there must be at least fifty of them!"

exclaimed the startled lieutenant. "Not only are they not zigzagging, but I don't even see any destroyer escorts. Shall I set up a firing angle, Captain? At least we can take out several of the largest vessels."

All eyes were on the Captain as Hirsacker backed away from the periscope to await his commanding officer's response. An eternity seemed to pass before Eisenbach's voice broke the strained silence.

"Down scope. There will be no attack."

"But, Captain," pleaded the lieutenant. "They are just sitting ducks up there. I'm certain that we could get away our torpedoes without them knowing exactly where we were. We could be back on our route southward in less than a quarter of an hour's time."

"I said that there will be no attack!" shouted the Captain firmly. "Now, that's enough of your impertinence, lieutenant, for the matter is closed. We will continue submerged until the convoy has passed. Then we shall ascend and continue at speed once more. Is that clear, Herr Hirsacker?"

Nodding his head dejectedly, the junior officer responded. "Yes, Captain. Your intentions are understood."

"That's more like it," observed Eisenbach, who turned towards the diving console. "Chief Keller, please inform me when we have these waters all to ourselves. I'll be in my quarters if needed."

"Yes, Sir," snapped the chief, as he watched the Captain duck through the forward hatchway.

With Eisenbach's exit, the tense atmosphere inside the control room noticeably lightened. Keller crossed the compartment to approach the sound cubicle. As he passed the periscope well, he met the bespectacled gaze of Hirsacker.

"They are just sitting up there, ripe for the pickings," mumbled the junior officer idly. "How could he pass up such a shot?"

Helmut could sense that Hirsacker's nerves were strained and answered carefully. "There's nothing that you can do about it now, sir. I'm certain that the Captain has his reasons. The Skipper loves a fight just as much as any of us. It must have hurt him to pass up this chance as well."

"No wonder Germany's losing the war." Hirsacker spat. "Why Command is wasting us on delivery duty is beyond me. We're a first-line man-of-war. Holding the U-313 back like this is inexcusable!"

Not knowing what else to say, Helmut patted his shipmate on the shoulder. Silently, the lieutenant looked up and met his gaze. Managing a bare smile, Hirsacker inhaled a deep breath and turned to get on with his duty. As the chief continued on to the sound room, he realized that their present mission had to have more to it than met the eye. Surely Admiral Donitz wouldn't waste them on a meaningless trip halfway around the world for nothing.

Two days later, as the morning of May 7, 1945 dawned off the coast of central France, U-313 continued its dash southward. The weather was mild, the air clear and warm with spring. From the exposed bridge, Helmut Keller was taking his turn as watch officer. The young lookout assigned to scan the eastern horizon was having problems seeing through the glare of the rising sun. The chief was giving the youngster a hand with his difficult assignment when he noticed the small advancing aircraft headed straight toward them. His heartbeat pounded rapidly in his chest as he identified this vehicle as an RAF Mosquito.

"Enemy aircraft! Dive! Dive! Dive!"

The Chief's frantic words of warning had their desired effect as the team of lookouts sprinted for the hatch. The last man inside the sail was Keller. The drone of the Mosquito's engine was clearly audible as he spun the hatch shut above him. This was followed by the staccato blast of the fighter's machine guns. The bow of the sub was already angled downward, toward the safety of the ocean's depths, when the chief climbed down into the control room. Waiting for him, at the bottom of the stairway, was Gunther Eisenbach.

"Sorry about that, Captain," said the breathless chief. "But he came right out of the sun. It's a miracle that I saw him when I did."

Shifting the well-chewed butt of his cigar from one corner of his mouth to the other, the Captain nodded. "It's not your fault, chief. Let's just button this little lady down in case that airplane is carrying a depth bomb."

Eisenbach turned and shouted toward the diving station. "Bring us down to two hundred feet! Secure the boat for depth charging!"

While the crew coolly went about their tasks, Keller positioned himself behind the planesmen. His glance had just registered that their depth gauge showed a rather meager sixty-five feet when a deafening explosion sounded. This was followed by a powerful shock wave. Sent to his knees by this concussion, Helmut groped in the darkness as the lights failed. When the auxiliary lighting system finally took over, the bulkhead was still quivering. Bits of paint and cork fell from the ceiling, and the sausages that hung beside the rear bulkhead swayed wildly. Well aware that a single sheet of steel, barely three quarters of an inch thick, was all that lay between them and the sea, Helmut looked at the room's center. Perched there at the foot of the periscope well was the Captain, his mouth turned in a relieved grin.

"That was a close one, my friends. Fortunately, we still seem to be in one piece. Now let's get some depth between us and the surface. Next time, we might not be so lucky."

No sooner had these words left his mouth, than the sound man's voice rose clearly for all to hear. "Surface screws, Captain! It sounds like a group of destroyers coming in with a bone in their teeth."

"Damn it!" cried the Captain, as he bashed his right fist into the open palm of his left hand. "With their sonar, we'll be a sitting duck out here. Lieutenant Hirsacker, what lies below us?"

U-313's second in command was in the process of picking up the navigational instruments that had fallen to the deck as a result of the depth bomb when the Captain's question arrived. Hastily setting down a ruler, he reached out for the latest chart and responded.

"There's at least twelve hundred feet of ocean beneath us, sir."

Again Eisenbach cursed, realizing that this was

well beyond their depth threshold. "Well then, we'll take her down to our maximum and hope for the best. Planesmen, make our depth four hundred feet. I want this boat buttoned up tight! Right now, silence is our only ally."

Keller remained behind the diving console as the planesmen began carrying out the Captain's orders. With eyes glued to the depth gauge, he monitored each passing foot. Soon, the hull itself was creaking and moaning under the stress of a pressure of immense proportions. The chief wiped the sweat from his brow, and issued the briefest of silent prayers. Not long afterward, the control room filled with the distinctive "ping" of the enemy's sonar. This was followed by the actual sound of their screws.

"They've got us for sure now," commented Hirsacker grimly. "It sounds like there are three of them. They won't stop dropping their depth charges until they see the blood in the water themselves."

These desperate words went unanswered as each man was lost in his own thoughts. Over 27,000 of their comrades lay at the bottom of the Atlantic, the victims of their adversaries. Conscious that there was little they could do to affect their cruel fate, the sub's complement could only prepare for the final reckoning. Keller was in the midst of making his own separate peace when a loud, whirring sound broke his concentration. This was followed by the excited shouts of the sound man.

"Captain, it's unbelievable! They're leaving!"

With eyes wide open, Eisenbach sprang for the sound cubicle. It wasn't until he had the headphones firmly covering his ears that he managed a relieved grin.

"I don't believe it, yet it indeed appears to be true," said the Captain. "For some reason, they've called off the hunt, right when they had us cornered."

"It's a trap," returned Hirsacker. "They're playing with us, just like a cat plays with a trapped mouse."

Continuing to listen to the headphones, the Captain shook his head. "This is no game, Lieutenant. As the Fuhrer is my witness, those destroyers are definitely headed back to port. What in the world could have precipitated such a thing?"

Though he didn't know how to answer the Captain's question, Chief Keller found himself smiling. He heartily agreed that it would be best to remain submerged for at least another hour. If it was indeed a trap, the enemy would surely play their hand by then.

The sixty minutes passed quickly. All too soon, they were back on the surface, with lookouts deployed. Helmut himself was on his way to the bridge when the radio suddenly chattered alive. Such dispatches were rare, and the chief followed the Captain's hand signal to join him at the receiver.

The message arrived in code, and was the longest that they had ever received. It was the Captain who translated it for all of them to hear.

Helmut was outwardly trembling as he took in Eisenbach's unbelievable words. The Fuhrer was dead, an armistice had been signed, and the war was over! A heavy feeling settled in his gut, and he didn't know if he should cry in despair or shout for joy. This emotional confusion was temporarily pushed aside by thoughts of a more immediate nature, for all U-boats were ordered to raise a black pennant and surrender to the nearest Allied port.

Hirsacker was the one who brought up the idea of heading for America. Fearing a hostile reception on the Continent, U-313's second in command reasoned that the charitable Americans would offer a more amiable reception. Gunther Eisenbach agreed, and soon the U-boat was headed westward, a triangular black banner flapping from its conning tower.

Three thousands yards off U-313's starboard bow, the attack sub USS *Abalone* silently approached. Only the upper tip of its periscope broke the ocean's surface, as the *Gato*-class, fleet-type submarine closed in for what appeared to be an easy kill. From the boat's hushed control room, Lieutenant Commander William Carrigan orchestrated the attack. One of the youngest skippers in the US Navy, the twenty-six-year-old Annapolis graduate draped his lanky arms over the extended handles of the periscope. He audibly sighed upon taking in the sleek target so clearly visible in the scope's lens. Oblivious to any threat, the German U-boat plunged on a course due westward, a mysterious black banner flapping from its conning tower. Taking in the four lookouts visible on the U-boat's bridge, Carrigan stepped back and beckoned his XO to join him.

"You've got to take a look at this, Pete. It looks like we caught them completely napping."

Lieutenant Peter Donner, the brown-haired executive officer, two years younger than his Captain, stepped up to the periscope. Quick to peer into the viewing lens, he immediately identified their quarry.

"That's one of their new Type Twenty-ones, all right. What the hell is that black pennant all about?"

"Maybe it's a Kraut skull and crossbones," offered the Captain, who caught his XO's excited gaze as he backed away from the scope. "How about sending that pirate ship down to visit Davy Jones's locker?"

"With pleasure, Skipper," answered Pete Donner.

Carrigan's right hand went for the corncob pipe he habitually carried in his shirt pocket. Only when he had the well-worn bowl in his fingers did he cry out his orders.

"Battle stations, Mr. Donner! Ready torpedo tubes one through four."

As the *Abalone*'s crew scrambled to their assigned positions, William Carrigan once more approached the periscope. There he was met by the boat's hefty, bald-headed chief, Stan Lukowski.

"Sorry to bother you, sir, but I thought you'd like to know that the radio is still on the fritz. We're doing our best, but we still can't receive or transmit a message."

With his mind on other concerns, Carrigan's answer was a bit distant. "Well, stay at it, chief. We're going to be wanting to inform Command of a very special kill shortly."

"Aye, aye, Captain," returned Stan Lukowski, who turned back to the radio room.

This left William Carrigan alone at the periscope well. He wasted no time peering back into the lens. His mouth was dry as he again spotted the U-boat.

He cleared his throat and shouted, "Bearing, mark!"

"Two-two-eight, Captain," answered Pete Donner, who was putting this attack information into their torpedo data computer.

"Range, mark!" continued Carrigan.

Again the XO responded. "Two-five-double-zero, sir."

Carrigan's words boomed out deep and clear. "Bearing—mark, set! Fire one through four!"

Peter Donner hit the fire-control switch and braced himself for the powerful jolts of compressed air that he knew would soon follow. When several seconds passed and the distinctive sounds of the torpedoes firing still were absent, he hastily scanned the panel. He saw a flashing red light.

"Captain, we show an electrical power failure in the TDC relay system."

"Well, damn it!" cried Carrigan angrily. "Get Mac Brady on the horn and have him punch that solenoid manually!"

Reaching for the sound-powered telephone, the XO contacted the *Abalone*'s weapons officer. What he heard from Mac Brady's lips caused a depressed tone to color his response.

"Lieutenant Brady is unable to feed a proper gyroangle into the firing system, Captain. He's working on the problem now."

"Oh, for Christ's sake!" screamed Carrigan. "Why now of all times? A boat could fight an entire war and never get an opportunity such as this one."

Carrigan's face flushed in anger. His hands twitched and he dropped his cherished corncob. As he bent down to the deck to pick it up, he strained to control himself. It certainly wasn't his crew's fault that their equipment didn't work properly. Earlier in the war, it had been torpedoes that failed to arm themselves and run true. Today they were plagued with such things as inoperative radios and faulty fire-control systems. The sophisticated equipment that they relied upon to bring them victory too often failed. An engineering student himself, Carrigan knew that this was the price one paid for hastily installed, improperly tested systems. If he could survive the war, he swore that he would do his best to insure that future crews never had to face such a wasteful, frustrating situation.

The deep voice of Chief Lukowski got Carrigan's attention. With pipe in hand, the Captain stood and turned toward the radio shack, where some sort of unusual commotion was going on. The chief was waving his hands wildly and shouting out at the same time.

"It's over, Captain! The damn war is over!"

Not certain what the pot-bellied chief was babbling about, Carrigan watched his XO hastily cross the compartment. Peter Donner took the dispatch Stan Lukowski had been holding and quickly scanned it. While he did so, the chief added, "One second the radio was as dead as a cold fish, and then, in the blink of an eye, it was operating once again. Not five seconds passed, when this message arrived from COMSUBLANT."

"It appears to be legit, Skipper," commented Pete Donner triumphantly. "As of an hour ago, an armistice was to be in effect, ending all hostilities between the U.S. and Germany. It really is over!"

A chorus of excited cries met this revelation. Caught off guard by the surprise disclosure, Carrigan showed a look of shocked relief.

"Jesus Christ!" exclaimed the young Captain. "That U-boat!"

"I guess it was a good thing that our fire-control system failed after all," added Peter Donner. "All German warships have been ordered to raise a black pennant and to surrender to the nearest Allied port."

"Well, I'll be," sighed the Captain thoughtfully. Placing the well-chewed stem of his pipe between his lips, he looked up to meet the XO's stare.

"Lady Luck was sure shining on those Kraut sailors today, Pete. If they only knew how close they came to being among the last casualties of the war. What do you say about giving them a proper escort back to the good ole' U.S. of A.?"

A rousing shout of approval met the Captain's words. Though part of him still had trouble accepting the fact that the war in the Atlantic was over, Carrigan realized that his prayers had at long last been answered. Ever mindful of the hundreds of thousands of men who had died so that this moment would finally come, Carrigan solemnly turned to begin charting the long cruise homeward.

CHAPTER TWO

The Soviet Far East — The Present

The sound of crackling underbrush echoed from that section of the forest that lay before him, and Vasili Burukan alertly halted. Scanning the tree line for the noise's source, the grizzled old trapper took in the massive pine trunks. A sudden movement caught his practiced gaze, and the woodsman caught sight of a full-grown buck. The deer carried a well-developed rack of antlers. Its brown coat was spotted with white. Though it was some fifty meters distant, Vasili knew that it weighed well over three hundred pounds. Since it was upwind, the animal continued grazing, completely unaware that it was being observed.

Vasili's trigger finger instinctively flexed, yet on this trip he carried no firearms. The prey that he was seeking would need no bullet to take it down.

There had been a serious shortage of meat this past winter, and the old-timer's mouth watered. Fresh venison was one of his favorite dishes. His Natasha's specialty was deer stew. Perhaps on his return he could rig a snare and yet capture this prize. With this in mind, he continued down the narrow footpath he had been following. He had been walking this trail for two days now, after leaving his village for the trip southward.

Tavricanka had been his home for the last sixty-two years. Except for a brief span of time when the Japanese had forced him to the north, he knew little else but these woods. This was fine with him, for he had no desire to live elsewhere. The modern world with its big cities and rush for riches was certainly not for him. Two years ago, he had taken Natasha on a trip to neighboring Vladivostok. From the moment they'd boarded the bus for the fifty-seven-kilometer drive to the fabled port city, he'd known that he had made a mistake. Chattering crowds and nauseous diesel fumes all too soon had him longing for the clean, silent solace of his woods.

Vladivostok had grown to an immense size since he had been there last. Not only was it the final eastern stop of the Trans-Siberian railroad but the city also had a massive naval presence. Dozens of Soviet warships crowded its harbor, and everywhere one looked the young sailors were busily going about their business. Vasili would never forget how happy he had been when their shopping bags were filled and they were boarding the homeward-bound bus once again.

Since that time, his travels had been confined to a rather small patch of Manchurian wilderness. Fortunately, the woods surrounding Tavricanka were still sparsely populated. This was true of most of the territory that made up the rectangular piece of land that stretched from Vladivostok to the Korean border. Barely thirty kilometers wide, this snake-like peninsula had been formed with China determining its western boundary and the icy Sea of Japan lying to the east. A single road and railway track stretched down the peninsula's length. These arteries connected the isolated towns of Kraskino and Posjet to the rest of the Soviet Union.

Vasili picked up his pace as the trail stretched out wide and flat. A raven cried out a harsh welcome and a cool breeze ruffled his full mane of silver hair. He carried an ashen walking stick that he had carved himself, and a medium-sized, canvas rucksack. Inside were enough provisions to last him a week and a dozen delicate steel traps.

His journey was taking him down into a portion of the peninsula that he hadn't visited since last summer. At that time he had hastily scouted the isolated countryside surrounding the port town of Posjet, and found them bristling with signs of the small mammals he was seeking.

For the last four decades, he had made his living trapping the beaver, otters, mink, and sable that proliferated in this wilderness. This was a trade that his father had brought with him when he'd moved to Manchuria not long after the Great Revolution. In those days, the game was unbelievably bountiful. A good season's work at that time could generate hundreds of shiny skins. Today, Vasili knew he was lucky to bring in but a few dozen animals after many months of hard work. Yet their needs were few, and the demand for the skins was still quite high. Thus, each pelt generated a substantial number of rubles. These skins were sold to Lev Litvov, a heavyset, bearded Jew who had a trading post in their village. Though Vasili could probably have received a better price in Vladivostok, such a trip was not worth the nerve-wracking aggravation it would inevitably produce.

Quite happy to be alone here in the hills of his birth, the keen-eyed trapper inhaled a deep lungful of crisp air, sweet with the scent of the pine woods. In the distance, the murmur of a babbling brook called out invitingly. He knew this stream and would halt there to drink and have a quick lunch. He couldn't tarry long, for his ultimate destination was still several kilometers distant. He hoped to begin laying the first trap by nightfall.

After a hasty bite to eat, Vasili was soon back on the trail headed southward. The portion of the woods that he now crossed was hilly. Gone were the massive pines that graced the wilderness to the north. In their place were thousands of gnarled oaks, many of which were hundreds of years old. There was an abundance of streams here, and the old trapper soon caught sight of the type of wildlife that had called him from Tavri-canka.

The first hint that a family of mink was close by came when he chanced upon a number of familiar tracks etched on the muddy banks of a tiny stream. The sun had long since fallen behind the western tree line, and the air was cool with the first hint of dusk. Vasili figured that he had reached his goal and decided that his first priority should be to search for a spot to set up camp. There would be plenty of time to lay down his traps under the proper light of the warm morning sun. The old-timer found just what he was looking for on the crest of a nearby hillside. There, someone had abandoned a crude, wooden lean-to. Not expecting such a simple luxury, he gratefully removed his knapsack. After stretching his sore leg muscles, he took a minute to survey that portion of the peninsula visible on the crest's opposite side.

Though the light was rapidly fading, he could just make out the village of Posjet down below. Surrounded by thick forest on three sides, the settlement overlooked the grayish waters of a huge bay. Two sleek destroyers lay at anchor there. Since they were only a few kilometers from the borders of China and North Korea at this spot, he really wasn't surprised at the Soviet Navy's presence. In a way, it was somewhat reassuring.

The first electric lightbulbs flickered on in the village, and Vasili yawned contentedly. Here he was, so close to civilization, yet at the same time so very far away. After a simple meal of dried venison strips, black bread, and cheese, the old-timer crawled beneath the shelter of the lean-to. Seconds later, he was sound asleep.

Vasili awoke to the eerie wail of an air-raid siren. He hadn't heard such a frightening racket since the closing days of the Great War, and for a second thought that he was dreaming. Yet when his eyes popped open and the high-pitched howling continued, he knew that this wasn't a nightmare.

The air was cold, and puffs of white steam emanated from his nostrils and lips. He sat up, and could see that the first light of dawn was already painting the eastern horizon. Since the siren seemed to be based somewhere in Posjet, it was in this direction that he turned. A few dozen meager lightbulbs outlined the village's location. Beyond, the waters of the bay were just visible, shimmering in a ghostly iridescence. As the sun continued to rise, he noticed that the destroyers were no longer in the harbor. They must have weighed anchor and set sail sometime in the night.

Did their leaving have something to do with the siren that continued to haunt the dawn? Vasili's pulse quickened as he considered the possibilities. Perhaps what they were facing was an invasion by either the Chinese or the North Koreans. Border incursions were a constant source of irritation in this region. Hundreds of kilometers of shared territory made such raids a frequent occurrence. Yet if this wasn't the case in this instance, could an enemy of an even greater stature be responsible for this call to arms? The American Imperialists had been arming themselves to the teeth for years now. Their brave leaders in Moscow had warned the Motherland's populace that the Yankee hordes wouldn't be satisfied until the Soviet Union was under their greedy domination. Had this feared day finally come to pass?

Vasili's terrified imagination ran wild as the throaty roar of powerful jet engines sounded clearly overhead. The sun had broken free of the horizon and was rising in a crystal-blue sky. Searching the heavens, Vasili caught sight of a trio of large, gray-skinned jet aircraft approaching directly from the west. They appeared to be bombers and seemed to skim the surface of the bay, only a few meters from the glimmering whitecaps. His mouth was dry as he watched the three airplanes suddenly pull upward. They rapidly gained altitude, all the while closing the distance that lay between them and the village.

Why in the world would even the ignorant Americans waste their bombs on such an insignificant target? Vasili contemplated this confusing question while bracing himself to meet the initial explosion.

The old trapper would take to his grave the incredible series of events that he next witnessed. Perched beneath the primitive lean-to, with his heart pounding wildly in his chest, Vasili looked on as a blinding shaft of intense white light shot out from the village's outskirts. This brilliant beam angled itself upwards and smacked into the nose of the lead aircraft. A deep-throated blast followed, and the jet was instantly enveloped in a cloud of fire and smoke. In the blink of an eye, it was falling from the sky, into the waiting waters of the bay below.

Vasili barely had time to catch his breath when the beam suddenly redirected itself. Fifteen seconds later, the two bombers that followed soon shared the lead aircraft's fiery fate. No sooner did the last plane smack into the waters than the beam dissipated as quickly as it had appeared. The air-raid siren halted its mad wail, and soon all was quiet except for the gentle howl of the gusting morning wind.

Stunned into inaction, Vasili tried to make some sort of sense out of what he had just seen take place. Had he just witnessed the opening shots of World War III, or was this all just some sort of horribly realistic test? And if it was but an exercise, what kind of weapon could down its quarry with a mere beam of light? Anxious to share his observations with his wife and neighbors, Vasili Burukan decided to return to Tavricanka with all due haste. The furry mammals that he sought would surely be here waiting for him when he returned. After hiding his prized traps under the corner of the lean-to, he shouldered his knapsack, picked up his walking stick, and immediately headed for the footpath that would take him back home.

The fifty-seven-kilometer journey from Vladivostok had taken Tanya Markova the better part of a day. The first bus she had boarded broke down soon after leaving the terminal. They were forced to wait on the stranded vehicle for over two hours until a replacement arrived. Tanya and her fellow passengers took this delay in stride. Many merely snacked on the treats they had purchased in the city, while others passed the time deep in conversation. Several of the old-timers pulled their overcoats tight and attempted to get in a nap. Tanya, who had a seat to herself in the back of the bus, had her thoughts to keep her company.

She had been in the port city for over a week now. During that time, she had stayed in the cramped apartment belonging to her uncle, Lev Litvov. The visit had provided a welcomed relief after spending the entire winter cooped up in Tavricanka. Just to see new faces once more reaffirmed her contact with the human race.

Tanya had spent her first day in Vladivostok sightseeing. The city had buzzed with activity. Everywhere she looked she'd found crowds scurrying off to their daily tasks. They traveled by bus, automobile, bicycle, and foot. Most were dressed in heavy furs or long leather coats. All in all they seemed a healthy lot, their ruddy faces showing a potpourri of racial backgrounds. Almond-eyed Tartars mixed freely with swarthy Uzbeks and big-boned Georgians. Interspersed among this mosaic of humanity was an occasional Great Russian. Appearing almost lordly with their blond hair, blue eyes, and fair skin, the Russians stuck out like a breed apart. Most aware of her own fair coloring, Tanya appreciated the vast racial diversity of her Motherland.

Apart from the scampering crowds, she found herself surprised with the amount of construction going on around her. It seemed that every corner held a new building site. The incessant pounding of the jackhammer merged with that of the pile driver. Like skeletoned giants, the bare steel frames of new high-rises dotted the landscape. Though most of these structures were unimaginatively designed, their mere presence gave the city a certain dynamism.

Situated far away from the cosmopolitan environs of Kiev, Leningrad, and Moscow, Vladivostok stood on the Rodina's last frontier. As the capital of the vast Soviet Far East, it would be from there that this new land would be developed. Of course, of great significance was its excellent harbor. Free from ice for all but a few months each year, the port at Vladivostok gave the Soviet Union a much-needed commercial and military outlet on the Sea of Japan. It was this facility that Tanya allowed herself to be drawn to.

The tavern that Lev had told her about was called the Red Pelican. It stood on the wharf, directly across from the entrance to the naval base. After checking out its location, she returned to the apartment, which was a mere kilometer inland. There she finished unpacking, and allowed herself the luxury of a hot bath. The sun was low on the western horizon as she dressed herself in her best outfit, a black leather dress that she had made herself, and carefully put on her makeup.

Her friends always said that she would have made an excellent fashion model. She'd inherited her tall, thin frame from her mother. Lately, she had been wearing her blonde hair cut bluntly short. With bangs lying naturally on her forehead, her dark, hazel-green eyes were that much more emphasized. She'd learned from the French fashion magazines just how to apply her makeup in order to enhance her prominent cheek bones, aquiline nose, and delicate chin. Checking out the results in the mirror, she nodded in approval.

Lev had given her a gorgeous full-length fox coat. It did an excellent job of sheltering her from the frigid chill as she left the apartment and began her way back to the docks.

The Red Pelican was bustling with activity as she entered. The majority of its patrons were uniformed naval officers. Tanya chose a table on the opposite side of the room, near a large picture window. She couldn't help but feel the intense stares of inspection upon being led to her seat by the maitre d'. Barely a minute passed before a tall, handsome officer was standing beside her, politely asking her to have a drink with him. Tanya replied that, although she was supposed to be meeting a friend there, she would be honored if he would keep her company until her date arrived.

She was surprised to find the officer younger than she had anticipated. His name was Mikhail Amazar, and he was a junior lieutenant aboard a Krivak-class guided-missile frigate. His ship had only recently arrived there, after spending the winter based out of Vietnam's Cam Ranh Bay. All too soon the vodka was flowing, and the twenty-four-year-old lieutenant was sharing a rather detailed description of life aboard a Soviet man-of-war. Doing her best to slowly sip her drink, Tanya took in each word of the young man's passionate narrative. She especially took note when he began explaining just how the Soviet Navy was adapting the former American naval facility to guarantee the Motherland a much needed warm-water port on the South China Sea.

When it appeared that her "friend" would be standing her up this evening, Mikhail Amazar graciously invited her to dinner. Tanya accepted, and soon both of them were wolfing down a hearty meal at a nearby restaurant. Afterwards, he walked her back to her apartment, leaving Tanya with a rather timid kiss on her cheek and an invitation to join him for lunch the next day. Thus began her week in Vladivostok, which had culminated in an actual tour of the frigate *Ivan Komarov* the previous afternoon.

Tanya stirred as she mentally recreated all that she learned during this time. There would be much to share with her uncle when she returned to Tavricanka. She fidgeted in the back of the stalled bus that was supposed to be conveying her homeward, and wondered if they would ever get going again. The other passengers seemed oblivious to the wait, satisfied to chatter or nap away the wasted hours. Patience was a virtue that her countrymen were well aware of. Whether it was waiting in line for one's daily bread, or facing the seemingly endless bureaucratic red tape that ruled one's existence, only by being tolerant could a Soviet citizen survive.

It was noon before the replacement vehicle arrived. Appearing at least three decades old, the battered bus endlessly belched sooty diesel fumes and rattled noisily. Because it contained fewer seats than their original coach, Tanya found herself sharing her hard bench with a plump, rosy-cheeked babushka. Clothed in layer upon layer of well-worn garments, the old lady gave Tanya a running commentary on the ridiculously high prices she had paid for such basic food items as cheese, bread, and canned fish. A good quantity of those treasures lay wrapped in the many sacks that were stored beneath her feet.

Glad to be moving once more, Tanya listened to her traveling companion's irritated babbling, occasionally nodding in compliance. As they left Vladivostok's outskirts, the road narrowed. Frequent potholes, and the vehicle's virtually nonexistent shock absorbers, made the ride far from comfortable. They were soon traveling through a thick pine forest. An occasional cottage dotted the landscape, yet it was quite evident that man's presence there was at a minimum. Though her visit to the city had been exhilarating, Tanya was happy to be back in the wilderness. Life seemed so much simpler there. The snores of the old lady came from her right, and Tanya saw that the babushka had fallen sound asleep. Returning her gaze back to the window, she thought about the fateful series of events that had led to this trip.

She supposed it had all started over twenty years ago, when her mother decided to leave her father and return to Tavricanka. Until that time, they had been living in the Siberian city of Chabarovsk, some 650 kilometers due north of Vladivostok. There, her father had been employed with the railroad. Though she was only a youngster at the time, Tanya remembered her father as a handsome, sad fellow who was unfortunately prone to fits of drunken violence. In was this vice that provoked her mother's rather drastic decision to leave him.

Tavricanka had been her mother's birthplace, and they found the townsfolk happy to take them in. Among Tanya's first memories of this confusing time was the warm, smiling face of her Uncle Lev. It was in his home that they settled, and there she grew to womanhood.

Uncle Lev had been there to comfort her on the icy night that her mother's lifeless body was brought in. They said that her death was caused by a tragic automobile accident, but Tanya instinctively felt otherwise. She was fourteen at the time, and was certain that her mother had been involved with some sort of clandestine activity. It wasn't until three years later that her suspicions were confirmed.

Because of their village's small size, schooling was the responsibility of a local collective. The proper State books arrived from Vladivostok, yet it was up to the teachers to interpret them properly. Unknown to Tanya was the fact that Tavricanka had been originally settled by a group of political dissidents who had arrived there shortly after the Revolution. More attuned to the principles of the opposing "White Party," the village elders had accepted the Red Communist yoke somewhat reluctantly. Resistance to Moscow had continued throughout World War II, and existed even now.

Uncle Lev was the person who initiated Tanya into their villagers' unique set of beliefs. To the founders of Tavricanka, socialism was a pure ideal, and its coming would signal a time of equality and great joy. The present Soviet State was no better than the out-of-date Czarist system that it had replaced. Corruption and graft were just as prevalent today as they were one hundred years ago. And just like then, it was the common man who suffered the most.

Careful not to let the government learn of their doctrine, many of the citizens of Tavricanka did their best to resist Moscow's rule whenever possible. Since the end of World War II, their greatest concern had been that the State's misguided leaders would lead them into a full-scale nuclear war with the West. It was common knowledge that this would be a conflict that would have no winner. The Rodina's arsenal had more than enough warheads to destroy the planet several times over. And to think that they were continuing to produce rockets and bombs at an unheard-of-pace! What kind of system could support such madness?

In an attempt to neutralize the omnipotent powers of the military, the elders of Tavricanka had decided to open up a channel to the Western powers. Since they were situated in one of the most strategically important areas of the Soviet Far East, it was hoped that this leaked intelligence would give the West a better idea of just what it was up against.

Tanya readily offered her services to the Movement, after Lev revealed that it was the tread of a Soviet Army armored personnel carrier that had caused her mother's death. The teenager's initial assignments were minor ones. Most of the time they involved surveillance of the road leading southward to Posjet. It was her responsibility to monitor all military movement. She also acted as a courier, and because her mother had taught her English early on in life, Tanya was the village translator.

More recently, she had been given assignments of a much more active nature. Last fall, she had been allowed to hike down to Posjet, to check on a mysterious military installation that was said to be under development there. After great effort, she had indeed found the site, yet was forced to abandon any hopes of penetrating the compound because of a sophisticated security system.

Her recently concluded trip to Vladivostok had signaled a radically new environment in which to apply her talents. Though the dangers of discovery were greatly enhanced, the risks were well worth it. Soon the West would know just how serious the Soviets were about keeping Cam Ranh Bay to themselves. She could also offer a detailed list of the present Pacific Fleet warships and a firsthand recollection of life aboard a *Krivak*-class frigate. All of this information had been amassed with the least bit of effort on her part. Surely the young lieutenant she befriended had suspected nothing unusual.

Tanya blushed upon recollecting Mikhail Amazar's awkward efforts at courting. A gentleman to the core, he'd treated her to almost a week's worth of drinks and meals without pressing her to go to bed with him. There was no doubting her loyalty to the cause, but just how far could she really go? She had tried to come to terms with this question earlier, and decided to let nature take its course. Her continued virginhood didn't help matters any. A time could very well come in the near future when such a gift could be priceless. Better she should lose her innocence to someone she genuinely cared for than a mere drunken sailor. As the bus rumbled over a wooden suspension bridge, she seriously considered letting Anton Bagdaran have his way with her. There was no doubting the lumberjack's interest. So he wasn't a man of the world. At least they'd practically grown up together.

Her benchmate's snoring sounded unevenly, and Tanya closed her eyes in an effort to clear her mind. Seconds later, she unwillingly joined the babushka in dreamland.

It was the sudden squeal of grinding brakes that snapped Tanya from her slumber. Her eyes opened and she realized with a start that it was dusk outside. Sitting up on the bench, she peered out the window for any familiar landmarks. Much to her dismay, the enveloping nightfall veiled the countryside in a cloak of mystifying blackness.

A voice came from her right, and Tanya turned to face her traveling companion. "Well, good evening, sleepy-head. You've been out for over a good hour now. Would you like some bread and cheese?"

Without waiting for a reply, the old lady broke off a heel of crusty black bread and a chunk of bright yellow cheese. "Here, my dear. You're already much too skinny as it is. What in the heavens is the matter with you youngsters nowadays? Here you go starving yourselves just to fit into a dress that's several sizes too small for you. Don't you realize that a real man likes a woman with a little meat on her bones?"

Though she had no appetite, Tanya took the food anyway. "Thank you, comrade. This is most kind of you."

"Nonsense," retorted the babushka. "As fellow citizens of the Rodina, it's the duty of each one of us to share with one another. Besides, I wouldn't want to be responsible for your starving to death."

Tanya couldn't help but laugh at this. Tearing the

piece of bread in half, she managed to consume a bite. It was fresh and tasted vaguely of yeast and rye seeds. Stifling a yawn, she asked, "Do you have any idea where we are? I sure hope I haven't missed Tavricanka."

The babushka put down the ripe green pear that she had been munching on and responded, "You have no worry, my dear. We have yet to reach our first stop. Your village is the one after. Have you lived there long?"

Ever cautious of needless questions, Tanya decided that the old woman was harmless. "Yes. I've spent almost my entire life there."

"Well, no wonder you're such a sight," reflected the babushka. "What you need is some meat and potatoes on those bones. This rocky wilderness is fit for the wild beasts only. We should have given it to the Chinese years ago. Now there's a people who have learned to live off the land!"

The old lady was in the midst of a sprited discourse on the strengths of Chinese communal farming over the Soviet way when a collection of flickering electric lights could be seen up ahead. Once again the bus driver applied the brakes and a deafening squeal filled the cramped carriage. The vehicle slowed and a sudden wave of activity stirred its occupants. Many of the passengers began gathering together their precious baggage. This included Tanya's talkative travel companion.

"Well, this is home for me, my dear. Take this old woman's advice and put a few more pounds on your bones. Then an attractive girl like yourself won't have to travel these roads by her lonesome."

The babushka winked wisely and stiffly got to her feet as the bus pulled into the terminal. With shopping bags in hand, she began shuffling her bulk towards the exit. Tanya couldn't help but notice how she bravely pushed away those passengers who tried to block the aisle and leave the vehicle before her.

A dozen or so individuals disembarked. After taking on a scraggly single replacement, they were soon back on the road headed southward. Relieved to have the bench all to herself now, Tanya stretched her cramped limbs. Setting aside the bread and cheese that the woman had given her, she turned her gaze back to the passing landscape. A quarter of an hour later, they crossed a familiar bridge and entered the tiny village of Tavricanka.

Tanya was the only passenger to exit the bus there. It was cold and dark outside. Leaving a cloud of fumes in its wake, the vehicle sped off into the night. As the grinding sound of its engine faded in the distance, Tanya was aware of the utter quiet. After the bustle of Vladivostok, this silence was a welcomed change.

She stood in the vacant town square, and studied the handful of sturdy wooden cottages that made up the village proper. A dog barked, and a gust of cool, fresh wind blew in from the northwest. The smell of ripe pine and the bare hint of the coming spring accompanied this draft. Pulling the high collar of her fox coat tightly around her neck, Tanya proceeded to Lev Litvov's abode.

Uncle Lev's residence was situated in the rear of his shop. She was surprised to find the front door to the office unlocked. Tanya entered and took in the familiar scent of tanning hides. A single light bulb blared from the ceiling. This adequately illuminated the workspace where the furrier bartered for pelts with the local trappers and processed those skins as well.

The sound of muted voices was audible in the background, and Tanya continued on to that portion of the structure reserved for the living quarters. There she found the furrier deep in conversation with the trapper, Vasili Burukan. Lev noticed her entrance, yet greeted her with a silent, solemn nod. Strangely enough, he was wearing his sleeping attire. Standing before the blazing fireplace, clothed in longjohns, slippers, and a long robe, Lev listened to Vasili's nervous babbling. The two men were a study in physical contrasts. Though both were approximately the same age, the trapper was short and slight in stature, his face cleanly shaven and his mane of white hair thick and long. Lev Litvov was his complete opposite. Standing well over six feet, five inches, he carried his massive girth, full gray beard, and shiny bald head in a stately, dignified manner.

It was evident that Vasili Burukan had just come in from the wilds. Not only did he carry his ashen walking stick in hand, but the grizzled old trapper still wore his knapsack on his back. As soundlessly as possible, Tanya peeled off her coat and cautiously approached the two men. Without halting to acknowledge her presence, Lev Litvov's deep voice boomed out clearly.

"I can assure you, Comrade Burukan, that we are not in the midst of World War Three. As far as I know, the Rodina and the United States of America are still deadlocked in the infamous Cold War that has prevailed for over four decades now. Surely what you witnessed was but a mere military test by our forces."

"But why would we waste three of our own bombers?" countered the confused trapper. "I tell you, Lev Litvov, as Lenin is my witness, I saw those massive aircraft with my own eyes."

Instantly curious as to the nature of their strange conversation, Tanya joined them before the fireplace. With her approach, the portly furrier broke eye contact with his guest. When his face beamed with a warm smile, Vasili Burukan turned also. He took in the tall, thin, blond-haired figure of Tanya Markova and found his own grin widening.

"Well, look what the wind has blown in," said Lev Litvov. "Welcome back to Tavricanka, my sweet niece."

He followed this salutation with a tight hug and a kiss to each cheek. Looking deep into her eyes, he added, "Is it my imagination, or have you grown even more beautiful since you left us?"

Tanya blushed. "Oh, uncle, I've only been gone a week."

"It seemed more like an entire year," returned the furrier. "I trust your visit was a success. Did you find my loft in order?"

"Yes I did, uncle. Everything was most comfortable."

"Good," sighed Lev, who returned his gaze to the leather-coated trapper who stood beside him. "Tanya, as a fellow admirer of the military sciences, I believe you'll be fascinated with the amazing report Comrade Burukan here brings into our parlor this evening. It seems Tavricanka's most skilled trapper stumbled onto a bit of a mystery while working the forest near Posjet. Vasili, my friend, would you mind repeating your tale?"

Anxious to be in the spotlight once more, Vasili Burukan shared the story of his encounter with Tanya. With no detail left out, he described the moment he awoke from the lean-to, roused from his slumber by the eerie wail of an air-raid siren. His voice rose in excitement as he told of spotting the three jet aircraft skimming the waters of Posjet Bay. Using his right hand to portray the lead plane, he showed it suddenly gaining altitude. It was at this point in the story that his eyes brightened and his very limbs seemed to tremble. Licking his dry lips, he went on to describe the moment when a blindingly bright shaft of light shot up from the outskirts of Posjet and proceeded to knock the three jets from the sky. His face was flushed, his pulse racing, upon completing this startling account.

Tanya absorbed the trapper's words and found her own heartbeat quickening. Though she dared not verbally admit it, she had a fairly good idea of just what Vasili had witnessed. If it were indeed true, it could have startling implications for each one of them.

She could see in her uncle's eyes that he too had grasped the significance of the trapper's report. Stifling a yawn, Lev Litvov turned his attention back to Vasili.

"It is getting late, my friend. I thank you once again for sharing your astounding tale with us."

"But, Comrade Litvov," said the trapper. "You still haven't been able to tell me just what I saw out there. Perhaps I should return to Posjet, to ask the authorities there just what has occurred."

"No!" snapped the furrier. "It is my opinion that such a move could lead to your arrest. If you know what's good for you, you'll keep this incident to your-self and stay well away from those woods. At least until I've been able to make some subtle inquiries of my own. If this is indeed but a routine military exercise, you'll be able to return to your traps in a few weeks time. Mark my words well, comrade. Otherwise, it will be off to the Gulag for you and your entire family."

This stern warning seemed to take the edge off of Vasili's passionate inquisitiveness. Lowering his eyes, he humbly bowed.

"As always, you are right, Comrade Litvov. It's apparent that I've stumbled onto something that's none of my business. I will listen to your advice and take my trapping elsewhere."

"Why not try the swamp outside of Primorski?" offered Lev. "I hear that there are beavers in those streams the size of small dogs."

"Primorski it will be," returned Vasili Burukan. As he turned to leave, he added, "Again, thanks for taking the time to hear me out, comrade. If it wasn't for you, I could have gone and done something that I would have later regretted."

The furrier answered while walking his guest to the door. "Not at all, my friend. That is what I'm here for. Now go and bring me back some thick pelts. My contacts in the city grow impatient, and now is the time for you to earn many rubles."

Accepting this with a nod, Vasili left through the shop's only exit. After setting the door lock and switching off the light, the furrier returned to his parlor. There he joined Tanya, who had seated herself before the fireplace.

"Well, my sweet niece, it indeed appears that you

have arrived back on a most auspicious occasion. So that laser battle station is not a rumor after all."

"We still don't know that for certain, uncle. It is no secret that Vasili Burukan is a lover of his vodka. Perhaps this is all an alcoholic hallucination."

Lev grunted. "I find that hard to believe. He saw something out there. I can see it in his eyes. Besides, you know as well as I that the military has been busy building an installation down at Posjet for some time now. Little did we realize how very significant this site would be."

Lev looked on as Tanya's glance centered itself on the fireplace's blazing embers. Her usually jovial expression looked weary, and for a second he couldn't get over how much she reminded him of her mother. Gone were her little-girl features. In their place were those of a woman. Well aware of the solemn mood that was prevailing, he did his best to lighten his tone.

"Say, now, what kind of greeting is this for my favorite niece? What do you say to a nip of my prized cherry brandy? Then you can tell me just what went on during your trip to the big city."

Catching her uncle's wise grin, Tanya couldn't help but feel her spirits rise. She grinned in response, and no further words were needed to send Lev off to the pantry for the promised refreshments. He returned with two delicate, lead-crystal snifters and a half-filled decanter of crimson-colored liquor. After carefully pouring their drinks, he raised his glass in toast.

"To life, my sweet niece. Now, tell me all about your adventures in Vladivostok."

Before responding, Tanya took a sip of the distilled spirits, which had been bottled thousands of kilometers distant, in the Ukraine. The fiery liquor burned her mouth and throat, and warmed her stomach. Smacking her lips together, she tasted the rich flavor of ripe cherries. She downed another sip, and went on to relate how she had managed to get settled in the port city. Her uncle was in the midst of pouring them refills when she described her visit to the Red Pelican. She had his total attention as she recounted her meeting with the young naval lieutenant, Mikhail Amazar. By the time she had drawn a detailed mental picture of her tour on board the Krivak-class frigate Ivan Komarov, her uncle was proudly beaming.

"My, my, little one. You certainly didn't waste any time getting to the heart of the matter. A trained KGB operative couldn't have done better."

Her uncle's words of praise did little to change the direction of her thoughts. "I imagine that the Navy's intention to develop Cam Ranh Bay as a permanent installation would be of some interest to our friends in the West, but surely all that I learned on my trip is overshadowed by Vasili Burukan's narrative."

With his gaze locked on the fire, Lev responded. "Your efforts are more important than you realize, little flower, yet your observation is a correct one. If a laser battle station is indeed operational at Posjet Bay, such astounding news must take precedence."

"Will you inform your contact of the possibility?" quizzed Tanya.

Lev answered directly. "Not until I see this site with my own eyes. I must be absolutely certain of its existence before sharing it with the others."

"Then you'll be going off to Posjet soon?"

"I plan to leave with the sunrise," replied Lev.

"I thought that would be the case," reflected Tanya. "Would another pair of eyes be helpful?"

Expecting just such an offer, the bearded furrier smiled. "Just who could be so crazy as to volunteer for such a dangerous mission?"

Tanya wasted no time raising her hand over her head.

"I thought as much," said Lev. "Since there's nothing I could say that would change your stubborn mind anyway, I'll accept your company."

A relieved smile etched Tanya's lips and she raised her glass in toast. "To the greatest uncle in the Rodina! May our efforts guarantee the peace of our planet."

They touched glasses. It took them a single gulp to finish off their brandies. Lev yawned and stretched his limbs.

"Well, then, if we're going to be doing some traveling tomorrow, we'd better be getting some rest. Sweet dreams, little flower."

Lev lifted up his bulk, kissed his niece on each cheek, and disappeared into his bedroom. As was her practice, Tanya would sleep before the fireplace. Her mattress was kept rolled up in the parlor's closet. Suddenly drained of all energy, she struggled to stand and retrieve her bedding. With Vasili Burukan's tale still fresh in her mind, she managed to lay out her bedroll, and soon was sound asleep.

The morning found the battered Zil truck belonging to the furrier barreling its way southward down the peninsula's sole roadway. A storm front had passed through during the night, leaving behind several inches of wet snow. Fortunately, it was not cold enough to ice over, which would have made driving conditions considerably worse.

Lev enjoyed being behind the wheel. He drove while whistling a spirited series of folk tunes celebrating Lake Baikal. Beside him, Tanya dreamily studied the passing landscape. Cloaked in a freshly fallen mantle of snow, the pines that lined both sides of the road looked like something out of a fairy tale. A family of deer, contentedly feeding on the shoulder, made this imagined vision complete.

They had been driving for over two hours now. During that time they had encountered not a single other vehicle. Both wore thick fox coats, and Tanya had an extra blanket thrown over her lap, for the truck's heater had long since gone dead.

A road sign passed on the right indicating that Posjet was seven kilometers distant. Taking in this information, Tanya sat up straight and studied the passing landscape with an increased intensity.

"Would you like a cup of tea, uncle?" she offered, while reaching under her feet for the thermos.

The furrier momentarily stopped whistling. "My dear niece, that would be excellent."

Tanya was in the process of carefully pouring some tea into the plastic cup that topped the thermos when the truck abruptly slowed. As a result, she spilled a good portion of the amber liquid onto the seat. It was her uncle who cursed.

"Damn it anyway! Just look at our greeting party on this godforsaken morning."

Tanya looked up and spotted the military roadblock that lay approximately a quarter of a kilometer distant. A pair of armored personnel carriers obstructed the snow-covered pavement there. Several soldiers stood beside the massive vehicles, their Kalashnikovs hung over their shoulders.

"What do you make of that?" quizzed Tanya, as she handed her uncle a half-filled cup of tea.

The furrier placed the plastic mug on the flat dashboard and proceeded to shift the truck into a lower gear. "Who knows, little flower. Perhaps a bridge has washed out, or maybe they're only checking papers. Whatever, just relax and leave all the talking to me."

Quite happy to do just that, Tanya sat back as the truck was braked to a slippery halt. A pair of bored-looking soldiers sauntered over to the driver's window. While they approached, Lev reached for his tea and took an appreciative sip. He smacked his lips and slowly lowered the window.

"Good morning, comrades," greeted the furrier. "Isn't it a bit nippy for morning maneuvers?"

The lead figure, a stocky, mustached corporal, leadenly nodded. "I wish you would tell our captain that. May I see your papers, Comrade?"

Lev kept his traveling documents in a brown leather pouch which he had tooled himself. He handed it to the sentry, and took another sip of tea.

"I'm certain that you'll find everything in order, young man. I've been taking this route for more years than you have of life. Perhaps you've seen some of my work. Posjet's garrison commander's wife wears a lynx coat that I crafted especially for her."

Not paying much attention to Lev's ramblings, the soldier hastily glanced over the documents and, before handing them back, took an extra minute to study the truck's sole passenger. The furrier noticed his interest and added, "This beautiful young creature beside me is my niece. It's her expert eye that helps me to purchase only the most stylish pelts."

Obviously liking what he saw, the sentry politely bowed. This motion coaxed the least bit of a smile from Tanya.

Relishing his moment of power, the young corporal returned Lev's papers and said, "I'm sorry to disappoint you, but this as far as all civilian traffic is allowed to go. There's a chance that the road will be reopened by the end of the week."

Lev's gaze narrowed. "Is there some sort of highway construction going on here? I must get down to Posjet to pick up a very important consignment which will be crafted into a garment for a member of the Politburo itself."

"I don't care if it's for Secretary Chernavin," snapped the sentry. "This is as far as you'll be going, old man."

From the tone of his voice, Lev knew that the soldier was adamant. Not wanting to make a scene, the furrier shrugged his shoulders.

"What can I say, but that we tried? Come now, Tanya, let's go back to the warmth of the fireplace that we should have never left this morning. Stay warm, young man. And if you should ever be in need of a fur, just look me up."

Without another word spoken, Lev rolled up the window, shifted the truck into reverse, and turned them around. The roadblock had just faded from the view of his mirror before he let go a deep breath and commented, "Well, there goes the easy way, little flower. That roadblock only means that the military is indeed up to something here. What would you say to taking a little hike this snowy morning?"

Tanya was well prepared for just such an excursion and was quick with her reply. "Lead the way, uncle. It's been much too long since I've explored these hills anyway."

The furrier guided the truck northward for another quarter of a kilometer. After passing over a narrow, wooden bridge, he braked, and carefully searched the forest to his right. The trees lay thick there, yet Lev soon caught sight of a bare passageway between them. He turned the steering wheel, shifted into first, and, while affectionately patting the dashboard, issued a single plea.

"Come on, little girl, see us into those woods. You won't have to go far."

The crunch of snow on the tires met their ears. Yet the snow wasn't deep, and all too soon they were completely hidden from the main thoroughfare. They entered a clearing formed from a number of previously felled trees, and slowed to a halt. Before switching off the ignition, Lev turned the truck around so that it faced the direction from which they had come.

"This is it, little flower. Not far from here is the footpath that Vasili Burukan traversed only yesterday. It will take us to that lean-to he told of and, if we desire, all the way into Posjet. If you'll be so good as to ready our things, I'll go and cover our tracks. No use in drawing the attention of a curious onlooker."

Fifteen minutes later, they were well on their way southward again, although their speed of travel was significantly slower. Lev led the way. Tanya followed, a few steps behind. Both were adequately dressed for hiking and wore shouldered day-packs.

Because the snow completely covered the footpath, Tanya relied on her escort to forge the proper trail. Never one to question her uncle's abilities, she proceeded without question, surprised at finding herself utilizing all her effort just to keep up with him. For a man in his late sixties, his physical prowess never ceased to amaze her.

The cold had been a bit uncomfortable at first, yet by now she was barely aware of it. So intense were her exertions that she even had a good sweat on her forehead. The fresh, icy air was like a tonic, and she found herself breathing in deep lungfuls.

When she was a child, such wintertime excursions had been among her most cherished experiences. Nothing was like walking through the deep woods after a recent snow. Appearing cleansed and pure, the very earth seemed to take on a new, enchanted luster. Tanya was surprised to find that this magical feeling still existed.

A gust of wind blew overhead, and the boughs of the surrounding pines stirred like a single entity. Far away a raven cried, and she could just pick out the gurgling chorus of a nearby brook. So powerful were these sensations that she almost forgot her purpose there, until her uncle's deep voice brought her quickly back to harsh reality.

"We will have to do a bit of climbing up ahead, little one. How are you faring? Are you warm enough?"

Conscious of his fatherly concerns, Tanya managed a broad smile. "I am just fine, uncle. How much further to that lean-to?"

Lev pointed to the summit of the tree-and boulder-covered hillside that lay in the near distance. "That is the crest where Vasili Burukan witnessed his mystery. We should have an excellent view of Posjet and the bay from there. Now look out for ice and pick your steps with care."

Tanya issued a mocking salute and followed on her uncle's heels. She was careful to take his advice as the path steepened and the footing became increasingly treacherous. Even the hefty furrier was forced to slow his progress. At a particularly sheer granite incline, he halted to let her go before him.

"Try to grab hold of a crevice with your hands and feet. I will be right behind you if you should fall, so have no worry."

Tanya faced the icy wall that stretched several meters upward. Though it took some effort, she managed to locate a series of narrow fissures in the rock and used them to gain leverage and stability. When the toe of her boot slipped from the shelter of one of these clefts, her uncle's firm grasp was quick to steady her. With her heart pounding away in her chest, she somehow resumed her climb, and eventually reached the top of the sheer rock shelf.

They took several minutes to regain their breath at this spot. Lev readjusted the fur cap that covered his bald skull, and pointed to the hill's tree-lined summit, which lay barely an eighth of a kilometer distant.

"That's the worst of it, little one. The path is more level now. We'll stop for some refreshments at the lean-to, which lies just over the crest of that hill. Can you make it, my dear?"

Before Tanya could answer, the woods filled with the distant, pronounced wail of an air-raid siren. This unexpected, alien sound was all that was needed to send the two hikers scrambling up the snow-covered trail. Minutes later, with lungs wheezing, they reached the crest.

Barely taking notice of the crude, wooden structure that graced the hillside there, Tanya peered out to the unbelievable vista visible before her. Filling the southern horizon was an immense, pine-filled valley, and beyond, the rippling waters of Posjet Bay. All of this took on a different dimension when the clouds parted and a beam of direct sunlight lit the earth below. It was her uncle who redirected her gaze to the west.

"Do you see those two silver objects skimming the water down there? My God, they're cruise missiles!"

Tanya followed the direction of her uncle's pointed right index finger, and seconds later caught sight of a pair of stubby, rectangular, rocket-shaped missiles complete with miniature wings and stabilizer fins. Because of their relatively small size and great velocity, they proved difficult to track visually. She could only guess that they were aimed at the collection of cottages and other structures that hugged the bay's northern shore and comprised the village of Posjet.

The siren was still incessantly whining in the background when both missiles suddenly veered upward. Tanya caught a glint of sunlight reflected off their fuselages. She watched breathlessly as they continued to climb towards the heavens, until a blindingly bright shaft of pure white light issued forth from the village's outskirts. In the blink of an eye, the lead rocket exploded. The swiftness of this attack had barely registered in her consciousness when the second cruise missile burst in a fiery cloud. Soon all that was visible

70

was a smoking shower of falling debris. With this, the wail of the siren dissipated, to be replaced by the howl of the gusting wind and the firm, deep voice of her uncle.

"Good heavens, they've done it! If I hadn't seen it with my very own eyes, I would have never believed it, yet here it is. Do you know what this means, little one? For the first time ever, a surprise nuclear strike can be undertaken with little risk of a counterstrike. The entire balance of military power will be upset, with World War Three all but inevitable!"

An immense bank of clouds veiled the sun, and Tanya shivered uncontrollably. Well aware of the truth of her uncle's apocalyptic observation, she found her gaze glued to the waters of Posjet Bay. There a trio of small boats could be seen setting sail from the village's pier. It was obvious they were bound for the spot where the debris of the cruise missiles had smashed into the waters.

A firm, warm hand grasped her shoulder and she redirected her glance to meet the serious gaze of Lev Litvov. He was more like her father than her own flesh and blood. She knew she would do whatever he asked in order to help him get knowledge of this momentous event to their contact in the West. She could only pray that it already wasn't too late.

CHAPTER THREE

The view from General Secretary Viktor Chernavin's office window was ordinarily an inspiring one. Clearly visible over the thick Kremlin walls were the gold-skinned, onion-shaped domes of the buildings that once housed the Cathedrals of the Annunciation, St. Basil's, and the Archangel Michael, and were now State museums. On a clear day, one could see beyond these massive structures, to the myriad of high-rises that shaped the profile of modern Moscow. Though the sky was indeed a deep blue, with the sun shining high in the heavens, the man who was responsible for guiding the Rodina's fate peered out of his office's full-length picture window and saw only his own reflection. The frame and figure of a tired old man met his weary eyes. Gone were the solid shoulders and tight gut of his youth. In their place were a full potbelly and a rounded back, stooped forward as if the very weight of his great office had altered his posture.

Running his hands through his thinning mane of silver hair, Chernavin wondered where the years had gone to. What had happened to that strapping, bright-eyed young man who'd come to the capital full of dreams and ideals? Was it really that long ago that he'd arrived in Moscow, with little more than the clothes he wore on his back? Yet, somehow, five decades had passed since that fated day he'd stepped off the railroad coach to begin his life's work.

He would never forget how exciting those early days had been. After all, he'd been a naive farmer's son who knew little of the world's cosmopolitan ways. It had been one of his father's wartime comrades who'd taken Chernavin under his wing and given the youngster his first position in the government. Though he was but a lowly bureaucrat in the State's Agricultural Ministry, he'd worked hard and tirelessly. This selfless effort had brought him under the scrutiny of the local Party leader, who'd recognized Chernavin's unique talent in getting things done. A quick series of promotions had followed, and soon it had been apparent that the young farmer from the Ukraine would never return to work the fields again.

How very innocent life had seemed in those days, thought the General Secretary with a heavy sigh. And who would have ever dreamed that his efforts would eventually lead him to the Rodina's highest office? Surely he had lived up his life's greatest potential and then some. Yet why was he so depressed lately? Instead of glorying in his long climb to power, he found himself sullen and cynical. Ever since his beloved Anna had died, five and a half years ago, this morose view had increasingly worsened. Today he had no real friends or outside interests. Filling his every hour were the seemingly insatiable demands of his job.

As Chernavin redirected his gaze to take in the copse of evergreens that were positioned outside in the courtyard, he could think of but one place where his worries temporarily escaped him. His dacha in Voronkl served as his lone solace. Situated a mere twenty-five kilometers due west of the Kremlin, this simple stone cottage was his last refuge. He knew he could take strength in the fact that he would be on his way there in a few more hours. He could only hope that this good weather held. After another long, frigid Russian winter, spring was finally in the air. Nowhere would this be as noticeable as in the birch wood that lay behind his dacha. There, on the banks of the Moscow River, new life would be emerging in the form of sprouting bulbs and newly born leaves. The ancient prophecy that his grandfather had spoken of would be renewed, as fresh life rose from the cold ashes of the old and Mother Russia once again fulfilled herself.

Merely contemplating such a primal vision, Chernavin felt his spirits lighten. He would go on with his duty tirelessly, knowing full well that his efforts guided the very fate of the Motherland. Soon enough, it would be his time to retire. Then he would have all of his remaining years to enjoy the countryside he so loved.

The clock that sat on the room's massive walnut bookcase chimed four times, and Chernavin turned away from the window. Slowly he walked over the magnificent Persian carpet that was a gift from the Turkmen citizens, and approached his desk. Its voluminous marble surface was cluttered with dozens of documents. On the top of this pile was a crimson-red folder, complete with an embossed hammer and sickle and the words "Top Secret" printed on its spine. Chernavin had been studying the contents of this report all afternoon, and was well aware of its significance.

The document had originated in the Ministry of

Defense. It concerned a detailed assessment of the progress of America's so-called Strategic Defense Initiative. As always, the determined Imperialists were throwing hundreds of billions of dollars into this effort. Three of their innovative programs were showing particular promise—lasers, particle beams, and kinetic-energy weapons.

The Soviet leaders who had come before Chernavin had vainly tried to warn the world of the dangers of such technologies. It was clear that a working ABM system would compromise the planet's already precarious balance of arms. The Imperialists had turned a deaf ear to their passionate pleas, and the Soviet Union had had no choice but to proceed with its own research program. Unlike the Americans, *their* scientists had concentrated their attention on a single area of study. This could have very well been a foolish decision, yet the Defense Ministry had been most convincing with its argument. In fact, all thirteen members of the ruling Politburo had given the Ministry the go-ahead to continue this effort.

As almost always seemed to be the case in such difficult programs, one delay had followed another. Already they were a full three months behind schedule. Chernavin knew they couldn't afford much more of a delay, for the report he had been scrutinizing warned that the Imperialists' strategic-weapons shield could very well be operational in less than a year. If the Americans beat them to it, it would be the Union of Soviet Socialist Republics that would be groveling at the Yankees' feet, completely impotent and begging for mercy.

The mere thought of such a scenario soured

Chernavin's stomach. Before he would allow such a thing, he would go to any extreme, short of a full-scale, surprise nuclear attack, to insure the Rodina's integrity. Lately, he was even beginning to reconsider this previously unthinkable option.

Chernavin was in the process of reseating himself behind the desk to take another look at the contents of the crimson-red folder when his intercom buzzed. This was followed by the familiar, nasal voice of his secretary, Olga Tisnevo.

"Comrade General Secretary, the Defense Minister has arrived. Shall I show him in?"

Chernavin took a quick look at his pocket watch, and saw that Marshal Alexi Kudikov was a good five minutes early for his appointment. This was just like the veteran officer, who would probably arrive at his own funeral early. Smiling at this thought, the General Secretary spoke into the intercom.

"Yes, Olga, show the esteemed marshal in. And would you please be so good as to serve us some tea."

"Of course, sir," answered Olga efficiently.

Chernavin was in the process of studying the opening page of the crimson folder when the double doors to his office swung open. The imposing figure of the Marshal stepped inside. The fifty-seven-year-old-Defense Minister was solidly built and wore his expertly tailored, forest-green uniform proudly. As he walked towards the desk, Chernavin noticed the full complement of medals that graced his chest. Many of those decorations were for valor, and were won on the bloody battlefields of Afghanistan. In fact, it could be said that it was because of that campaign that Alexi Kudikov had risen so quickly to his current position.

The General Secretary stood to greet his illustrious guest. It was as they traded hugs of welcome that Chernavin spotted the large envelope that the Defense Minister was carrying at his side.

Good afternoon, Comrade Marshal," said Chernavin gracefully. "You're certainly looking as fit as ever. Please take a seat and share some tea with me."

"Thank you, comrade," responded the Defense Minister. "In my mad rush to prepare myself for our meeting, I was forced to miss lunch, so the tea will be most appreciated."

Chernavin grinned and beckoned him to take a seat in one of the two high-backed chairs that were placed before his desk. The General Secretary chose to seat himself in the chair directly across from his guest. He settled himself in just as Olga Tisnevo entered, pushing an ornate silver tea cart before her.

"I hope you've included plenty to eat, Olga. It seems both myself and the marshal have a bit of an appetite this afternoon."

"It's no wonder. You barely touched your lunch, sir," retorted Chernavin's personal secretary for over three decades now. "As luck would have it, there's herring, sour cream, chopped onions, and some ham slices as well. The rye bread is fresh, and there's even some poppyseed cakes for dessert."

As he beamed at the tray of goodies that was soon set beside him, Chernavin's voice rose approvingly. "As always, you provide just what the doctor prescribed. I hope you have such an angel on your staff, Marshal. I don't know how I would get along without mine."

Olga blushed at this unexpected compliment. "There's plenty more if you're still hungry. You only have to ring."

With this, she turned to exit, and efficiently closed the doors behind her. Viktor Chernavin wasted no time picking up a cocktail fork and spearing a slender piece of pickled herring. He swallowed it with a single gulp and grinned.

"Ah, it's indeed excellent, my friend. Please help yourself. Now, do you desire tea or something a bit more stimulating?"

"I believe this occasion warrants the latter, Comrade General Secretary."

Surprised with such a response, Chernavin searched his guest's gaze. "It sounds as if you're the bearer of glad tidings, Marshal. Do I understand you properly?"

Marshal Kudikov answered while patting the envelope that lay in his lap. "That you do, comrade. I do hope that your video cassette recorder is working properly. I have a tape here which I'm certain you'll find most fascinating."

His curiosity piqued, Chernavin fumbled for the crystal decanter that graced the cart's lower shelf. He filled their tea cups with vodka and quickly returned his attention to the Defense Minister.

"Must you keep me in suspense so?" he queried.

The marshal smiled and tore open the envelope. He then removed a single, unmarked black video-cassette tape from its interior.

"It's all here, comrade. I'll guarantee that you won't be disappointed."

Chernavin reached forward and carefully grasped the cassette. Without further delay, he rose and proceeded to his desk's rear. There he faced what appeared to be a solid walnut panel. Yet, when his finger hit a switch recessed beside the coping, the wall opened, revealing a fully stocked entertainment center. This included a stereo, television monitor, and video-cassette recorder, which he was quick to access. After loading the tape, he picked up a hand-sized remote control device and returned to his seat beside the marshal. It was only then that he hit the remote's on switch.

Almost instantaneously there was a loud clicking sound. This was followed by the television monitor's sudden activation. Both men looked on as the screen filled with what appeared to be a large body of water. It was at this point that the Defense Minister began his commentary.

"What we are viewing is the Bay of Posjet, in the Far East. At this point, we are only a few dozen kilometers from the borders of North Korea and China, and are directly south of Vladivostok. This particular site was chosen for its relative anonymity and its proximity to an abundant source of nearby hydroelectric power.

"This film was shot from the cockpit of a Mil Mi-8 helicopter. The first segment that we shall watch was recorded three days ago. The segment that follows it was filmed only yesterday. It arrived in my office only a few hours ago and we are the first in Moscow to view it. Please pardon the lack of a sound track, but I'm certain that you'll find the action that you're about to witness more than sufficient."

Not really certain what he was about to see, the General Secretary sat anxiously forward. He looked on as the monitor filled with a shot of a portion of the land mass that surrounded the bay. He identified a solid forest of evergreen pines and what appeared to be some sort of small village tucked beneath the wall of thick boughs.

The angle of the lens once more returned to the bay and he caught sight of a trio of low-flying jet aircraft. They appeared to be moving at a great speed, and nearly skimmed the water's surface. Again the Defense Minister supplied the narration.

"Those are Tupolev Tu-22 supersonic bombers. They are being piloted by remote control and are following a flight plan similar to known US Air Force attack procedures. It is their strategy to approach their targets as low as possible to escape radar detection. As you will see, they will rapidly gain altitude as they near their weapons' release point, in order to escape the shockwaves produced by their ordinance."

True to this observation, the silver-skinned, swept-winged aircraft abruptly began pulling upward. The camera closed in on the lead jet and held on its fuselage. Still surprised that such vehicles could be piloted by remote control, Viktor Chernavin watched as a bright beam of intense white light flashed from below and focused itself on the plane's sharply angled nose. Barely a second later, the fuselage was enveloped in a veil of fire and smoke. This was followed by a violent explosion and the jet awkwardly cartwheeled from the sky, in a mass of showering debris.

This scenario was repeated two more times on the two aircraft that followed. Each time the results were the same. The final frames showed a number of patrol boats searching the blue, choppy waters for what was left of the three jet bombers.

Clearly impressed, yet puzzled all the same, Chernavin hit his remote control's stop button, and the picture froze in mid-frame. "May I ask for an explanation of the event we just witnessed, marshal?"

The Defense Minister was expecting such a confused reaction, and was direct with his reply. "What we have just seen is the destruction of a trio of modern, supersonic aircraft by means of a ground-based, free-electron laser."

"Then we've done it!" returned Viktor Chernavin excitedly. "All the billions of rubles and thousands of hours of research have finally paid off!"

"Just wait and see," added the marshal, who pointed to the screen. "Continue the tape and view for yourself the true extent of our project's advancement."

Chernavin needed no more urging to hit the button marked "forward." Again the screen filled with a shot of the Bay of Posjet. Yet this time when the camera panned the surrounding countryside, the General Secretary noticed that the woods were covered with a blanket of snow. The snow was not visible in the earlier segment, and must have fallen sometime between the two tapings.

The view returned to the bay and centered on a portion of the white-capped waters several kilometers from the shoreline. Only when the lens pulled down for a close-up did Chernavin spot the two stubby-winged, rocket-shaped objects shooting over the waves. He knew at a glance that they were cruise missiles, one of the latest additions to the Rodina's arsenal and an extremely potent strategic weapon. Like the jet aircraft, they were flying low to prevent radar detection. It was as they pulled up for the final segment of their attack scenario that a now-familiar, blindingly bright beam of light hit the lead vehicle. In response, it exploded almost instantaneously.

Chernavin marveled at the speed with which the laser beam redirected itself. Only a fleeting few seconds passed before the second cruise missile was nothing but a cloud of debris, raining down on the waiting waters. With this, the tape went unceremoniously blank.

After hitting the remote control's rewind button, Chernavin reached over for one of the two filled tea cups. He handed it to his bright-eyed guest, and then picked up one for himself. Holding the delicate china vessel before him, he made a spirited toast.

"To the Motherland, Comrade Kudikov! Once more, our brilliant scientific and military communities have done the impossible. What a momentous day this truly is!"

The Defense Minister nodded and, following his host's lead, downed a hearty mouthful of the fiery spirits. The sting of the vodka had yet to dissipate as the erect Army officer lifted his cup to make a toast of his own.

"To the foresight of our country's leaders! Without their vision and support, this glorious project might have never come to pass."

"Well said," prompted the General Secretary proudly. He then downed a second mouthful of spirits. Gazing directly into his guest's dark eyes, he added an almost fatherly request. "Now, you must take something to eat, Comrade Marshal. All this drinking on an empty stomach will give you nothing but ulcers."

This was all that was needed to send the Defense Minister reaching over to the silver tray. He chose the heel of the rye bread, and topped it off with a herring filet, some sour cream, and a sprinkling of chopped onion. A look of satisfied delight painted his face as he bit into this concoction and audibly sighed.

"There is nothing as tasty as the Rodina's own bounty," he observed between bites. "For this is a treat fit for a king."

"How about a czar?" jested Chernavin, in the midst of making a herring sandwich of his own.

Alexi Kudikov answered with a grin and finished off his snack. After washing it down with another drink, he again caught his host's attention.

"Now that you've seen the success of our country's first laser battle station against the fixed-wing aircraft and cruise-missile threat, how would you like to personally witness the final phase of our great experiment? If it is within the confines of your busy schedule, we'd be honored if you could visit the Posjet site in three weeks' time. If all proceeds on schedule, we'll be ready to attempt the ultimate test—the actual destruction of a flight of ICBM warheads as they descend over the waters of Posjet Bay."

Clearly impressed, Chernavin shook his head in wonder. "Of course I'll be there! I never dreamed that this project would bear fruit so quickly. It is a proud day for all of us."

"It's more than that," added the Defense Minister. "For, if this final phase is successfully completed, it will mark a turning point in history. Just think of it, comrade, a world in which the Motherland would no longer find itself threatened by the West's triad of strategic weapons! At long last, we could take the offensive, without the fear of Imperialist reprisals. Lenin's prophetic dream of an entire planet bonded together by the strengths of socialism will finally come to fruition!"

This lofty projection was still ringing in Viktor Chernavin's ears, when his Defense Minister leaned forward and locked his hypnotic gaze on that of the General Secretary. When Kudikov again spoke, his well-thought-out words flowed out smoothly.

"It is at long last time for you to take your rightful place in history, Viktor Chernavin. Never again will the Rodina have such an opportunity. It is common knowledge that America's own SDI package won't be operational for at least another year. Because of our daring gamble to concentrate our efforts on a single element of this same system, we have gained not only time, but the initiative as well.

"In the closing days of World War Two, it was the United States that beat us to the atomic bomb. During the years that immediately followed, when we desperately sought our own atomic weapon, the Americans were free to do just as they pleased. In one fell swoop, our entire socialist experiment could have been reduced to mere ashes. Yet the weak-minded Western leaders failed to take advantage of their sworn enemy's one vital weakness, and by 1949 the opportunity had been lost for all time.

"Unlike those idealistic fools, we Soviets have a better understanding of our place in history. No unrealistic visions veil our way. The Rodina has lost too many of its sons and daughters to aggressors, and we've made it a point to never forget their sacrifice. Thus, Viktor Chernavin, it has fallen upon your worthy shoulders to lead us from fear for the final time.

"What I propose is a preemptive nuclear strike against the United States of America, once the final test of our ABM system has been accomplished. The targets will be carefully selected to include only military command posts and communications relay stations. This will cripple the Imperialists' ability to launch a counterstrike. Yet, even if they do manage to release a selected load of warheads, our laser battle station will be put into action and their threat instantly negated."

Though such a suggestion hit Viktor Chernavin with a jolt, he found his mind, surprisingly, weighing the consequences. "Of course this attack would have to take place before the Americans deployed their SDI system," reflected the General Secretary. "Since that it only a mere year away, how do you propose building additional laser stations to protect the Rodina's borders to the north, west, and south?"

Thrilled that the old leader had not rejected his daring plan outright, the Defense Minister answered, "You are extremely perceptive, Comrade General Secretary. As you've so cleverly deduced, there will unfortunately be no time to build additional battle stations. Thus, in the unlikely event that our preemptive strike fails to totally cripple the Yankees, and they are able to launch some sort of counterattack, we merely have to move the country's most valued citizens under the protective umbrella of the Posjet installation. Vladivostok would be an excellent choice for a temporary capital."

Wincing at the thought of possibly exposing millions of the Rodina's citizens to the horrors of an atomic attack, Viktor Chernavin hesitated. Could he in all good conscience make such a decision, whatever good might eventually come of the outcome?

Seemingly reading his mind, Alexi Kudikov pleaded. "I realize that there are many risks involved, yet please look at the overall picture! Even if we were forced to sacrifice some of our own, surely they would readily go to their graves knowing that their deaths were not in vain. The important element is that the country's leadership would survive. Freed forever from the threat of Imperialist aggression, the Motherland would quickly heal its wounds and a new, glorious chapter in humanity's history would unfold. The question now is if you can dare pass up such a once-in-a-millennium opportunity. At least consider it thoroughly before making up your mind one way or the other."

With his gaze still locked on the distinguished face of the Defense Minister, Chernavin inwardly debated the pros and cons. He was well aware that the Americans had indeed lost an irreplaceable opportunity in the years immediately after the Great War. If the Yankees had dared to take the initiative, as their brilliant generals Curtis LeMay and Douglas MacArthur had proposed, the current Soviet Union would not exist. Today the tables were reversed, and it was the Rodina that held the technological advantage. Since this advantage would only be a temporary one, could he stand by and watch their efforts all go for naught? For, the moment the Americans deployed their own strategic defense system, the same old nuclear stalemate would prevail — and with it an even more costly episode of the arms race would be upon them.

One thing that he was certain of was that the Rodina was sick and tired of sacrificing the majority of its industrial output for one wasteful weapons system after the other. There could be no ignoring the grumbles of the average citizen, who faced continuous shortages of basic foodstuffs and other consumer products. Since it was evident that the Imperialists would never agree to a nuclear weapons treaty, there was little hope for the future. Yet here was the hand of fate offering him an unparalleled chance to break this tragic stalemate once and for all. A single window of opportunity existed to take advantage of this unique combination of circumstances. Even if it did mean exposing the Motherland to a limited nuclear attack, could he neglect the vast long-range benefits such a daring move on their part would entail?

Conscious that the poker-faced Defense Minister must be well aware of his quandary, Chernavin decided to further contemplate the consequences of Alexi Kudikov's proposal. His dacha at Voronkl would offer him the perfect environment to determine his alternatives and come up with a proper decision. Of course, there were still some very important considerations that had to be cleared up. Most of these were of a military nature. Since the Defense Minister would be the individual whom he would be relying on for the answers to these questions, he would have to trust Kudikov implicitly. One element came immediately to mind, and the General Secretary decided to waste no time with his inquiry.

"Comrade Marshal, have you completely thought out the manner in which we will negate the Americans' ability to order a counterstrike? I fear that I could never promote a plan that could result in an unprecedented slaughter within our borders."

Well prepared to answer just such a question, Alexi Kudikov sat forward. "Neither could I, comrade. That is why I've made such an attack plan the focus of my study for a good part of the past decade. With the assistance of our intelligence community, I have come up with a mere one hundred targets within the continental United States, the elimination of which will almost completely deny them the ability to launch two elements of their strategic triad. By knocking out their NORAD Colorado Springs headquarters, and taking out their alternative flying command posts and ground-based SAC airfields, we will severely cripple their fixed-wing capabilities. A simple pin-down strike, followed by a barrage of accurately placed, silo-busting warheads, will do the same to their ICBM fields. This leaves only one leg of their triad to be reckoned with.

"It has long been recognized that the Imperialists' submarine fleet offers us our most serious challenge. Their Trident submarines carry well over half of the West's available nuclear warheads. For years these vessels have been practically untraceable. Yet, just as with the laser battle station, we have applied our total effort to this problem and have come up with an extremely practical solution.

"To seek out and destroy the Tridents as they soundlessly cruise the depths of their patrol stations, a new class of Soviet attack subs has been created. The Akula vessels incorporate the latest state-of-the-art high-tech systems. Not only do they run deeper, quicker, and with just as much stealth as their Yankee equivalents, but they also carry a new sonar array that will tag the Tridents long before they release their missiles. A new design of torpedo has been put into service that will insure the enemy subs' destruction once they have been found.

"As a backup to the Akula, we have taken the liberty of stationing various older-model submarines in the waters near America's naval bases. It is their responsibility to monitor the Tridents as they leave port and head for the open seas. In most cases, the Akulas have taken this information and utilized it to silently follow the Tridents all the way to their patrol stations. Thus the majority of their fleet lies within our sights at this very moment."

It was clearly evident that the Defense Minister had indeed given this much thought. Chernavin couldn't help but be impressed. Yet the weighty consequences of his decision still had to be completely considered. To properly insure his objectivity, he would leave for Voronkl as soon as possible. There the Defense Minister could always be brought in to provide additional details, and at least he would have the peace and serenity of the birch wood to guide the course of his difficult, all-important choice.

Once again reaching over to refill their glasses, Viktor Chernavin knew that the responsibility was now all his. Never one to shirk his duties, he could but study the alternatives and then reach a decision to the best of his abilities. Even though the fate of the entire planet now rested squarely on his worn shoulders, his hand barely shook as he raised his glass in silent toast and downed the spirits that were the Rodina's lifeblood.

At the same moment that General Secretary Viktor Chernavin was in the midst of his difficult deliberation, the Soviet Whiskey-class attack submarine *Dnieper* was penetrating Washington's Strait of Juan de Fuca. Having left its pen in the Soviet Far East ten days before, the vessel had crossed the Pacific by way of the deep waters of the Kuril and Aleutian trenches. The boat had momentarily ascended off the coast of Vancouver Island. There, under the cover of night, it had turned due southward for the short trip to the nearby strait of water separating the countries of Canada and the United States.

The *Dnieper* was almost thirty years old. Based on the primary design of the German Type XXI submarine, it had come from one of the most successful classes of underwater vessel ever produced. Beginning in 1951, and continuing on until 1964, the Soviet Union had launched 260 of these reliable, sturdy craft. At present, 50 of these boats remained in service, with a further 100 in reserve.

Specially adapted for use in shallow waters, the *Dnieper* was an excellent representative of those surviving Whiskey-class subs that still earned their keep. It was 250 feet long, from its v-shaped bow to its tapered stern, and was staffed by a complement of fifty men. Unlike the majority of modern submarines that were powered by nuclear reactors, the *Dnieper* gained its propulsion from a pair of diesel-electric motors. Thus, like the boats of World War II, it was forced to surface from time to time to replenish its supply of oxygen. To keep from being detected at this time, the sub made use of a snorkel device that sipped in air without compelling the vessel to completely break the water's surface.

Captain Dmitri Zinyagin had been the commanding officer of the *Dnieper* for the past year and a half. A ten-year naval veteran, Zinyagin looked at his present command as the high point of his career. Though others may have sailed newer, more modern vessels, the *Dnieper* was a special boat, manned by a handpicked crew. Their current assignment was indicative of the confidence his superiors had in them. For few other Soviet submariners had ever ventured into the waters they were presently penetrating.

Upon first reading his orders, Zinyagin had thought that there must be some mistake. The Strait of Juan de Fuca was amongst the most closely monitored waterways on the planet. To successfully remain undetected there would take not only near perfect seamanship, but a good deal of luck as well.

As the captain stood in the rear of the *Dnieper*'s control room, watching his crew busily work at their stations, he felt confident in their proficiency. No group of sailors in the entire Rodina was as competent as his men. When he had informed them of their ultimate destination, only two days before, they had taken the news of their dangerous assignment all in stride. Not a single voice had been raised in dissension. If anything, they had seemed to apply themselves to their work even more than before.

The boat's Zampolit, Ivan Koslov, took this as an excellent sign of morale. The chubby, pasty-skinned political officer had requested a conference with Zinyagin immediately after the Captain had shared knowledge of his orders with the crew. At that time the Zampolit had warned him to be on the lookout for any signs of emotional overload. Zinyagin knew his men and shrugged off the paranoid Koslov's words of caution. Yet now that they were about to undergo the most critical part of their mission, he couldn't help but wonder if the Zampolit's observation could have substance.

For several hours now, they had been within the territorial waters of the United States. As if this weren't reason enough to cause the crew to be overly anxious, their present course was taking them due east. With each kilometer they traveled, the *Dnieper* was finding itself that much further from the shelter of the open ocean.

On the average the strait they were currently penetrating was barely twenty kilometers wide. Though they had an adequate depth, the waters were frequently traveled, particularly by military vessels. Of course, it was because of such traffic that they had been sent there in the first place.

As Zinyagin scanned the compartment's various consoles, from which every aspect of the boat's operational ability could be monitored, he found his gaze halting on the metal table that lay to his left. There, at the navigational station, the ship's senior lieutenant stood. Sergei Volzhnin's mournful eyes were glued to his own. When the thin, bearded officer grimly nodded, the Captain knew that it was time to join him.

From the boat's helm, the diving officer's muted voice routinely called out their course, speed, and depth. Subconsciously taking note of each figure, Dmitri Zinyagin approached his second in command.

"I take it that we're nearly there, Sergei," said the Captain solemnly.

In response, the senior lieutenant pointed to the detailed chart that lay on the table before them. "If the last bearing was a correct one, we will be passing Callam Bay in five more minutes. From there, the inlet that we're to station ourselves in will be only seven and a half kilometers distant."

The Captain bent over to study the chart that had been his frequent companion for over a week. Yet now that they were actually in the straits, it seemed to have taken on an additional degree of realism. Starting at Cape Flattery, he traced the meander of the waterway eastward. It was at the cape that they had ascended to periscope depth, and made their initial bearing. Since they were hugging the southern shoreline, which was in American waters, they had used the lights of Canada's Port Renfrew to determine their exact position. Once this was known, they had again descended and continued with their penetration.

A pocket watch lay beside the chart. He could hear the ticking of each passing second, which meant that they were that much closer to their final goal. Dmitri Zinyagin had surrendered his gaze to the sweep of the second hand when a low-pitched voice called out behind him.

"Surface screws, Captain! Range one thousand meters and closing. It sounds like a pair of destroyers headed right at us from the east."

Instinctively, Zinyagin's pulse quickened. He looked upward, as if he could spot this threat visibly. His throat became dry and he began contemplating a worst-case scenario. Had they triggered some sort of underwater sensor that had pointed to their presence there? Or perhaps the sound of their E-motors had been picked up by the sensitive hydrophones of the Americans' SOSUS monitoring system. If any of these scenarios proved true, it was already too late to effect an escape.

While hastily considering his limited alternatives,

the Captain noticed that a newcomer had joined them. Seeming to be his usual snide and conceited self, the Zampolit stood by the navigational station. The political officer's forehead, cheeks, and neck were soaked in sweat, and his small, beady eyes were gleaming with curiosity.

"Is something occurring here that I should know of, Captain? Why, the tension's so thick in here that I could cut it with a knife."

A muted, alien, whirring sound was suddenly audible in the distance, and the political officer looked to the control room's cable-lined ceiling. "Ah, so we have visitors topside," he observed.

As if to confirm this, the sonar operator again spoke out. "That range is down to five hundred meters, Captain. From the screw pattern they appear to be powered by gas turbines, most likely of the Spruance class."

Dmitri Zinyagin knew such vessels to be extremely effective ASW platforms. Doing his best to ignore the distracting presence of the newcomer, the Captain listened as the sound of the advancing destroyers continued to intensify.

"Can't we do something, Captain?" whined the Zampolit. "Surely we're only sitting ducks here!"

Disgust painted Zinyagin's face as he responded. "And what would you like me to do, Comrade Koslov, blow them from their own waters? Don't forget who's doing the trespassing here."

Straining to control himself, the Captain turned toward the sonar console. Thirty seconds passed and the buzzing vibration seemed to rise even louder. Suddenly the sonar operator shouted excitedly, "They're turning back into the channel, Captain! The new range is six hundred meters and fading."

Concrete proof of this fact became apparent when the sound of the whirring screws gradually lessened. After a full minute, the noise of the passing destroyers could barely be heard, and Zinyagin knew that the threat was temporarily over. Only then did he allow himself a sigh of relief.

Beside him, Ivan Koslov had taken out his handkerchief and was doing his best to mop up the moisture that was dripping down his forehead. To the Zampolit, the interior of the sub always seemed to be at least ten degrees too warm. Thus his uniforms were consistently wrinkled and sweat-stained. As he patted dry his flushed cheeks and neck, the political officer turned his attention to the chart the Captain was bent over.

"That was a close one, Comrade Zinyagin," said the Zampolit. "Yet Lady Fortune remained with the *Dnieper* in this instance. Still, I thought that we would have arrived at our goal by this time."

The Captain grunted. "Have patience, Ivan Koslov. These waters are tricky and we must proceed warily."

Sergei Volzhnin checked the pocket watch and then drew a minuscule extension to the line that indicated the *Dnieper*'s present position. "It's time to take the final bearing, Captain."

"Very good, lieutenant," offered Zinyagin. "Bring us up to periscope depth, comrade. I'll be utilizing the attack scope to offer as little a profile as possible."

While the senior lieutenant relayed these instructions to the diving officer, Dmitri Zinyagin strode over to the periscope well. The Captain was somewhat upset to find the fat figure of the Zampolit waddling in his wake. His present mission was difficult enough, without having the nosy political officer to deal with constantly.

The firm voice of Sergei Volzhnin shouted out, "Periscope depth, Captain."

Zinyagin countered with a quick, "Up attack scope!"

In response to this directive, there was a loud hydraulic hiss as the periscope rose from the boat's bowels. With well-practiced rapidity, Zinyagin extended the scope's arms, hunched over, and nestled his eyes into the rubberized lens coupling. Hastily he turned a complete circle to make certain that there were no surface vessels lying close by. Once he was assured of this fact, he turned the lens to examine the southern shoreline.

Under maximum magnification, the tree-covered hills of this portion of America's Washington State seemed to be within touching distance. He spotted what appeared to be a small fishing camp comprised of a one-story, wooden lodge, a ramshackle pier, and a battered old trawler docked beside it. A gentle plume of smoke rose from the cottage's chimney, giving this scene a homelike quality. A quick scan of the coast to the immediate east of this compound revealed nothing but a solid expanse of isolated forest land. Fearing that they had missed their mark, the Captain turned the lens even further to the east. He was forced to do a double take when a flashing green beacon beckoned in the distance like the smile of a long-lost friend.

"I believe we've got it!" cried the Captain triumphantly. "Down scope. All ahead one-third."

Zinyagin stood straight and backed away from the well, as the periscope hissed downward. The compartment filled with the sudden soft whir of their E-motors. There was the slightest sensation of forward movement, and the Captain's eyes went immediately to his wristwatch. His total attention was riveted on this timepiece's second hand, when the gruff, irritating voice of Ivan Koslov came from his right.

"Are you certain that this is the proper inlet, Captain? A miscalculation at this point of our mission could prove disastrous for us all."

Hardly believing the man's audacity, Dmitri Zinyagin caught the beedy glance of the Zampolit. "If you have no faith in my seamanship, Comrade Koslov, just say so outright, and I'll be happy to let you try your hand."

There could be no mistaking the hostility of the Captain's tone, and the political officer responded carefully. "I was not challenging your ability to run the *Dnieper*, Captain Zinyagin. I was only recommending additional caution during this the most critical portion of our long journey."

Not taking the time to answer him, the Captain returned his total attention to his watch. "That should do it, lieutenant. All stop! Up scope."

The submarine slowed and its periscope hissed upward. No sooner did the lens break the water's surface then Zinyagin bent over to peer through its reflective coupling. His line of sight was still focused on the adjoining coastline, and it took only a few seconds for him to reorientate himself. From this new perspective, the beacon he had previously viewed was nearly in front of them. It appeared to be anchored to the floor of the strait and was situated a mere quarter of a kilometer from land. Beyond its flashing green strobe, a good-sized cove was visible. There was no doubt in his mind that this was the very inlet that Command had chosen for them to carry out the next portion of their mission.

Not desiring to proceed blindly, the Captain issued his orders while still perched before the periscope. "Come hard aport to course two-zero-zero. All ahead one-third."

Volzhnin repeated these directives and the *Dnieper* began slowly altering its direction. All the time the Captain was watching their progress unfold. He shouted out in warning, "Watch the depth under our keel, lieutenant! I know the charts show us with plenty of headroom, but this is no time for surprises."

"I'm on the fathometer now, Captain," Volzhnin answered alertly. "So far, all appears to match up with the chart perfectly."

Thankful for what appeared to be excellent intelligence data, Zinyagin exhaled in relief. Still hunched over the periscope, he looked on as the beacon passed on their starboard. Their present course was taking them into the exact center of the rapidly approaching inlet. This channel had apparently been formed millions of years ago, when a major river poured into the strait here. Today the river was no more, yet the channel still existed. It would be within this estuary that they would descend, to take refuge on its sandy bottom.

Zinyagin took a moment to scan the hills that were beginning to surround them on three sides. With the benefit of the attack scope's maximum magnification, he could see that these slopes were formed from what appeared to be limestone. This carbonated rock provided an adequate footing for the thousands of pine trees that comprised the encroaching forest. With fond memories of the similar stands of pines that made up the Siberian woods of his youth, he felt strangely at home here. In such a way, his first close-up view of America wasn't so alien after all.

The Captain clicked the scope back to normal magnification, and realized that they were making excellent progress. Well into the shelter of the inlet by now, he prepared to give the orders which would stop their forward progress, turn their bow back towards the strait, and then take them to the channel's bottom. Seconds away from relaying these directives, his gut unexpectedly tightened. This was followed by a sudden, jarring concussion, which knocked the Captain's forehead hard into the scope's coupling and sent him reeling to his knees.

The lights to the control room blinked off and then on again, and the bow of the sub noticeably dipped downward. As he struggled to stand, Zinyagin was sent slumping to the deck by a wave of nauseous dizziness. His thoughts clouded, and all that he was aware of was the intense pain that pounded in his forehead.

Though he had smacked into the periscope well alongside the Captain, Koslov had escaped major injury. Not knowing what had caused this collision, he kneeled down beside his fallen commanding officer.

"Captain?" implored the Zampolit. "Captain, can you hear me?"

When Zinyagin failed to respond to his plea, the political officer knew that the Captain was hurt seriously. Suspecting a concussion, Ivan stood to determine their status.

He was surprised to find the control room in shambles. Loose equipment lay scattered on the decking, with several prone sailors sprawled among the debris. The bearded figure of Sergei Volzhnin was in the process of picking himself up from the floor, on the opposite side of the compartment. Relieved to find him apparently uninjured, the Zampolit called to him passionately.

"Lieutenant, the Captain appears unconscious. This means that you are now in command of this vessel. What is the *Dnieper*'s status? Are we sinking?"

Spurred instantly into action, the bearded officer faced the boat's helmsmen, who had been held in their chairs by seatbelts. A quick scan of their instruments showed the sub to be hanging motionless in the water. Volzhnin wasted no time telephoning the engine room. He listened to the chief explain their condition, and went on to query damage control. By the time he was off the telephone, the Zampolit was positioning himself at Volzhnin's side.

"Well, Lieutenant?" prompted the sweating political officer. "Just what has befallen us?"

Volzhnin answered while looking at the compartment's far side, where a kneeling corpsman was working on their still-prone Captain. "It appears that we have run into a fishing net, Comrade Koslov. As it stands now, the *Dnieper*'s dual propeller shafts are completely jammed."

"Well, can they be repaired?" asked the red-faced Zampolit anxiously.

The senior lieutenant thoughtfully stroked his beard. "The chief feels that a diver may be able to cut us loose."

"Then what are we waiting for?" queried the eager Zampolit.

Not appreciating the political officer's aggressiveness, Volzhnin challenged him directly. "I am quite aware of our precarious situation, Comrade Koslov, and I plan to attempt to extricate us from our predicament as soon as I feel it's safe to do so."

"And just when is that?" snapped the Zampolit curtly.

Trying hard to keep his control, the senior lieutenant took a deep breath and exhaled it fully before answering. "In order to effect such a repair, the *Dnieper* will be forced to surface. To do so now, under the light of day, will be tantamount to suicide. Thus, we will wait for the cover of night before ascending."

Satisfied with this response, the Zampolit nodded. "That sounds like an adequate plan, lieutenant. Your competence shall be noted. If I can be of any help to you, please don't hesitate to ask. Now, I'd better see to the condition of our esteemed Captain. That knock he took on his forehead was a nasty one."

Without further comment, Koslov turned again to cross the compartment. By this time most of the debris had been picked up and the injured attended to. Only the Captain was still prone on the deck. Relieved that Volzhnin had apparently risen to the occasion and accepted full command, the political officer approached the periscope well to see to Dmitri Zinyagin's condition.

The night fell clear, yet moonless. After waiting for the last drop of color to fade from the dusk, Senior Lieutenant Sergei Volzhnin gave the order to surface.

In instant response, a gurgling surge of seawater was vented from the *Dnieper*'s ballast tanks and the crippled sub popped upward.

For almost two hours the interior of the sub had been bathed in an eerie red light. This precaution had been taken to insure that the crew had the full benefits of night vision. To further expand their range of sight, the deck crew had been outfitted with the so-called "see-in-the-dark" binoculars.

When it was determined that Captain Zinyagin's concussion would keep him from reassuming command, Volzhnin had assumed total responsibility for the repair attempt. With the moral support of the Zampolit, the *Dnieper*'s second in command had called together the boat's senior ratings. It was during this desperate conference that a plan had been finalized.

Proud of their effort, Volzhnin stood in the control room clothed completely in black oilskins. Beside him, dressed in similar outfits, was a handpicked seven-man deck crew. Standing behind these anxious figures were their two wet-suited SCUBA divers. Each of these brave men waited for the moment when the boat's deck would emerge clear of the inlet's waters.

It was the boat's diving officer who gave Volzhnin the go sign. Ever true to his new leadership role, the lieutenant was the first to climb the sail's ladder and pop the hatch. A cold spray of still-draining water soaked his face as he emerged topside. Wiping this moisture from his eyes, he took in a deep lungful of fresh night air, and found it heavy with the scent of the surrounding pine forest.

Two lookouts joined him. It would be their responsibility to continually scan the waters for any signs of unwelcome visitors. This left Volzhnin free to monitor the movement taking place on the deck below him. There the other portion of the repair crew had popped the hatch cut into the sail's base. A safety line was rigged and the men began the dangerous job of transferring themselves to the boat's stern. Fortunately, the waters were calm and this transit took place without incident.

By use of a two-way radio, the lieutenant was given an up-to-the-minute report of their progress. He was impressed with the swiftness with which the divers were able to take to the waters. When the chief reported the lead diver's initial visual scan of the clogged shafts, his spirits further lightened, for the obstructions didn't appear to be as serious as they had feared. In fact, the divers were already well into the process of cutting the net free.

Volzhnin took this opportunity to view the full expanse of stars visible above him. Back in the Rodina, he had spent entire nights in such a manner, his mind totally lost to the vast universes visible beyond. Breathing the fresh night air, he could easily fool himself into believing that he was merely back home once again. Yet there could be no ignoring the seriousness of their current predicament.

For a solid hour, the divers worked on freeing the frozen shafts. Without the benefit of a single break, they worked tirelessly, until the final strand of netting had been finally cut loose. Only after a preliminary test of the propulsion system showed it to indeed be working perfectly did Volzhnin order the deck crew below, with a hearty "Job well done!"

The men were in the process of transferring themselves back to the sail when one of the lookouts who stood beside Volzhnin cried out in alarm. "Surface ship approaching off the port beam!"

These words struck the lieutenant like a clenched fist. Hurriedly following the young man's pointed finger, Volzhnin had no trouble locating this unexpected visitor. The ship was rounding the inlet from the waters of the strait. The gathering roar of its engines and the powerful beam of the spotlight that was mounted on its bow surely indicated that this was a military vessel. Not desiring to waste a single second in learning for certain, Volzhnin screamed into the intercom. "Dive! Dive! Dive!"

The repair crew was just disappearing into the base of the sail, as the lieutenant followed the two lookouts down from its top. Volzhnin sealed the hatch above him and scurried down the tubular steel ladder. He entered the control room and found it filled with activity. The wet-suited divers and their helpers were clearing the compartment, while the crew members on station were carrying out his frantic order. Volzhnin rushed to the diving console and found a familiar, portly individual waiting for him there.

"The *Dnieper* is sealed and ready to dive, Comrade Volzhnin," said the sweating Zampolit. "What in the world did you see up there anyway?"

"Actually, I didn't wait around to check for certain," returned Volzhnin, who relished the sound of venting air and onrushing seawater ballast.

"Then perhaps all this fuss is over a mere fishing boat," offered the political officer.

Ignoring this observation, the *Dnieper*'s acting Captain locked his concentration on the planesmen. "Take us down, comrades, for our very lives!"

Seeing that they were doing everything within their ability to do just that, he turned to address the sonar operator. "Well, Nikolai, just who do we have up there?"

With one hand pressed to his headphones, the experienced petty officer answered, "It sounds like one of their Coast Guard cutters, sir. She's cut her engines and seems to be just sitting there at the mouth of the inlet."

"Then perhaps Lady Fortune is still with us," reflected the Zampolit. "After all, there's always the chance that they saw absolutely nothing."

Again Volzhnin attempted to ignore the political officer's ramblings. Instead he returned his glance to the depth gauge that was set between the planesmen. He was just about ready to believe that they could escape detection when the room filled with the sickening ping of the enemy's sonar.

"They've restarted their engines!" shouted the sonar operator.

Volzhnin found himself wishing that their Captain were beside him. Dmitri Zinyagin would know just what to do. Yet fate had elected Volzhnin to get them out of harm's way. This was a task he could not refuse.

Snapping him from his brief reverie was the ever-present voice of Ivan Koslov. "Well, Comrade Volzhnin, now what?"

The lieutenant's response was ultimately determined by the cries of their sonar operator. "They're heading into the inlet!"

It was apparent that they had but two options. One was to remain where they were, which was as good as surrendering. The other was to run for the relative shelter of the strait and the open ocean beyond. Well aware of the sensitivity of their mission, Sergei knew he had little choice in the matter.

"Engineering, we're going to need full power! Helmsmen, prepare the boat for a one-hundred-and-eighty-degree turn!"

Silently appraising this passionate outburst was the Zampolit. Though he would have been more comfortable with Zinyagin at the helm, the lieutenant was displaying his share of spunk and spirit. Koslov wondered if these qualities would be sufficient to see them free. Suddenly the *Dnieper* lurched forward. He found himself having to hold on to the chart table's edge as the boat attempted a canted, high-speed turn.

Sweat poured down Koslov's forehead and his mouth was dry with fear. This was a sensation that had been long absent from his life, yet in a strange way he found it somewhat stimulating.

They were well into their tight turn, with a look of hope in the command crew's expressions, when the *Dnieper* plowed into a newly formed sandbar. So intense was this collision that the vessel was abruptly stopped dead in the water, its bow firmly embedded in the shoal's innards. The resulting jolt sent a spasm of uncontrollable energy throughout the vessel. The majority of the sub's crew found themselves lying bruised and shaken on the equipment-cluttered deck. Several of the men weren't so lucky. This included their radio operator, who was crushed to death by a falling transmitter in the first fleeting seconds of the accident.

Panic rose. Among those who tried to quell the alarm was the Zampolit. Though bruised and cut himself, Koslov organized the first damage-control surveys. Once the integrity of the boat was assured, he quickly walked the length of the *Dnieper*, spreading hope and confidence wherever possible. As he was passing through the torn remains of the officers' quarters, he found the corpse of Dmitri Zinyagin. Their Captain's neck had been broken, and Ivan guessed that the poor man had never known what hit him. The political officer spent little time in the mourning, for a much greater priority dawned in his consciousness.

Locked in the boat's safe was a full set of top-secret, ultra-sensitive orders. Since the American Coast Guard cutter was presently lying in the waters directly above them, it was evident that they would all too soon be boarded. Thus it was his duty to destroy these documents at once. Thankful that one of the two keys to this safe was in his possession, he got on with this chore, confident that he could make up a story to relate to the gullible Yankees. After all, he could always tell them that the ship had gotten lost, while in the midst of an innocent cruise homeward!

CHAPTER FOUR

The office of Admiral Walter Lawrence, the current Chief of Naval Operations — CNO, as he was more commonly known — was located in the Pentagon's exclusive E-ring. Built as one of the world's largest office buildings, with a capacity of well over 30,000 people, the Pentagon was not actually one building, but about fifty. Each of these were interconnected, in the shape of five complete pentagons, placed one inside another in a series of concentric, five-sided rings. The outermost, and therefore largest of these rings, was the E-ring.

One of the benefits of having an office there — in addition to the ornate marble columns, terrazzo floors, and private elevators that were unique to this section of the structure — was the marvelous exterior views. It was this feature that Walter Lawrence was admiring on this hectic Monday morning.

With coffee cup in hand, the CNO stared out at the city of Washington, D.C., visible before him. It was a gray, rainy day, and he could barely make out the 555-foot-high, white-marble obelisk of the Washington Monument peeking through the mist in the distance. On the other side of this structure, not visible from this vantage point, was the White House, from which he had only recently returned.

The call informing him of the National Security Council briefing had come as a complete surprise. In fact, he had just been emerging from the shower barely four hours ago, when the phone rang and the President's National Security advisor issued the curt invitation. Two hours later, he was in the Oval Office, seated among an illustrious grouping of individuals which included the Secretaries of Defense, State, and Navy, the Director of the CIA, the NSA Director, and, of course, the President.

The meeting began with the Chief Executive issuing a brief greeting. Keeping to his character of not being one to waste words, he then introduced Samuel Morrison, the head of the CIA. Well-respected by his fellow colleagues, Morrison stood and got the briefing off to a rousing start with an astounding revelation. Only hours before, a communiqué had arrived from one of their most dependable operatives in the Soviet Far East, informing them that the Soviets had successfully tested a ground-based laser battle station. What made this report even more important was the fact that these tests had apparently taken place under wartime conditions, and that the lasers had been responsible for the downing of both fixed-wing jet aircraft and cruise missiles.

Though the Agency had been well aware that the Soviets were actively engaged in such research, the speed with which they had actually deployed this equipment had caught the U.S. completely off guard. America's own laser battle station was well over a year from completion, thus giving the Russians a tremendous head start. Of course, all this could be of even greater significance if the Soviet installation could prove effective against ICBM warheads. Morrison concluded his remarks by warning them all that it was the CIA's belief that such a test against descending warheads could take place shortly. If successful, this would give the Soviet Union the first active ABM shield in existence.

There was a hushed silence as the distinguished CIA director seated himself. The CNO's gaze went to the Secretary of the Navy, the man he answered to. The two men seemed to share a silent moment of concern. Then the President introduced the Secretary of State.

The country's chief diplomat went on to give them a quick update on the recently signed ABM treaty between the US and the Soviet Union. This intensely negotiated document had established a concrete set of guidelines concerning such technology. Both countries had agreed to the principle that research and development in this difficult, costly field was to continue, though well short of actual deployment. It was the Secretary's opinion that if such a test had indeed occurred, the Soviets had definitely exceeded the limits of the treaty.

Following him was the grim-faced Secretary of Defense. His voice's tone was ominous as he revealed the results of the latest reconnaissance satellite photos of the Soviet Union. Deteriorating weather conditions had made it impossible to get photos of this rumored laser installation. Yet other intelligence shots showed a somewhat alarming increase in Russia's strategic nuclear-delivery posture. Of particular concern were photos showing Soviet ballistic missile submarines being fitted with some sort of new warhead, and then these submarines' sudden departure to sea. Before this, the Russians had been content to station but a small percentage of their subs on actual patrols. Yet the latest assessment indicated that an unprecedented eighty percent of Soviet strategic missile-carrying vessels were now cruising beneath the planet's oceans.

Walter Lawrence anxiously stirred at this. He knew that most of these submarines could loiter silently in their own waters and still be able to hit targets anywhere in the continental United States. Others would be assigned to cruise beneath the cover of the Arctic ice pack, where they would be extremely difficult to locate—and if need be eliminate. And then there were those vessels which would be stationed only a few miles off America's coastline. In the event they remained undetected, such subs could hit American cities with missiles in less than ten minutes.

The CNO was already beginning to contemplate how the US Navy would counter these threats, when the President's deep voice caught his attention. Walter looked on as the Chief Executive lifted his lanky frame upward, cocked his hands behind his back, and continued to speak while pacing the floor that lay before his desk.

With direct ease, he listed their alternatives. The first one he offered was to merely ignore the Soviet test as inconsequential. But because a comparable US installation was at least a year away, he immediately discounted this thought as being much too dangerous to even consider.

His next option was to contact the Soviet General Secretary on the hot line and directly confront him. From what little he knew of Viktor Chernavin, he was pretty certain that the veteran leader of the Politburo was not the type to be easily intimidated. Because of the Soviets' technological advancement, Chernavin would be holding the stronger hand anyway. Thus the President could only take this course if the laser base were somehow put out of action.

This led the Chief Executive to put forth a plan first offered by his National Security advisor. Because the very balance of power would be upset in the event that the Soviet laser base were indeed able to eliminate all three legs of America's strategic triad, it was vital that the US be given the option of clandestinely destroying this installation. Much to Walter Lawrence's dismay, the responsibility for planning such a mission was rather unceremoniously dumped into his lap. With the CNO's promise that he would get to work on drawing up such an operation at once, the meeting was adjourned.

This had all taken place barely an hour before and Walter Lawrence had hurriedly returned to the Pentagon to get on with this new assignment. His first duty upon arriving back at his office had been to inform his top subordinates of the Soviet strategic posture. It would now be their duty to inform the various fleet commanders. In such a way, the country's naval ASW forces could be better prepared to meet any type of Russian threat. He took it solely upon himself to come up with a method of taking out the Soviet laser battle station.

His first move had been to draw up a map of this

installation's exact location. He pulled out his charts of the Soviet Far East. As he searched for the coordinates that lay to the immediate south of Vladivostok, utilizing the data that the CIA had provided, he found himself somewhat surprised to lay his eyes on a familiar geographical formation. He realized with a start that it had been over forty years since he had last studied these very same waters. At that time the name had been different, yet how amazingly similar were the missions!

The Strait of Posjet was currently under Soviet rule, yet forty-three years before it had been the exclusive domain of the Japanese. Walter Lawrence had first learned of this godforsaken corner of the earth during the closing days of the war in the Pacific. He was but a young, somewhat idealistic lieutenant in Naval Intelligence, and Command had given him his biggest assignment to date—to see to the destruction of a top-secret Japanese weapons facility that lay on the banks of Posjet Bay.

Still shocked by what appeared to be an incredible coincidence, Walter Lawrence suddenly remembered the officer who had overseen his work forty-three years before. Samuel Morrison had been a full commander at that time. It was under his auspices that the mission had been conceived and subsequently carried out.

No wonder the President had chosen him for this task. Certainly he had been recommended by the Director of the CIA, who knew that Walter was uniquely qualified to handle this mission. Mentally chastising himself for not realizing this sooner, he turned from the window and picked up the chart

113

that lay on the desk top before him.

Today the tiny peninsula of land that formed Posjet Bay was enclosed by the borders of China and North Korea. Four decades ago, this had not been so. Known simply as Manchuria, it had been under the supreme sovereignty of Japan. Compared to the satellite-enhanced chart that he presently held, the maps of forty-three years ago had been crude representations. In fact, if he didn't know otherwise, he would be hard-pressed to find any similarities between this chart and the older maps. Yet there could be no doubting it — the Soviet laser station was located close by the same site where the Japanese weapons facility had stood. And now, four decades later, he had been called upon to draw up yet another mission into these very same waters, this time to destroy a facility run by their ex-ally!

His pulse quickened with this thought, and Lawrence closed his eyes to return to the past. Could he ever forget that fateful afternoon when he had ordered "Carrigan's Raiders" to enter the strait and blow up the Japanese munitions factory? As if it had occurred in another lifetime, he visualized the faces of the USS *Abalone*'s crew as they cruised back into Pearl after the mission's conclusion. Embedded forever in his memory was the determined expression of the sub's young skipper as he stood on the boat's exposed conning tower, his trusty corncob pipe in hand. William Carrigan had gotten the Navy Cross for his efforts, yet the lanky commander had found little joy afterwards, so concerned was he for the handful of individuals he'd been forced to leave behind. Carrigan's preoccupation with this loss was one of the reasons the promising officer left the Navy soon afterward. Though he had certainly been of important assistance to them in his civilian duties since then, he was the type of man the Navy hated to lose.

The CNO remembered well the last time he had seen William Carrigan. It had been a year ago, on the eve of his installation as the Chief of Naval Operations. Looking dashing in a smartly tailored, pin-striped suit, Carrigan had arrived at the reception with nothing but good things to say about his World-War-II colleague. Walter was amazed at how little Carrigan had seemed to change through the years. Though his hair was streaked with gray, he was as fit and robust as ever. One thing that was apparent was that his success in business certainly didn't seem to have gone to his head. Even though he was the Chairman of the Board of one of the largest defense contractors in the nation, he still took the time to share a moment of pleasant conversation with all those he met.

They had parted with a promise to see each other on a more regular basis. Yet all too soon the great demands of their jobs had possessed their time like a jealous lover. And here it was a year later, and they hadn't even spoken to one another since.

Looking back to the chart that lay on his lap, Walter Lawrence decided with a grin that it was time to remedy this. He would need all the help he could get now, and could think of no better source of assistance than the ex-skipper of the USS *Abalone*.

The board meeting began at eight a.m. sharp. Seated at the head of the conference table, William Carrigan brought the session to order. Looking at least ten years younger than his actual age of sixty-nine, the silver-haired founder of Carrigan Industries welcomed his eight fellow board members to their Sunnyvale, California, headquarters. He then introduced the company's VP of finance, who briefed them on their current monetary position. Record last-quarter sales had significantly improved their position from the previous board meeting. Cash flow was adequate, and even their common stock was once more on the rise.

The mere mention of stock attracted the attention of their general counselor. Only the previous day their arch-rival, Jet Star International, had put into effect yet another hostile takeover attempt against them. Only a massive, last minute buy-back of their own common stock had saved them the last time this had occurred. Since current market conditions could make such an effort difficult this time, he proceeded to caution them that Jet Star's challenge was a very serious one.

This brought an immediate emotional response from the company's founder. Not about to merely sit back and watch his life's work go for naught, Carrigan urged the board to adopt a "poison-pill" anti-takeover strategy. Such a maneuver had been discussed at their last meeting. It was not only extremely time-consuming, but costly as well. If special warrants were issued to present common stockholders, shares of their preferred stock could be exchanged when the board deemed necessary.

This would make the price of the company far too expensive for Jet Star.

A vote was taken, and through the force of Carrigan's personality the "poison-pill" option was unanimously approved. With this out of the way, the discussion turned to current business.

First to speak was the VP in charge of the new, advanced-capability—ADCAP, for short—torpedo for the Navy's Seawolf attack-submarine program. He proudly reported that the research and development had been completed a full quarter early, and production of a prototype was already in the works. If all remained on schedule, actual field testing of this weapon could begin as early as this summer.

This brought a satisfied murmur from the others. Unfortunately, the mood was soon soured when the manager of their second most important project reported serious difficulties in their initial research stage. This project concerned using a blue-green laser to link the Seawolf with a communications satellite, even while the sub was deeply submerged.

Since the advent of the submarine as a vessel of war, one of its prime weaknesses had been communications. This included the modern Trident boats, which were forced to ascend toward the surface and launch a specially designed buoy when radio contact was desired. Such submarines survived by running deep and silent, and any unnecessary movement on their part only made them more vulnerable to the ever-lurking enemy.

The development of a device which would permit even deeply submerged subs to communicate with Command would revolutionize naval warfare, and thus was one of Carrigan's pet projects. Not only had he worked on the original concept himself, he had also been responsible for recruiting several of the designers who currently worked on the project for them.

Carrigan was forced to speak up when the project manager blamed their current delay on their team's newest member, a twenty-four-year-old, self-avowed "hot-shot" designer from Caltech by the name of Peter Lowell. Carrigan had worked hard to recruit Lowell and was well aware of his genius. If Lowell was holding up their efforts, there had to be a good reason for it. Carrigan promised to check on this personally, and was in the process of initiating a discussion of future business when his intercom line rang once. His secretary was well aware of the importance of the meeting, and wouldn't dare interrupt him unless something extremely important had occurred. Curious as to what had taken place to warrant this, he excused himself and picked up the red plastic receiver.

The Lear jet belonging to Carrigan Industries soared on a course northeastward 29,000 feet above the Ozark foothills. From the plane's passenger compartment, William Carrigan peered out a window to the rugged landscape visible far below. In this part of the continent, it was a sunny, cloudless afternoon. Even from this great height, he could make out vast, rolling tracts of virgin forests. Interspersed among these woods were snaking rivers and several good-sized lakes. During the summer of his twenty-ninth year, he had spent a full month in this area. Fresh out of the Navy, with visions of his wartime experiences still vividly engraved in his mind, he had used this time to rediscover his inner self. The camping and fishing here had been excellent, and he had emerged from these hills with a better idea of where he had been and, more importantly, where he was headed.

Well aware of how relatively simple life had been at that time, he contemplated today's hectic activities. He had arrived at his office at 6:30 a.m. The sun was just breaking the eastern horizon, when he pulled into the plant to ready himself for the all-important board meeting. Everything was going right as planned, when the surprise call from Washington, D.C., arrived. From that moment onward, his carefully thought-out schedule was torn asunder. This morning's tour of the plant and the afternoon luncheon all had to be placed in the capable hands of his subordinates.

Several of the visiting board members were long-time friends, who visited Sunnyvale but a single time during the year. Thus he could understand the looks of puzzlement they showed when he suddenly had to excuse himself. Unable to explain the real motive behind this unexpected call to duty, he could only plead a personal emergency, and left them with that.

The Lear jet momentarily vibrated under the influence of an invisible pocket of turbulence, and Carrigan shifted his line of sight from the window. He sat in the rear of the passenger compartment, which could hold up to twelve individuals. Today, it contained only him. Looking past the series of thickly padded, leather armchairs that lined the fuselage, he could see all the way into the open cockpit. A clear blue sky beckoned before them, and he could just make out the right hand of the pilot as he reached out to make a minor throttle adjustment. Confident that he was in expert hands, Carrigan found his line of sight straying to that portion of the plane's bulkhead that lay to his immediate right. There was hung a simply framed, eight-by-ten-inch, black-and-white photograph of his first and only Naval command, the USS *Abalone*.

The photo had been taken in Pearl Harbor, a week after the Japanese surrender. The *Abalone* had just come in from its last war patrol. Though its cigar-shaped black hull was splotched with fingers of rust, the vessel still looked sleek and deadly. Upon a closer examination of the picture, William spotted two khaki-clad individuals visible on the vessel's exposed bridge. They were Pete Donner, his XO, and the boat's Chief, Stan Lukowski. He had seen both these men just three years ago, during the last reunion of the *Abalone*'s surviving crew members. At that time it had been forty years since this photograph had been taken.

These reunions had been held every ten years or so since the end of the war, and sadly, with each meeting, their ranks had gradually thinned. These gatherings were an excellent indication of the rapidly passing years. Silver hair—or none at all, wrinkled skin, and bulging waistlines were traits now shared by all of them. Yet no one could miss the way their eyes lit up like young men again when the stories of their war exploits were told with intricate detail. These shared life-and-death experiences would keep them linked forever, for the sub force was an exclusive club, and its members were initiates for life. Proof of this fact had been demonstrated barely three hours before. Little did Carrigan's fellow Board members realize that it was a voice from his naval past that had called him so abruptly away.

Carrigan hadn't spoken to Walter Lawrence since the day he was installed as the Chief of Naval Operations, over a year ago. Of course, even to this day, they had much in common. Many of the top-secret projects that Carrigan was currently working on were well-known to the CNO, and the two had parted with a promise to keep in touch. Yet, as inevitably happened, the months had shot by and their paths had never seemed to cross. That was why he'd been even more surprised when Walter's familiar, gruff voice had greeted him this morning.

The CNO had been direct and asked Carrigan for his assistance in a matter of utmost national urgency. His tone had hinted at the importance of this request and Carrigan didn't hesitate to volunteer his services. Oblivious to his present responsibilities, he had accepted the CNO's plea to meet him at his Pentagon office with all due haste. No other information had been shared, and he had left Lawrence with a promise to inform him of his exact arrival time.

Carrigan couldn't help but find himself extremely curious and somewhat stimulated by this mysterious request. He was certain that something of extreme gravity had occurred to warrant such a call.

The constant, muted whine of the Lear jet's engines filled the background with their monotonous sound, and Carrigan stifled a yawn. With his leaden gaze still centered on the photo of the *Abalone*, he allowed his thoughts to soar back in time, to that fated day when he had first met Lieutenant Walter Lawrence.

It was in July of 1945 that Carrigan arrived in Pearl Harbor. With V-E Day having taken place two months earlier, the *Abalone* had been one of those Atlantic-based subs chosen to help out in the war against the Japanese. They had arrived in the Pacific by way of the Panama Canal. Anxious to experience the sunny tropical skies that these seas were famous for, the crew looked forward to their new assignment, for surely it was only a brief matter of time before the Japs too surrendered.

After duty in the stormy Atlantic, Hawaii indeed seemed like a paradise. Yet this was no vacation, and COMSUBPAC wasted no time giving them their first mission. Carrigan remembered the day well. They had been in Pearl for barely a week when the orders arrived sending him scurrying to headquarters. It proved to be no admiral who greeted him, but a weary-eyed captain and a young, straight-faced intelligence officer by the name of Walter Lawrence.

The captain commended the *Abalone*'s record, and particularly noted her successful reconnaissance operations off the coast of Norway. After pulling out a well-worn chart of the western edge of the Sea of Japan, he pointed to a tiny bay of water lying on the coast of Japanese-controlled Manchuria that appeared to be shaped much like the fjords of Scandinavia. It was at this point that the young lieutenant took over.

Intelligence had only recently discovered a highly sensitive Japanese munitions factory somewhere on the banks of this bay. It would be the *Abalone*'s job to take it out. They would do so with the help of a squad of specially trained Army commandos and a Soviet operative, all of whom the *Abalone* would be conveying into these waters.

It was immediately after this briefing that Lawrence introduced him to the Soviet national they would be taking along. Carrigan was shocked to find her, not only a woman, but a young, attractive one as well. Her name was Lydia, and Carrigan learned much more about her over dinner at the Royal Hawaiian.

Lydia's parents had both been teachers, and had been exiled into Manchuria during one of Stalin's purges. When they were subsequently murdered by the invading Japanese, Lydia had sworn revenge. With the help of a group of local dissidents, she'd secured passage to Australia, and eventually made it to Hawaii, where she worked for Naval Intelligence as a translator. She'd subsequently volunteered for this mission only after learning that it would take place only a few kilometers from the village she grew up in.

By the end of their meal, Carrigan was totally infatuated. It was not only her tall, trim figure, shiny blond hair, and exotic facial features which prompted this attraction, but also the very force of her intense personality. All in all she was unlike any girl he had ever met before. Well accustomed to adversity at an age where most kids were still absorbed by their toys, Lydia was a survivor who had been through hell and back.

He found himself somewhat surprised that this fascinating woman, who had already seen so much of life, seemed to have a genuine interest in his rather staid background. Over rum-and-pineapple-juice cocktails, he explained what it was like growing up in a rather typical middle-class American family. Because his father had been a career naval officer, they had managed to escape the ravages of the Depression era and, true to the family tradition, he had enrolled in the Naval Academy at Annapolis. He was a rather average student, whose passion was inventing things.

He remembered how her face lit up with laughter when he told her the story of one of his first inventions. To increase the speed of their dormitory's archaic elevator, William had designed a special governing device which more than doubled its velocity. Yet little did he realize that this elevator was not designed to take such additional strain. Of course, it had to be during the visit of the Academy's second-in-command that the elevator went haywire, trapping the officer between floors for over two hours.

Carrigan had been quick to admit his guilt and somehow hadn't been thrown out of the Academy altogether. Resigned to limiting his scientific curiosity to the laboratory, he had graduated with a degree in engineering. Since the clouds of war were already gathering on the horizon on the day they had received their diplomas, he had decided that he would do his part on a frontline man-of-war. Though his father had begged him to apply for duty aboard a battleship, he'd chosen submarines for the unique engineering challenge they presented.

By the time he finished his brief, autobiographical tale, he noticed a strange gleam in his date's dark eyes. Though he'd had little experience with members of the opposite sex, Carrigan couldn't help but feel the powerful attraction that they shared for each other. It was Lydia who brought up the idea of a walk on the beach.

The idea of becoming romantically attached to a virtual stranger, whom he was about to convey into a war zone, didn't really appeal to the young officer, yet these were special times and very special circumstances. After all, both were young and full of life. As it turned out, neither had ever felt the true passion of physical love before. The mission they faced was fraught with danger, and the chances were great that they'd never survive. They owed it to themselves to experience the gratification of a desire both had dreamed of yet neither had fulfilled.

The night was warm, the air sweet with the scent of the sea. Waikiki beckoned, and hand in hand they followed their destinies to the tide line. All was quiet except for the slap of the waves on the beach as they stripped off their clothes and entered the Pacific. Both were strong swimmers. Matching each other's strokes, they swam seaward until reaching a depth where Carrigan could just stand on the sandy bottom and keep his shoulders above water. As he did just that, Lydia was suddenly in his arms. The smooth feel of her tight, naked skin hit him like an electric shock, and hungrily their lips met. He needed no coaxing when her legs slipped around his waist and he plunged his stiffness upward to fill her void. Time halted, and with it the worries of war and death, for this was a ritual of life itself.

An eternity had passed when Lydia's body stiffened, her kisses intensified, and she moaned in utter delight. Conscious of her pleasure, Carrigan felt his own desire rise, and with this ascension the secret that all lovers shared was given. Contented and satiated, they floated in the warm Pacific, like infants secure within the confines of the womb.

Carrigan could almost taste the salty essence of the seawater and feel the effects of his spent passion. Suddenly he was jarred from his thoughts by an intense, rattling vibration. Instantly returning to the present, he instinctively pulled his seat belt tighter as the Lear jet plummeted into a pocket of extremely unstable air. He turned to the window just as the pilot's voice came over the intercom.

"Sorry about this rough stuff, Mr. Carrigan, but I'm afraid the good weather is over. There's a low-pressure system stalled over the Appalachians and those storm tops look pretty high. It'll be a bit bumpy, but nothing that we can't handle. So hang in there, sir."

Visual proof of this warning lay immediately outside. There the horizon was filled with thick layers of roiling cumulus clouds. From the base of the largest of these formations, staccato forks of lightning emanated. Soon the sun itself was blotted out, and the tiny jet felt the full brunt of this angry, late-winter storm. Tightly grasping the arms of his chair, Carrigan looked to his right, back to the photograph of the USS *Abalone*. Once again he turned his thoughts to the past and a storm that easily rivaled this one in intensity.

It was late in July of 1945 when the *Abalone* entered the Sea of Japan and approached the shores of Manchuria. At that time there were no weather satellites to warn them of the nearby typhoon, only a falling barometer, a pitch-black noontime sky, and a sailor's constant tendency to anticipate the worst that nature could deal out. The seas were already running high and the *Abalone* pitched to and from like a child's toy. No sooner had Carrigan climbed up into the exposed conning tower than his oilskins and body underneath were completely soaked. He only needed to take a single look at the horizon to make up his mind. Though it would cost them speed, the *Abalone* had to take shelter beneath the ocean's surface. Screaming into the intercom, he gave the order to dive.

Ten minutes later, they were down to 100 feet, and barely noticed the storm's presence topside. This provided quite a relief for the majority of the crew, who were green-faced with seasickness.

As they continued slowly closing in on their goal, Carrigan met with his XO/Navigator, Peter Donner. Together they studied the chart that Intelligence had furnished them. It was most apparent that, once this typhoon was gone, their greatest obstacle would be penetrating the narrow strait that led into the bay where the Japanese munitions facility was located. Since the chart gave them no hint as to the nature of the enemy defenses there, they could only suspect a probable mine field and a waiting sub net. To find out for certain, they would have to make a visual scan once the weather had sufficiently cleared.

Twelve hours later, the *Abalone* ascended to periscope depth. Carrigan's scan found that the storm had passed and that the strait they hoped to enter lay only a couple of miles distant. As fortune would have it, a Japanese tanker approached from the south, seemingly headed toward the same strait they wished to enter. Quick to take advantage of this, Carrigan ordered "full ahead," and soon the *Abalone* was silently cruising a mere sixty-five feet beneath the tanker's hull.

Working closely with the helmsmen was their sonar operator. Together, they were able to plot the tanker's zigzag course, which indeed seemed to be leading them through a mine field. The atmosphere inside the *Abalone*'s control room was thick with tension as they blindly followed their escort toward the bay's narrow entrance. Again it was the sonar operator who first heard the grinding sound of a sub net being opened. Keeping close beneath the tanker's stern, they safely passed into the unknown waters of their goal.

Suspecting that this bay was fed by several freshwater river estuaries, Carrigan closely monitored the *Abalone*'s trim. With the help of Chief Lukowski, they made certain that a sudden, insidious change in the water density wouldn't make the sub many tons overweight in a matter of seconds.

When the Japanese tanker made a sharp turn toward what was apparently its dock, Carrigan ordered the *Abalone* to the channel's bottom. There they waited for the cover of dusk before ascending to periscope depth. It was at this point that Lydia was called forward.

Carrigan had seen relatively little of her since leaving Pearl. Living conditions within the sub were difficult enough without the additional burden of having a woman along. Thus it was decided that it would be best if the Captain gave up his cramped cabin for Lydia's benefit. This arrangement seemed to work out, and the blond-haired Soviet national was content to limit her wanderings to the officers' area. On those occasions when they did confront one another, they were careful to disguise their shared passion. Neither would forget that magical evening on Waikiki, but they could only gain satisfaction by being silently aware of each other's presence.

Lydia's arrival in the control room was hardly noticed by the crewmen, who were busy with their individual duties. Carrigan escorted her to the periscope well and briefly explained how the device operated. It was strange seeing her tight figure draped over the lens coupling, yet the precariousness of their current situation kept the Captain's thoughts solely on their mission.

Lydia needed only a quick glance to confirm their position. She backed away from the viewing lens and explained exactly where the Japanese munitions facility was located. Carrigan took a look for himself. The rapidly falling dusk provided just enough light for him to see the tree-lined hillside beneath which the enemy installation lay. After determining the most efficient drop-off point, he ordered the group of Army Rangers to ready themselves.

Under the cover of a moonless night, the *Abalone* approached as close to the shoreline as it dared. They surfaced, and Carrigan quickly led the squad of commandos and the blond-haired operative out onto the boat's exposed deck. As their black-rubber life raft was readied, Carrigan took a last look at his newfound love. Their gazes briefly met, and the Captain found his gut heavy with an emotion he had never before experienced. A tear dropped from Lydia's cheek, and she silently turned to follow the Rangers into the waiting raft.

Carrigan would never forget the moment he last saw her. Perched in the raft, she looked fragile and unimposing beside the burly squad of armed soldiers. This final glance would have to live with him forever, for none of the raft's occupants ever made it back to the sub. Presuming that they had been either captured or killed, he reluctantly gave the order to return to Pearl Harbor.

It had been forty-three years since that fated night, and Carrigan could still visualize it as if it had happened only yesterday. In fact, whenever he recreated the incident, a familiar heavy feeling possessed his gut and he found himself longing for a soul mate he would never see again. Well aware that they had been forced to squeeze a lifetime of love into a single evening, Carrigan sighed heavily.

He returned to the present, called into renewed awareness by the increased whine of the Lear jet's engines. His eardrums registered the distinct sensation of changing air pressure, and he yawned wide to clear them. Looking outside, he saw that the darkness that was painting the sky was not caused by weather but by the advancing dusk. He angled his line of sight downward and found that the clouds had cleared. Lush green woods gave way to illuminated strips of houses and shops. They crossed over an Interstate highway and continued to lose attitude, until the jolting sound of the jet's landing gear locked into place. This was followed by a sudden activation of the plane's intercom.

"We've just received our final clearance from National, Mr. Carrigan. We'll be down in just a few more minutes."

Carrigan picked out the broad Potomac snaking its way to the sea down below, and all too soon noticed that the woods of Virginia were giving way to the city. Anxious to finally learn what had called him these thousands of miles, Carrigan sat back in his seat in anticipation of the landing.

CHAPTER FIVE

Admiral Walter Lawrence was hunched over his desk, lost in his work, when the intercom rang and he was informed of William Carrigan's arrival. Instructing his aide to show his newly arrived guest in, the CNO checked his watch and found it hard to believe the late hour. Somehow he had managed to work through lunch and then dinner. For that matter, he only now realized how dark it was outside. The day had been a full one, starting with the morning's wake-up call from the Oval Office. Though he had learned to put in his share of twenty-hour working days during the war, the project that he was currently involved with had a peculiar urgency to it. After all, it wasn't everyday that he received an assignment right from the President's own lips.

He looked up when the door to the office opened and William Carrigan entered, wearing a dark blue suit and carrying a briefcase. As on their last meeting, his guest looked robust and vigorous, even though he had surely put in as many hours that day as the CNO had. Of course, this was pretty impressive for a guy pushing seventy. He could easily pass for an individual ten years younger.

"Welcome to Washington," said Lawrence, as he stood to shake his old friend's hand. "I want you to know how much I appreciate your presence here. I hope it wasn't too much of an inconvenience."

"Not at all," returned Carrigan. "Actually, you saved me from a day that was to be spent with my board of directors. I got what I needed from them, and anyway, there's those overpaid VPs of mine to take care of the board. I'm glad to see that they finally got a chance to earn their full keep for a change."

"Well, thank the Lord that you were available," added the CNO. "Now I'm certain that you're curious to know what this ruckus is all about. How about letting me fill you in over chow? I let my work get the best of me today and now I'm famished."

Carrigan grinned. "That sounds good to me, Walter. We didn't have much time to take on supplies at Moffett this morning, and I could do with some real Chesapeake seafood."

"I know just the place," offered the CNO, who went for his hat. "I'll have my aide call for a table while we get going."

Less than a half-hour later, the two men were seated beside a huge picture window, with an unobstructed view of the Potomac River and the country's capital beyond. Both had started with a glass of white wine and were now well into their meals. The CNO had chosen a fresh, charbroiled swordfish steak, while Carrigan had decided on a "Fisherman's Platter." This delectable combination of seafoods included steamed shrimp, fresh oysters, and two fried, soft-shelled crabs. Along with this came a hearty serving of french fries, a scoop of cole slaw, and a basket of piping-hot corn bread.

During the ride over to the restaurant Lawrence had

described his morning's meeting at the Oval Office. He'd included the exact nature of the unusual mission that the President had personally asked him to plan. He'd then revealed the location of this so-called Soviet laser battle station. He'd described the bay of water that it presumably bordered, and Carrigan's eyes had lit up. Both men had been well aware of the significance of this godforsaken spot. As they'd sipped their wines, Carrigan had revealed that he'd been contemplating those same waters that very afternoon.

The CNO had allowed his esteemed guest to absorb this information. Now that they were well into the meal, he sat forward and softly asked, "Well, William, what do you think? Can we get another sub through that infernal strait?"

After thoughtfully chewing a bite of crab, Carrigan answered. "I would think that you would be in a much better position to answer that question than I, Walter. What do you know about the Soviet harbor defenses there?"

The CNO solemnly shook his head. "That's the tough part. All we know for certain is that they seem to have some sort of minor naval installation near Posjet itself. Our recon photos show what appears to be a newly installed sub-net system protecting the strait itself."

"Well, then, I'm sure that you can expect to encounter mines as well," reflected Carrigan. "The Soviets just love to play with those little fellows. And then there's always the possibility of encountering some sort of permanently moored hydrophone arrays down there, similar to our SOSUS system. That's one obstacle I'm sure glad we didn't have to face in '45. The *Abalone* was lucky back then. If you ask me, if we had to undertake that mission today, it would be virtually impossible."

Lawrence digested this, and made certain to catch his guest's glance before responding. "I agree with you, William. Even our latest 688-class nuclear attack subs would be just looking for trouble if they attempted to penetrate that bay. Yet what would you say if we were able to negate the problems with that sub net and the hydrophones?"

"How could you do that?" quizzed Carrigan alertly.

The CNO grinned slightly as he answered. "Several days ago a fully operational, Soviet Whiskey-class submarine ran aground in Washington's Strait of Juan de Fuca. This is all on the hush. Because of an inoperable radio, not even the Russian High Command knows that its sub is missing. How would you feel about the mission if we were to use this sub to penetrate that strait and land a SEAL team to take out that installation?"

Shocked into silence, Carrington looked on as the CNO continued. "I'm sure that you're aware of the fact that the Soviet Whiskey-class submarine is but an adaptation of Germany's XXI-C boats of World War Two. Do you remember a vessel by the name of U-313, commander?"

Carrigan's eyes were wide with wonder, and his inner thoughts whisked back into the past. Once again he was aboard the *Abalone*, yet this time they were afloat in the Atlantic, in the midst of setting up a torpedo attack. Their inviting quarry was a battered black submarine. From its conning tower flew a mysterious black pennant.

"You know that type of vessel, my friend," prompted the CNO. "After all, you did escort one all the way back to Portsmouth. And then, if I remember correctly, didn't you return there after V-J Day to initiate a full study of that particular boat?"

Carrigan absentmindedly nodded while Walter Lawrence went on, his tone rising. "Of course you did, commander! Why there's hardly anyone in this entire country who knows that class of vessel better than you. So what do you say to training a crack crew of current US Navy submariners in that Whiskey's operation? Why, we'd even be willing to help you contact some of your ex-shipmates to assist you with this top-priority, rush instruction."

Still dumbfounded by the sheer audacity of such an attempt, Carrigan hastily went over the facts that had just been presented to him and commented, "You say that this Whiskey is in full operational condition, Walter?"

The CNO responded, "Except for that inoperable radio, and a little gash in her bow, she's ready to take to sea this evening if needed."

"And the Soviets know nothing about its capture?" continued William incredulously.

The CNO shook his head and smiled. The cocky glow that painted the old Admiral's face was enough to lift even Carrigan's weary spirits. His tanned face filled with a grin of his own, and he voiced his thoughts.

"Though it sounds like the weirdest mission that I ever heard of, you can count on me, admiral. When do we get started?"

Lawrence's eyes glowed. "I knew that we could depend on you for a hand, Carrigan. We leave for Bangor, Washington, in an hour. Welcome aboard, commander!"

Norton Military Academy was located in the hills of Brentwood, California. Founded at this same location in 1897, the institution specialized in college-preparatory instruction. For decades many of the finest families on the West Coast had counted on Norton to instill discipline, character, and self-control in their spirited youngsters. Scholastic endeavors were also stressed. For several years running the Academy had produced one of the highest SAT score averages in the nation. Such grades were mandatory for those students who desired to attend the Air Force Academy, West Point, or Annapolis.

Because many of Norton's pupils were from military families, a strict, martial environment prevailed there. Most of the faculty were retired from the armed services themselves. This guidance insured a proper, no-nonsense atmosphere.

Peter Donner had joined the teaching staff at Norton fifteen years ago. At sixty-seven years of age, the former naval officer was the current dean of the history department. Before this assignment, he had taught at such prestigious institutions as Annapolis, the Naval War College, and the Citadel. Though he could have easily retired several years ago, the white-haired professor thrived in his chosen occupation. His enthusiasm was contagious, and his courses were among the most popular at Norton.

Teaching had always come easily to Donner. Even

in the Navy, he had enjoyed sharing his knowledge and insights with those who desired it. After his twenty-year tour of duty had been completed, he'd decided to go back to college himself for his Masters in military history. Because of his years of service, his interests revolved around the Navy. At Annapolis, he had taught courses about America's short but glorious naval history. At the Naval War College, his specialty had been US submarine tactics during World War II.

He'd found that even in today's nuclear, high-tech Navy, there were valuable lessons to be learned from the past. Surprisingly enough, most of his students at the War College, for the most part young officers, had known absolutely nothing about America's sub effort during World War II. This was particularly true of the Pacific theater. It was as if, after Pearl Harbor, the US fleet had ceased to exist. Of course, Peter Donner knew otherwise. Though he had fought against both the Germans and the Japanese, the sub war in the Pacific had become his special course of instruction. He was presently giving a toned-down version of this series of lectures to Norton Academy's senior class.

The morning was clear and crisp as Peter Donner left his on-campus residence for the short walk to the lecture hall. The air smelled of sage and cypress, and he took a moment to scan the serene setting that surrounded him. The hustle and bustle of Los Angeles were only a few miles away, yet these hills guaranteed privacy. Separating the west end of LA from the San Fernando Valley, this range was officially known as the Santa Monica Mountains. Because of its steep, rugged terrain, the normal development that had completely eaten up the Los Angeles basin was absent here. Sure, there were a few residential and commercial developments in these hills, but most of the land remained in its natural state.

Thick mountain scrub grew alongside groves of oak and cypress. Deer still roamed, along with coyotes, possum, lizards, and plenty of rattlesnakes. Donner had a personal run-in with this last species of reptile. He had almost stepped on one of the sleeping serpents while taking a hike just the previous week. Though the rattlers certainly had the potential to injure, like most wild species they only desired to be left alone.

As he remembered the moment when he'd first spotted the snake and yanked his foot backward, only inches from its body, Peter Donner shook his head. Fortune had been with him on that outing. No one would have to remind him to be extra-cautious on the next one.

Spurred by the call of the chime tower that rang nine times, the white-haired veteran turned and crossed the quadrangle. He arrived at his lectern in plenty of time to prepare for his 9:30 class.

This morning's lecture concerned the manner in which the US Navy had taken the sub war deep into Japan's home waters in the closing days of the war. He planned to open with a detailed account of the Barb's amazingly successful patrol in the northern reaches of the Formosa Strait. He then planned on explaining the strategy behind the tactics of eliminating the enemy's all-important convoys in the South China Sea, the cutting of the Japanese shipping lanes to Manchuria, and the ensuing blockade of their Pacific ports. He would conclude the hour with an account of his own vessel's exploits.

Though some of the details of the *Abalone*'s excursion into Manchuria were still classified, there remained much that he could share with his students. This included several excellent photographs taken during the mission by himself and another member of the crew. As he arranged these slides in their proper order, he accidentally dropped the final picture of the series. Donner reached down to pick it up and momentarily studied its contents. Even without the benefit of the projector, he could make out the rust-splattered hull of the *Abalone* as it pulled into Pearl Harbor from its final war patrol. He knew that it would take additional magnification to make out the two familiar figures standing on the open bridge.

Too often lately he'd found it hard to believe that forty-three years had passed since the day this photo was taken. He remembered the exact moment well, for Stan Lukowski had just joined him on the bridge to inform Donner that he had finally fixed the flush mechanism on their toilets. The portly chief had been struggling with this nasty problem for a good part of their voyage homeward. Lukowski had been bubbling with pride in this accomplishment, yet it was much too late in their cruise for the XO to share his chief's enthusiasm.

Chuckling at this flashback, Donner dropped the photo back into its proper place in the slide series. He reached over to make certain that the projector was plugged in as a gangly, red-headed figure entered the classroom and approached him. The professor recognized Danny Meyerson, one of his top students.

"Good morning, Danny. You're a bit early this morning, aren't you?"

The uniformed young man reacted coolly to Donner's greeting by presenting him with a sealed envelope. "I realize that, sir. Dr. Norris asked that I drop this off to you, professor."

Donner wasted no time tearing it open. His eyes skimmed the envelope's contents and his pulse quickened in response.

The message was from William Carrigan. It simply stated that a matter of the utmost urgency necessitated Donner's immediate presence at the sub base at Bangor, Washington. No additional details were given. Though he was puzzled by this enigmatic request, Peter Donner knew that he would obey his ex-skipper without question. Seeing that he still had a quarter of an hour until class time, he rushed from the room to see about getting a proper substitute to take his place.

Stan Lukowski was a happy man. This morning's grand opening would mark his twelfth "Pit-Stop" auto tune-up center in the Dallas area. For a guy who'd left the Navy with but a dream and a thousand bucks in his pocket, he was living proof that capitalism worked well.

His dad had always told him that hard work would pay off in the end. As a kid, Stan watched his pop work their family farm in Allen, Texas, a rural community lying approximately thirty miles due north of Dallas. He was up before sunrise and still in the fields at dusk, the rich black soil of north Texas absorbing his every effort.

In those days, the farmer faced a different challenge than he did presently. A wartorn world begged to be fed. Corn and grain could be as effective as bullets, and Stan's dad sacrificed his all to squeeze all that he could from his two-hundred-acre spread.

Stan would never forget the day that he told his folks that he had enlisted in the Navy. He was an only son and now just as he was coming of age, they had been counting on his help more than ever before. Yet Stan saw a different priority. Unless America's youth shouldered arms together to stop the Axis threat, farms such as the Lukowskis' would no longer be free. Eventually his parents saw it his way, and he left for the Great Lakes Training Center with their full blessings.

Stan only wished that his folks could be here today to see how he had turned out. Both his mom and dad had died over twenty years ago. At that time, he was still struggling with his first garage, a cramped, jury-rigged affair in downtown Dallas. When his pop took sick, his mother practically begged him to give up his business and return to work the farm. Though at the time he was tempted to do just that, his commitment to his partner kept him focused on his original goal. Not long afterward his father died, to be followed quickly by his mother. Stan sold the farm to a real-estate developer and came away with more money on the transaction than the farm had ever netted in its lifetime. The Navy veteran pumped this new infusion of cash into his garage, and the first "Pit-Stop" tune-up center was the result.

Well aware of his roots, Stan sat silently in the

driver's seat of his brand-new Cadillac Eldorado. Before him was their newest location. Balloons decked the stucco-walled structure, and there was even a clown on the sidewalk to draw the attention of all those who passed this portion of busy Preston Road. In a few minutes, representatives of the press and Chamber of Commerce were due to arrive for the grand-opening ceremonies. It had been Helmut's idea to invite along a contingent of local cheerleaders to add to the party atmosphere. These youngsters were presently in the back parking lot, going through their last minute warm-ups.

Stan looked on as the door to the shop opened, and his tall, red-haired business partner walked crisply outside. The erect German hastily scanned the lot, then disappeared around the building's far side. He still found it hard to believe that Helmut Keller was about to turn sixty. Not only was his physical appearance more indicative of a man much younger, his sheer vigor and unceasing drive had remained constant for as long as Stan had known him.

Their relationship had begun most inauspiciously. In fact, if the hand of fate hadn't intervened, it was very possible that they might have never met in the first place. For Helmut had been the chief engineer aboard U-313, the submarine that Stan's boat, the *Abalone*, had almost sunk on the day the war in the Atlantic concluded.

They first met in Portsmouth, New Hampshire, several days later. Helmut was the only German on board who could speak English, and he was asked to give the Americans a complete tour of his vessel. Since Stan was the chief of the boat that had captured

143

them, he was invited to accompany the brass during this extensive tour of inspection.

From the very beginning, the two got along like long lost brothers. Both had similar interests and, of course, similar technical responsibilities in keeping their respective boats running. Helmut didn't show the least hint of resentment towards his captors. If anything, he seemed thrilled that the war was finally over.

Stan was soon off to the Pacific to take care of their remaining adversary, and didn't meet with Helmut again until a month after V-J Day. Sent back to Portsmouth to continue his study of the captured U-boat, Lukowski was pleased to find that the big-boned German chief was being allowed to remain in the US indefinitely. The Navy was anxious to know just what made the new type XXI-C boat tick, and Helmut Keller was quite happy to divulge each of its secrets. It was while crawling inside the U-boat's engine room one day that they first came up with the idea of going into business together. Since neither of them felt comfortable unless he had a good coat of grease beneath his fingernails, they decided on a garage.

It took a good ten years of working for others to come up with an initial down payment. Stan wisely picked Dallas for their first site. Not only was it conveniently near home, but he had great faith in the area's future growth and development. As it turned out, this was a decision that they had yet to be sorry for.

The 1950s and 1960s saw an unheralded economic boom in America. Fueling this era of amazing industrial growth was the country's passionate love affair with its automobiles. These vehicles came in all shapes, colors, and sizes, and poured off the assembly lines in the hundreds of thousands. It was inevitable that they would eventually need service. Too often, the local garage just couldn't handle the bevy of new cars that were coming its way.

Stan and Helmut had come up with the idea of the "Pit-Stop" concept while facing a cramped garage full of cars to be worked on. The basis of their notion was to apply modern, assembly-line methods in a field that was still ruled by a "mom and pop" philosophy. Specialization was the key. At "Pit-Stop," the customer would come in for one thing only—a tune-up. This work would be completely guaranteed for both quality of workmanship and time of completion. Working by appointments and on a first-come, first-serve basis would insure that both parties knew just when the job would be done. Thus, there'd be no work overload, for, when the daily schedule was full, additional projects would only be taken on when time allowed.

Though it took a bit of time for the public to catch onto the idea of taking one's car in for a tune-up only, in the age of fast-food and convenience stores "Pit-Stop" fit in perfectly. Business was soon booming. Dallas continued to grow, and its new suburbs were ripe for outlets of their own. To cope with this demand, it was decided to come up with a standard prototype structure that would be exactly copied in each new location. Only young, industrious mechanics were recruited to man these sites. Before any of these individuals ever touched a customer's car, they were required to undergo both a rugged training period and a thorough examination. Only then did they become a part of the "Pit-Stop" team.

Lately, Stan and Helmut were even thinking of selling franchises. Their familiar red, white, and blue logo could soon be visible from coast to coast.

The mere thought of such a thing stimulated Stan immensely. He had never showed a particular mind for business, and this whole thing had just sort of fallen together. Of course, there could be no denying Helmut Keller's contribution. Together they produced a unique chemistry that had made this success possible.

Stan was in the process of leaving the comfortable environs of his car when the familiar voice of his partner came from the building's rear.

"So there you are, my friend. I didn't recognize you in this new car of yours. My, she's a beauty!"

"Wait until you drive her," added the pot-bellied Texan. "It's just like cruisin' on air. The only trouble is that we're going to need some new computers to tune these babies up with. It's like a fuckin' IBM workshop in there."

The German appreciatively patted the Eldorado's streamlined roof, then suddenly spoke out. "I almost forgot the reason why I'm out here looking for you. You've got a phone call inside."

"Couldn't you have just taken a message?" queried Stan, as he attempted to smooth down the two perpetually wild strands of hair that framed his balding skull.

"They said that it was urgent," returned his partner.

Lukowski started toward the building. "I bet it's

146

another lawyer hot for those franchise rights. What do you say about raising the ante another hundred grand?"

Helmut Keller's response coincided with the arrival of a large, white van. "Don't be too greedy, Lukowski, or we'll end up with nothing again. Hey, here's the press. Take care of that phone call and then get your keester back out here. And bring those cheerleaders with you. Free publicity like this comes around once in a lifetime."

Happy to let his personable partner take care of the PR chores anyway, Stan scurried off to the office. He wasted no time picking up the phone.

"Hello, this is Stan Lukowski speaking."

The faraway clatter of static sounded in the receiver and Stan wondered if there was anyone left on the line. He was about to hang up when a deep, somewhat familiar voice greeted him.

"Jesus, chief, you're harder to reach than the President. This is William Carrigan speaking. Did I catch you at a bad time?"

"Of course not, Skipper," returned the pleasantly startled Texan. "You wouldn't believe this, but not five minutes ago I was out in my car thinkin' of the *Abalone*. We sure shared some times, Skipper."

"That we did," responded Carrigan. "I know that this is coming out of the blue and all, but something important has come up and I need your help."

Lukowski didn't waver. "Just name it, Skipper."

Carrigan's tone lightened. "By the way, are you still in business with that big, red-headed Kraut?"

"I sure am, Captain. In fact, it was Helmut who answered the phone. Today we're celebrating the

147

opening of our twelfth Pit-Stop tune-up center."

"No kidding. Well, congratulations, chief. I always knew that anything that you two put your hands on would be a success." Carrigan cleared his throat before continuing. "Now, I hate to ask this of you, but do you think that it's possible that you could join me in Bangor, Washington? Your country and I would be most appreciative."

Not certain what Carrigan was implying, Lukoswki responded, "I guess that I could, Skipper. What's come up and when do you need me?"

"Let's just say it's a little unfinished submarine business, chief. I'd appreciate it if you could meet me at the naval base tomorrow evening. And by the way, I'd also like you to bring along your partner. I'm certain that both of you won't be disappointed."

Still caught off guard by Carrigan's offhand request, Stan mumbled, "I'm sure that we won't be, Skipper. Is there somewhere we can reach you to give you our travel plans?"

Carrigan gave his phone number, and once again thanked Stan for his help. With that, the line went dead.

A dumbfounded look painted Stan Lukowski's face as he stood by the receiver, his mind trying hard to make some sort of sense out of the strange conversation he had just concluded. All that he knew for certain was that the Skipper wouldn't ask for help unless he was really in a bind.

There was a sudden commotion outside and he looked out of the window to trace its source. A line of short-skirted cheerleaders stood in the middle of the driveway. They were in the process of waving their pom-poms over their heads as a line of reporters and local business leaders admiringly looked on. Even from the office's interior, he could clearly hear their spirited chant.

"Pit-Stop, Pit-Stop, read all about it! Give us your plugs and go out and start it!"

Though this was surely a day for celebration, somehow Stan was no longer in the mood. For something in William Carrigan's voice had expressed a concern of a much more vital nature. The Skipper had said that it concerned a little unfinished submarine business, and that both he and the country would appreciate their assistance. Carrigan hadn't said so outright, but this could only mean that the Navy needed their services once again. When he'd taken his oath to enter the Navy, he'd sworn to offer his nation a lifetime of duty if necessary. He would never forget how good his country had been to him since leaving the uniformed ranks. Now it was his turn to repay the favor. Without further deliberation, he picked up the phone and dialed his travel agent.

His skiff's seaworthiness was proving beyond Mac Brady's greatest expectations. He had designed the twelve-foot, wooden-plank vessel precisely for the waters of the Straits of Florida. To get him to the edge of the Gulf Stream, where the really big fish lurked, he'd added a centerboard, outrigger, and small sail, which Martha had sewed up according to his specifications. Mac had included a small, gas-fed outboard engine only for emergencies, for it was his desire to keep his vessel as basic as possible.

Today had marked his first complete day of sea

trials. After working on the skiff all through the summer, fall, and most of the winter, today's events had been most anticipated. Like an anxious child on Christmas morning, he'd emerged from his bed long before sunrise. Dressed only in his skivvies, he'd gone immediately outdoors. Mac had found it a warm, crystal clear morning. The barometer was rising and the sea appeared calm and inviting. He'd put on a pot of coffee, then gone off to the bathroom. Fifteen minutes later, with coffee mug in hand, he'd been sitting on his favorite high-backed rocker, perched on the end of the battered pier, watching the sun inch its way over the eastern horizon.

Dawn was a momentous event here in the Florida Keys. Mac had always bragged that his perch on the end of the pier offered him one of the most spectacular views of the sunrise in the entire country. This morning's dawn had certainly proved him right.

The morning stars were still visible in the heavens when he'd first arrived. Ever so gradually they'd faded from sight and the sky had lightened from the black of night to the rich, deep blue of dawn. Then, in a crown of gold, the sun had peeked its way out of the Atlantic and the new day had been born.

All had been quiet except for the slight gust of the trade winds and the gentle slap of the sea upon the pier's abutments. This silence had taken on an almost holy quality for the sixty-three-year-old Navy veteran, as his thoughts had risen with a clarity he could not recreate the rest of the day. That peace of mind was one of the reasons he had bought this place a decade ago.

When he'd finally left the Navy after thirty years of

service, Martha and he were free to settle wherever they chose. They tried San Diego and found the city growing too fast for their tastes. Their next stop was Apple Valley, California, a sprawling, residential community located in the state's High Desert country. Before buying a place permanently, they decided to rent first. This proved to be a wise move for, although they enjoyed the Joshua trees, quail, fresh air, and spectacular scenery, the summers were a bit too hot and the winters too cold. So, after a year there, they packed up their trailer and began crossing the continent, stopping in whatever location looked promising. Two months after leaving California they somewhat wearily pulled into Key West, Florida. Finding themselves with nowhere to go but back north again, they decided to camp there for a while. As it turned out, they hadn't left the Keys since.

Mac had stumbled upon the Breakers Motel quite by accident. He was tarpon-fishing at the time, and rowed up to the pier when the outboard he had been renting suddenly gave up the ghost. The owner was a grizzled old-timer who was too ill to take care of business. As a result, Mac found the motel complex in sore need of attention. Most aware of its potential, he took a gamble and asked the old man if he wanted to sell. His timing was perfect, for the octagenarian was finding the place much too difficult to manage. A price was hastily negotiated and the deal closed with a handshake, even though Martha had yet to set her eyes on the place. Anxious to have her check it out, he borrowed the old man's 1957 Ford pickup and rushed down to the trailer park to get his wife.

Martha indeed saw the resort's potential, yet was all

the same conscious of the immense work that needed to be done here. The entire complex was situated on a five-acre rectangular plot, set on the island's eastern shoreline. There were twelve individual guest cottages scattered amidst the mangroves. Each of these gabled structures had a screened-in porch and an unobstructed view of the adjoining beach and the ocean beyond. Their own hut was the largest of these structures and contained the motel's office. Though six of the units were at the moment uninhabitable, they moved in three weeks later.

Limited resources forced them to concentrate their initial work on the most important projects. As an ex-submariner, Mac was used to determining his priorities and sticking to them. On a submarine, this could make the difference between life and death. Here at the Breakers, it meant drawing up a work schedule that would lead to some income flowing their way as soon as possible.

Their initial efforts were focused on the cottages that were presently inhabitable. Mac worked hard fixing leaky roofs, rusty plumbing, and torn screens. Martha concentrated on cleaning, sewing new curtains, and buying fresh linens. It wasn't long until they were able to place their first advertisement, and soon tourists were able to rediscover the Breakers once again.

Their income wasn't much, but it was enough to keep them going. Mac was even able to afford the major structural repairs on the units that were out of commission. All in all the northerners found their resort "a hidden jewel," as one New Yorker so aptly put it. The cottages were clean, comfortable, private, and offered one of the most beautiful views in all the Keys. Many of their customers were repeats. Several were retirees who stayed months at a time. Martha turned out to have a wonderful head for business. She was content to keep the books and supervise a staff of two cleaning women, a gardener, and an assistant night manager in season. Since the cottages were now in decent shape, this left Mac with plenty of time to indulge in his lifetime's passion—fishing.

Several years before, he had bought a used, twenty-eight-foot cabin cruiser. With such a boat he was able to go after the sailfish, marlin, and tuna that abounded there. Yet there was one elusive species that generally eluded him. The tarpon was the unheralded king of the local fish. This elusive species was most likely encountered in the shallower waters, where his cruiser had trouble penetrating. Thus he had the idea of designing his own skiff.

As he sat on the pier's end, sipping his coffee and watching the morning continue to develop, Mac decided that it was time to see what his season's effort had produced. With the help of their gardener, he transferred the newly crafted vessel from the garage to the water's edge. The first test was passed when the boat was plopped down into the sea and it floated, its interior bone-dry. With a triumphant shout, he then climbed into the skiff and, utilizing a paddle, guided the vessel into deeper waters. He was a good fifty feet away from the shoreline before he attempted to raise the sail.

The onshore winds were light yet constant, and they were more than sufficient to propel him forward. He proceeded to tack and found the steerage stiff, yet adequate. It had been much too long since he had sailed, and he enjoyed the challenge of anticipating the wind's direction. The almost silent hiss of the water hitting the skiff's sharply angled bow would surely get him close to the tarpon. Then he would use a set of lightweight tackle to make his pursuit a fair one.

He was in the midst of turning his skiff around, so that he could return for his rod and reel, when he noticed the figure of Martha standing on the end of the pier. Though he was a good distance from land now, he could see that she was waving her hands over her head. He doubted if this was a mere greeting, and charted a course due westward. Ten minutes later, he was within shouting distance of his wife.

"It's Captain Carrigan!" screamed Martha.

Not certain what she meant by this, Mac yelled in response, "What's he doing down here?"

All this time the skiff continued its approach, and Martha found herself able to answer without having to raise her voice. "He's not here, silly. He's on the telephone for you. Says it's urgent."

Mac's surprised expression turned to puzzlement as he guided his boat onto the beach. He hadn't spoken to his ex-skipper since their last reunion. Even then, it was only light banter, far away from anything that one could possibly label urgent. Since William Carrigan's present business venture was strictly Navy-orientated, he could only guess that the *Abalone*'s commanding officer needed some help with a design problem. Mac's specialty was weapons, and, if he remembered correctly, Carrigan Industries was bidding for the new ADCAP torpedo project. Surely this was what this unexpected call was all about.

A broad grin returned to Mac's tanned face as he stepped onto the sand and greeted his wife with a wink. "She handles like a real beauty, honey. Can I take you out later on?"

"We'll see about that, Mac. Right now, you'd better get on up to that telephone. William has been waiting long enough."

Hand in hand the two strolled over the beach and up toward the office. They were in excellent physical shape because of an active schedule and wise diet. Their strides were long and matched each other's perfectly. Martha remained at her husband's side as he picked up the receiver and mouthed a greeting.

She knew Mac's face like the back of her own hand. Forty years of marriage had given her this ability. As he stood there with the receiver by his ear, silently absorbing his caller's words, she imagined she caught just a hint of both bewilderment and concern in his expression. Her instincts said trouble when he muttered a terse reply, hung up the receiver, and vacantly looked off into space.

"Well, Mac, what in the world did William Carrigan want from you?"

He voiced his response carefully. "Oh, it's nothing, honey. It seems the Skipper needs my assistance with a project his company's having troubles with. Will you be all right here by yourself while I jump on a plane to help him out? It will only be a few days at the most."

Though she could have sworn that he was somehow keeping the entire truth of the matter from her, Martha gave Mac her approval to help William Carrigan in whatever way he could. She was surprised with his swiftness as he fumbled for the Yellow Pages and hastily looked up a listing. Without wasting a second, he dialed a number and asked for the time of the next flight leaving Miami for Seattle, Washington.

The Lockheed C-130 transport zoomed in low over the waters of the Outer Santa Barbara Passage. In the plane's central compartment, Navy Lieutenant Vince Paterson, strike leader of SEAL team Alpha, peered out the open hatchway. To the grinding roar of the C-130's four Allison T56 turboprops, he studied that portion of the Pacific visible beneath them. The ocean was choppy, with three- to four-foot swells. He could just make out the fog-enshrouded palisades of the east end of Santa Catalina Island. Lying approximately twenty-five miles due south of Catalina was their current goal, the island of San Clemente.

There was a loud, metallic buzz, and the crew-cut commando turned away from the hatchway to pick up the intercom. "Peterson here."

Quick to answer him was the plane's pilot. "Just wanted to let you know, lieutenant, that the head winds have picked up to twenty-five knots. Since that's at the limit of your safety perimeter, do you want to scrub the mission?"

"Hell, no!" Paterson shot back. "We've come to fight, and nothing short of a full-force gale is going to send us back to Coronado now. Just bring us in low and quiet. We'll take care of the rest."

"Aye, aye, sir," responded the pilot. "We have an ETA on that jump point in two and a half minutes."

With this the intercom went dead. Vince Paterson

replaced the plastic handset and pivoted to face the three men who waited behind him. Seated on one of the two benches that lined the compartment's length were the other members of Strike Team Alpha. Each of these individuals was dressed in identically camouflaged wet suits and wore not only a parachute, but a watertight kit containing full battle gear as well.

Perched closest to Paterson was Ty Meadows, who was known simply as "Indian." A full-blooded Dakota Sioux, Meadows was at home in the wilderness, a natural point man and as tough as they came. Beside the bronze-skinned Native American sat Billy Joe Miree, whose handle was "Gator." A starting quarterback with LSU, the bayou-bred Louisiana native was a crack shot, a powerful swimmer, and their explosives expert. This left the team's electronic specialist, Ed "Wizard" Sanger, seated nearest the cockpit. Sanger was easily the brains of the outfit and the only Annapolis man amongst them. Yet, when things got messy, he could hold his own and then some.

As Paterson scanned their alert faces, he knew that he was fortunate to lead such men into battle. They were undoubtedly the Navy's best, able to fight from the sea, the air, and the land with equal ability. Their training was extensive, ranging from underwater demolitions and hand-to-hand combat to electronic warfare. Added to this vast technical knowledge was one of the most demanding physical regimens in the entire Armed Forces. It could honestly be said that only a handful of world-class athletes shared their strength and stamina.

A series of loud chimes rang overhead, and Paterson knew that they were approaching their drop-off point. He somberly nodded, and his three teammates stood to join him at the hatchway. Beside this opening were two lights, one red, the other green. Only the red one was presently lit.

After hastily scanning the scrub-filled, dry, mountainous terrain of San Clemente Island visible below them, Paterson turned his head to address his men. He had to shout to be heard over the C-130's engines.

"It's show time, gentlemen. We've got a twenty-five-knot westerly wind, so it had better be heads up on this descent. You all know the attack scenario, so let's go kick some ass!"

The plane was in the process of rounding the northern end of the island when the red light abruptly switched to green. Paterson stepped back and beckoned Indian to lead the way. Meadows flashed him a thumbs-up and jumped. He was followed in rapid succession by Gator, the Wizard, and finally Paterson himself.

The SEAL leader was a natural-born paratrooper. From the first time he'd jumped at the tender age of sixteen, he'd found himself more at home during free-fall than he was on solid land. This morning's jump proved no different.

The air was brisk and intoxicating as he cleared the plane and stabilized himself. The rest of Alpha team was visible below him, falling in identical tuck positions. It was only when he spotted the white-cap-tossed waters that marked the submerged reef of their target that the first chute triggered. Seconds later, another parachute billowed open, and then another followed. All too soon Vince Paterson's joined them.

After hastily checking that the rails were clear,

Paterson became aware of the gusting winds. It took the full utilization of his steering mechanism to keep him from being blown onto land. Not only was the rugged, uneven terrain there ill-suited to receive them, but such a landing would also most likely cost them the element of surprise. Of course, they also had to be extra-careful not to fall too closely to rock-strewn shoreline.

So busy was Paterson with his steering problems that he didn't notice when his first man hit the water precisely on target. Nearly crashing onto Indian's back were Gator and the Wizard. Seconds later, Vince Paterson entered the water beside them with a re-sounding splash.

Even with their protective wetsuits, the penetrating chill of the Pacific there was most noticeable. Careful to get completely clear of their parachute rigs, the commandoes wasted no time heading for the beach that lay several thousand yards distant.

Gator led the way. To accommodate their gear bags, which were worn strapped to their backs, the breaststroke was utilized. Even though each of the SEALs was an accomplished swimmer, the commando from Louisiana gradually outdistanced them. He alertly halted after noticing the first signs of a vicious riptide ahead. Signaling the others to halt, he went on to probe the waters to find the best angle of approach, for to enter the riptide head on could prove disastrous. Several hundred feet down the coastline he found what he was searching for, and waved the other members of Alpha team onward.

Sheltered by a partially submerged ledge of rock that led from the beach, the riptide was substantially countered there. The surf was negligible and they had no problem swimming up to shore. As each SEAL emerged onto the pebbly beach, he scrambled to his knees, and sprinted for the cover of the nearby palisades. No words were exchanged as they ripped off their wetsuits, opened their gear bags, and donned identical sets of camouflaged fatigues. Next, they pulled out their armaments.

Paterson and the Wizard shouldered lightweight Beretta PM 12S submachine guns. This was in addition to .45-caliber pistols and the satchel of electronic "goodies" that Wizard wore at his side. Meanwhile, Indian deftly assembled an Ithaca "combat" shotgun, while Gator Miree put the finishing touches on his Colt Commando, a specially designed M16 complete with flash suppressor and telescopic sights.

Now that they were properly outfitted to "party," Paterson pulled out a map. They quickly oriented themselves, and found a trail that would presumably take them to their objective, on the opposite side of the island. Indian led the way, followed by Gator and the Wizard. Vince Paterson was content to bring up the rear. The trail they had chosen was a narrow pathway, little more than a goat track. It led from the beach directly into the hills above. With precious few switchbacks, it snaked its way up the steepening, ever-ascending grade.

Alpha team's leader did his best to match the brisk pace that their point man was establishing. Even with the benefit of his excellent physical conditioning, the climb strained Paterson's legs and lungs, causing thick sheets of sweat to mat his forehead. He had learned long ago that under such extreme circumstances it was best to focus one's concentration on establishing a rhythmic pace, matching both stride and breaths. After a while, one learned to merely ignore the pain.

They climbed to a height of nearly 1,000 feet above sea level before stopping for their first break. The trail was substantially level there, the path having merged with a wider, more developed one. Vince Paterson didn't need his map to know that this new footpath would follow the spine of the surrounding mountains all the way across the island. Though they still had over seven miles to travel, most of the heavy climbing was now over.

Vince sat down on top of a smooth rock ledge and took in the landscape visible around him. Being a Southern Californian by birth, Paterson knew the identities of many of these plants. He had gone to Boy Scout camp on nearby Catalina Island. There he'd learned that much of the flora was endemic to these islands only, found nowhere else in the world. He spotted several stunted Catalina manzanitas with their distinctive, oblong, leathery green leaves and dark-red bark. Clumps of shrub-like St. Catherine's lace grew beside several wild tomato plants. This last was deceptively labeled, for its purplish berries were highly poisonous. Paterson also identified a holly-like Toyon tree, a sprawling Catalina currant bush, and several species of cactus and other succulent plants.

The aroma of ripe sage scented the warm air, and Vince felt right at home there. He scanned the northern horizon and could just view the eastern end of Catalina Island, rising above the mist-covered waters. As a youth, he had wondered those distant palisades, looking out to San Clemente and wondering what it would be like to explore there. It was in these waters that he'd seen his first real destroyers at work. Much of San Clemente was a Navy gunnery range, and when the warships had raised their big guns and let them blast, Vince had been in second heaven. How he'd bragged that evening around the Scout campfire!

This boyhood encounter with the Navy was not soon forgotten. Equally as fascinated with each new warship that he was fortunate enough to view, Vince Paterson couldn't wait to enlist. By taking advantage of UCLA's Naval ROTC program, he was able to get both an education and an officer's commission at the same time. It was while stationed in San Diego that he learned about the SEALs. To the impressionable ensign, this program was the epitome of Navy excellence. It took a bit of work, but eventually he was admitted into the Navy's special forces program.

The distinctive chopping clatter of a helicopter's rotor blades broke Paterson's musing. Without hesitation, he screamed, "Take cover!" He then ducked beneath the rock ledge he had been sitting on. Barely thirty seconds later, a massive Sikorsky Sea Stallion assault transport shot overhead, only a bare three hundred feet above them. The dark-green Marine chopper seemed to be following the same ridge as the SEAL team was now headed on. Taking this in, Vince Paterson crawled from the shelter of the ledge, stood, and addressed his men, who were also emerging from their various hiding spots.

"Well, it looks like the enemy's here, gentlemen. Shall we get on with our little surprise party?"

This question needed no answer as the team reassembled itself, with the supple figure of Indian once again leading the way. The trail was indeed more level, and they were able to make excellent progress. Even Mother Nature proved cooperative. With the sun's descent towards the west, the fog was able to more fully develop. Soon thick fingers of gray fog completely veiled their presence. This was fine with Vince Paterson because it allowed them to make use of the path to a much greater extent than he had expected.

Under normal circumstances, the trail's lack of cover would have forced them to use one of the canyons that lay to either side. The going there would have been extremely difficult, with steep, slippery grades and the ever-present rattlesnakes as constant sources of worry.

Feeling as if he were walking among the clouds, Paterson kept a close watch on the time. One hazard of the poor visibility was the chance that they could easily overshoot their intended goal. He had just figured that they had less than two more miles to go when the trail began losing altitude. Five minutes later, the fog lifted as abruptly as it had arrived.

The SEALs found themselves in the middle of a saddle, a narrow ridge connecting two mountainous summits. It took Vince only a single glance at the peak toward which they were headed to know that they had just about reached their destination. Conscious of how exposed they suddenly were, he flashed Indian a hand signal to proceed at double time. They had to sprint nearly an eighth of a mile before finding adequate cover.

Sheltered by a grove of grizzled oaks, they decided on a final strike plan. Their goal was a Marine Recon position situated on the mountain's summit, which lay another 700 feet above them. Though the trail led directly there, they didn't dare use it. To insure that their attack caught the "enemy" by complete surprise, they chose to climb the peak's most treacherous face, its rugged western side. This would also allow them to have the sun at their backs when it came time for the final phase of their assault.

It didn't take Indian long to find a goat trail that led to the peak's western exposure. Looking almost straight up from this spot, they spied their distant goal and realized that they had their work cut out for them. It was most evident that not even the goats had dared to attempt such a route. Yet the Marines were also well aware that this side of the mountain offered them the least threat, and it would be practically undefended. Hoping that this was indeed the case, the SEALs initiated their ascent.

Two hours of grueling labor followed. The mountain's rocky face cut and bruised them. In several spots it was so sheer that they were forced to clip metallic crampons onto the soles of their combat boots and use a nylon hand rope for additional support. Halfway up, the Wizard lost his footing and slid feet first into a clump of prickly cactus. Somehow he kept from screaming out in pain, and the others got to his side and did their best to remove the razor sharp needles that had penetrated his pants leg. Waving away the offer to wait for them down below, he wiped the blood from his shins and continued on with the climb.

Twenty-five feet from the summit, the grade began to lessen and the footing improved significantly. They briefly halted there and studied the wall of boulders that seemed to circle their goal. To check on the Marines' exact deployment, Wizard volunteered to crawl up to this wall and utilize one of the special gadgets that he had lugged up the mountainside with him. Paterson gave him the go ahead, and the Annapolis grad proceeded further upward. At the base of a particularly massive boulder, he positioned himself in a crouch and slowly extended what turned out to be a lightweight, tubular periscope device. It was thus that he was able to share with them a detailed description of their adversaries' defenses.

Having paid the western access route absolutely no attention, a dozen Marines were gathered near the eastern wall. It was to this portion of the peak that the trail directly led. This vantage point also afforded them an excellent view of San Clemente's northern, eastern, and southern flanks.

The majority of the leathernecks seemed to be but raw recruits who were in the process of field-stripping their M-16s. The others present were gathered around a two-way radio. This observation got a grin out of Vince Paterson, who decided to give their final assault a bit of additional realism.

While Gator Miree began the task of setting up a series of weak explosive charges beneath the boulders they perched under, the Wizard pulled out yet another device from his bag of tricks. After switching on this hand-sized, battery-powered transmitter, which would be able to jam the Marines' transmission, he fiddled with the frequency selector, then handed it to Vince Paterson, who beckoned his men to take their positions.

The attack began when Paterson turned up the jamming device's volume gain and spoke clearly into its transmitter. "Excuse me, but did somebody up here from Charlie Company order a large pepperoni pizza?"

Vince knew his cryptic remark had been received when a loud, bass voice emanated from the summit screaming, "What the fuck?"

This was all Paterson needed to hear to get the party going in earnest. His first signal was to Gator Miree. With a snap of his wrist, Alpha team's explosives expert activated the miniature detonator and the peak's entire south wall was taken out in a muted roar of smoke and dust. The blast was far from being a really powerful one, and as the rocky debris showered to the ground, Alpha team sprang up the hill — scrambled over the remaining boulders, raised their weapons, and began spraying the heavens with ear-splitting blanks. Needless to say, the shocked Marines were caught completely off guard, and the SEALs were able to surround them before the leathernecks were able to raise a single weapon.

As it turned out, Alpha team had little time to revel in their hard-earned victory, for no sooner had the smoke cleared than a white Navy Seahawk helicopter soared in from the southeast. To a swirling whirlwind of blowing debris, it landed on the summit and the SEALs were ordered inside. Seconds later, they found themselves being whisked off the mountaintop, to a new assignment in faroff Washington State.

CHAPTER SIX

William Carrigan and Walter Lawrence had arrived in Bangor in the wee hours of the morning. They were fortunate to land at nearby McChord Air Force Base, since an almost solid wall of fog had descended upon the Puget Sound area earlier.

This was Carrigan's second cross-continental airplane trip within the last twenty-four hours, and he took advantage of the spacious MATS transport to get in a four-hour nap. When they arrived at the sub base, they were shown immediately to their quarters. Both had individual rooms in a special VIP residence. Carrigan found it comparable to a first-class hotel room, and because of the still-early hour was able to get in another couple of hours of shut-eye.

He awoke at eight a.m. After soaking himself in the shower, he found a thermos of coffee and a copy of the *New York Times* at his door. By nine, he was ready to make the first phone call. Peter Donner was the easiest one to locate. He was still on the staff of Norton Military Academy and Carrigan had no trouble calling information for the phone number. Tracking down Stan Lukowski and Mac Brady proved to be a bit more difficult. Fortunately, he was able to use the services of his ever-faithful secretary back at Carrigan Industries. He dialed the office and Sally filled him in on yesterday's activities. It seemed that his executives had had no trouble handling the visiting board members in Carrigan's place. The luncheon and plant tour had gone right as scheduled. After receiving a quick rundown on the latest production and sales figures, he gave Sally the assignment of tracking down the former chief and weapons officer of the *Abalone*. Much to his surprise, she called back with their respective phone numbers barely a half-hour later.

Each of his men had responded to the sudden call to duty without question. Regardless of their personal concerns, they unhesitatingly volunteered their services. William had almost forgotten about Helmut Keller. Having the benefit of his expert services was an unexpected stroke of luck. He was confident that they would arrive in Bangor just as they had promised, and his outlook brightened. When the Base Commander's office called to invite Carrigan to breakfast, he immediately accepted.

The Bangor sub base was a relatively new installation. It was built primarily to service the new Trident class SLBMs that were steadily being placed into duty now. With this task in mind, the Navy had done an excellent job creating an efficient, comfortable facility. Primarily set within the shelter of a surrounding forest, the structures were modern and built with the future in mind.

William found himself impressed with the officers' mess hall. Again he could only compare it to a first-rate hotel or private club. The tables were spread out with privacy in mind, and he had no trouble sighting the figure of the CNO, seated against the far wall. Walter Lawrence was sipping a mug of coffee and was deep in conversation with a young uniformed officer.

"Well, good morning, William," greeted the Admiral. "I hope you've got this jet-lag figured out. William Carrigan, I'd like you to meet Commander Ronald Barry, our host here at Bangor."

The officer stood and exchanged handshakes with Carrigan. He was of average height and build, and his inquisitive glance didn't seem to miss a single detail. As Carrigan seated himself, the Commander addressed him.

"I hope your quarters are sufficient, sir."

Carrigan grinned. "Actually, I don't think that I could have done much better at the Marriott. This is quite a facility you've got here, Commander."

"Why thank you, sir," said the fair-skinned officer. "We're certainly proud of the place and would love to show you more later."

"I'd enjoy that," said Carrigan, and he accepted a cup of steaming hot coffee from a bright-eyed steward.

"By the way, William, do you need any help with those phone calls that you wanted to make?" asked the CNO.

Carrigan sipped his coffee and found it Navy strong. "Actually, admiral, that's all been taken care of already. With a little outside assistance from my office, I've been able to contact Peter Donner, the *Abalone*'s XO; her weapons officer, Mac Brady; and

169

her chief, Stan Lukowski. To help out even more, Lukowski is bringing along Helmut Keller, the ex-chief of U-313. With their combined expertise, we should be able to determine just what makes that Whiskey-class vessel tick."

"Excellent!" Lawrence beamed. "The Commander here was just filling me in on the sailors we've chosen to become your students. Commander, why don't you continue?"

Ronald Barry responded succinctly. "As I was saying, we hope to man the *Dnieper* with the crew of the USS *Stingray*, one of the three remaining diesel-electric subs in our fleet. They are presently steaming up from their home port of San Diego, and are due in here later today.

"Since the rest of our subs are nuclear-powered, the crew of the *Stingray* has a special legacy all their own. They're proud and smart. Only last month, the boat received its latest battle-efficiency award. That makes two years straight now. There is no finer crew when it comes down to being open to training, and they've demonstrated well the abilities of conventional power in exercises with the rest of the fleet."

"Sounds like just the kind of boys that we're looking for," observed the CNO. "Having just stood back and watched the nukes get all the juicy assignments, I'll bet my pension that those kids are ready to show their stuff with a real mission. By the way, what's the latest status of the *Dnieper*?"

"The Soviet vessel is presently encased in a sub pen in dry dock," said the Commander. "She's got a pretty good gash in her bow, yet nothing that we can't handle. Though it's hard to say for certain, all

170

her systems appear to be functioning properly except for the radio transmitter."

"Lukowski and Keller will know soon enough if she's fit for the sea," added Carrigan. "One thing has still got me puzzled, though. What have you done with that Soviet crew?"

With this question, the Commander looked to Lawrence for help. The CNO cleared his throat and carefully responded.

"Here's where it gets a bit sticky, William. When we pulled them out of Juan de Fuca, we took into custody forty-six surviving crew members. Four sailors were apparently killed during the initial collision. This included their Captain.

"Believe it or not, their Zampolit, or political officer, tried to give us some cock-and-bull story that they were merely lost while in the midst of a peaceful cruise home. I don't have to tell you how this bag of BS went down in Washington. We believe that their most likely mission was to monitor the advance of our Tridents as they put to sea. Since such a clandestine operation would need the strictest secrecy, it's doubtful that Soviet Naval Command would dare attempt to contact them while they were in the strait. Thus it's fair to say that the *Dnieper* is alive and well as far as Vladivostok is concerned.

"We've estimated that we have at least another three weeks until they begin to get suspicious. Meanwhile, we've taken the liberty of locking up the *Dnieper*'s crew in the local brig. This facility has only just gone on line, and although it's a bit cramped in there, the security is first-rate. As it stands now, we plan on holding them there indefinitely."

Carrigan shook his head at this. "Brother, those Russkies sure must be upset."

"You don't know the half of it," observed the Commander. "Screaming that their human rights were being flagrantly violated, that Zampolit has threatened to take their case to the United Nations. We've managed to shut him up by reminding him where they were caught, and that the US Navy considers such an intrusion an act of war."

William Carrigan was in the process of wondering if it indeed just might lead to this unthinkable state when the CNO brought up the idea of ordering breakfast. Carrigan's thoughts were far from his physical needs, yet he hadn't eaten anything since last night's seafood platter, and some chow would be welcome. Their orders were taken and, while they waited for the first course to be served, Commander Barry briefly outlined their day's activities.

Twenty-eight nautical miles due south of the entrance to the strait of Juan de Fuca, the Captain of the USS *Stingray* was in the midst of his own breakfast. Randall Spencer had been commanding officer of the diesel-electric attack sub for the last year and a half. Since such assignments were generally for two years at the most, he knew that he would soon be transferred elsewhere. As he spooned in his oatmeal, he reflected on the fact that when he'd first received his orders for his present command he'd been somewhat disappointed. As with most young officers on their way up in the sub force, duty aboard a 688-class nuclear attack vessel was the ultimate draw. Such boats were crammed with the latest high-tech gear and could dive deeper and faster than almost any sub on the planet. In contrast, the *Stingray* was almost thirty years old.

Commissioned in 1959, the vessel was well advanced for its time. One of the radical design changes that separated it from the subs of World War II was its "teardrop" hull and single propeller. Such innovations allowed vastly improved submerged performance. Through the years the boat had also been equipped with the latest word in torpedo fire-control, radar, sonar, and navigational gear. Yet because its power plant was run on fossil fuels, it was still forced to surface from time to time to "breathe." This dependency too often led to detection by the enemy's sophisticated ASW sensors, and with the advent of the nuclear reactor, the *Stingray* saw its best day come and go.

Surprisingly enough, Randall Spencer had since developed a definite attachment to his boat. He was proud of his special crew, who were also well aware of the *Stingray*'s uniqueness and had a morale of extremely high proportions. Though they were forced to prove their worth time after time, they rose to the challenge without complaint. Often they were even able to turn the tables, and hunt down the nukes that had been sent to "sniff" them out.

Spencer finished off his cereal and began working on a platter of bacon and eggs as the boat's navigator ducked into the wardroom. Lieutenant Stephen Monihan had only recently arrived on the *Stingray*. So far, the Captain was impressed. The lieutenant was the no-nonsense type, who prided himself in doing a thorough job. This was a quality that was a must in navigation, and Monihan was one of the best.

"Sir, I have those charts of our approach," said the lieutenant shyly. "Shall I bring them back after you've finished breakfast?"

The Captain looked up at his navigator and took in the youngster's slight frame, sallow complexion, and round, wire-rim glasses. He decided that Monihan reminded him of a typical scholar. "No, lieutenant, you may spread them out before me. Since the morning paper failed to arrive, I could use some decent reading material anyway."

Failing to find any humor in his Skipper's words, the serious-faced navigator carefully spread out his charts. The one closest to Spencer showed their current position. A line was traced northward showing their route to Juan de Fuca. Several reference points were marked along their way, where they could ascend to periscope depth to double-check their bearings. After scanning it for accuracy, the Captain signed it in the lower left-hand corner. He then reached out for the second chart, which was drawn in greater scale. He was in the process of studying their route through the straits themselves when the intercom rang. The handset was placed conveniently at his side, and Spencer didn't even have to take his eyes off the chart while he cradled the black receiver up to his ear.

"This is the Captain."

The familiar voice on the other end was deep and powerful. "Skipper, it's the XO. Minutes ago we were routinely clearing our baffles when sonar picked up an unidentified contact following in our wake. Mariani is working on a positive, but I smell the bad guys."

"Good show, Tim. I'm on my way up there now."

Spencer hung up the receiver and pushed away the chart he had been scanning. "Looks like we could have an unfriendly on our tail, lieutenant. Bring along those charts and let's see what we can do about shaking them off before we lead them straight into Bangor."

The Captain scooted out from his seat at the head of the table, stood, and began his way forward. As he ducked through the hatchway leading from the wardroom, he passed down a narrow, cable-lined passageway, which held the locked radio room on his left and the boat's office to his right. He rounded a stairwell headed downward and, seconds later, entered the control room. There could be no ignoring the frantic activity taking place there. Seemingly orchestrating this movement was Lieutenant Commander Tim Kelly, the *Stingray*'s Executive Officer. The six-foot, muscular Nebraskan stood behind the seated diving officer, Chief Pat McDaris. Both were watching the two helmsmen, who were perched before them, steering columns in hand. Quickly the Captain took in their current depth and speed as he approached his XO.

"Any news from sonar yet, Tim?"

The XO seemed relieved with the Captain's presence. "Negative, Skipper. The last we heard from Mariani, the contact was smack in our baffles, approximately six thousand yards away. Do you

175

think we should zap them with active to get a positive?"

Active sonar meant transmitting a powerful pulse of sonic energy out into the surrounding waters and waiting for an ensuing reflection. Though it could accurately tag any pursuers, Spencer was well aware that such a method would allow their quarry to detect them earlier than they could detect their quarry.

"Let's hold on that, Tim," advised the Captain. "There's no use giving away the store yet. Let's see what kind of water we've got around here to play with."

The XO followed him over to the nearby navigational station. There Lieutenant Monihan had alertly spread out a bathymetric chart showing the ocean's depth in that portion of the Pacific. As the three officers studied the ocean's contour, the seaman responsible for manning the sound-powered telephones spoke out clearly.

"It's sonar, Captain. Mr. Mariani has a definite on that contact. He IDs the footprint as a Soviet Akula. Range remains at six-triple-zero yards, sir."

Nodding at the receipt of this news, Spencer caught his XO's glance. "So it's an Akula! Here's a classic matchup for you, the Soviet Union's latest attack sub versus one of the last of her kind. Shall we show those Russkies just how much kick this grand old dame still packs?"

The XO grinned and the Captain continued, "See if you can find us a decent thermocline, Tim. Chances are that the Soviets still don't know that we're on to them. To spoil their day, let's put a little knuckle in the water. Not even the Akula's super-sensitive sonar will be able to track us through the turbulence we'll soon be leaving behind in our wake."

This maneuver sounded fine to Tim Kelly, who pivoted to get on with the Captain's bidding. Battle stations were sounded, and the rest of the crew scurried to their assigned positions. Thousands of hours of practice soon paid off as the *Stingray* suddenly plunged its nose downward. With its screw turning at full throttle, the sub began a tight, spiraling turn. Like a fist plunged into a basin of calm water, the sea behind them filled with a sizzling vortex of alien sound.

At 850 feet the *Stingray* pulled from its dive. There they made the best use of a well-pronounced thermocline. Hopefully, this thick layer of cold water would further veil them from the Akula's sensors. Their daring maneuver seemed to have produced its desired effects when sonar reported picking up the mad rush of the enemy's screws as they vainly searched in the exact opposite direction from where the *Stingray* was now headed. Confident that they had successfully made their point, the Captain ordered the navigator to draw up a new course to Juan de Fuca. Under the near-silent propulsion of their electric motors, they turned to the north to continue on with their mission, this time with the seas all to themselves.

Less than twenty-four hours later, Captain Randall Spencer and his XO found themselves in a drastically different environment. They had arrived in Bangor late the previous afternoon. While entering the waters of Puget Sound, they had passed a 688-class attack sub in the process of escorting one of the huge Ohio-class Tridents out to sea. The Trident was well over twice the size of the *Stingray*, and Spencer had gotten great satisfaction from warning them of the Akula's presence outside the strait.

The Captain allowed several of the enlisted men up onto the exposed bridge to watch the two nukes pass. Whistling in astonishment, they couldn't help but feel proud to be in the same Navy with those awesome strategic platforms. Spencer was in the process of briefing them on the incredible amount of nuclear firepower stored within the Trident's missile magazine when the tug arrived to escort them to their proper berth.

The Captain's orders read that he was to stay with his vessel until contacted by the Base Commander. He was a bit surprised when night fell and the *Stingray*'s presence was still not officially acknowledged. The next morning, Spencer was just rolling out of his cot when a dispatch from Commander Ronald Barry arrived. Apologizing for not greeting him earlier, the Commander invited both Spencer and his XO to a special briefing at his office that afternoon at 1400 hours. With this in mind, Spencer spent the rest of the morning shuffling paperwork.

At the appointed hour they left the *Stingray* under the watchful eye of Lieutenant Stephen Monihan, and made their way to Barry's office. This was their first visit to Bangor, and they couldn't get over the

178

base's well-designed, modern facilities. Since they were a few minutes early, their escort drove them by the dock where the Tridents were serviced. Triangular in shape, the massive structure handled all aspects of the Ohio class's refitting. A single such vessel was berthed there. Well over the length of three football fields, the sub loomed like a beached behemoth. Wondering how such a giant handled, they passed the security gate and headed back toward the thick stands of woodland that the installation was built around.

They were led to a briefing room, set in the rear of what appeared to be a contemporary two-story office building. Huddled around a rectangular conference table there were an assortment of animated figures. Five were substantially older, and were dressed in civilian garb. Though their faces were unfamiliar, Randall Spencer was able to identify the distinguished-looking officer seated at the table's head. He was none other than Admiral Walter Lawrence, the Chief of Naval Operations. A full Commander, seated to the CNO's left, caught sight of the *Stingray*'s Captain and XO as they entered. This relatively young officer rose and greeted them.

"Captain Spencer and Lieutenant Commander Kelly, I presume. Welcome to Bangor. I'm Commander Barry, your host here. Sorry I wasn't able to introduce myself earlier, but things have been unusually hectic lately. I'd like you both to meet Admiral Lawrence, and then we'll get started."

The CNO momentarily broke off his spirited conversation with the distinguished, white-haired civilian seated to his right. He warmly greeted the

Stingray's senior officers and proceeded to introduce them to the other six individuals present here. In quick succession they met William Carrigan, Peter Donner, Stan Lukowski, Helmut Keller, Mac Brady, and Lieutenant Vince Paterson—a US Navy SEAL. They were seated in the two remaining empty chairs that were set up beside the lieutenant. As they settled themselves in, the animated hum of conversation that had greeted them upon entering gradually subsided. This was soon replaced by the firm voice of the CNO.

"First off, I want to thank you for your prompt attendance here this afternoon. Many of you have had to travel thousands of miles to get to Bangor, with less than twenty-four hours' notice and no idea what this impromptu meeting was even about. Your unselfish devotion to your country shall never be forgotten.

"What is discussed today in this room is for your ears only. It's not to be repeated to either family, friends, the press, or your lovers. Our gathering concerns a matter of the utmost sensitivity. For not only is the nation's security at stake, but the rest of the world's as well. In a nutshell, this meeting was precipitated by a weapons test that recently took place in the Soviet Far East. At this time the Russians successfully fired an earth-borne laser device, which succeeded in taking out both a flight of jet aircraft and cruise missiles.

"As far as we know, this is the first time that such a device has been tested under actual wartime conditions. Its success has caught our Intelligence people completely by surprise. It is feared that their next step will be to use the laser against descending ICBM warheads. If they are successful in this effort, the fragile balance of arms that has managed to keep the peace for the last four decades will be directly threatened. For no longer would the Soviets have reason to fear our strategic triad.

"Since the deployment of America's own laser battle station is still well over a year distant, and because the Soviet installation directly violates the newly signed ABM treaty, we have decided to draw up a scenario to take this prototype facility out. Thus, the reason you have been called together today is to draw up just such a plan."

With the conclusion of these words, a nervous murmur of chatter rose amongst the CNO's audience. The admiral allowed his guests a minute to emotionally vent themselves before continuing.

"If you'll be so good as to direct your attention to the screen on the far wall, I'll share with you some slides which should substantially clarify our intended operation."

As all heads turned to this screen, the CNO picked up the remote-control switch that had been placed on the table before him, and utilized it to turn off the room's lights. He activated the projector, and the screen filled with a detailed map of the Soviet Far East. Circled in red was the city of Vladivostok and the narrow peninsula of Soviet territory that extended to its south. The admiral provided the commentary.

"This is the sector where the laser battle station has been situated. Vladivostok is the home of the Soviet's Pacific Naval Command. Because of the proximity of this installation, Intelligence feels that the Navy is playing an instrumental part in the system's development."

The CNO hit the remote switch and the slide was replaced with another chart. This one was of a much greater scale and showed the extreme southern portion of the peninsula visible on the previous map.

"We believe that the laser base is situated here, on the Bay of Posjet. This body of water is protected by a strait and leads directly into the Sea of Japan. A small Soviet Naval facility has its home in the bay and is rumored to be the home of an attack-submarine squadron."

Again Lawrence switched slides. This time the screen filled with the photograph of a black-hulled submarine.

"Before you is a vessel of the Soviet Whiskey class. Such boats began production in 1951 and are among the most successful classes of sub ever produced. They are loosely based on the German Type Twenty-one boats, which were designed in the closing days of World War II.

"Several days ago, a boat of this class ran aground in the Strait of Juan de Fuca. The Coast Guard was able to remove the crew before they were able to inform Soviet Command of their misfortune. The *Dnieper* is presently in dry dock here in Bangor. Her bow is being repaired and the vessel will soon be seaworthy once again. The coincidental capture of this craft offers us a unique opportunity."

The photo of the Whiskey-class vessel was replaced by one showing another submarine. Yet this one had a much more sharply angled bow and several gun platforms mounted on its deck. Two uniformed figures could be seen on its exposed bridge, as the boat approached an awaiting pier. Excited by this shot, the admiral quickened his commentary.

"In the closing days of the war in the Pacific, the USS *Abalone* was sent into that same bay to land an Army Ranger squad, whose job was to take out a Japanese munitions factory that was situated there. Captain William Carrigan was the skipper of that mission. He was invaluably assisted by his XO, Peter Donner; his weapons officer, Mac Brady; and the boat's chief, Stan Lukowski.

"As fate would have it, the *Abalone* also participated in the capture of a German Type Twenty-one U-boat on V-E Day. Helmut Keller was the esteemed chief of that vessel, which was guided into Portsmouth Harbor. Here this subsequent prototype of the Soviet Whiskey-class line of boats was picked apart and studied. With the invaluable aid of Chief Keller and William Carrigan, Stan Lukowski, and other US Navy personnel, we were able to learn just what made that U-boat tick.

"Today we hope to utilize this knowledge to train the current crew of the USS *Stingray* in the operation of the *Dnieper*. Under US command, the Whiskey class boat will then set sail for the Bay of Posjet, where she will land a squad of Navy SEALs. It will then be the SEALs' responsibility to take out the laser installation and return to the *Dnieper* without being detected. The sub will then return to Bangor, with the Soviets none the wiser."

The conclusion of this statement caused a renewed

wave of hushed chatter to possess the onlookers. Well aware of the cause of this commotion, Lawrence turned off the projector and switched on the lights.

Randall Spencer was stunned into silence as the lights popped on. He looked to the drawn face of his XO, then turned to study the chattering civilians who sat opposite him. With renewed respect, he took in each of the veterans who had known what it was like to fight a real war. With the CNO's unorthodox plan still whirling in his mind, the *Stingray's* Skipper vainly attempted to grasp its scope. Though his first impulse was to reject it as being ridiculously impractical, he forced himself to remain open-minded.

From the head of the table, two intense stares caught his attention. Spencer returned their stares and realized that both the CNO and the distinguished-looking civilian who sat to his right were attempting to gauge his initial reaction. Spencer solemnly nodded and Walter Lawrence took this as a sign to continue.

"Excuse me, gentlemen, but there's one important addendum that must be made absolutely clear. As of this moment, this entire operation is merely an option which our government shall feel free to apply only if it deems absolutely necessary. If the President does choose such a drastic course of action, we must be ready to carry out his will without hesitation. Thus we shall proceed just as if the mission were a definite go.

"William Carrigan and his associates will have two weeks in which to thoroughly train the crew of the

Stingray in the *Dnieper*'s operation. During this time, all those concerned will be confined to the base. There will thus be no contact with the outside world.

"I know this is asking a lot from each one of you, but we have no other choice. The very security of our nation is the bond which must motivate us. For if the Soviet laser facility succeeds in the final phase of its test, there will be nothing that we can do to counter any offensive moves on their part. Without our strategic weapons to keep them contained, the Russians will run rampant. By the grace of God, an unbelievable opportunity has come our way. We would be fools to ignore it, and we won't!

"I have asked Commander Barry to coordinate the training schedule. We'd like to begin tomorrow morning at zero-eight-hundred hours. Time is of the essence, and I don't intend to waste a precious moment of it. Now, I want to thank you again for your patience. The next couple of weeks will be difficult for each of us, yet our duty is clear. We have already lost too many brave men in the defense of freedom, and it would be an utter sacrilege to merely stand by and do nothing now that democracy faces its greatest challenge ever."

These somber words concluded the CNO's presentation. As his audience thoughtfully absorbed his closing remarks, Randall Spencer once again returned the probing stare of the man sitting to the admiral's right. As the ex-Skipper of the USS *Abalone* silently appraised his new pupil, Spencer decided to accept his challenge. After all, hadn't he always dreamed of participating in a real operation?

185

Yet never in his wildest vision did he ever expect to lead his men into battle from the bridge of one of their enemy's own vessels. It would take some getting used to, but he would succeed, just as he had consistently proved the *Stingray*'s worth to the hightech Navy.

CHAPTER SEVEN

The skies had begun blackening soon after they had left Moscow. By the time they were preparing to land at Voronkl, it was all that the General Secretary's pilot could do to set the helicopter down in one piece. Viktor's senior aide had advised against attempting such a landing at all, once it was apparent that the storm front would arrive at the same time they would. Yet Viktor Chernavin would hear of no such thing. He had been anticipating this trip all week long, and wasn't about to let a little thing like the weather interfere.

Whipped by the dual Isotov turboshaft engines, the Mi-8's five rotors bit into the gusting northerly winds. The fuselage vibrated and tilted, causing its occupants to grab onto their safety harnesses. Confident that his hand-picked pilot would see them to the earth safely, Chernavin peered out of the nearest porthole. The northern horizon was almost black as night, even though the sun was not scheduled to set for at least another hour. Cursing at the misfortune of missing out on the magnificent spring-like weather that had settled upon the capital these last few days, the General Secretary angled his line of sight downward. What he saw there caused a slight smile on his face.

Oblivious to the ever-advancing storm front, the

Moscow River snaked its way through the thick forests of encroaching birch. Human habitations were few and far between, for there the forest reigned unchallenged. When another gust caused the Mi-8 to shudder, Chernavin noticed how this same breeze coursed through the woods. Like the masts of an immense fleet of sailing ships, the stately, leafless trunks swayed and bobbed in unison. A splattering of precipitation struck the porthole and Chernavin knew that the full fury of the storm would soon be upon them. Fortunately, though, their goal was close by, the throaty pitch of the Isotov's further increased, signaling their impending descent.

They landed with a moderate jolt. As Chernavin ripped off his harness and stood, he noticed that most of his staff were still stuck to their chairs, their knuckles white and faces flushed with fear. This included his faithful secretary, Olga Tisnevo. Remembering her dislike of air travel, Chernavin attempted to lighten the tense atmosphere.

"What are you waiting for, Comrade Tisnevo? Would you like me to ask our esteemed pilot to attempt an encore landing in your honor?"

This remark soon had its desired effect as Olga quickly removed her seatbelt and moved herself out into the narrow aisle. "Heaven forbid, Comrade General Secretary. This citizen has had enough flying for one day."

Olga's words were delivered tensely and Chernavin instinctively softened. "Have no fear, my dear. For the rest of the week we travel only by foot, and if that sky remains true, even then we'll have to wear either skis or snowshoes."

The truth of this observation struck home when the hatchway was popped open and they were greeted with an icy blast of Arctic air, thick with swirling snow. By the time they had made it down to the footpath leading to the dacha, a virtual blizzard was blowing. Yet at least they could take comfort in the fact that they were safe on solid land.

The snows continued well through the night. To properly celebrate their safe arrival, Chernavin had ordered a special dinner party for his entire staff. As they gathered around the blazing fireplace, with their bellies full and the vodka flowing, the storm was soon forgotten. They played charades, told jokes, and, after the usual gossip was exchanged, took off for the warmth of their beds.

Chernavin was the last one to leave the crackling hearth. Soothed by the flickering flames and the persistent howl of the wind, which could be heard even inside, the General Secretary allowed himself to further relax. Even with the snowstorm, Voronkl had once again been able to weave its magical spell on him. Moscow and its incessant pressures were soon forgotten, to be replaced by concerns of a much more basic level.

There in the deep forest, clever city ideas and political machinations were of little use to a man. A vastly different code of survival existed. So basic in its primal simplicity, this code was the same that ruled the wolf and the bear. In a matter of speaking, it was identical to the principles that had guided prehistoric man, long before the creation of city-states and governments.

Survival of the fittest was its basis. A starving predator which took pity in its prey's plight would not be long for this world. Thus the wolf's reputation as an unmerciful, ruthless killer.

Modern man had somehow strayed from this universal law. As a result, the world was rife with wasteful, foolish political stalemates. Such a condition was against the very principles that guided nature, and man as a species was paying the price.

Only a few hours ago, his Defense Minister, Alexi Kudikov, had come to him with a plan to do something about this ridiculous deadlock once and for all. Yet fear of risk kept Chernavin from immediately giving the marshal his blessings on the daring project. In the forest, the wild beast had no time to consider risk or even fear for that matter. It only went forward guided by an instinctive longing for self-fulfillment. Had Chernavin forgotten this basic longing? Or perhaps it had been bred from his species generations ago. Miraculously, Voronkl had reestablished the ancient bond, and Viktor Chernavin's vision was no longer veiled.

The wind howled like a pack of hungry wolves on the trail of a weakened deer. Channeling his gaze into the fireplace, the Rodina's most powerful man mentally recreated the video tapes that had been shown in his Kremlin office earlier. Like crippled eagles, the trio of jet bombers had tumbled from the sky. And how could he forget that fated moment when that pair of cruise missiles had followed these aircraft into the surging waters of Posjet Bay? If the laser battle station indeed proved successful against a flight of ICBMs, could he afford not to back Kudikov's carefully worked-out scheme? With the Imperialists' own ABM system still a good twelve months away from deployment, this would be the chance of a lifetime.

A nuclear attack, no matter how limited, meant that hundreds of thousands would perish. If their preemptive strike failed to cripple the Americans completely, many of those dead would be the Motherland's own. Would those poor souls knowingly go to their graves if they knew that their deaths would not be in vain? For the world that would eventually emerge from such an inferno would be cleansed of all past sins. With only the tenets of pure Communism to guide them, all men would finally be free from their shackles. Just think of all the great things such a society could accomplish! With the burden of foolishly high military budgets no longer holding them back, starvation would be no more, and mankind could focus its energies on combating disease and then exploring the heavens. Was this but a dream, or could he attain such a state within his very own lifetime?

Viktor Chernavin had never been a gambler, yet there came a time in one's life when a fellow had to put his money down and roll for what he believed in. His time on earth was limited. He had worked hard and gained much, and now he had a chance to go for it all.

The wind howled and Chernavin stirred. Like a wolf on the prowl he would let his instincts go. Satisfied with this decision, he reached over to call Alexi Kudikov. Snow or no snow, the marshal would find a way to join him in Voronkl with the dawn — for there was an attack to plan and a new world to begin making preparations for!

Tanya Markova left for Vladivostok on a crisp, clear morning. The snow that had fallen several days earlier had long since melted, and once again there was a hint of spring in the fresh air. Since returning to Tavricanka, after their brief excursion to the hills surrounding Posjet, both Tanya and her uncle had been extremely busy. Of course, their first task had been to get hold of their contact in the West. Once news of the laser test had been conveyed, they'd gotten to work organizing a proper surveillance operation. A pair of operatives was sent to the Posjet region to keep a lookout for further tests, but Lev Litvov felt that Tanya could help out elsewhere. It was decided that she would be their eyes and ears in Vladivostok.

With her fox coat around her shoulders, and two weeks' worth of clothing inside her suitcase, Tanya boarded the bus for the fifty-seven-kilometer ride back to the capital city. She wasn't surprised to find this vehicle to be the same battered, old carriage that had acted as the replacement on her recently concluded return trip. In a cloud of black diesel exhaust, it chugged out of the village of her birth. She had been fortunate to get a seat by herself at the very back of the bus, and was able to get a last look at the massive figure of her uncle as he stood by the curb waving goodbye.

There could be no ignoring the lines of worry that had etched the furrier's face these last few days. He had slept fitfully and was far from his spry, jolly self. Tanya knew it was the test that they had personally witnessed that was bothering him. He talked incessantly of it. He was fearful that such a device would lead directly to World War III, and his only hope was that the West would be able to act before it was too late. The monitoring of such preparations was one of the reasons Tanya had been sent packing for Vladivostok.

Tavricanka was soon no longer visible, and she turned her attention to the passing landscape. Endless stands of giant pines hugged the roadway. Fat, grayish squirrels could be seen playing in their boughs, and above, a large group of black ravens circled. With such a peaceful scene before her, she found thoughts of the world's destruction hard to contemplate. Yet she had seen the laser blast those cruise missiles from the sky with her very own eyes, and knew the threat was a real one.

Tanya was suddenly chilled and she pulled her coat tightly around her thin body. She stifled a yawn and leaned her head against the seat's torn headrest. With her glance still pointed toward the passing forest, her inner vision went back to a time of innocence and joy. Though her childhood had been interrupted when her mother and father had split up, she still had many fond memories of these early days. Most of these recollections centered around her mother.

Her name had been Lara and she was a kind, gentle soul. A full-time teacher by profession, she still managed to keep a warm, spotless home. More importantly, she always had time for her daughter. When Lara returned from the classroom, young Tanya was constantly at her side, doing her best to help her mother with her chores. They made dolls together and cooked. It was her mother who taught her not only to read and write Russian, but English as well.

One snowy winter's night, when Tanya had just turned thirteen, her mother brought out a dusty old photo album. Tanya remembered this evening well, for they had only just left Chabarovsk and her father, to return to Tavricanka. It was before Uncle Lev's blazing fireplace that she first saw a picture of her grandmother. Taken at the Great War's conclusion, somewhere in these very woods, the photo showed an attractive, tall, trim woman. She was dressed in what appeared to be an Army uniform, her short blonde bangs emphasizing a pretty, alert face that seemed to belong to anyone but a soldier.

Another picture showed a tall, muscular, bearded officer who was also dressed in green Army fatigues. He looked vaguely familiar to Tanya, and her mother explained that this man was her grandfather. Though both of her grandparents had been killed long before Tanya's birth, his virtual twin seemed to appear before the teenager's startled eyes when Uncle Lev entered the room. She soon learned that the furrier was actually her step-uncle, for Lev had been her grandfather's son by a previous marriage.

Tanya went on to study the album's other contents. These included several pictures of her mother and father in happier times, and even a snapshot or two taken when Tanya was but an infant. As it turned out, it wasn't until a year later that she once again opened the album. That fated evening was far from a happy occasion, for it was only hours earlier that she had learned of her mother's tragic death.

Tears wet her eyes when the grinding squeal of the bus's brakes broke her sad musing. Tanya wiped her cheeks dry and sat up straight. They had reached their first stop of the morning, and a half-dozen weary passengers soon climbed aboard. These bedraggled

194

newcomers settled in front of the vehicle. They mechanically stowed their belongings while the driver exited for the restroom.

Fifteen minutes later, they were on their way northward once more. A stream followed the roadway here, and Tanya watched its gurgling current smash white upon the boulders that shaped its course. Two heavily bundled children could be seen ahead, playing on the stream's banks. Supervising their every move was a middle-aged woman, who was most likely their mother. Seeing her caused Tanya to again return in time. For could she ever forget her last fond look at her own mother?

The coffin had been laid out in Uncle Lev's shop. Tanya hadn't been allowed to see the body until the local women had finished washing and dressing the corpse. Even in death, she looked beautiful. Lara's smashed body had been covered in her prettiest dress, and if one didn't know any better, she appeared to be merely sleeping.

The hushed, tense chatter of those who came to view the body first gave Tanya the hint that something regarding her mother's death was being kept from her. Later, after Lara had been buried in the cemetery that contained the remains of her own parents, Tanya confronted Uncle Lev. One look at her face and the furrier knew that his niece was serious. After swearing her to secrecy, he went on to explain the real cause of Lara's demise.

Her mother and a neighbor had been sent to monitor a military exercise taking place in the hills to the immediate west of Tavricanka. They thought they had found a safe observation point, but an armored personnel carrier suddenly burst from the woods behind them. As they scrambled to get out of the way, Lara fell and was run over. Since the soldiers hadn't seen her, they merely kept on moving. Yet even if they had stopped, it was already too late, for her neck had been broken.

So that her death would not be in vain, Tanya instantly volunteered to help the same Movement that her mother had been involved with in whatever way possible. Tears were falling from her uncle's eyes as he reached out and pulled her hard to his swelling chest. The very next day she was indoctrinated.

All this seemed to have taken place a lifetime ago, yet Tanya knew otherwise. She had grown up quickly in these last six years. Not only had her physical body matured, but her political consciousness as well.

To stop the mad arms race that was draining their country dry, they had to go to any extreme. This was the principle that her mother had dedicated her life to. Tanya was thus proud to be able to follow in her footsteps.

The bus seemed to slow down, and she looked out the window and caught the sight of the reason why. Approaching them from the other direction was some sort of military convoy. With a deafening squeal, the bus pulled onto the narrow shoulder and halted. Seconds later, an eight-wheeled BTR-60 armored personnel carrier passed them. A flashing red light was set on its sloped roof. On its tail was another BTR-60. Tanya knew they each carried up to fourteen troops. An assortment of vehicles followed. She identified several

BTR-40 scout cars, a lumbering 122-mm self-propelled howitzer, two BMD air fire-support vehicles, and a half-dozen Main battle tanks. To see such a heavily armed convoy on this road was unprecedented, and Tanya wished she could somehow inform her uncle of its approach. She could always make a phone call at the next stop, yet there was always the chance that it would be overheard. Well aware that the Movement would all too soon know of its passage anyway — if they didn't know of it already — she decided that her upcoming mission took precedence. If there were really a full-scale military alert on, as indeed it appeared, she would soon know for certain when she entered Vladivostok.

She checked her watch and silently cursed at the late hour. The bus driver seemed to have all the time in the world as he slowly guided the ancient vehicle back onto the roadway. Taking a deep breath to calm herself, Tanya closed her eyes with the hope that a nap would cause the hands of time to move quicker.

It was dusk before they finally lumbered into Vladivostok. For the last hour and a half, Tanya had been forced to share her bench with an unkempt old man who reeked of cheap vodka and sweat. Though he kept well to himself, his scent was sickening. The night air never smelled so good as Tanya gratefully climbed out of the bus.

The terminal was located in the center of town, and even Vladivostok had its version of that modern phenomenou called rush hour. Tanya took in the assortment of vehicles that completely clogged the city's streets. Interspersed among the tangled web of automobiles, buses, and trucks were hundreds of scurrying pedestrians. Horns honked, engines roared, brakes squealed, and humans cursed. Thus went the sounds of the city.

With her suitcase at her side, Tanya began her way to the apartment. Even though the traffic was fierce, she enjoyed this chance to stretch her legs. She knew the way from her last visit, and arrived at the proper building without a single wrong turn. Inside, she was greeted by the rosy-cheeked concierge.

"Ah, so you're back so soon, miss. I guess that your village seemed a bit tame after your week's visit here."

Lev had warned her that the nosy old woman was curious and sharp as a tack. To keep on her good side, he had made her a beaver stole, which he had given to her this past fall.

"That it did," returned Tanya with a smile. "I imagine that you never have a dull moment around here."

"You can say that again," answered the concierge. "Why, only last night a group of hooligans robbed a woman of her purse right outside this very door. The poor thing ran into here sobbing, yet what could I do but call the militia? Do you know that it took over an hour for them to respond? Why, she drank all of my tea, and then started on my dinner!"

Shaking her head in sympathy, Tanya began her way to the stairs. "Well, I'll certainly be careful. Thanks for the warning."

"That's the least I can do for the niece of my personal furrier," added the old-timer. "Now, don't forget to lock your door behind you."

Tanya took in this motherly advice while climbing the stairway. The apartment was on the third floor, and by the time she reached it, she was puffing for breath. Inside, it was just as she had left it.

There were only two rooms, which her uncle had decorated simply yet efficiently. She placed her suitcase on the kitchen table, which doubled as a desk, and turned up the steam heat before unpacking. She had initially planned to return to the Red Pelican that same evening. There she hoped to renew her contacts with the Navy. Unfortunately, the concierge's warning had forced her to rethink her plans. To go out alone now would only arouse the old lady's suspicions. Anyway, a group of hooligans wasn't something to take lightly. Not desiring to be their next victim, Tanya decided to hold off her visit to the wharves until tomorrow afternoon. By that time she would be rested and ready for action.

She had brought along a parcel of food and made herself a light dinner of canned fish, bread, and an apple. She ate while listening to the radio. A violin concerto by Tchaikovsky proved to be her dining companion. By its finale, she was sound asleep.

She forced herself to stay in bed late, for there was certainly no reason to get up early on this morning. The establishment she would be visiting didn't open until noon. She allowed herself a long soak in the tub and had a breakfast of an orange, some tea, and the rest of the bread. After carefully choosing her outfit, she dressed and, trailing her fox coat over her arm, began her way down the three flights of stairs.

The concierge was in the process of sweeping out the foyer. This was the first time that Tanya had seen her away from her desk. Though she was barely five feet tall, she pushed around her broom like a virtual giantess. It didn't take her long to notice the new-comer's presence.

"Well, good morning, miss. Or should I say good afternoon? I hope that you found all in order."

Tanya nodded that she had, and looked out the window that was set beside the door. That portion of sky that was visible showed it to be an almost cloud-lessly clear day. Noticing the direction of her glance, the concierge added, "And a truly magnificent day it is, miss. Why, this morning the birds were singing and I could have sworn that I smelled spring in the air. It won't be long in coming now, my dear. May I ask where you're off to, dressed so pretty like you are?"

Tanya answered cautiously. "Of course you may, comrade. Soon my uncle will be bringing the season's pelts to town. Today I will be going down to the wharf to see about arranging transport for these skins. You don't think that I'm dressed too provocatively for such a place, do you, comrade?"

Eyeing her from head to toe, the concierge was quick with her response. "Of course not, my dear. You look as pretty as a doll. You'll be a sight for sore eyes to those sailors. Did I ever tell you that my beloved husband was a longshoreman? Before he passed away, I spent many an afternoon down on those docks, and I was always careful to fix myself properly beforehand. When a man's been to sea for a time, just seeing a pretty woman is a gift all in itself. As long as the vodka's not in them, they'll behave all right and you'll be just fine."

Thanking her for this timely advice, Tanya excused herself. Outside, the air was indeed quite mild. Since there was not even a hint of a breeze present, she wore her coat over her shoulders, leaving her arms and body uncovered, except for her black-leather, long-sleeved dress. The city looked different under the direct light of noon and she walked down the sidewalk with assured confidence. After passing a series of crowded food stores, she turned directly toward the docks.

The wharf area was buzzing with activity. Lines of trucks clogged the streets there, anxiously waiting to take on or drop off their loads. To a series of whistles from men she crossed Front Street, and got her first clear view of the docks. Though there were a good dozen cargo ships berthed there, most of the vessels were military. The largest of these was a Kresta-II-class cruiser. This massive ship easily dwarfed the various destroyers, frigates, and tenders that surrounded it. After noting that the *Ivan Komarov*, the Krivak-class frigate that she had toured earlier, was still docked there, she proceeded straight to the Red Pelican.

The bistro had been open for barely an hour, yet there was already a good-sized crowd inside. The table by the window that she had occupied during her last visit was vacant and she asked to be seated there. No sooner had she settled herself in than a tall, dark-eyed, mustached officer approached her. He slyly grinned and clicked his heels together.

"Good afternoon, comrade. Please excuse my forwardness, but I believe we've met before. Aren't you Lieutenant Amazar's friend?"

She nodded she was. He continued, "I thought so. You see, I never forget a pretty face. I'm Senior Lieutenant Grigori Kisnev, communications officer aboard the *Ivan Komarov*. We met briefly when you graced our ship with your lovely presence last week."

She had seen many new faces on that day, and though his was not a familiar one, she smiled anyway. "Why of course, lieutenant. I was fortunate enough to be sent back to Vladivostok sooner than I had expected and was hoping to bump into Mikhail this afternoon."

Eyeing her with more than a passing interest, the lieutenant shook his head. "I'm afraid that your wait could be a long, lonely one. You see, the lieutenant is on special watch now. I seriously doubt that he'll be getting any additional leave for the rest of the week."

A look of disappointment clouded Tanya's face. "Oh, that's too bad. He is such a nice young man, and I was looking forward to spending my extra time with him once again."

Taking this as the cue that it was meant to be, the lieutenant winked. "So that your day won't be a complete loss, why don't you let me buy you a drink? By doing so you would make this lonely old officer most happy."

The lieutenant had a devilish gleam in his eye. As he stood there, twirling the ends of his mustache, Tanya could see his air of cocky self-assurance. This one thought of himself as a lady killer, there was no doubt about it.

"I'd be proud to share a drink with you, lieutenant. Please have a seat."

"Only if you'll promise to call me Grigori."

"Very good, Grigori. I'm Tanya."

They exchanged handshakes and she found his grasp firm and warm. As he pulled the chair back, he beckoned a passing waiter.

"We'll be having a bottle of your best champagne, my friend, with a liter of Ukrainian potato vodka on the side."

With this he seated himself and smiled. "I hope that's all right with you, Tanya. This day's such a beauty that I feel like celebrating."

"Champagne is my very favorite, Grigori. How did you guess?"

The lieutenant's eyes sparkled. "Actually, it was quite easy. The first time that I saw you I said to myself, Grigori old man, there goes a woman with champagne tastes."

Tanya couldn't help but blush. "You are much too kind. In reality, I am but a simple country girl."

"So that's where you get your innocent beauty," reflected the officer. "You may be from the country, but simple you're not. I knew from the start that you were a deep one."

Not really certain what he meant by that, Tanya was nevertheless relieved when the waiter arrived with their order. The mood shifted as the cork was popped and their drinks were poured. Before allowing her to take a sip of the golden effervescent wine, he broke the seal on the vodka bottle. He then poured just a slight portion of the clear liquor into their glasses. Only then did he hand her one.

"This champagne-vodka cocktail is an old family tradition of mine. You'll see that the vodka effects the taste in no way whatsoever, but what an additional kick it gives!"

This was the first time that Tanya had ever heard of such a thing, yet, being open to new experiences, she lifted the glass to her lips and listened to the officer's toast.

"To the most beautiful woman in Vladivostok! May

health and happiness be with you always."

Tanya shyly nodded and took a sip. "It's indeed delicious," she commented. "How very decadent I feel drinking champagne with the sun still high in the sky."

"That's merely the country girl in you talking," responded the officer. "In Kiev, where I was born, it's not uncommon to have champagne for breakfast, lunch, and dinner. Now that's living!"

Tanya sat back to carefully appreciate her drink, while Grigori Kisnev began to discuss his background. It wasn't until they were nearly finished with the bottle, and he had begun a description of his naval experiences, that Tanya's complete interest was reawakened.

Not only was her drinking companion a graduate of Vladivostok's prestigious Makarov Naval School, but he had also attended postgraduate courses at the Order of Lenin Academy in Leiningrad. Such superior training put him well on the way to career advancement. He had only recently been selected to specialize in communications.

Grigori was just beginning to explain his current responsibilities aboard the *Ivan Komarov* when he noticed that their bottle was empty. Tanya was anxious for him to go on talking. She was about to urge him on, but decided against it. The drop of vodka that he subsequently added to each glassful of champagne seemed to channel the alcohol into her brain that much faster. Not much of a drinker to begin with, she had done her best to sip her cocktail as slowly as possible. Yet even with this strategy, she could feel herself losing control.

Her escort seemed to notice this, and a mischievous spark painted his glance. "Shall we have another bottle, my beautiful Tanya? Then perhaps I'll shut this big trap of mine and let you tell me a little about yourself."

Tanya strained to reply without slurring her words. "I'll agree to that bottle only if you'll promise to go on with your fascinating story. You'll soon enough find that my life has been dull compared to yours."

"I don't know about that," offered Grigori. "But if I'm indeed not boring you to death, I'll order us that bottle and continue on with my tale."

A new cork was soon popped and the naval officer kept to his word. As he continued on with an explanation of his present duties, Tanya realized that he was telling her things about radio waves and frequencies that had to be classified information. Surely the champagne had loosened his tongue and he was trying hard to impress her with his importance. Though most of the technical details were beyond her comprehension, she sat forward attentively when he mentioned a test that the *Ivan Komarov* would soon be involved with. When he added that General Secretary Chernavin would personally board their frigate to witness this test, she knew that she was on to something of vital importance. Being careful not to overplay her hand, she probed guardedly.

"Does that mean that the *Ivan Komarov* will be transferred to the Baltic?"

Thinking that Tanya was already worried about losing him, the lieutenant answered, "No, my little beauty, there will be time for us yet. For the General Secretary is flying here to Vladivostok. Why, we'll have a good sixteen days together before our esteemed leader arrives and we take off to sea."

"What kind of test could prompt such a trip?" asked

Tanya.

Relishing his power, Grigori hesitated before replying. "You probably wouldn't believe me if I told you. Yet this isn't the place to talk of such things. If only we had someplace more private."

Tanya was quick to take the bait. "My apartment is less than a kilometer from here. It's not much, but at least we'll have it all to ourselves."

Grigori grinned. "Well, whatever are you waiting for, my beauty? Lead on!"

With a bit of effort, Tanya managed to stand. The lieutenant was quickly at her side. Before leaving the bar, he managed to secure two more bottles of champagne. With one hand on the bag holding these treasures and the other around Tanya's narrow waist, Grigori led them outdoors.

The sun had already fallen behind the line of warehouses that lay to the west and the air was quite chilly. Before continuing on, Tanya put on her jacket. Grigori had no overcoat, yet he seemed oblivious to the weather. When they passed a group of young, uniformed seamen, he suddenly stiffened and became serious. He returned their salutes and only after they were well behind did he exhale a sigh of relief. Seconds later, he burst out in laughter.

"For a moment there, I almost forgot that I was in the Navy. Some example I am to the brave lads of the Rodina's fleet! Now do you see what kind of effect you have on me, my pretty one?"

His tone was so innocent that Tanya couldn't help but laugh herself. They struggled to contain themselves as they crossed Front Street and began their way into the city proper.

It was Grigori's idea to stop in several of the food stores that lined the street there. Since the hour was late, the lines weren't all that bad, though the selection was rather limited. They chose a tangy wheel of goat cheese, a fresh loaf of coarse pumpernickel, several sour pickles, and, of all things, a fresh pineapple. Tanya had only had such a delicacy once before in her life, and even then it was canned. Grigori explained that his frigate had escorted the ship that had carried the pineapples up from Viet Nam. They ate this delicious fruit quite often in Southeast Asia, and he volunteered to show her how to properly prepare it.

Feeling a bit more sobered, Tanya led them to the apartment building. As they approached the brick structure, she suddenly remembered the nosy concierge. There was no telling how the old lady would react if she saw Tanya bringing in a strange man. At least he was in uniform, yet would even this stop her from making trouble? While deliberating whether or not to make up a story, she decided that it would be best to let nature take its course. As it turned out, her worries were all for nothing.

Tanya pushed open the front door and heard the snoring. Grigori followed close on her heels, and both caught sight of the old lady sound asleep in her rocker. This innocent slumber didn't keep her from loudly breaking wind, and the two onlookers fought hard to contain themselves. Three flights of stairs later, they exploded in laughter behind the locked door of Tanya's apartment.

While Grigori prepared their drinks, Tanya excused herself to use the bathroom. Once inside this tile-lined cubicle, she wasted no time slapping some cold water onto her face. She would need all her wits now more than ever before. The water proved to be stimulating, and she took an additional minute to study her reflection in the mirror. The little makeup that she had used earlier was hardly visible. But her natural looks would be more than sufficient to lure her quarry into the snare.

She took a series of deep breaths and tried desperately to clear her mind. The man who waited for her outside held secrets of untold importance. Above all, she had to find out more about this mysterious test that was calling the likes of their General Secretary all the way out to Vladivostok. She wondered if it could have anything to do with the laser battle station she and Uncle Lev had seen in operation. She knew she would have to use any means at her disposal to get the truth from her guest. This even meant going to bed with him.

When she had stayed in Tavricanka the last time, she had not had time to visit Anton Bagdaran. She had chosen the handsome lumberjack to initiate her in the ways of a man and a woman. Yet the fates had not willed it, and here she was still a virgin.

The lieutenant seemed to be a decent enough fellow. He was tall, good-looking, and sure of himself. He also had a good sense of humor and even though Tanya hated to admit it, she did have fun with him. But could she really go to bed with him merely for the Movement? Was any amount of information worth such a sacrifice?

Just then, Tanya fleetingly saw her mother's reflection take the place of her own in the mirror. And on top of that merged the fatigue-wearing figure of her grandmother. Her forebears had sacrificed their very lives for the Cause. Surely she could offer her own meager oblation. With this in mind, she turned away from the mirror and returned to the other room.

Grigori had made himself right at home. Having lit the two candles that graced the kitchen table, he had turned off the electric lights. Spread out on the counter were the goodies that they had purchased. Tanya chose a spear of pineapple. It was tart and juicy, and tasted of a faroff land. Grigori poured them each a drink and beckoned her to join him on the couch. She did so without question.

They sipped their drinks silently for a while. Tanya was trying to figure out a way to get him talking about his duty once again when she felt his hand reach around her back and touch her shoulder. It was evident that there was only one thing on his mind and she had to get him talking first.

"Are you sure you won't be just taking off on the morning tide, Grigori?" cooed Tanya, her eyes wide. "I don't know if my heart could take such a thing."

Grigori pulled her closer. "Oh, my little sensitive beauty, don't worry so. You'll have your full share of me for at least sixteen more days. Believe me, the *Ivan Komarov* is going nowhere until that time. And even then, it promises to be but a short cruise."

"Then you won't be sailing off to the Baltic?"

"Hardly, little one. Why, we'll hardly be leaving these waters. Now, enough of your insecurity. Surely you don't think I'd open myself to losing you now that we've only just gotten together. Why, that would be unthinkable!"

Emptying his glass in a gulp, he bent over to kiss her.

His lips were moist and hot upon her own, his tongue probing madly. Tanya felt revulsion, yet she didn't dare push him away. Remembering her vision in the bathroom mirror, she closed her eyes and let her imagination run rampant. In a heartbeat, she was no longer in the arms of a virtual stranger. Rather, she found herself in a spring meadow, with her handsome lumberjack initiating her into the mysteries of womanhood.

His desire was strong, and she lost all will to resist. Helping him with the buttons of her dress, she shivered in ecstasy when his hands went to her bare breasts. Strong and experienced, his fingers gently rubbed against her budding, erect nipples, and she audibly sighed when they were replaced by his lips and tongue. Magically, his hands found their way between her thighs. They peeled off her panties and stroked the hairs of her womanhood. Gently, urgently, his fingers probed the dark, moist recesses that had never been violated before. When they found her clitoris, her entire body quivered as if it had been touched by an electric shock.

He laid her on her back, and took only a few fleeting seconds to rip off his own clothes. He was heavy and hot above her, yet his smell and touch were exciting beyond belief. His lips met hers just as an alien stiffness pressed against the smooth skin of her upper thigh. She reached down to identify this object and found her hand dwarfed by a thick, throbbing shaft of tight skin. Instinctively, she stroked it even stiffer.

This stroke further inflamed her lover, who placed his hands beneath her buttocks and guided her hips outward and apart. Then there was a brief, searing pain, as sharp as a knife thrust. Yet how quickly this

210

hurt turned itself into another sensation, far removed from pain!

She knew he was in her now. Slowly he inched himself forward until her entire insides were filled. With equal dexterity he pulled himself back, only to plunge himself forward once again. Time after time he repeated this mad dance of passion, and an odd, tingling warmth began gathering in her loins. Somehow she knew that it would be his touch alone that would bring this erotic sensation to fruition. Pushing her hips forward with each of his thrusts, the tingling intensified until she finally exploded in a whirlwind of awakened pleasures. She cried out when his coupling intensified, only to be abruptly cut off by a final deep thrust that brought forth a pumping current of hot, molten seed. She soaked in this stream and felt his pleasure merge with her own.

They lay spent and satisfied. They slept, and sometime late that night made love once again. She was sore, yet found herself swallowed by a series of orgasms soon after he entered her. It was only after he was fully satisfied that he hugged her close and voiced his innermost thoughts. Strange as it seemed at the moment, they were not of love, passion, or desire. They were rather of his duty, and his fear that the Rodina would soon be going to war. Tanya calmed him and urged him to sleep, knowing that he'd willingly reveal to her all that he knew with the new dawn. Of this fact she was now certain.

CHAPTER EIGHT

At 0800 hours William Carrigan was escorted into the concrete sub pen where the *Dnieper* was being repaired. At his side was Commander Ronald Barry. It was a cold, rainy morning. Thick fog had enveloped the Puget Sound area most of the evening and the CNO had had trouble getting a flight back to Washington, D.C. Carrigan had traveled with Admiral Lawrence to nearby McChord Air Force Base, where the CNO's flight had originated. It wasn't until midnight that the MATS aircraft had finally lifted off.

After yesterday's briefing, Carrigan had spent most of the day with his ex-shipmates. They were housed in the same quarters he was staying in, and this allowed them to see much of each other. They had shared a spirited lunch together. Though the primary topic of conversation had been the mission that was bringing them together, the discussion had soon turned back to World War II. William was sitting at the head of the table at the time, and had had a chance to sit back and study each of his old friends. Since he had seen them at the last reunion, time had certainly left its mark. Peter Donner had been seated opposite him. His XO's curly hair was almost completely silver now. There were slight bags gathering beneath his eyes and his neck was ceased and wrinkled. Yet his mind was as sharp as ever, his recall of events long passed precise and exacting.

Seated beside Donner had been Stan Lukowski. The *Abalone*'s chief was almost completely bald, his gut as swollen and extended as ever before. Though his appetite was certainly healthy, the chief's personality was somewhat dampened. In the old days they could always count on him to bring joviality to even the darkest of situations. Today he seemed distracted and preoccupied. Wondering if his thoughts were still back in Texas with his business, Carrigan turned to examine his partner.

Of all those present, Helmut Keller seemed to have changed the least. The big German's build was still solid, his skin tight. Even his red hair looked the same, cut short in a spiky crew cut. As in 1945, U-313's chief was a man of few words. He voiced himself only when he was certain that he had something unique to offer to the conversation.

Mac Brady had been seated to Carrigan's left. Tanned and fit, the weapons chief seemed genuinely happy to be there. It was as if his ideal life-style down in the Florida Keys had somehow been lacking. The *Abalone*'s ex-Skipper thought he knew what this missing ingredient was. Mac had always been the type who constantly craved adventure and challenge. He had reluctantly left the Navy only after reaching the mandatory retirement age. Thus this unexpected trip to Bangor was like a reprieve for him.

Together they had talked all afternoon. Last night at dinner, the CNO had informed them that his duties were calling him back to the Pentagon. Admiral Lawrence had again thanked them for coming, and pledged his assistance in anything they needed. He had

213

left Carrigan his private phone number.

Carrigan had awakened this morning ready to get down to work. The others had already taken off for the sub pen by the time Commander Barry had arrived to pick him up.

The immense, rectangular structure was situated in a remote corner of the sprawling base. It sat beside the water, its entrance protected by a seven-foot-high, barbed-wire-topped, chain-link fence. Even the Base Commander was forced to show his ID at the sentry station that was located there.

Once inside the compound, Carrigan noticed a number of armed guards alertly strolling the grounds. Several of them led guard dogs. As they approached the closed doors of the pen's entrance, Commander Barry pulled out a plastic key card. He inserted it into a slot placed beside the doorjamb and there was a muted buzz, followed by the loud click of the lock mechanism being triggered. Barry pushed the door open and beckoned his guest to enter.

The interior of the pen was cold and clammy. The air smelled of diesel oil and the nearby sea. After passing down a short corridor, they found themselves on one of two narrow ledges that completely lined the structure. Before them, perched on the V-shaped slots that were cut into the pen's floor, was the *Dnieper*.

By the dim interior lighting, Carrigan scanned the vessel. He started at its angled bow. There a platform had been rigged, and a group of goggled yard workers were visible, their welding torches cutting blindingly bright arcs of white light. They were apparently in the process of repairing the damage caused when the sub had gone aground. Other than a few buckled plates that they had yet to replace, the hull appeared in pretty good shape. Dozens of free-flood holes lined its length, and splotches of rust were visible where the primer was scraped off.

She certainly looked seaworthy enough, thought Carrigan, who took in the boat's elongated sail. He was studying this portion of the vessel when a hatch set into the bottom of the conning tower popped open. Squeezing his bulk out onto the deck was the portly figure of Stan Lukowski. Quick to spot Carrigan, the chief screamed out to him.

"Morning, Skipper. You won't believe this little lady. Why she's almost the spitting image of U-313. Helmut's having a field day!"

Anxious to take a closer look himself, Carrigan sought out his escort. He found Commander Barry in the midst of an animated conversation with the supervisor of the repair crew. Not wishing to interrupt him, he turned to the gantry that connected the sub's deck with the ledge he stood upon. Seconds later, he joined his ex-chief at the sail's base.

"Well, Lukowski, can we sail her?" quizzed Carrigan directly.

The chief didn't hesitate with his response. "No trouble at all, Skipper. The engine room is a bit of a mess, but it's nothing that we can't handle. The control-room crew might have some difficulties though. All the gauges there are in metric and labeled in Russian."

Carrigan noticed a new level of excitement flavor Lukowski's tone. It was as if just being back on a sub again had reawakened his old, jovial personality. Returning his animated glance, Carrigan grinned.

"We'll see to that, Chief. Now, how about giving me a quick tour of this old rust bucket?"

Lukowski mockingly saluted. "Yes, sir! It will be my pleasure."

He turned and pulled back the hatch that he had just climbed through. "Heads up once you're inside, Skipper. That stairwell is steep and tighter than the inside of a phone booth."

Taking in this warning, Carrigan ducked through the hatchway. He faced two stairwells. One ascended up to the sail's top, the other led straight downward. It was in this latter direction that he chose to travel.

The steel rungs were cold and slick, yet he handled them without difficulty. He managed to complete his climb without incident, and found himself in the control room. The deck was made of latticed steel. Directly before him was the periscope well, with the torpedo fire-control console set on the wall to his left. It was on his right side that the helm was situated. Two upholstered chairs faced the forward bulkhead there. Before each of these seats was an aircraft-style steering wheel and the all-important depth and level-of-ascent gauges. Behind the helm was the diving station. This portion of the compartment held a large console comprised of two horizontal rows of lights, one red and the other green. Carrigan identified this as the old-fashioned "Christmas tree" that would show whether the various ballast tanks were either in the open or closed positions. Completing this portion of the room was the navigational station and the radar cubicle.

All this looked familiar enough to Carrigan, who felt himself a bit relieved. He really didn't have any idea what he'd find here, but so far, it appeared to be nothing out of the ordinary. He was in the process of checking which gauges would have to be relabeled when there was the sound of a loud human grunt behind him. He turned and caught sight of Lukowski attempting to squeeze his corpulent frame out of the stairwell.

"Need some help, chief?" asked Carrigan lightly.

Lukowski managed to free himself, with a bit more effort. He slowly entered the control room, all the while tucking in the grease-stained shirt and wiping the sweat from his forehead.

"All these Russians must be little guys, Skipper. Why I never had that much trouble climbing down the sail of the *Abalone*."

Not wishing to remind him of the additional weight he had put on since, Carrigan nodded. "That they must be, chief. You know, I was just checking out the floor plan of this compartment and it's not really that much different from the *Abalone*. You're right about those gauges, but it should be no trouble relabeling them. What's the quickest route down to that engine room?"

Lukowski pointed to the descending stairwell that was set behind the periscope. "If you'll just follow me, Skipper. I'll have you there in no time at all."

Beckoning him to lead on, Carrigan climbed down the stairwell behind the chief. This passageway was a good deal wider, and Lukowski managed it without difficulty. They soon found themselves on the *Dnieper*'s bottom floor. Carrigan glanced forward.

"What do we have up there, chief?"

"That's the crew's quarters and head, Skipper. It sure ain't the Hilton, but I guess it's adequate. And further up is the torpedo room."

Carrigan's eyes widened. "I'd like to see what kind of armament they're carrying. Let's check it out."

Not waiting for a response, he turned toward the sub's bow. Hastily checking the enlisted men's quarters, he ducked through the hatchway that led into the torpedo room.

This compartment was dominated by two massive steel pallets, one laying on each side of the deck. Strapped on these platforms were eight torpedos, stowed four to a side. They seemed to be encased in some sort of dark green, protective wrapping and Carrigan could see that they were wire-guided. There was a loud scraping sound coming from the front of the room. Continuing on past the pallets, Carrigan soon found its source. Totally absorbed in his study of the four twenty-one-inch torpedo tubes here was Mac Brady.

"Good morning," greeted Carrigan.

Surprised by another's presence, Brady momentarily flinched. "Jesus, Captain, you caught me far away."

Carrigan joined him beside the shiny brass tube that he had been studying. "Sorry about that, Mac. What do you make of this system?"

Brady took out a rag from his back pocket and replied while wiping the grease from his hands. "It's an antique, all right. She's a far cry from the new automated systems, but with a little more human attention, I'll guarantee you that she'll get the job done just as effectively."

"Let's just hope that Captain Spencer and his gang don't have the need to find out. Yet all the same, we'd better have them prepared for the worst."

"Can do, Skipper. Once I figure out how this loading system operates, all I have to do is pick apart the fire-control mechanism. Then I'll be ready to teach those youngsters how to defend themselves."

"That's all I ask, Mac," returned Carrigan. "Just holler if you need an extra hand."

"Aye, aye, sir," snapped Brady, whose attention was already drawn back to the tube's loading system.

Confident that Mac Brady could handle himself, Carrigan turned to rejoin the chief, who had stopped off in the head. They proceeded toward the *Dnieper*'s stern now. Both men took in the vessel's cramped sonar room, galley, and mess hall. They passed by another stairwell leading upward, and Lukowski mentioned that this led to the officers' quarters. Continuing aft, they entered the maneuvering compartment. It was lined with various consoles. Each of them was filled with dozens of dials and gauges. There all aspects of the sub's various power systems would be monitored. This included the regulation of both the battery and diesel-powered engines. The proper understanding of these consoles was of the utmost importance. Carrigan knew that it would take a total effort to figure this out in the time allotted to them. Of course, if anyone could do it, it would be Stan Lukowski and Helmut Keller. Well aware of this fact, he followed the chief into the engine room.

The smell of diesel fuel was strongest in this portion of the boat. It also seemed several degrees warmer there. Carrigan thought that this had to be his imagination playing tricks with him, since the engines had long since been allowed to go cold. Lukowski was in the process of explaining the purposes of the myriad of snaking lines, pipes, and valves visible around them when Helmut Keller crawled out from underneath one of the huge engine blocks. The muscular German was dressed in blue coveralls and completely smeared in black grease. He put down the tools he had been working with and approached Carrigan.

"I'm afraid that we have a real mess here, Captain. One of the exhaust manifolds appears to be cracked."

"Can you repair it?" asked Carrigan.

"Get me the proper parts and I can fix anything," returned the confident mechanic.

"We'll get you a replacement if we have to make one ourselves," responded Carrigan. "Tell me, Helmut, is this layout familiar to you?"

The German grinned. "It's like stepping back in time, Captain. Though there's a few modern improvements present, the Soviets seemed to have copied our original design most thoroughly. Once we complete the repairs, a minor overhaul is in order. By the time we accomplish that feat, those young sailors will be ready to handle these engines all by themselves."

"Excellent," said Carrigan. "Start making a list of those parts that you'll be needing at once. Then we'll really see what the machine shop crew here in Bangor is made of."

Helmut Keller nodded. "Very good, Captain. Now, if you'll be so good as to let me have my associate back, we'll be getting back to work."

Carrigan looked over at Lukowski and winked. "Sounds like you're needed, chief. Take care in those tight places, and by all means get in touch with me if you run into any more problems. I'll be up taking a closer look at that control room if you need me."

"Will do, Skipper," replied the chief, who turned sidewise to squeeze his way further into the compartment.

Carrigan decided to proceed to the control room by way of the officers' quarters. To do so, he utilized the stairwell that lay outside the maneuvering compartment. He climbed up to the next deck and emerged into the passageway separating the officers' staterooms. There were two cramped cubicles with three bunks apiece. Both of these rooms had a single folding desk, above which hung a print of Lenin and a recent photograph of their present General Secretary.

Viktor Chernavin looked more like a kindly grandfather than a demanding despot. Carrigan had read what little was available about Chernavin and found him still somewhat of an engima. The silver-haired General Secretary seemed content to stay out of the public's eye as much as possible. This was in vast contrast to his younger predecessor, who'd thought of himself as something of a worldwide media star. When a scandal had subsequently brought his liberal regime down, Chernavin had stepped in, with his rather old-fashioned, yet internally stabilizing ways. Unfortunately, with his ascent came a new chapter in Soviet arms development. The present full-time work load at Carrigan Industries was proof enough of this new leader's intentions.

Carrigan passed by the Captain's spartan cabin, which consisted of a narrow cot and a desk, above which hung the same two pictures that graced the officers' quarters. Continuing forward, Carrigan passed the wardroom. He was totally surprised to find a single uniformed figure seated there, sipping a mug of coffee and leafing through some sort of manual.

Carrigan had met Captain Spencer the previous day, during the briefing. Though they had said little to each other, William had carefully watched the way the young officer had reacted to the vast challenge that was abruptly thrown his way. He'd seemed cool as ice, yet sensitive—just the type of individual they'd need if they were going to successfully see this difficult mission through. Later that evening, the CNO had briefly shared with Carrigan a few tidbits from Spencer's service record. It was evident from this information that he was the type of person who saw a project through to its very end. He was a natural motivator, and his men followed him without question.

Spencer sensed his presence and looked up from his study. He seemed to be relieved on identifying this newcomer as his mentor.

"Good morning, Mr. Carrigan. There's coffee in the officers' galley if you'd like a cup."

"Sounds good," returned Carrigan as he poked his head around the partition to retrieve a mug. "Is it Russian?"

"Yep," answered Spencer. "And it's as powerful as jet fuel."

Carrigan savored the aroma rising from his cup. "That's the way I like it, strong and black. Have you been aboard long?"

Spencer nodded. "Actually, I got here around zero-seven-hundred hours. I took a quick walk through with my XO and chief engineer, and then I came across this little gem."

He showed William the cover of the manual that he had been reading. Its title was in Russian, and there was a large, crimson hammer and sickle imprinted on the book's spine. Carrigan didn't have the least idea what it said and could only shrug his shoulders.

Spencer noted his confusion and added, "My Russian's only at the college level, but it was enough for me to spot this manual when we chanced upon it in the officers' head. Believe it or not, what I have here is an elementary operations manual covering all aspects of the Whiskey-class line of vessels as a whole."

"Wonderful!" exclaimed Carrigan, who seated himself opposite Spencer. "We should get it fully translated and distribute it to the men. By the way, have you chanced upon Peter Donner yet this morning?"

Spencer grinned. "If you mean your XO, he was waiting for us when we first got here. He's really a remarkable guy. He was able to fully brief us on the Whiskey's history. He was extremely helpful during our initial walk-through, and went off with my senior lieutenant to pick up the rest of the men."

"Pete's a natural teacher, all right," offered Carrigan. "We're fortunate to have his services. Now that you've seen the *Dnieper*, what are your thoughts on driving her?"

Spencer deliberated a bit before answering. "Two weeks isn't a hell of a lot of time, but with your expert help, we should be able to just get by."

"We'll do our best to get you ready short of going along ourselves," said Carrigan.

With this, the young officer beamed. "You know, that's not a bad idea. Do you mind if I bring that up with the CNO?"

Carrigan couldn't help but laugh. "I don't think the US Navy, or even the Russians for that matter, are ready for the likes of us again. No, son, I'm afraid this war is all yours."

In another section of the sub base, situated in an adjoining valley, was Bangor's guardhouse. Originally constructed to hold up to two dozen individuals who were confined for minor infractions or while awaiting court-martials, the brig had been recently cleared of its US Navy prisoners. In their place had arrived the surviving crew members of the Soviet submarine *Dnieper*.

To accommodate twice the number of men that it was designed to hold, a large tent had been raised in the facility's exercise compound. Even with the day's cold rain, the Russian sailors who were assigned to this temporary shelter were able to remain dry and fairly warm. Meals were served in shifts, while the bathrooms remained hard-pressed to keep up with the constant flow of humanity.

The *Dnieper*'s Zampolit had just finished a tour of the tent facility. Whenever he could, Ivan Koslov attempted to spread hope for the best. Many of the enlisted men he visited were bruised and cut as a result of their grounding. Several of them had broken bones. Though the Americans had so far been deaf to his demand that he be able to speak with a Soviet diplomat, they did provide adequate medical care.

The political officer had a good-sized gash on his forehead. It had taken over a dozen stitches to close properly. Fortunately, this cut hadn't incapacitated him, for his men needed him now more than ever before.

Since their capture, a wave of insecurity had possessed the *Dnieper's* complement. Captain Zinyagin's death didn't help matters any. To bring back some sort of discipline, Koslov made the rounds as much as he could. Above all, he fought to dispel panic. By reinstilling in the crew pride in service for the Rodina, he hoped to keep them from telling everything when it came time for the inevitable interrogations. So far, only he and Senior Lieutenant Volzhnin had been subject to formal questioning by the enemy.

The Americans had been strict, yet polite. Both of the *Dnieper's* senior officers had decided to maintain that the sub had merely been lost. Though he doubted that the Americans believed such a tall tale, the Zampolit knew that it was up to them to prove it was a lie. He had been able to shred the orders from Command which had directed them into the strait in the first place. This left no concrete evidence behind to help the Americans determine their real intentions.

Of course, there was always the possibility that their interrogators would resort to drugs to get the truth from them. During his six-month stint at a KGB-supervised training camp, he had seen the effects of Sodium Pentothal on even the strongest dispositions. And then there was the chance that the Imperialists would resort to cruder types of physical torture, which would serve to loosen their tongues just as well.

Koslov knew that if he could only contact a representative of his government, some sort of diplomatic deal could be eventually worked out. As it stood now, no one in Moscow even knew that they were captured. Cursing that inoperable radio transmitter, the Zampolit guided his portly figure back into the thick, timber-framed guardhouse. Compared to the tent, it was substantially warmer inside this permanent structure. Thus, it took him only a few seconds to work up an uncomfortable sweat.

With handkerchief in hand, Koslov reentered the communal cell where the officers had been sequestered. Vainly attempting to mop his forehead and neck dry, he approached the cubicle's far corner, where Sergei Volzhnin slumped, his face buried dejectedly in his hands.

"Come now, lieutenant," said the Zampolit. "Things can't be that bad. Just think, you could be sharing an adjoining slab beside the Captain."

"Sometimes I think that I would be better off in just such a condition," said Volzhnin softly.

Conscious of his associate's depression, Ivan cautiously probed. "Now, why would you say such a foolish thing, comrade?"

The lieutenant looked up and caught the Zampolit's beady stare. "Oh, be sensible, Koslov. It's easy for you to shrug off our predicament and put on a happy face. You forget who will be held responsible for our capture. Why, my entire career will be ruined!"

"So that's what's got you down," reflected the Zampolit. "I know you see things otherwise now, but I can almost guarantee you that you will not be held at fault. If anything, your quick reaction to Zinyagin's concussion will gain you nothing less than the Order of Lenin. Why, your actions saved the lives of each one of us! Now you must snap out of this selfish introspection, for once more the Rodina is counting on you to rise to the occasion."

"And what occasion is that?" queried the bearded officer gloomily.

Koslov patted his forehead dry before answering. "It is most evident that the Americans plan on keeping us in confinement indefinitely. My every plea to be allowed to speak with a member of our government has been met with a curt rejection. Since Vladivostok surely has yet to find out about our misfortune, as far as Command is concerned we are merely still on duty. Until they know the truth of the matter, we'll be forced to remain prisoners here. Thus it is in our best interest to figure out a way to somehow get word to an authorized representative of the Rodina with all due haste. If my memory serves me correctly, we presently have a consulate in nearby San Francisco."

"Whatever are you getting at, Comrade Koslov?" quizzed the astounded lieutenant.

The Zampolit was well aware that he had broken Volzhnin from his pitiful stupor, and his dark eyes glistened. "Why, I would think that's fairly clear, my friend. For, if any of us ever want to see Mother Russia again, someone must attempt to break out of this compound to inform our nearest consulate personally."

This rash proposal hit Sergei Volzhnin like a slap in the face. "Are you crazy, comrade? This compound is buttoned up as tight as the Kremlin. Besides the barbed-wire-topped, chain-link fence that completely surrounds us, there are guards watching our every movement. Why, it would be instant suicide!"

The Zampolit reacted coolly to this emotional outburst. "Easy, my friend. You will soon see that there are ways to effect an escape without having to resort to such crude methods as going over the fence or burrowing tunnels like rats. Trust me with this, lieutenant."

Volzhnin still wondered if it was worth the great risk involved. "But surely the Americans can't keep us here forever. Command has to find out about us eventually."

"That is true," offered Koslov. "But you are forgetting one major consideration. Until that time comes, our sworn enemy has the services of one of the Rodina's first-line men-of-war. The *Dnieper* may be old, but think of the havoc she could cause if she were to be taken over by an American crew. They could sail her right into Vladivostok, and Command would never be the wiser. Can we just sit back and wait for such a thing to happen? Of course we can't! It is our sworn duty to protect the Motherland with our very lives if necessary. Thus it's imperative that this escape is at least attempted. Otherwise our countrymen will indeed have justifiable grounds to brand you both a traitor and a coward. With such a condemnation eternally branding you, even our Captain's present state would be envied."

Having completely forgotten about the *Dnieper*, Volzhnin absorbed the Zampolit's warning. In addition to saving their own lives, saving their boat from the enemy would be reason enough to listen to the political officer's plans. He resolved to do so. Volzhnin caught Ivan Koslov's piercing glance, and nodded for him to continue.

Meanwhile, from the sheltered confines of an adjoining valley, the crew of the USS *Stingray* boarded the dry-docked vessel that was to temporarily be their new home. Looking forward to their assignment as a great adventure, they entered the *Dnieper* through the hatch that was cut into the base of the vessel's sail. Once inside the control room, the young sailors were greeted by Pete Donner. This gray-haired civilian had a commanding, no-nonsense attitude about him. With the direct ease of an officer, he had them introduce themselves and divulge their specialties. Donner recorded this information in a notebook, and then directed each sailor to that portion of the boat where he would begin his individual instruction.

Before long, the passageways of the *Dnieper* were buzzing with action once again. All of this activity was currently being monitored from the wardroom. There William Carrigan and Randall Spencer sat facing one another across the rectangular table. Kept up to date by frequent visits from Tim Kelly, the *Stingray*'s XO, they were able to sketch out a flow chart. This plan showed where the current classes were taking place and which areas of the boat would offer them the greatest difficulties.

They were initially concentrating on three areas of operation. In the torpedo room, Mac Brady was introducing a handful of weapons ratings to the new system they would have to learn to operate. This equipment was vastly different from the gear that graced the *Stingray*. Closer in design to World War II than that carried by the modern Navy, the fire-control system demanded human supervision in almost every phase of its operation. Even the actual loading of torpedoes was by hand. Since the youngsters had been spoiled by computerized automation, Mac found himself having to teach them all over again.

In the vessel's control room, Peter Donner faced a different problem. His job was to introduce his select portion of the crew to the various operational functions monitored there. Yet none of the men, including himself, could read Russian. Thus, many of the gauges and dials were completely unintelligible. Captain Spencer had promised to help him with the translation as soon as he had time. Then they would see about relabeling the various consoles in English. Until this came to pass, Donner could only instruct his men in the theory that made this submarine unique to operate. He was presently concentrating on the main differences between the manner in which the *Dnieper* ran and that of the *Stingray*.

In the boat's engine room, the crew's concerns were of a much more practical nature. No strangers to working with young mechanics, Stan Lukowski and Helmut Keller wasted no time putting their men to work. Engines were engines, as Lukowski so aptly commented. As long as spare parts were available, these diesels would do the job just as well as any others. While the hefty Texan put a group of sailors to work on the overhaul, Helmut Keller showed the *Stingray*'s chief how he intended to repair the cracked manifold. It was decided to deal with the instructional problems that faced them in maneuvering once these mechanical concerns were completed.

William Carrigan and Randall Spencer didn't try to fool themselves into thinking that the next two weeks would be easy ones. For, in a mere fourteen days, the youngsters would have to be ready to solo. To make the best use of every available minute, they would have to create a strict training schedule and be certain to stick to it. Only then would they have a chance to achieve the impossible.

Captain Spencer was in the midst of explaining the operational areas that gave him the most worry when Commander Ronald Barry entered the wardroom from the aft hatchway. From the solemn look that painted this newcomer's face, both Carrigan and Spencer knew that their guest was the bearer of bad news.

Barry wasted no time with pleasantries. "Gentlemen, less than a quarter of an hour ago I received a scrambled phone call from Admiral Lawrence. The CNO had just emerged from a crisis meeting at the White House and conveyed the following information. Intelligence has learned that not only is the Soviet strategic alert being intensified, but that the final test of the laser battle station will be in a mere sixteen days. More concerned with this installation than ever before, our Commander-in-Chief has given us the go-ahead to take out the facility before the test is finalized."

"But that's only a little over two weeks away!" observed Spencer. "Since the cruise over there will take at least ten days, when are we supposed to be able to learn how to operate this vessel? Six days of instruction won't even get our feet wet!"

"Then perhaps we'd better rethink the mission," offered the stern-faced Commander. "Since you won't have enough time to become familiar with the *Dnieper*, the *Stingray* is just going to have to do."

"That's insane!" interjected Carrigan. "You know as well as I that the *Stingray* wouldn't have a chance in hell of successfully penetrating that bay."

Barry didn't flinch. "Then maybe we should bring in a 688."

"The type of platform makes no difference," continued Carrigan. "The only vessel that can possibly pull

231

this thing off is the *Dnieper*."

Taking in this observation, Barry glanced at each of the men who sat before him. "Well, then, can anyone tell me how we're going to be able to get this sub operational in a mere six days from now?"

Spencer was at loss for an answer and turned to his mentor for assistance. Carrigan returned his stare, cleared his voice, and answered, "The way I see it, there's only one way to pull this thing off. My group is just going to have to accompany the *Dnieper*'s new complement to the objective."

A moment of stunned silence followed this surprise offer. Carrigan found himself astounded that he had summoned the audacity to even mention such a thing. Yet the more he thought about it, the more he realized that it was the only course open to them.

"Well," he prompted. "What do you say?"

Barry's expression remained impassive as he looked first to Carrigan and then to Captain Spencer. "My initial reaction is that if it will allow the mission to go forward as planned, I'd say take them along. How do you feel about it, Captain?"

Spencer answered thoughtfully, "Having Captain Carrigan and his men along would sure make a difference, but would the Navy ever approve of such a thing?"

Barry beamed. "There's only one way to find out. Why don't I bounce it off the CNO?"

As the commander excused himself to initiate the phone call, Carrigan contemplated the can of worms that he had just opened. Not only had he just committed himself for an entire month, but he had also volunteered for a dangerous mission, deep into Soviet

232

territory. And then there was the "minor" fact that he had so graciously offered his ex-shipmate's services without even allowing them the courtesy of making up their minds for themselves. Though he was certain that each of them would willingly agree in an instant, it was still a lot to take for granted.

As it turned out, he had little additional time to ponder this decision, for no sooner had Commander Barry exited the wardroom than another uniformed figure entered from the opposite hatchway. Lieutenant Vince Paterson seemed relieved to have found this particular compartment. The SEAL crisply saluted the seated Captain and spoke out loud and clear.

"Sir, I have that preliminary attack plan that you asked for yesterday."

"At ease, sailor," instructed Spencer. "Since conditions are so close aboard a submarine, saluting is not necessary here."

"I'm sorry, sir," stuttered Paterson. "Some habits are just going to be hard to break."

With this, he handed Spencer a large envelope. Inside was a single sheet of paper. Drawn on its surface was a somewhat messy conglomeration of squares, arrows, circles, and x's.

"I know that it's not much, sir, but right now we really don't have very much to go on," added the commando.

Spencer passed the sheet on to Carrigan, who also tried to make some sort of sense out of the mixture of symbols. "I imagine that this all has something to do with taking out that laser battle station," said Carrigan.

Patterson nodded. "That it does, sir. What you see

before you is a diagram of a standard assault on a fixed position. Of course, we'll know a lot more about what we're up against once we link up with those Soviet operatives outside of Posjet."

"Do you know anything about lasers, son?" asked Carrigan.

"I've seen them at work on the battlefield guiding smart munitions," answered the SEAL.

Carrigan shook his head. "Well, this little baby that we're after is a whole different ballgame. It will probably be placed in a structure as large as this sub pen, with a variety of support facilities nearby. It's vital that each of these separate installations be taken out also."

The SEAL didn't seem the least bit fazed by this challenge. "We can do it, sir. My explosives team is the best in the Navy."

Knowing that it would take much more than a first-rate demolition team to cripple the facility beyond repair, Carrigan got a sudden inspiration. Since it would be foolish to take the risk of sailing all the way across the Pacific only to fail to properly take out their ultimate objective, he knew that it would be to their advantage to call in another civilian expert. And as fate would have it, he knew just the individual for the job. Yet this time, before playing God, he decided to call this person and ask him if he were interested, before bringing up his name to the others.

CHAPTER NINE

Peter Lowell had never intended to be a weapons designer. In fact, as an undergraduate, he had looked at such work with abhorrence. His original intention was to be the designer of the world's first laboratory X-ray laser, which would be applied to medical research only. With such a device, he had hoped to produce three-dimensional holographic images of the human body's smallest molecules, in order to unlock the mystery of cancer.

He had first gotten the idea for such a project soon after entering the California Institute of Technology in Pasadena. Peter was originally drawn to Caltech for its excellent physics department. Being a National Merit Scholar, he had little trouble gaining admittance to this, one of the country's toughest, most prestigious schools.

From the moment he'd had his first high school calculus class, Peter knew that the physical sciences were for him. He had been but an average student until that time, when higher mathematics opened his eyes to the wonders of chemistry, astronomy, and physics. It was as if he were suddenly aware of a major part of his brain that had been long dormant.

Having been raised in San Diego, Peter drove up to Caltech as a high school senior to see if the curriculum there was for him. He had been on the campus for less than an hour when he was immersed in a spirited discussion with a bearded undergraduate on the possibility of running a futuristic computer on laser light instead of electricity. Peter had argued that such a system's great speed would revolutionize the computer industry. Though their debate had no official outcome, he knew that at long last he had found others his age who spoke the same language. He was accepted to Caltech three weeks later.

Peter found his work load challenging and the staff most accommodating. His freshmen class was made up of just over two hundred students. The faculty-student ratio was one to three. Twenty of the faculty were Nobel laureates.

The competitive pressures were extremely tough, and Caltech was infamous for its high rate of undergraduate suicides. Thus the administration tended to turn its back on student pranks that helped to relieve this great stress. In his junior year, Peter and another student became involved with just such a prank—one that was talked about even today, seven years later. While enrolled in an electrical circuitry class, they had succeeded in hacking into the Rose Bowl's computer system. Not only did they rearrange the score in the midst of a Super Bowl game, but they had gotten credit for it as well!

After four years of study, Peter graduated with both bachelor's and master's degrees. He ranked at the very top of his class. The twenty-one-year-old was anxious to get on with his Ph.D., and it was while looking through Caltech's fellowship file that he chanced upon the Carrigan Foundation. Since he was in need of financial aid, and since this organization offered one of the highest stipends of all, he immediately set up an interview.

This took place in Sunnyvale, California, and it proved to be Peter's first visit to the infamous Silicon Valley. He couldn't help but be intimidated as he drove up to the gates of Carrigan Industries. It was a sprawling complex, protected by an ever-present security force. While waiting for the interview to begin, he hastily scanned the corporation's quarterly report. It was most evident that the majority of their business was with the military.

He was called into a conference room and introduced to the man who would initially interview him. Peter was relieved to find him a Caltech grad himself. They talked about the latest changes on campus, and briefly went over Peter's course of study. To clear the air completely, Peter offered to explain just the type of research he desired to become involved with. Before he was allowed to do just that, another individual was called into the room.

This was to be his first meeting with William Carrigan. Peter was completely snowed under by his charm and savoir-faire. Impeccably dressed, the silver-haired founder of Carrigan Industries talked to him more like a long-lost uncle than the stranger he was. He seemed genuinely interested in Peter's interests, and soon had the recent graduate revealing his innermost dreams and desires. This included his hopes of working on an X-ray laser.

As it turned out, he was eventually offered the fellowship, but not before being forced to accept a number of preconditions. The most major of these was that his primary work was to take place at the Lawrence Livermore Laboratory. This federally controlled installation was located some forty miles east of San Francisco, and had gained world-wide notoriety as a principal designer of America's nuclear arsenal.

Peter immediately balked at this idea. Carrigan had been apparently anticipating his recalcitrance, and phoned him personally. He explained that Livermore would offer Peter the ideal place to initiate his research, for they already had an advanced X-ray-laser project in actual development. Before he turned down the offer altogether, Carrigan begged him to go out to the lab and have a look around. Somewhat reluctantly, Peter did so.

The Caltech graduate arrived at Livermore and found the well-guarded installation staffed with some of the most interesting people he had ever met. The facilities were first-rate, and the laser program unparalleled. With the realization that he really didn't have anywhere else to go, Peter agreed to make Livermore his home at least temporarily.

He found it somewhat hard to believe that he stayed on at the lab for the next six years. With America desiring to produce a ballistic-missile shield, millions of dollars were being pumped into Livermore for research. Much of this money made its way into Peter's department, where they worked with X-ray lasers as a possible defensive weapon that would be fueled by the power of a nuclear explosion. In such a way ascending ballistic missiles would be shot down.

Peter had access to a huge network of super-computers, and a 25-million-dollar laser known as Shiva. He worked late into the night mastering quantum theory, developing new ideas, and writing computer programs. Often inspired by the work of his brilliant colleagues, he never gave up his dream. Yet an incident occurred soon after he entered the facility that was to change his very outlook on life.

William Carrigan sent him a three-volume set of Alexander Solzhenitsyn's *The Gulag Archipelago*. The nightmarish world of Soviet concentration camps affected the sensitive researcher greatly. He had never given the Russians much thought until this time. He was therefore somewhat shocked to read of their barbarity and utter contempt for the basic human rights that he so often took for granted. Because the Soviets had publicly admitted their desire to place the entire planet under their control, Peter began to look at nuclear weapons in a different light. After all, since their inception over four decades ago, the Russians had been forced by the sheer weight of the West's strategic arsenal to keep their intrigues far from America's shores.

With this in mind, he applied himself to his daily work with an even greater degree of diligence. For three years straight he worked almost exclusively on developing a nuclear-pumped X-ray laser, to be shot into space and utilized as an ABM platform to negate a preemptive Soviet strike. He became so involved in this effort that his dream of using this same laser as a medical tool no longer preoccupied him.

All had been going smoothly until six months ago, when his research group got a new director. From their first meeting, Peter knew that there were going to be serious problems. Not only did their personalities clash, but this newcomer was a stickler for details who demanded reams of useless paperwork and created a disciplinary system second only to the military in strictness.

Peter couldn't work under such tight confines. He was a free spirit who needed space for his thoughts to come together. Bringing this up to the Lab's head administrator, Peter was offered a transfer into the nuclear-weapons program. Such work was not to his liking and he turned it down. Not certain what he would do now, he called the only person whose advice he truly respected. As he hoped, William Carrigan had a quick fix for his predicament. Peter Lowell would go to work for Carrigan Industries.

Lately, the twenty-eight-year-old scientist wondered if he had made the right decision. Sure, his salary had more than doubled and he had a huge office, with his own secretary. Yet working for a corporation was proving much too structured for his liking. The manager he presently answered to was turning out to be just like the administrator he had run from at Livermore. He would set a deadline and expect results without any excuses for tardiness allowed.

As a systems designer, Peter was constantly working with unknowns. This was especially true in the case of his current area of responsibility. Since there were no precedents in this field, how could he be expected to meet an arbitrary time schedule? For no one had ever succeeded in doing what they were currently attempting.

Carrigan had personally assigned him to the blue-green laser project soon after he'd arrived there. Since their inception as a strategic weapons platform, one of the weaknesses of the nation's fleet of submarines was in the area of communications. Water was an extremely impenetrable medium as far as radio signals were concerned. Thus, to pick up orders from Command, the same subs that depended upon the ocean's depths to veil them from attackers were forced to ascend toward the surface when it came time to operate their radios. Unlike low-frequency radio signals, a blue-green laser could cut through the ocean's depths like a knife through warm butter. When mounted on a satellite, such signals could reach a submarine wherever it might be.

The Navy was particularly anxious to incorporate such an unprecedented system on their new Seawolf-class·attack subs. Such a contract could be extremely lucrative, and Carrigan Industries was one of two firms which had been picked to go ahead with the preliminary research and development.

So far, they had succeeded in designing a blue-green laser to do the job. Yet the stumbling block remained the creation of the supersensitive detector that would be incorporated into the submarine to pick up the modulated laser beams as they filtered through the water. The design of such a device was Peter's current assignment.

He had already missed a trio of deadlines, and doubted that he could meet the fourth, which was rapidly approaching. Peter had never been a quitter. Such behavior just wasn't in his makeup. He also wasn't the type who liked to give excuses, or ask for help from those above him. He knew that all he had to do was make a single call to Carrigan's office to get the pushy project manager off his back. Yet he couldn't keep running to Carrigan every time he faced a problem that he couldn't manage. It was time to stand on his own two feet and face the consequences, for the better or for the worse.

This was his decision as he sat before his computer console and prepared to have another go at the design problem. Before entering the access code that would draw up the equations he had last been working on, he paused a moment to take three deep breaths. Only when his mind was completely clear would he continue on. His thoughts at first drifted randomly, and he concentrated harder on centering them. For some apparent reason, he found himself preoccupied with the laboratory X-ray laser that he had once dreamed of designing. Though the advent of the electron microscope made such a device no longer practical, this first great dream of his youth would forever haunt him. How very innocent he had been in those early days! At that time, working on a weapons system would be the farthest thing from his mind. Had he sold himself out, or had he merely reawakened to a vaster responsibility? Peter was in the process of confronting such a lofty concept when his intercom chimed. Called as if from a dream, he quickly activated it.

"Yes, Maria."

His secretary responded, "Sorry to disturb you, Peter, but the chief's on the line."

Lowell instinctively sat up straight in his chair, thanked his secretary, and reached for the telephone receiver. "Mr. C., this is Peter. To what do I owe this honor?"

William Carrigan's voice was mixed with a slight hiss of static. "Afternoon, Mr. Lowell. How would you like a nice change of scenery?"

Peter listened on in wonder as his boss invited him to Bangor, Washington. When he offered to pull Peter from the blue-green laser project to work directly with him, Lowell took this opportunity as a dream come true. He instantly accepted and was surprised when William Carrigan made him swear to keep all the details to himself. For the only one who would be privileged to know his true disposition would be Carrigan's executive secretary.

All this secrecy only served to arouse Peter's curiosity that much more. Anxious to get to the root of it, he signed off with a promise to be on the next day's first flight to Seattle.

The jet carrying Peter Lowell landed at SEA-TAC International airport at 10:45 a.m. Dressed in a well-worn pair of jeans, a Caltech sweatshirt, and a windbreaker, the sandy-haired researcher carried a fully stuffed overnight bag and a battered briefcase along with him as he exited the aircraft. This was his first visit to Seattle and he was somewhat concerned as to how he'd find his way around the city. As it turned out, his worries were for nothing, for a uniformed Navy seaman stood at the rampway holding a sign with Lowell's name printed neatly on it. In such an efficient manner, he met his personal driver.

The trip to Bangor took them through the nearby city of Tacoma and over the Tacoma Narrows bridge. A storm front had recently passed through the area, and the surrounding landscape glistened in a light coat of wet snow. Beyond appreciating the scenery, Peter had an enjoyable conversation with his chauffeur. The lad had only recently enlisted. Fresh out of high school, he was hoping to save up enough money to go to college, where he planned to study engineering.

Peter did all that he could do to urge the youngster on. He related several stories about his own experiences with higher education, and emphasized the many opportunities open to the graduate.

By this time they had passed over Puget Sound and were approaching the Bremerton Navy Yard. Though Peter had never been in the service himself, he always did have a passion for ships and the sea. Growing up in San Diego, he had toured many a warship, including several aircraft carriers, destroyers, and even a battleship. Thus he was no stranger to the assortment of vessels that they were soon passing.

It was rapidly closing in on noon as they pulled up to the gates of the Bangor sub base. The heavy security visible there reminded Peter of his years at Lawrence Livermore. Only after the civilian's name was checked off a clip board by an efficient sentry were they allowed to proceed.

Peter was surprised to find the facility spread among a tree-covered valley. He spotted the fuel depot, several modern barracks, and an administrative complex. As they drove down by the water, he got a brief view of a massive triangular wharf where a single submarine was docked. He was genuinely astounded by this vessel's mammoth size and audibly expressed his amazement. Relishing his guest's wonder, Peter's driver identified it as the Trident-class sub USS *Michigan*.

Peter had read much about the Tridents. He had even seen several pictures of them, yet nothing was as sobering as seeing one of these giants with one's own eyes.

The scientist couldn't help but stir excitedly. It was one thing to work with submarines in the confines of his laboratory. It was another thing altogether to actually be this close to one. Since William Carrigan hadn't given him a hint as to what he'd be doing there, Peter could only sit back and let fate lead him onwards.

They didn't have to travel much longer before they faced another security gate. At this stop, Peter had to hand over his driver's license. Even his escort was forced to display his military ID. Their names were checked off of another list, their car briefly searched, and only then was the barbed-wire topped gate opened.

They proceeded at once to the water's edge, where they pulled up to a cavernous, concrete structure. Since this rectangular building extended out over the water, Peter guessed that it was some sort of sub pen.

Following his driver's lead, Peter exited the vehicle. It was good to stretch his legs and breathe in the crisp air that was fresh with the scent of the nearby sea. No sooner was his baggage removed than he was greeted by a khaki-uniformed ensign. The driver was excused and Peter was led to the structure's entrance. A plastic key card gained them access there.

After passing down a somewhat narrow corridor, they emerged into what indeed proved to be a sub pen. Lying in dry dock before the wide-eyed researcher was a single submarine. It appeared more like the kind of vessel that saw service in World War II. The boat had a sharply angled bow and was no longer than 250 feet. This was in vast contrast to the modern nuclear vessels that had sleek, "tear-drop" hulls and were well over twice this size. A welding crew was busy at work on the bow, while various other figures could be seen on the sub's deck. Beckoning Peter to follow him, the ensign began crossing one of the gantries that led directly to the boat.

Peter entered the sub through a hatchway that was cut into the base of its sail. The cramped interior was cool and smelled vaguely of diesel oil. He had never been known for his physical agility, and had a somewhat awkward time climbing down the steep stairwell. Twice he cracked his elbow on the ladder's smooth iron rungs. Thus he was relieved to conclude this short descent and find himself in the boat's control room.

He scanned the compartment and found it packed

with equipment. Various consoles held dozens of gauges and dials, while the ceiling was completely lined with snaking cables. Perched before this gear were a number of young sailors. They wore blue overalls, and were in the midst of a teaching session. Their silver-haired instructor was considerably older than his attentive students. He had been mentioning something about diving angles, when he noticed the newcomer's presence.

"Excuse me, but you must be Mr. Lowell," said the instructor with a cordial tone. "I'm Pete Donner. Welcome aboard the *Dnieper*. The Skipper's waiting for you in the wardroom. The ensign will show you the way."

Peter nodded in acknowledgment, and the instructor wasted no time turning his attention back to his students. Not really certain just who this so-called Skipper was, he followed his escort further into the sub's bowels. Lowell was impressed with the amount of gear that was stashed there. So much equipment lined the passageways that there was not even enough room for two men to pass shoulder to shoulder. When they passed by a cramped cubicle holding some type of office, he spotted a small sign mounted on the bulkhead there. Much to his astonishment, it was printed in what appeared to be Russian. He was just about to bring this fact up to his escort when the ensign ducked through a hatchway. Peter followed him and entered a private dining area. Seated at the head of this table was the familiar figure of his boss.

Upon sighting his visitor, William Carrigan put down the report that he had been studying. His face

247

lit up in a smile, and he reached out to offer Peter his handshake.

"Good afternoon, Mr. Lowell. It's good to see you. Please sit down. Would you like some coffee?"

"Greetings to you, Mr. C.," returned Peter, who scooted into the booth directly opposite his boss. "I'll pass on that coffee. I already had my caffeine fix on the airplane this morning."

With this, the ensign who had served as Peter's escort nodded toward Carrigan and left the wardroom. This left them alone.

"And how are things back at the ranch?" queried Carrigan lightly.

"As busy as ever," said Peter. "I guess you know that I missed my latest deadline. Right now, I just seem to be at an impasse."

Carrigan shrugged his shoulders. "Relax, Peter. Such things happen, and there's no use fighting them. The artists call it creative block. The way I like to deal with it is by a drastic change of scenery. That's one of the reasons I invited you up here."

Peter seemed relieved. "I appreciate your concern, Mr. C."

"It's the least that I can do for one of my most talented employees," countered Carrigan. "Yet I must be the first to warn you that there's an ulterior motive behind my invitation for you to join me here. By the way, how do you like the *Dnieper* so far?"

Peter surveyed the wardroom while answering. "She's a beauty. You know, this is my first visit to a real submarine, and I never realized how packed with equipment they were. There is one other thing that I noticed, though. I could have sworn that I saw a sign printed in Russian back in the passageway."

"What else would you expect to find on a Soviet submarine?" replied Carrigan matter-of-factly.

Peter's brow tightened. "What do you mean, Soviet submarine?"

Carrigan's expression turned serious. "I'm not going to BS you, son. You're much too smart for that type of thing, so here it goes. The vessel that we're currently sitting inside of belongs to the Soviet Pacific fleet. She recently ran aground in the waters not far from here, and because of an inoperable radio we were able to board the vessel without Soviet Command learning of its plight. The original Russian crew is presently being held in seclusion. It is the US Navy's desire to use the *Dnieper* for a mission of its own. To do so, a substitute American crew is currently being trained in the sub's operation.

"In five days time, the vessel will be on its way to the Soviet Far East. There it will penetrate Russian waters and proceed to land a commando team, whose purpose is to destroy the world's first operational laser battle station. I have just received clearance to be co-commander of this operation. I was counting on you to come along with us. Because of your knowledge of laser weapons systems, you can be of enormous value in showing our operatives where their explosives will do the most harm.

"Now I know that this is a lot to hit you with, Lowell, but I've got no other options. You're free to walk right out of here and forget that this whole thing ever happened. In a way, I wouldn't blame you if you did. Yet, if you should agree to come along, your country would be most grateful. For not only do we face a drastic imbalance in the current state of U.S.-Soviet relations, we also face a definite strategic threat. That is why this mission must come down with all due secrecy and haste."

Stunned into silence, Peter vainly attempted to make rational sense out of Carrigan's abrupt plea. Meeting his boss's concerned glance, the twenty-eight-year-old scientist strained to reevaluate what Carrigan was asking of him.

The revelation that the Soviets had an operational laser battle station was shocking in itself. Peter knew that an American equivalent would be well over a year away. At Livermore some of his closest friends had been nuclear weapons designers. Many an all-night rap session had centered around the horrifying reality of strategic warfare. One scenario was based on the premise that the first country to put on line an effective ABM shield would then be in an excellent position to launch a preemptive strike. With no fear of retribution, such a country could win World War III, and the control of the entire planet, in a matter of minutes. Well aware of Russia's desire to win its battle against capitalism at any cost, Peter shivered. Though he definitely wasn't a soldier, and had never dreamed of going to war before, he knew that if it ever came down to it, he'd fight until his last drop of blood to defend the American way of life. Surely the United States would never attempt such a rash operation as the one Carrigan had just presented to him unless the country were desperate. And to think that civilians such as Carrigan and himself were being asked to accompany the Navy was astounding in itself. Peter never thought of himself as the hero type, yet found his chest swelling in a sudden surge of patriotism.

"If you really think that the outcome of this mission could depend on whether I was along or not, I'd be proud to accompany you, Mr. C."

Peter could hardly believe that these brave words actually came from his mouth. Still attempting to understand the full implications of his instinctive decision, he looked on as Carrigan's face lit up in a compassionate smile.

"I knew that we could count on you, lad. God bless you!"

Any further comments on Carrigan's part were interrupted by the sudden appearance of a solidly built Navy officer at the wardroom's aft hatchway. He saw that Carrigan had another civilian present, and was quick to excuse himself.

"I'm sorry, sir. I didn't realize that you had a visitor."

"Nonsense, lieutenant," answered Carrigan. "In fact, I was just about to call for you. Lieutenant Vince Paterson, I'd like you to meet Peter Lowell. You two had better get to know each other, because as of this moment you're on the same team."

While Peter Lowell began his initiation into the ways of the U.S. Navy, Tanya Markova nervously paced the floors of her uncle's apartment, all the while pondering the moral dilemma she had gotten herself into. Her plight centered around Senior Lieutenant Grigori Kisnev. Since the night she had lost her virginity to the mustached officer, barely a moment had gone by without her feeling cheap and dirty. It had all started on the morning after their initial evening of debauchery.

Tanya had awakened hung over and with an alien soreness between her thighs. Her lover had left some time earlier, and hadn't even bothered to leave her a note. Visual proof of their night of sin came when she examined the bloodstained bed sheet. She immediately ran into the bathroom to fill up the tub with hot water. She soaked herself for over an hour. Yet, even when she emerged from the tub, she still felt dirty.

After some aspirin and several cups of tea, she began to pull herself together. After all, there had been a practical reason motivating her whorish behavior. She pulled out a pad and pen to scribble down all that she had learned from the drunken sailor.

It had been sometime late that previous night, after he had mounted her for the third time that evening, that the Senior Lieutenant had opened up to her like a bragging schoolboy. Though she was tired and bruised, she had managed to take in his every slurred word.

The officer had been most proud that his ship, the *Ivan Komarov*, had been chosen to convey Secretary Chernavin down to the Bay of Posjet in sixteen days. There they would witness the test of an amazing new weapons system that would allow the Motherland to go ahead with a preemptive nuclear strike against the United States of America. The senior lieutenant had cleverly learned of these astounding facts while transcribing a scrambled radio message meant for his Captain. He was the ship's Communications Officer, and it was his job to decode the message. He was not supposed to read the directive in its entirety, yet how could he resist such a thing!

Except for Tanya, he had yet to share this information with another soul. He explained that he was only telling her because he feared for her life should hostilities truly come to pass. He eventually passed out, mumbling that she could always hide out in Siberia, to be united with him after the war's conclusion.

Tanya finished writing down this all-important report. If it indeed proved true, surely her virginity was but a small price to pay for saving hundreds of millions of lives.

Her next task was to figure out a way of sharing this information with her uncle. Since she couldn't possibly trust either the telephone or the post office, she decided that the only course open to her was to return at once to Tavricanka. As it turned out, this wasn't necessary. Soon after she made the decision there was a knock on the door, and in walked the lumberjack, Anton Bagdaran.

She flushed in embarrassment on setting eyes on her childhood sweetheart. For here was the man she had planned to give the gift of her womanhood to! Why, she had even fantasized about him only the previous night, and in a way it had indeed been Anton who had made love to her.

The handsome woodsman was also a member of their Movement and had been sent into Vladivostok to deliver an important dispatch. Uncle Lev had instructed him to stop off at the apartment to check in with Tanya before heading back.

Over a cup of tea, she shared with him every last detail of the senior lieutenant's revelation. Anton was as shy as he was good-looking, yet somehow he summoned the nerve to ask her how she had learned these incredible things. Sensing just a hint of jealousy, Tanya said how she had managed to gather the intelligence was not important. What was significant was the fact that its source was high in the military and, for all she knew, extremely reliable. It was now up to the lumberjack to convey it to Lev Litvov with all due haste.

He left her hurriedly with a kiss on each cheek. No sooner had he closed the door behind him than Tanya broke down in a fit of tears. Flashes of the previous night's lovemaking rose in her mind's eye, and she inwardly cursed herself for allowing her body to actually experience pleasure from a stranger's embraces.

Tanya decided to stay in for the rest of the day. She was all set to go to bed early when there was a knock on the door and in walked Grigori.

He was the last person she wanted to see, yet she had to act civil so as not to make him suspicious. He had thoughtfully brought along some groceries and another two bottles of champagne. No sooner had he taken off his coat than he pulled her roughly by the arm and tried to embrace her. His breath was sour, his touch cold, and Tanya dared to pull herself back, pleading illness.

The senior lieutenant slyly grinned, yet let her go. Saying that he had the perfect cure for what ailed her, he went to open the champagne. She forced down a glassful and complained that the sparkling wine only made her feel that much sicker. Her suitor could sense that there would be no lovemaking on this day and soon excused himself.

Tanya was instantly relieved. To celebrate she consumed another glass of champagne, bolted the door, and then crawled into bed. For the first time in months she slept a solid twelve hours.

The next day she spent exploring Vladivostok. It proved to be another warm, spring-like day, and she spent much of her time walking the dock area. Though several sailors tried to pick her up, she readily shunned their advances by telling them that she was already engaged to a jealous admiral.

Her flirting failed to get her admitted into the naval base. Yet, even from the outside of the security perimeter, she couldn't help but see the frantic activity taking place there. Unlike her last visit, hundreds of civilian dockhands now worked the piers alongside an equal number of Navy personnel. They were busy unloading various supplies from a long line of trucks and railroad boxcars. Waiting for this material were dozens of berthed warships.

Tanya played with the idea of attempting to contact the *Ivan Komarov*. Surely Senior Lieutenant Grigori Kisnev would have no problem getting her onto the base. Deciding that she had seen enough for one day, she turned around to begin the short walk home. She was soon glad that she had made this choice, for waiting for her in the apartment building's foyer was the portly figure of her uncle.

The furrier had been in the process of giving the concierge a rabbit hat when Tanya entered. The old lady had given Tanya the cold shoulder when she had left that morning. Tanya knew that this was in response to the string of men that had been visiting her lately. The furrier's gift was the ideal peace offering, and soon it was apparent that all was forgiven.

Lev didn't hug his niece properly until they were safely behind the doors of his apartment. After kissing her on each cheek, he stepped back and examined her from head to toe.

"Are my eyes deceiving me, or have you grown even more beautiful since we've been separated?"

This was her uncle's standard greeting when she had been gone for a time, yet she still blushed. "Oh, come now, uncle. I think that it's time that you had your eyes examined."

Lev grunted. "That may be so, but this time I really think that you have somehow changed. By the way, let me be the first to offer you a hearty congratulations from the others. Anton Bagdaran arrived in Tavricanka with your incredible dispatch. I must admit that even I was astounded by this report's essence. Nevertheless, because Anton swore to your source's reliability, I wasted no time communicating with our contact in the West. The Americans must have believed it also, for only a couple of hours ago I was paid a rare personal visit by my contact.

"It seems that they are taking this war alert very seriously. They feel that the whole crisis revolves around Posjet's laser facility. To redress the situation, they've decided to eliminate the installation. Though the plans are still being finalized, we can expect our friends to visit us sometime before the final test that you warned of takes place. Since it will all be done undercover, if this surprise raid is successful, the authorities here will never know what hit them. Without the laser facility for protection, they will call off this preemptive strike, and once more the world will be saved from certain annihilation. Perhaps then we can reveal the plot to the people, and the great change that we seek can at long last take place. It is this outcome that my prayers beseech."

Her uncle's emotional discourse hit home and tears were cascading down Tanya's cheeks as she fell into his strong arms. His very touch comforted her, and in an instant she knew that her sacrifice had been well worth the great price paid.

CHAPTER TEN

It was a dark, moonless night when the sub pen holding the *Dnieper* was reflooded and the vessel again returned to its intended medium. With fanfare kept to a hushed minimum, the boat entered the cold waters of Puget Sound. A Coast Guard cutter escorted the sub into the Strait of Juan de Fuca. There it attempted its first test dive. Veiled by sixty-five feet of black water, the *Dnieper* passed Cape Flattery with only the rounded tip of its periscope breaking the ocean's surface. Its dual propellers whirred with a near-silent hiss as it penetrated the Pacific and pointed its bow on a course due westward.

Submerged in these very same waters, the Soviet Akula-class submarine *Baikal* drifted noiselessly. With its nuclear reactor scrammed and the boat buttoned up in a state of ultra-quiet, the *Baikal*'s sensors were free to scan the surrounding waters without any outside interference of their own.

The vessel's Captain couldn't help but be tense and frustrated. These waters were heavily patrolled by their enemy and, so far, their mission hadn't been the least bit successful. The commander's problems had all started over a week ago, when they had first arrived there. At that time they had been shadowing one of the Imperialist's few remaining diesel-electric subs. All appeared to be going splendidly until the Yankee vessel apparently picked up their presence. An abrupt, death-defying maneuver followed as the Americans suddenly dove for deeper waters in a tight, spiraling turn. Caught completely off guard by this surprise tactic, the Captain of the *Baikal* could only order his boat to descend also. Yet try as they could, no trace of the enemy sub was ever detected. Only the mad hiss of agitated seawater remained.

Supposing that they had escaped under the power of their near-soundless electric motors, he directed the *Baikal* back to its patrol station at the strait's mouth. Not an hour passed before yet another contact was heard. This signature was of a vastly different nature. Their computer showed that it belonged to an American 688-class, nuclear-powered attack sub. Their sonar operator could have sworn that another vessel trailed in this boat's wake, but they had little time to learn the validity of this fact. For no sooner had the *Baikal* attempted to close in than it was hit by a solid sonar ping. It was as if the Americans had been expecting them, and it was all the Captain could do to turn the *Baikal* northward to escape the now-charging 688.

Twelve long hours later, the Soviet sub creeped

back to its precarious patrol station. Though there was no excuse to being caught off guard as they had been, the Captain couldn't help but wonder why the *Dnieper* hadn't informed them of this hunter's presence. After all, this was their job. He could only assume that the Americans had managed to sneak by the *Dnieper* as it lay hidden in an adjoining inlet listening for any approaching traffic.

The Captain had initially questioned the wisdom of Command's decision to use the thirty-year-old vessel for such a sensitive assignment. Yet there could be no doubting the reliability record of the Whiskey-class boats as a whole. They had served the Rodina extremely well and continued to do so. Looking forward to bringing up their close encounter with the 688 next time that he saw Dmitri Zinyagin in Vladivostok, the *Baikal*'s skipper focused his entire attention on their current reconnaissance.

Since it was almost impossible for a sub to be so delicately trimmed that it would remain indefinitely static, neither rising or falling, the *Baikal* was currently "riding a layer." It did so by finding a pronounced layer of cooler and therefore heavier seawater, and "balancing" on the boundary between it and a warmer strata. Because of this maneuver, they were able to keep engine noise at a minimum by cruising under the power of their emergency E-motors only. This would offer their sonar operators near-perfect listening conditions.

To insure that their attentions remained completely focused, the Captain currently stood behind this very console. The two men who manned the headphones had the *Baikal's* most acute hearing. This had to be the case for they were presently utilizing the boat's passive hydrophone array. This series of sensitive microphones was set alongside the sub's hull. They recorded sounds ranging from the click of spawning shrimp to the pulsating moan of passing whales. Yet the cavitational hiss of a man-made propeller had a pitch all its own. It was this unique sound that they were seeking.

The Captain looked on expectantly as the senior technician suddenly sat forward and pressed his headphone to his ear. This abrupt move was followed by a quick increase in his volume gain selector. To find out for himself just what had attracted the operator's attention, the *Baikal's* commanding officer hurriedly slipped on an auxiliary set of headphones.

For the first several seconds he could hear nothing out of the ordinary. To further increase his concentration, he tightly closed his eyes. At this point, a bare, distant surge became audible. Though the untrained observer would have had trouble just hearing this muted sound, the Captain immediately recognized its significance. He opened his eyes and caught the glance of the senior sonar technician.

"Well, comrade, what do we have out there?" he questioned.

The operator answered cautiously. "It's a bit early to say for certain, sir, but it sounds to me as if we've got a submerged diesel-electric coming at us from the east."

This revelation caused a broad grin to paint the Captain's face. "Excellent, comrade. Perhaps our

261

American friends have returned. This time they won't be getting away so easily. Run that signature through the computer and let me know for certain. Then we'll show the Yankees that we too can play their game of cat and mouse."

While the technician reached forward to carry out this directive, the captain considered his alternatives. If it indeed was the same sub that had successfully run from them earlier, he couldn't possibly pass up this chance to get even. Drifting silently as they were, the *Baikal* would be impossible to pick up. Thus the element of surprise was solely theirs.

One tactic would be to blast this contact with a burst of their active sonar. This deafening ping would startle the enemy crew, showing them that their opponents could track them down in their very own waters. If the Captain desired to prove his point in a more dramatic manner, the *Baikal* could always give them a little "love tap." This maneuver was first perfected in the Mediterranean, when a 688-class attack sub was located snooping close on the heels of a Soviet surface fleet. The Akula-type vessels had only been operational for a few months at that time, and a pair of these boats were sent in to intercept the unsuspecting 688. Because the bow of the Akula was specially reinforced, the lead vessel actually rammed its nose into the American sub's vulnerable, fiberglas sonar sphere. Not knowing what had hit them, the Yankees were last seen limping back into Sardinia for emergency repairs.

Anxiously, the Captain peered down at the sonar console to see what was holding up the technician. The operator was in the process of typing a series of commands into his computer's keyboard. When a coded response lit the green-tinted monitor screen, the *Baikal*'s skipper queried, "Well, comrade, is it the Americans?"

The technician pushed back his headphones and nervously scratched his forehead. "I've initiated a footprint scan twice now, and each time the results have been the same. We show an eighty-seven-percent probability that the submarine approaching us is a Soviet Whiskey-class derivative."

"Then it's the *Dnieper*!" said the astounded Captain. "I'll bet my retirement pension that they've experienced some sort of mechanical difficulties. Why else would they be pulling out early? Perhaps they've had a malfunction of their radio transmitter. This would explain why they never informed us of that 688's passing. I'd like to attempt to contact them, but our orders strictly forbid us from doing so. We'll have to wait until we return home ourselves to find out for certain."

Somewhat disappointed that this contact wasn't the enemy after all, the *Baikal*'s Captain silently wished his fellow countrymen a safe voyage back to the Motherland. Leaving the sonar operators with strict orders to continue their diligent scan, the skipper returned to his stateroom. There he would log this encounter with the *Dnieper*, and then see if the cook had any leftovers remaining from the dinner that he had missed.

It wasn't until they had successfully completed their first test dive that William Carrigan could issue a sigh of relief. Until then, he had no way of knowing whether or not they had mastered the Soviet vessel's alien operational systems. Their week of rushed training appeared to have paid off as the sub descended to its periscope depth without incident.

Carrigan had been in the control room when Captain Spencer gave the order to dive. Though he had witnessed more efficient descents before, the crew went about their difficult individual assignments without hesitation. This included their current diving chief, Helmut Keller. Merely having the knowledgeable German at the ballast controls induced a shared feeling of confidence. As it turned out, Keller handled the red and green switches of the "Christmas tree" as if he were back on U-313 again. He had no trouble trimming the boat, which had all too soon entered the cool waters of the Pacific.

It had been decided that both Carrigan and the young skipper of the *Stingray* would share this command. Since this arrangement could prove confusing to the men, Carrigan willingly handed over the everyday control of the *Dnieper* to Randall Spencer. He would be close by to offer his opinion when necessary.

Meanwhile, his recently reactivated ex-shipmates had been taking a more active role in the sub's daily operation. This was especially true of Lukowski and Keller. Both veterans had been of enormous value in getting them to sea so quickly.

After repairing the engine's cracked manifold and supervising the overhaul, the two chiefs wasted no time initiating a vigorous training program. Much of this took place in the vessel's maneuvering compartment. There, with the help of Captain Spencer's knowledge of Russian, the dials and gauges that monitored the propulsion system were relabeled. Then began the tedious task of reeducating the young engineering staff. Fortunately, they proved to be quick learners. Within a couple of days they were capable of manning their stations with a minimum of supervision.

This also proved to be the case in the *Dnieper's* torpedo room. There Mac Brady had worked overtime teaching his men how to operate the boat's outdated fire-control system. Though there was still some question as to their torpedoes' capabilities, Mac was confident that they could provide some sting if needed.

Carrigan had left the training of the control room's staff in Peter Donner's capable hands. Working closely alongside him was Tim Kelly, the Stingray's XO. Between them, they were able to make the best use out of the operational manual that Captain Spencer had translated for them.

The men responded to Donner's instruction with the same eagerness that characterized most of his students back at Norton Academy. They were anxious to meet the challenge, and didn't seem to fear the tight time restraints that caused many of their sessions to extend well into the night. By concentrating on individual specialties, they began manning the various stations. These included the helmsmen, sonar, and radar operators. All the while, coordinating their progress was the ever-present Randall Spencer.

There could be no questioning the young Captain's role in allowing them to get on with the mission so quickly. Carrigan was genuinely impressed with his unceasing efforts. Spencer's knowledge of the Russian language helped them time after time. His translation of the Soviet training manual alone saved them hundreds of hours of dangerous trial and error. Added to this was a cool inner confidence that seemed to rub off on all those he worked with. Not afraid to pitch in when the going got tough, Spencer inspired his men to face the impossible almost daily. Because of this, no challenge proved to be too difficult for his subordinates to handle.

Proud of each man's contribution, Carrigan could only pray that all of the *Dnieper*'s mechanical systems remained operational. A breakdown now could put them out of commission as quickly as an enemy torpedo would. Well aware that worrying about such things was a complete waste of energy, he took a last look at the control room and found all to his liking.

As the present officer of the deck, Tim Kelly stood beside the periscope well, alertly monitoring their progress. On the opposite side of the compartment, Peter Donner perched between the two seated helmsmen, his eyes locked on the depth guage. Immediately behind the helm was the diving station. There Helmut Keller was in the midst of teaching Pat McDaris, the *Stingray*'s chief, the fine art of keeping a Whiskey-class vessel in trim. To their rear, Randall Sepncer was bent over the navigational charts, with the bespectacled figure of Lieutenant Stephan Monihan close at his side.

Conscious of the paperwork that awaited him in his stateroom, Carrigan began his way aft. As he walked down the equipment-lined passageway that led from the control room, he felt himself being transferred back in time. In the blink of an eye, forty years disappeared. The sights, smells, and sounds that surrounded him no longer seemed to belong to a foreign vessel, but rather to his first and only command, the USS *Abalone*. This fantasy guided his steps past the sub's office. It was there he briefly caught sight of his face's reflection in a small, wall-mounted mirror. Nothing else was needed to bring him abruptly back to reality.

Over four decades had come and gone since he had last gone to sea. During this time span, he had created an entirely new way of life. He knew that he could be proud of Carrigan Industries. At the war's conclusion, he had made a promise to himself to become involved with the design and production of reliable, innovative weapons systems. With this thought in mind, he had enrolled in Stanford University to become better acquainted with both engineering and practical business doctrines. Immediately after graduating, he had briefly gone to work for the Electric Boat Company and become familiar with the designs of the first nuclear-powered submarines that were already on the company's drawing boards. Not long afterwards, he had attained the financing to open up his own shop, in which elements of the New Mark 101A fire-control system were produced. He had soon become known for excellent work at a fair price, one contract had followed another, and the rest was history.

Carrigan had never realized how completely he had immersed himself into his business until that fateful phone call from Admiral Lawrence arrived. His subsequent trips to both Washington, D.C., and Bangor had helped to give him a fresh perspective on life.

Today he felt like a different man. New priorities had emerged and, for the first time in forty years, he found himself involved with something other than his business. He had not even taken the time to marry and raise a family. Carrigan had dedicated his life totally to the firm. He'd never realized how much he had been missing until this moment.

Conscious that he had not even called the office to say goodbye, he ducked into the wardroom. The compartment was empty, yet there was a small sealed box sitting before his place at the head of the table. He glanced down at this object and saw that it was addressed to him. He peeled off the tape and removed a brand-new corncob pipe. Carrigan didn't need a note to inform him who this gift was from.

He hadn't smoked such a pipe since the day the *Abalone* had last sailed into Pearl. Now that he had returned to sea, his men had taken it upon themselves to continue on the tradition. The pipe felt good in his hand, and he packed its bowl with a pinch of aromatic tobacco that was sealed in an accompanying pouch. Though he didn't light it, he slipped its bit into his mouth and again found his thoughts traveling back in time. But his rememberances were brief, for another individual soon ducked into the wardroom.

Peter Lowell had a sickly green tint to his cheeks.

His eyes were bloodshot, and from the way that he stood beside the table Carrigan knew what was ailing the young man.

"I gather that you're not much of a sailor, Mr. Lowell?"

Peter weakly nodded, and his boss continued, "Well, just have a seat, and I'll take care of you."

While Lowell plopped onto the booth, Carrigan walked over to his cabin, situated directly across from the wardroom. There he removed a tiny adhesive patch from his medicine chest. He returned to this patient and stuck his patch on the skin directly behind Lowell's earlobe.

"It's known as a puss pad, to us in the trade," offered William with a wise wink. "But since even the hardiest sailors feel the sea from time to time, with modern science's advancements, there's certainly no reason for suffering."

Lowell looked as if he might throw up any minute, and Carrigan decided that he'd better see about getting his employee into his bunk. Hopefully he'd be getting his sealegs soon. Otherwise these next ten days would be sheer hell for the innocent lad.

While Peter Lowell slept off his first bout with seasickness, Ivan Koslov anxiously paced the containment cell in which he had been placed. With each day's passing, it was evident that the Americans would be keeping them in confinement indefinitely. Lately, their captors hadn't even showed up to interrogate their prisoners. They seemed content to just let the Soviets rot in their drafty cells.

When the Zampolit first brought up the idea of escape, Senior Lieutenant Sergei Volzhnin had been quick to reject it. Understanding the young officer's natural fears, Koslov began subtly working on him to change his mind. Since their only hope was to get to their consulate in San Francisco, the Zampolit volunteered to attempt this dangerous trip himself. Only this afternoon did the senior lieutenant finally throw in his total support.

Now that the hour had come for their plan to go into action, Koslov found himself strangely calm. He had even stopped sweating. Stimulated by the mere thought of what he was soon to do, the Zampolit felt totally alive. It was almost as if the closeness of danger had somehow reawakened him. Doing his best to remember the drama classes that he had attended in upper school, he took in a deep breath and mentally recreated the scene he wished to act out. Only when it was clear in his mind did he grab the right side of his abdomen and scream out in pain.

A pair of guards was in the process of making their nightly rounds when they heard the initial cries. It was Sergei Volzhnin who guided them to the Zampolit's cell.

"It's our political officer!" screamed the senior lieutenant. "He's been feeling ill all day, but this fit is the worst of them all!"

Before the cell was opened, two more guards were called into the containment room. Both of them held M-16s and kept these rifles pointed squarely at the other prisoners as the door was slid back. The Zampolit was sprawled out on his cot. He lay on his

270

back, with his right leg extended straight out and his hand gripping his right side. His screams of agony continued and, by this time, his pale forehead was completely soaked in sweat.

One of the guards tried to get him to bend his right leg upwards. Koslov attempted this movement, yet screamed out in agony when he vainly tried it.

"It seems to be his appendix, all right," observed the guard to his companion calmly. "You'd better keep an eye on him while I call in an ambulance."

Fifteen minutes later, the Political Officer was being wheeled out on a stretcher. His pained howling could be heard even as he disappeared from the containment area. Satisfied that the Zampolit's act had been a most convincing one, Volzhnin wondered what would happen next. For, even though Ivan Koslov had detailed his plan as if it were a mere walk in the woods, Volzhnin knew otherwise. Impressed with the man's daring, the senior lieutenant sat down on the edge of his own cot, to begin the long wait.

CHAPTER ELEVEN

Lieutenant Scott Sanger had been flying his Lockheed P-3 Orion out of Alaska's Shemya Air Force Base for a little more than a month now. Duty here was in vast contrast to his previous assignment in balmy Hawaii. Sanger knew that his sudden transfer was instigated by a single foolish incident. His father had always warned him that his passion for the opposite sex would get him in trouble sooner or later. But how was he to know that she was the new commander's wife?

They had met off base at a cozy little pub run by a pair of expatriated Brits. Sanger really wasn't on the prowl the afternoon he met her. Instead he had a taste for the excellent English ale that only that pub served.

She hit on him initially. They talked about their mutual love of the United Kingdom. Under the dim lights of the bar he failed to see the heavy makeup that so skillfully covered her age lines. All that he could remember taking in was her long blonde hair and a figure that could easily rival Dolly Parton's. She seemed lonely, and Sanger thought nothing of inviting her back to his apartment after both had drunk their fill.

She was a wild woman in bed. Wasting no time on small talk, she began stripping off her clothes, and then began working on his own. They lay on the couch naked, and Sanger couldn't resist her massive breasts. He slurped on her huge nipples like a hungry baby, while her lips did their own exploring. Soon he was erect and ready.

She preferred to stay on top and rode him unmercifully. As her orgasm began gathering, she began screaming passionately. Afraid that she could be heard by the neighbors, Sanger was about to warn her to keep her voice down when she burst in a hot, juicy climax. Seconds later, he too was satisfied and they lay silently beside each other, temporarily spent and satiated.

She left not long afterwards, without leaving either her complete name or phone number. As luck would have it, the very moment that she closed the door behind her Sanger's neighbor was just walking down the hallway. Being a young aggressive lieutenant commander on the rise, he recognized the new commander's wife and thought nothing of mentioning her visit to Sanger's quarters later that afternoon.

Forty-eight hours later, the orders arrived sending him off to the Aleutian Islands. He learned of the apparent reason for this hasty transfer only after he had landed at Shemya. If scuttlebutt could be believed, he soon found out that he wasn't the first officer to be compromised by his lover's uncontrollable horniness. Unable to vent his frustrations officially, Sanger did his best to accept his fate. At least he was still being allowed to fly.

He had been admitted to the P-3 Orion program early on in his eight-year naval career. Adapted especially for long-range marine patrol, the Orions specialized in anti-submarine warfare (ASW) operations. Powered by four Allison single-shaft turbo-props, the P-3 was built around the frame of the now-out-of-date Electra airliner. Though the design of this frame was over three decades old, the current fleet of Orions were packed with the latest in sophisticated computerized hardware. Manned by a crew of ten, the aircraft also carried an assortment of ASW weapons, from torpedoes and depth bombs to the lethal Harpoon missile.

Not knowing what he would do if the Navy took away his wings, Sanger carefully prepared himself for this morning's patrol. His record could not take another black mark against him. He rose early and was the first one in the briefing room. Today's assignment was the waters directly south of Shemya. Command had warned them of an unusual amount of Soviet submarine traffic in this sector. Since this was the shortest enemy route to America's western coastline, it was up to the P-3 Orion to tag those vessels long before they reached US waters.

Sanger got an inhospitable reminder of the location of his present home upon leading his crew out to their airplane. The frigid Arctic winds were howling in icy, forty-mile-per-hour gusts. It was all that he could do to get them safely airborne. Once this was achieved, he got them quickly to the calmer air at 28,000 feet. Approximately 800 miles later, the Orion descended once again. They were a little under two hours into their flight and it was time to deploy their first field of sonobuoys.

The sonobuoy was their primary ASW sensor. It contained an extremely sensitive hydrophone. This microphone-like listening device was designed to pick up the noise of a passing submarine. Carried in forty-eight externally loaded chutes in the plane's lower fuselage, the sonobuoys were dropped in pre-arranged patterns. With the aid of on-board digital computers, up to sixteen of the hydrophones could be monitored and analyzed at a time.

The sky was clear, yet the winds were still ferocious as Sanger guided the P-3 down toward the choppy, white-cap-tossed waters. He found it hard to believe that this wave-tossed portion of the Pacific belonged to the same ocean that surrounded Hawaii. The 140,000-pound aircraft was buffeted around like a child's toy as it broke the 200-foot threshold and the first load of buoys was dropped.

Sanger had just returned the plane to 10,000 feet when the intercom buzzed. Their chief sensor operator was known as a mellow type of guy, yet on this occasion his voice rose excitedly.

"We've got something, lieutenant! I show an unidentified submerged contact moving due west. Its signature is still too weak for us to get a definite, so I'd advise attempting a MAD pass to pin them down."

MAD was short for magnetic anomaly detector. This device was carried in a long, tubular "stinger" that protruded from the Orion's tail. Its purpose was to pick up the magnetic disturbance created when a sub's metallic hull cut through the natural lines of force that formed the earth's magnetic field. Though MAD wasn't suitable for a general area search, it was invaluable in locating the exact location of a target tagged by another means.

Once more Sanger guided the P-3 downwards. It took them a half-dozen bumpy passes to precisely locate the contact. When this was determined, they merely had to drop another sonobuoy on top of their target to accurately copy its footprint.

Several minutes after this buoy was dropped, the intercom again buzzed. "Lieutenant, big brother has got that definite. We show our contact to be a Soviet Whiskey-class vessel. She's down about one hundred feet, and sure's got a bone in her teeth. Must be doing a good twenty knots."

Beaming at the fact that they had tagged an enemy vessel so quickly, Sanger had his communications officer notify Command of their find. As it turned out, he was both astounded and puzzled by their reply. Instead of instructing them to continue to closely monitor the submarine for the rest of their patrol, Command ordered Sanger to break off their engagement at once. Without a word of explanation, they were directed to renew their search in a more southerly sector.

This made absolutely no sense to the confused pilot. Sure, Whiskey-class boats were older diesel-electric models, yet they still belonged to the Soviet Union. In past instances, they would have been instructed to closely monitor such a boat's progress

276

until either another P-3 or an attack sub arrived to take over. In that way the vessel's ultimate destination could be determined. Sanger wondered if he should ask for a clarification of these orders. He brought up the matter with his copilot. Between the both of them, they agreed that such a move would only make waves. Already well aware of his precarious standing with Command, the pilot shrugged his shoulders and proceeded to guide the aircraft to its new patrol position.

Oblivious to the P-3's presence above them, the *Dnieper* continued its mad dash across the North Pacific. It had been four and a half days since they had left Bangor. In that time the crew had done their best to settle into their new environment. Slowly but surely they were becoming adept with the boat's alien systems. Though they continued to have their fair share of problems, nothing of a serious nature had yet to arise. Thus they were able to continue making excellent progress.

The officers had decided to hold daily review sessions in the wardroom. It was such a meeting that brought them together on this afternoon. Seated at the head of the table, William Carrigan opened the forum for discussion. The smooth-talking veteran pulled his pipe from his lips and invited Randall Spencer to give them an update of their current position.

Spencer informed them that they were nearly halfway to their goal. This revelation caused a relieved chorus of chatter to begin among all those present.

Carrigan allowed the men a full minute before calling the meeting back to order. When it was determined that the various section chiefs had the boat well under control, Lieutenant Stephen Monihan was given the floor.

The young navigator was still a bit nervous expressing himself before the others, but he managed nevertheless. Monihan had been instructed by Carrigan to pull the charts on the narrow expanse of water lying between Hokkaido, Japan's most northerly island, and Soviet-controlled Sakhalin. Known as La Perouse Strait, this twenty-three-and-a-half-mile-wide channel would be the corridor the *Dnieper* would utilize to enter the Sea of Japan. From this point, a mere thirty hours of travel separated them from their ultimate destination, the Bay of Posjet.

Peter Donner was the first to offer his suggestions for penetrating La Perouse Strait. He recommended hugging the Soviet side of the channel whenever possible. Carrigan was quick to support this suggestion. Both the Russians and the Japanese were known to have those waters heavily monitored with underwater sensors. But they were presently traveling in a Soviet vessel, so the Soviet side would be safer. They could only pray that the Soviets would be fooled.

Lieutenant Monihan was given the task of drawing up the course. With this finalized, the meeting was adjourned. Five minutes later, the wardroom was empty except for a single figure seated at the table's head.

A look of determination painted Carrigan's weary expression as he focused on the chart that the navigator had been asked to leave behind. He traced the narrow expanse of water separating Sakhalin and Hokkaido, and determined that their second greatest challenge would soon be upon them. By the grace of God, they had been able to pass the first test. Somehow the *Dnieper*'s secrets had been unlocked. Their current position was proof of this. Yet it still remained to be seen if the Soviets would be fooled by their ploy. Three days from now they'd know the answer to this pivotal question, for the Russian hydrophone operators would surely be announcing their arrival then.

The Sunshine Mission for the Homeless was located on Tacoma's west side. On the average day it was home to over 100 desperate men and women who for one reason or another found themselves unable to afford their own room and board. The mission's occupants included derelicts, winos, the mentally ill, and many legitimate hard-luck cases. Unbeknownst to its management, for the last three days it was also sheltering a fugitive Soviet citizen.

The hand of fate had drawn *Ivan Koslov* to the mission's door. He had arrived there late at night, attracted to the establishment by the line of raggedly dressed individuals waiting patiently outside on the sidewalk. Since he was covered only by his hospital garb and a blanket at the time, he would blend in well with the unkempt crowd, and he wisely took his place among them.

The Zampolit had read about the social inequality that was so prevalent in American society. Little did

he ever dream that such an assemblage of unfortu-
nates would be his unlikely saviors.

His precarious road to the Sunshine Mission had
started off at nearby Tacoma General Hospital. This
was the facility that the Navy medics had rushed
him to when he had faked his attack of appendicitis.
The doctors at the emergency room had been bright
and perceptive. So that they would not decide to do
exploratory surgery, Koslov had begun playing down
his symptoms once he was admitted. Thus, their
initial diagnosis was that his appendix was inflamed—not ruptured, as they'd first feared. Just to
make certain, they'd decided to keep him in the
hospital under observation while further tests were
run.

Koslov made his move while he was in the midst
of being wheeled up to the protective custody ward.
The Navy had left but a single guard to watch over
him. He was a youngster who seemed to be distracted by the strange environment he now found
himself in. The Zampolit pretended to be dozing as
an orderly and this sentry pushed him into the
elevator. No sooner had the doors hissed shut than
he snapped into action.

His first move was to hit the light switch situated
on the elevator's control panel. Just as the lights
blinked off, he also activated the emergency stop
button. Taking advantage of the resulting panic, he
utilized the gurney that he had been lying on as a
battering ram. His very first blow made solid contact and there was a loud gasp, followed by the
sound of a body falling to the floor. Koslov swung
out wildly when a pair of hands grabbed at him

from behind. Again his aim was true, for his fist smashed blindly into the side of a man's jaw. All was still as he groped for the light switch.

The fluorescent unit popped on, and for a second the direct illumination stung his eyes. They quickly adjusted and he scanned the elevator's interior. The orderly had taken the full brunt of the gurney, and was still gasping for breath with the wind knocked out of him. On the other side lay the Navy sentry, who was definitely out for the count. Inwardly beaming with pride, Koslov wasted no time before redirecting the elevator down to the basement.

As he sprinted down the tiled corridor he alertly grabbed hold of a blanket. Wrapping it around his portly frame, he ducked out an emergency exit and found himself in an alleyway. A thick night fog allowed him to slip into the shadows.

His ultimate goal was the interstate highway that conveniently connected Tacoma to all points south. San Francisco was located in that direction. Yet first he had to gather his wits, and then get some proper clothing—and a map if possible.

Police sirens haunted the darkness with their banshee-like wail. Very likely there was a full-scale search being organized to track him down. Ivan knew he needed a safe place where he could hide for a while. Then he chanced upon the flashing neon cross of Sunshine Mission. Taking in the mass of grubby humanity perched before its door, he knew that he had found his refuge.

Though he both read and spoke basic English, in order to not draw attention to his accent he pretended to be a mute. This worked out perfectly when it came time to assign bunk space. The next day he was given a denim workshirt, some Levi jeans, a jacket, and a pair of sneakers. All this was offered with a bare minimum of questions. Impressed that some Americans still had an inkling of social justice, the Zampolit consumed a hearty meal before returning to his mattress.

As his fourth morning at the mission dawned, Ivan knew that it was time to be on the move once more. He decided he was going to wear out his welcome at the shelter shortly. In addition, the police search had no doubt lost some of its intensity by that time. Again lady luck was with him. A long-haired young man was assigned to the bunk beside him. This wild-looking individual carried a backpack with him. While Ivan pretended to be napping, he saw the lad remove a book of maps from his pack and begin studying them. When lunchtime came, the Zampolit waited for him to amble off to the dining room before reaching into the pack for the maps.

They were printed by an organization named the American Automobile Association, and were organized into something called a Triptik. They were drawn with remarkable detail and extended from the Canadian border southward to San Diego, California. He smiled upon finding the very route he had been seeking highlighted with a green felt-tip pen. Called Interstate 5, the thoroughfare conveniently passed right through Tacoma.

Forty-five minutes later, he was walking up the shoulder of this same highway. Ivan soon saw another young man wearing a backpack. This fellow held his right thumb up in the air, while in his left hand he held a cardboard sign with the words "San Francisco" printed on it. The Zampolit remembered that this was called hitchhiking. He looked on as a colorfully painted van pulled off to the side of the road and the young man sprinted over to board it. No sooner had he shut the door behind him than the van merged back into the traffic with the young man apparently well on the way to his destination.

Excited with how easy this process appeared, Ivan stood at the young man's spot on the shoulder. He held up his thumb and stared out at the approaching traffic. Never had he seen so many vehicles traversing the same thoroughfare before. He couldn't begin to count the number of cars and trucks that zipped by him. Yet, much to his dismay, nobody displayed even the slightest sign of halting to pick him up. Most likely this was caused by his failure to draw up some sort of sign.

He was out there for well over an hour when the weather started turning for the worse. It had been a warm, crystal-clear day when he had first started out. But as the afternoon developed, a solid wall of menacing black clouds began blowing in from the northwest. With their arrival, the temperature dropped a good fifteen degrees. His light jacket proved inadequate to keep the chill off, and soon his teeth were chattering. His condition worsened when a light drizzle began falling. He cursed the utter insensitivity of the capitalists as they whizzed by him without any compassion, and was about to give up. He had decided to give it another five minutes at the most when the sound of squealing brakes caused him to look up. He could hardly believe his eyes as he viewed a huge semi-tractor trailer pull off onto the shoulder. He wasted no time running up to its cab.

The driver had cranked the passenger window down and Ivan could hear the loud strains of fiddle music emanating from inside. As he peered up into this window, a bright-eyed, bearded face suddenly appeared. This was accompanied by a deep, bass voice.

"Well, what are ya' waitin' for, stranger? You're not goin' to tell me that you're standin' out there in that rain for your health, are ya'?"

Tanya had been genuinely surprised when Grigori Kisnev showed up at her apartment after a two-day absence. The grinning senior lieutenant had two customary bottles of champagne at his side. Demonstrating his usual cocky self-assurance, he invited himself in.

Unlike the previous time, Tanya was glad to see him. Her uncle had reminded her how vitally important the officer was to the Movement. In order to find out exactly when the next laser test would be attempted, they had to rely on Kisnev. She had to get him to disclose the departure time of his ship. Once this was known, Tanya would be free to return to Tavricanka to await the arriving American commandos.

Grigori seemed to be in a hurry, for he went straight into the kitchen to pour their drinks. No sooner had they consumed them than the officer pulled her toward him and began kissing her hard on the lips. The cold swiftness of his advances caught Tanya completely unexpected.

"Easy now," she warned as she struggled to push herself back. "After all, a girl does have to breathe."

"Since when has that stopped you?" returned Grigori icily.

Seeing that she had hurt his feelings, Tanya softened. "You know, I missed you these past couple of days. I was beginning to wonder if I'd ever see you again."

"I'm afraid that you won't be getting rid of me so easily," jested the officer, who reached over to put his arm around her shoulder.

Tanya allowed him to caress her.

"Relax, little one," he added with a whisper. "The way you're so jumpy, it would appear that you were the one under all the pressure these last two days."

"What pressure is that?" cooed Tanya gently.

Grigori began massaging the back of her neck. "The Rodina's Navy has a funny way of wanting to possess its sailors completely. Even though I have leave time coming to me, the Captain was all but deaf to my requests. Just because the *Ivan Komarov*'s been chosen to transfer the General Secretary down the coastline, he feels that I'm needed to see to the ship's final preparation. As if he couldn't manage it."

"It's good to be needed," offered Tanya.

Grigori took this comment in as his hands reached under her sweater and touched the bare skin of her back. "Do you need me, little one?"

Tanya sighed with his touch. "Of course I do, Grigori. It's just that I never know for certain when

285

I'll be seeing you next."

"That's what you get for falling for a Navy lover," he offered. "Once we get back from our little cruise, I promise that I'll have more time for you. Yet meanwhile, we must make the most of each available moment."

He reached around to caress her bare breasts. Her nipples hardened and she managed a single breathless query. "Then you'll be leaving shortly?"

Grigori slipped his hand into her crotch. "Easy now, my little one. Don't worry so. If all goes as planned, the Secretary will be here tomorrow. Our cruise is but a short one. And then I promise you an entire week of nothing but lovemaking."

Wincing at the thought of such a thing, Tanya forced herself to relax. After all, she now knew the exact date of the General Secretary's arrival. Her next goal was to get rid of her paramour before he became too far involved.

As he tried to nestle his fingers in her underwear, Tanya reached up and gagged herself by quickly forcing her finger down her throat. Grigori was so involved with his advances that he failed to catch sight of this move, which caused her to retch. She issued a mouthful of thin vomit. As she expected, this did much to cool his ardor. He backed off while Tanya struggled to catch her breath.

"Oh, I'm so embarrassed!" pleaded Tanya, who was close to tears. "My flu has ruined everything."

Disappointment etched the senior lieutenant's flushed face. "Why didn't you tell me that you weren't feeling good, little one?"

Tanya answered while covering the vomit-stained

couch with a napkin. "We get so little time together as it is. I couldn't bear to turn you away."

"Nonsense," answered Grigori firmly. "Your health is much more important. We will have plenty of time together. Can I get you some tea? Or perhaps you'd like some soup?"

Tanya rubbed her forehead. "No, my dearest, all I need is to get some sleep."

"Then to bed it will be," continued the officer, who stood to turn down her sheets. "Now, are you sure that you don't need anything else?"

Tanya shook her head. "No, Grigori, you've been an understanding sweetheart and I think it's best if you left me alone before you too come down with this bug."

The officer had been thinking of this very possibility as he stood to exit. "Get better, little one. The next time we're together there will be much to celebrate!"

He left without even giving her a kiss on the cheek. As the door slammed shut, Tanya exhaled a breath of relief. That had been much too close for comfort. Surely one time was enough to give of herself. She doubted if she could have kept her sanity if he had been able to have his way with her again.

Proud of her acting performance, Tanya rose to get a wet towel to clean the vomit-stained couch properly. Once this was done, she decided that bed indeed sounded like a good place to be. For she would have to be up with the dawn. At that time she would pack, and then be off to catch the morning bus to Tavricanka.

It seemed that she had just fallen off to sleep when the whine of an ambulance siren passed close by her window. She didn't give this alien sound much thought until the next morning. It was as she was descending down the apartment building's stairwell, with her suitcase at her side, that she heard the rumble of voices coming from the lobby. She instinctively halted. With heart pounding in her chest, Tanya took in the conversation.

Two militia detectives were in the process of interrogating the concierge. This questioning concerned the body of a man found not far from the apartment building late the previous night. Tanya froze when the victim was described as a mustached naval officer. He was apparently stabbed to death while resisting a gang of hooligans. Well aware that the concierge could connect this officer with herself, Tanya silently made her way back up the stairs. To get involved with a police investigation now would not only be dangerous, it would also delay her arrival in Tavricanka. Barely taking a second to mourn the death of her lover, she headed immediately for the fire escape. Tanya eventually made it to the alley that was in back of the building just as the two detectives were knocking on her apartment's front door. She wasted no time heading straight for the bus station.

CHAPTER TWELVE

The truck driver introduced himself to Koslov as Big Mike, and big he was. His muscular figure was well over six feet, five inches in height, and he had to weigh at least three hundred pounds. His bulging torso filled the cab, which also contained an excellent stereo, leather-padded consoles, and even a small sleeping area in back complete with refrigerator, hanging pictures, and a hotplate.

Mike handled the rig as if it were a toy. Koslov had never seen the interior of such a vehicle before and was surprised at the amount of dials, gauges, levers, and gears present. In a way, it looked more like an airplane cockpit than a mere truck.

Koslov introduced himself as a recently arrived Polish immigrant from Gdansk. Thankful for his knowledge of English, he explained that he had been sightseeing in the state of Washington, and was on his way to San Francisco to stay with relatives. The gullible American accepted his story without question. After welcoming him to the United States, he asked what it was like living in a Communist country.

So as not to arouse the man's suspicions, Koslov chose his words of response carefully. He described Poland as a rather backward country void of opportunities, and praised America as a place where a man could get a new start in life. He went on extolling both the virtues of the American people and the magnificent land they lived in.

This caused a proud gleam to sparkle in the trucker's eyes. He smiled and told a bit more about his own life. Though Big Mike was a fast talker, Ivan caught the gist of his words.

The trucker had been born in Hollywood, California, and was a Vietnam veteran. Ivan's stomach turned as he bragged about the "commies" he had killed in that jungle hell. After the war, he'd come back home, only to find that the times had changed. His friends and family didn't seen to understand him anymore, and he had trouble holding a regular job. With the help of the Veterans Administration, he became enrolled in a truck driver's school. The solitude of such a life suited him fine, and he soon got a job hauling produce across the country. By saving many of his hard-earned dollars, he'd been able to buy his own rig three years before. This was the truck that they were in presently, and it was solid proof that the American dream could still be attained.

Koslov could tell that the man was indeed quite proud of his lone achievements. Of course, this was just like a greedy capitalist. Concentrating solely on satisfying his own desires, while ignoring the larger needs of the people around him, the trucker was symbolic of the decadent West. Though he fought his country's wars, he really didn't know what he was risking his life for. He had spoken of the "commies" he had killed as if they were some sort of mutated, diseased organism. Little did he understand the tenets of universal brotherhood and equality that made Communism the world's last hope.

Wishing that he could really open his heart and share the brilliant ideology that his beliefs were based upon, Koslov held his tongue. To do otherwise would bring certain trouble. He decided to watch the countryside they were currently passing through, and took in the vast tracts of virgin pine forest that filled both sides of the road. The trucker noticed his new preoccupation and mentioned that they would soon be passing near Mt. Saint Helens, an active volcano that had erupted with devastating force only a few years before. Ivan absorbed this rich landscape, and couldn't help but compare it to similar woods that graced the Rodina's Siberia.

As the daylight faded, the weather continued to deteriorate. Soon the rains were falling with a vengeance. The cab was dry and warm. The monotonous slap of the windshield wipers had a soothing effect on Koslov, who soon fell fast asleep.

He awoke to find that the rains had ceased. He also realized with a start that they had stopped moving. He fought off a brief wave of panic as he searched the darkness to reorientate himself. There was a thick fog present, yet he could just make out a large, elevated neon sign in the distance. It read, "Angel's Truck Stop." Parked nearby were dozens of other tractor trailers. Since he was presently alone in the cab, Koslov guessed that he'd have time to stretch his legs.

It was chilly and humid outside, yet the fresh, pine-scented air was stimulating. He stood on the asphalt lot, and soon caught sight of the facility's diesel pumps and the brightly lit building housing its restaurant. Ivan's stomach growled with hunger. He hadn't eaten since breakfast, and even then it was only a glass of apple juice and some tasteless oatmeal. Though he'd love a hot meal, he had only a few coins, which he'd have to save for phone calls later on.

He was imagining the meal he'd have the consulate staff serve him once he arrived in San Francisco, when a voice whispered directly behind him.

"Hey, Pops, would you like some nose candy?"

The startled Zampolit turned and saw a leather-coated black man. Even though it was the middle of the night, the man was wearing sun glasses. This stranger studied Koslov's face and questioned him again. "Are you hip, brother? I said I'm the man with the blow."

"Blow?" queried Koslov cautiously.

The black seemed astounded. "What are you, some dude from another planet or something? I've got the coke, my man, as in c-o-c-a-i-n-e."

Koslov put these letters together and made the connection. "Ah, cocaine. No, sir, I don't believe I'm interested."

The black shook his head. "It's your loss, my man. When you get out on that long, boring road and your eyelids start to get heavy, think of me and

292

the wake-up powder that you passed by. Adios, bro."

As quickly as he had appeared, the black man merged back into the fog. Koslov stifled a laugh. Wait till he told his party colleagues about his first visit with an American drug dealer! Surely this was definite proof that the decadent capitalist system was on its way to collapsing.

The Zampolit had read about the West's addiction to the coca plant. Brought up from South America, the plant's leaves were then dried and processed. The result was a powerful crystalline-alkaloid narcotic that hit the nervous system like a jolt of electricity. Hundreds of thousands of Americans used this drug daily and, because of its great expense, went to any extreme—including crime—to satisfy their habits.

The Rodina had had its own problems with drug addiction back in the days of the Afghanistan war. At that time, hashish, opium, and marijuana use had spread rapidly into the ranks of the Army. Realizing the great dangers of such substances, the party had acted swiftly. Even the KGB was utilized to root out the dealers, and users faced extremely harsh penalities. In such a way, the Rodina's drug problem had been stifled.

The foolish Americans had been far too lenient. They were certainly paying for it now—the cost being countless broken homes and wasted lives.

A lonely train whistle blew in the distance. He was chilled, and to get his blood moving he began walking quickly around the truck. Koslov was just about to pass by its massive chrome grill, when another voice called out to him from the blackness. This one was one-hundred-percent female.

"Hey, honey, lookin' for a little somethin' to warm you up properly?"

He looked up as an unbelievably attractive redhead slithered out of the fog. She couldn't have been more than a teenager, and even though she wore a full-length trench coat, he could see that her figure was full and shapely.

An alien stiffness instantly triggered in his groin, and Koslov wished that he indeed had some more American dollars on him. While wondering if he could somehow work out a trade, he was distracted by the shrill, deafening blasts of a series of sirens. This was followed by the loud, amplified voice of a man.

"This is DEA raid! You are ordered to remain still under further notified. I repeat, this is the Drug Enforcement Agency—"

Not waiting around to listen any further, Koslov did his best to duck into the fog and get out of that den of decadence. He slid beneath a nearby rig as a bank of powerful spotlights suddenly triggered on. Sweat painted his forehead, and he struggled to control his pounding heartbeat.

To be picked up now by the authorities would signal the end of his all-too-short journey. Without proper papers, they would certainly incarcerate him. To insure his continued freedom, he had to get away and quick. With few alternatives to choose from, he took the only course of action available. He began sprinting away from the spotlights.

Though he could have sworn that he heard the scuffle of footsteps close behind him, Koslov made it into the surrounding woods. Not taking the time to gather his breath, he pushed himself further into the forest. The underfooting was muddy, and his going considerably slowed, yet no one followed. Still, he dared not to stop, until he suddenly saw a railroad track. Like a gift from Lady Luck, a train was moving slowly on the track with a long line of boxcars. One of them had its door cracked open, and Ivan caught up with it and dove inside.

He lay on his back on a bed of straw. Beyond the sound of his lungs gasping for breath he heard the steady, metallic clickety-clack of the train's wheels on the rails. A good five minutes passed before he realized that he shared his refuge with another human being. Seated contentedly at the head of the boxcar was a single individual, calmly chewing on an apple. Though he wore the remnants of a three-piece suit, it was evident that he hadn't bathed or shaved for quite some time. When he saw that he had been spotted by this newcomer, he pushed the broad-brimmed hat that he had been wearing back off his forehead and nodded. This was followed by a simple greeting.

"Evening, pilgrim. Welcome aboard the California Express."

Pete Donner was the current officer of the deck as the *Dnieper* penetrated the narrow strait separating Soviet-controlled Sakhalin to the north and the Japanese island of Hokkaido to the south. The veteran XO had sailed these same waters on one other occasion. Though it was over forty years ago, his memories of that eventful voyage would be fresh in his mind always.

To see them safely into the Sea of Japan, the *Dnieper* was running at periscope depth. In this way they were able to record frequent visual bearings. Donner had only recently concluded the last of these sightings. His brief scan found them directly opposite Sakhalin's Bay of Aniva.

It had just turned dawn topside. The sky appeared cloudy, with the seas running with a slight chop. He spotted a group of Soviet fishing trawlers anchored outside the waters of the bay. The OOD couldn't help but wonder if any of these vessels were carrying hydrophone listening arrays. If he knew the Russians, they most likely were.

The seas lying between Sakhalin and the Soviet mainland were militarily sensitive. Not only were they safe havens for Russian strategic-missile submarines, frequent weapons tests also took place there. It was in this general vicinity that the Korean Airlines 747 had been shot down. That disgraceful incident had offered certain proof of Soviet paranoia at its worst.

Donner knew that it was just like the Russians to shoot first and ask questions later. He supposed this characteristic indicated a basic insecurity in their system as a whole. Having been invaded by foreign armies throughout history, Russia had good reason for caution. Yet their current leadership took this prudence to an extreme.

Often in his classes, Peter tried to give his students a real feeling for what it was like to live in the Soviet Union. He himself had visited there on two occasions. His first trip had only gotten him as far as beautiful Leningrad, but it wasn't until his most recent visit that he was able to tour Moscow. Known simply as "the center" to its inhabitants, the capital city was the Communist world's showcase. Almost any item produced in the Rodina was available there.

Peter had stayed near Red Square. It was in the midst of summer when he arrived, and every occupant of the city seemed to be outdoors. After the usual tour of museums, he took some time to just walk the streets. There were construction projects on almost every corner, and everywhere he looked he viewed a people in the midst of social transformation. Blue jeans, transistor radios, and sneakers were signaling their arrival in the modern world. It just remained to be seen how long it would take their leaders to recognize this change and adapt to it.

The voice of the navigator called out a suggested course change, and Donner acted on it accordingly. He was surprised at how quickly he had adjusted to his new duty. It was almost as if he had never left the Navy at all. Yet the young, alert faces of those he sailed with couldn't be ignored. It was their war. He was only along to lend a temporary helping hand.

Donner knew that back at the Norton Academy his boys would be getting ready for midterms. He couldn't help but wonder how his substitute was holding out. Thankful that the administration had given him this sudden leave without too many questions asked, he scanned the helm and double-checked their course, speed, and depth. He was satisfied with what he saw, looked down at his watch, and calculated that in approximately twenty-four hours they would reach their intended goal.

As the *Dnieper* continued its penetration of the La Perouse Strait, a bored Soviet sonar technician, assigned to Aniva Port Command, sat at his console. The twenty-three-year-old Ukrainian conscript stifled a yawn and wondered what was keeping his replacement. This was the third day in a row that the Uzbek was late. The midnight-to-dawn shift was hard enough without having to be forced to work overtime.

From the first day he'd arrived in the Navy, he'd faced nothing but aggravation. When he was found out that he got seasick on the smallest body of water, at least Command had had enough wisdom to station him on land. But then he was sent to Sakhalin, in one of the most remote corners of the Rodina. Why couldn't he have been fortunate like his brother, who was stationed on the balmy Black Sea? Now that was the kind of duty that a guy dreamed of! But his brother had always had more luck anyway.

Consigned to at least a year in this frigid wasteland, he knew that he'd just have to make the best of it. He could try asking for a transfer, yet this would only draw attention to himself. One thing that he had learned early in his Navy career was that it was much better not to be too conspicuous. After all, he only had eleven months to go. Surely he'd get by.

A burst of painful static emanated from his bulky headphones, and he reached forward to turn down the volume control. By pounding his open palm against the side of the console, he soon got the receiver working properly once again. The hydrophone that he was presently monitoring was anchored some twenty kilometers distant, on the floor of Aniva Bay. With this sensitive device he was able to detect a variety of objects, from a passing whale to a fleet of approaching fishing trawlers. Though each and every detection was to be logged, only one sound signature warranted an immediate call to Command. This distinctive footprint belonged to the surging hiss of a submarine. So far, he had only made such a call seven times. In each of these instances, the computer verification system showed these vessels to be the Rodina's own.

What would really make his record shine would be to detect a passing American sub. Such a discovery would not only earn him a commendation, but also make his superiors more open to an eventual transfer. His hearing was above average, and since he wasn't the type who slept on the job, there was always the chance that his time would come. Meanwhile, he reached forward to turn up the transducer's digital volume gain again.

The sound that was soon streaming through his headphones made him instantly alert. It was the distinctive whir of a pair of churning propellers. Quickly identifying it as a submarine, he activated the signature-processing unit. This high-tech device had only recently been installed, and would run the sound he was hearing through the computer's memory banks. In this way the contact's audible footprint could be analyzed and its nationality and even class determined.

Immediately after activating this system, he reached out to pick up the telephone to Command. In a matter of seconds, he was in direct contact with faroff Vladivostok. There an equally bored technician picked up the receiver. This second conscript jotted down the exact time that the contact was initially detected, and waited while the sound signature was subsequently broken down and analyzed. Three minutes later, he was able to officially record the passage of a Soviet Whiskey-class submarine into the Sea of Japan.

A quick check of the day's operational manifest showed no such boat due in the bay that morning. Though this log's accuracy was daily questioned, the conscript followed standard operating procedure and reported the discrepancy to his superior, who was in this case a warrant officer.

It had already been a hectic morning for this junior officer. With General Secretary Chernavin due to arrive in Vladivostok any minute now, there didn't seem to be enough hours left in the young day to complete the final preparations for his visit. Filing the report of the unauthorized passage of the Whiskey class vessel at the very bottom of his "urgent" file, he sent the technician scurrying back to his post, with strict orders not disturb him unless the entire American Pacific fleet showed itself.

The flight from Moscow had so far been uneventful. After catching up with his paperwork, Viktor Chernavin had passed the time either chatting with his staff or peering out of one of the "Flying

Kremlin's" windows. As he gazed down to the vast tracts of raw wilderness visible far below him, he formed a better understanding of the great immensity of the nation he ruled. This seemed to almost always be the case when duty called him way out here to the Soviet Far East.

His current means of transport was a specially adapted Ilyushin IL-76 airliner. It was packed with a variety of sophisticated gear, and Chernavin could easily run the Rodina from this vantage point if he so desired. The distant roar of the plane's four Soloviev turbofan engines had a soothing effect on him, and he sat back in his seat to put the frenzied events of the last couple of weeks into their proper perspective.

His stay at his beloved dacha in Voronkl had been most enjoyable. Though he accomplished a great deal of important work there, he did have a chance to get out alone into the woods. The snowstorm that had greeted them on their arrival soon passed. Two days later, the precipitation was completely melted and, when the skies eventually cleared, once more there was the sweet scent of spring in the air.

One of his favorite hikes took him down to the banks of the Moscow River. The birch forest was budding with new life as he followed the snaking trail that beckoned him onward like an old lover. He could just hear the river gurgling in the distance when he came across a carcass blocking the pathway.

The torn corpse was that of an adult deer. The buck had a sizeable set of antlers and appeared to have been taken down only recently. Searching it for wounds, Chernavin soon saw that the deer's entire belly had been ripped open. The blood was dry, yet the organs were still wet with fluid and were barely steaming in the cool air. He knew that its killer had to be close, and turned suddenly when his instincts warned that he was being watched.

He spotted the wolf only seconds later. The animal was perched alertly beside a clump of fallen birch limbs. It appeared to be a full-grown male that still had a good bit of blood staining the gray fur around its angled muzzle. It growled when his glance met its own. No words were needed to translate this primal message.

Once again the law of the woods had prevailed. The strong had successfully hunted and made the kill. Now it would feed to grow even more powerful. Respectful of the beast's victory, Chernavin carefully stepped over the carcass and continued down to the river. There he looked out to the surging current and sighed at the utter irony of it all.

Like the wolf, he too had decided to once more go on the hunt. The Rodina was hungry for the great prize that only a total victory over the Imperialists could bring them. Freed from the yoke of decades of military stalemate, the Soviet Union would grow to its full potential, with the entire planet alongside with it. Defense Minister Kudikov had been over-joyed to receive his blessings on the operation that would end this wasteful deadlock once and for all. Now, it only had to be implemented for all of their hard earned dreams to come true.

Seeing the wolf was a definite sign to Chernavin. His decision had been a difficult one, yet at that moment he knew without a doubt in his mind that it had been a correct one.

Not long afterward, he returned to Moscow for a busy week of meetings and planning sessions. These events had come to a head only a few hours before, when he'd boarded the IL-76 for the flight to Vladivostok. All too soon he'd know the results of his efforts. Of course, the operation still depended upon the success of one more series of tests, which he would be personally witnessing shortly. So far, his military staff seemed to be taking it for granted that their laser battle station would dispose of the descending ICBM warheads without any difficulties. Such an act was itself unprecedented, and he could only wait and see if their scientists had made the breakthroughs they had boasted of.

And if the test were indeed successful, what would follow afterwards? Chernavin shuddered to think of the answer to this question. The way the marshals had described it, their preemptive strike sounded like some kind of neat, bloodless game. A few dozen carefully placed nuclear warheads, and America would be unable to answer with a responding strike. Yet Chernavin knew otherwise. He studied their maps for hours on end, and utilized his imagination to replace the drawn red x's with individual mushroom-shaped clouds. Regardless of their strike's accuracy, hundreds of thousands would die. Many of these casualities would be right here inside the Soviet Union. While they proceeded to die a dreadful death, he and his cronies would be safe under the protective umbrella of the laser facility. Was such a thing fair? Couldn't they come up with a less costly solution?

Chernavin needed only a second to remember the face of the wolf he had seen feeding to know that there were no other alternatives. If the Rodina wanted to reach its full potential, now was the time to act. Otherwise, they might never have such an advantage again.

The giant airliner was slightly buffeted by a pocket of turbulence and Chernavin looked out the window for any signs of approaching weather. Nothing but powdery blue sky and a few distant black clouds to the south met his glance. When his line of sight angled downward, he spotted a large body of water lying on the eastern horizon. This could only be the Sea of Japan.

The intercom chimed and a steward's voice began to prepare them for their imminent landing in Vladivostok. Two of Viktor's burly security guards rose to personally check that the Secretary's seat belt was securely fastened and that his chair was in its upright position. Chernavin waved them away and returned his glance to the city passing below.

Vladivostok had grown immensely since its first days as a frontier outpost. Dozens of tall buildings gave it a cosmopolitan flair. Many of these structures were situated near the harbor area. There dozens of vessels were visible. Many of these were warships of the Soviet Navy. Feeling confident and proud, Chernavin sat back when the grinding noise of the landing gear lowering sounded beneath them. It wasn't long afterward when they touched down, with the barest of jolts. All remained seated as the IL-76 taxied over to the terminal. After congratulating the pilot on a most comfortable flight and a superb landing, Chernavin exited via an enclosed walkway.

First in line to greet him was his Defense Minister, Alexi Kudikov. After the usual hugs and salutations, the entourage was led to a line of awaiting limousines. From the airport they proceeded straight to the naval base. There they would spend the night, before embarking on the frigate *Ivan Komarov* for the short cruise southward to Posjet.

CHAPTER THIRTEEN

Ivan Koslov had certainly met his share of eccentric characters since making good his escape. He wondered if all Americans were as strange as the assortment that he had met so far. The Zampolit's latest traveling companion was a grizzled, middle-aged fellow who went by the name of Prince.

Prince was proud to be what he called a hobo. With no permanent address or employment, he made his way around the country via open boxcars such as the one they shared. Though the hobo never asked Koslov anything about himself, the political officer willingly related his tale of being a Polish refugeé. It seemed that Prince had some Polish blood on his mother's side of his family, and he invited the newcomer to share some dinner with him. Koslov instantly accepted.

The can of cold beans that they shared was like the finest of gourmet meals to the Zampolit. It was accompanied by a crust of stale bread and a tangy apple. Savoring this feast, Koslov lay back on the layer of dry straw that covered the floor. He did his best to understand the hobo's words as he went on to relate the story of his life.

The man had had a tough, tragic life. He was just the type of individual whom Communism would set free. Raised in an orphanage after his mother died, he'd never known his father. As a teenager, he'd run off to join the circus. It was at this young age that he'd been swallowed by that vice known as alcohol. Prince had subsequently lost his job, and had been a wanderer since.

As Koslov lay in the boxcar absorbing this story, the Zampolit couldn't help but wonder how many hundreds of thousands of Americans shared Prince's lonely plight. For, since being loose on the streets of the United States, he had seen little but social unrest and deviance. It had all started at Tacoma's Sunshine Mission. He would never forget the moment he'd turned the alley's corner and caught his first sight of the ragged mass of unkempt humanity gathered outside the mission's doors. This phenomenon was more indicative of some third-rate country than the so-called land of opportunity.

And how could he ever purge from his memory his experiences at Angel's Truck Stop? He had read about America's drug problem in Party literature, but little did he ever dream that someday he would actually be asked to buy such poison. How nonchalant the black dealer had seemed about the whole transaction. It was as if it were all just a game to the man. Didn't he realize that he was ruining the lives of others? How could the authorities permit such a thing to take place right in the open?

Koslov guessed that the whore that followed the dealer must have been addicted to cocaine herself. Why else would such a beautiful girl stoop to such a degradation as selling her body for money?

And now to chance upon the poor hobo only

made the picture that much more complete. America was in the midst of a social crisis, there could be no doubt about it. Much like the Rodina before the Great Revolution, the rich got richer while the poor sank lower into hopelessness and despair. For all its lofty talk, the so-called democratic United States failed to practice what its propaganda preached. This was no home of the free, no land of opportunity. Rather it was a system dominated by vast social disparity. The masses here couldn't help but be ripe for change. Holding them in line was a government that relied upon its military might to insure social control. No wonder the Imperialists desired a war with the peace-loving peoples of the Rodina. In that way they could distract their citizens from their real concerns.

Ever mindful of the cold, inhuman way in which the crew of the *Dnieper* had been taken prisoner, the Zampolit vowed to see his mission out to the very end. He stretched out on the straw mattress, and realized that with each rattle of the rails beneath him he was getting that much closer to his goal. Anxious to see the astounded faces of his countrymen when he related the startling story of his capture and escape, Koslov drifted off into a deep sleep.

In his dream he was a boy again, romping through the wheat fields that surrounded their communal farm. His father had just returned home from the Great War and peace ruled the land once again. It was while running past the golden stalks of waving grain that he viewed a figure beckoning him in the distance. Sighting this stranger instilled fear in Ivan's being, yet he approached anyway.

Gustav Limenko waited beneath a lone, craggy oak. Dressed in a black cape, the pencil-thin beady-eyed leader of Ivan's Young Pioneer group commanded the youngster to sit down and listen. The lad did so, and Limenko pulled out a drawing that held an odd, mushroom-shaped cloud on it. The elder's tone was grim as he related to his captive audience the horrors of the new weapon that the Imperialists had just invented. Able to instantly incinerate this farm and all those who lived within a thirty-kilometer radius of it, it was called an atomic bomb. It could very well kill them all. Their one hope was with Ivan.

In a heartbeat, the youngster was transferred to his bedroom. At the side of his bed was his mother, who was bent over in tears. Pacing the floor before him was Papa, his usually jovial face filled with fear and worry.

"What's the matter, Papa?" screamed the lad vainly.

Ivan's stomach was heavy as his father looked down to him and pointed. "It's the bomb, son. The Americans are on their way to attack and only you can save us."

At that moment there rose the sound of roaring jet airplanes overhead. Struggling to rise and make his way to the window, Ivan looked up and viewed a sky filled with thousands of bombers flying in formation. He knew this was the end, yet cried out anyway, "What can I do to save us, Papa? Tell me, how do I send them away?"

There was a loud metallic jolt, and the Zampolit awoke with a start. His heart was pounding in his chest, his forehead matted with sweat, as he strained to reorientate himself. He felt straw beneath his stiff body, and could hear the steady clicking of the rails in the background. Startled into reality by his nightmare, he found himself calmed by the snores of his traveling companion.

The interior of the boxcar was indistinct in the blackness, and Koslov peered out into this void in an attempt to make some sort of sense out of his vision. Yet all too soon it faded from his consciousness, as he again fell back asleep.

He awoke to find that the dawn had arisen. After rising stiffly, Koslov joined the hobo, who was squatting in front of the partially opened doorway. As the Zampolit peered outside, he found it to be a perfectly clear day. Even from this vantage point, the sun was warm and soothing. They passed by a huge, open-roofed stadium of some sort, which Ivan soon learned was the Golden Gate Fields horse-racing track. Beyond this massive structure was a vast body of dark water.

"What sea is that?" quizzed the Zampolit innocently.

The hobo chuckled. "That's no sea, pilgrim. What you're lookin' at there is San Francisco Bay."

These last words caused the hairs on the back of Ivan's neck to raise excitedly. "Then I'm there already!"

"Easy does it, pilgrim," said his calm host. "If it's San Francisco that you're wantin', then the next stop is where you'll be hittin' the road again. That will put you in Oakland. Since we'll be stoppin' at the produce market there, your best bet is to hitch a ride

310

on one of the food trucks. They'll take you over the Bay bridge and that will put you practically in the heart of the Golden Gate City."

"I can't thank you enough," said the hopeful Zampolit.

Prince shrugged his shoulders. "That's the least I can do for someone who could be carryin' some of my own blood. Take care, pilgrim. Maybe I'll be seein' ya' around the rails sometime."

The last Koslov saw of the hobo was as he slipped out of the boxcar and cautiously began his way through the rail yard. Still squatting beside the barely opened doors, the man known simply as Prince seemed a strangely dignified figure dressed in the remnants of the gray, three-piece suit. Still thankful for his help, the political officer soon sighted the produce market that he had warned of.

Koslov felt at home as he walked among the various stalls of this spacious market place. As in his homeland, there was an abundance of fruits, vegetables, livestock, poultry, and fish to choose from. Buying these wares were hundreds of scurrying customers. Seeing that each of them carried several filled sacks at their side made Koslov feel even more homesick.

In the back of one stall, the Zampolit spotted a long-haired man busy loading a van with melons. It appeared that he had much work before him and Koslov dared to approach this individual and question him.

"Excuse me, sir, but would you be taking these fine melons over the Bay bridge?"

"What's it to you, bub?" shot the worker, who

didn't even look up from his toil.

Ivan nervously cleared his voice. "Well, if you happen to be doing so, I'd be willing to work off my passage by helping you load the rest of your purchase."

The denim-clad driver looked up as if he were hearing something he couldn't believe. "Let me get this straight, amigo. All you want is a lift into Frisco in exchange for helping me load my van?"

Ivan nodded and the pony-tailed young man sized up the portly stranger and continued. "I'll tell you what, bub. If you help me unload them as well, you got yourself a friggin' deal."

Less than an hour later, Ivan found himself standing on San Francisco's Fisherman's Wharf. His back was a bit sore, but his expectations were high. The air was fresh with the sea. Surrounding him were dozens of quaint shops and thousands of bustling tourists. Many members of this crowd were foreigners. He spotted camera-toting Orientals, and heard languages ranging from German, French, and Italian, to one group that was babbling away in what sounded like Croatian. Situated amid this crowd were numerous musicians, singers, and jugglers, and on one corner he even sighted a white-faced mime. This didn't appear to be a city at all. Instead it looked as if he had arrived in some sort of strange, freewheeling circus.

In the lobby of a hotel he found a working telephone booth. The directory book had been ripped out, but as he read the plastic card that was stuck by the dial, he saw that he only had to access three numbers to reach a service that would look up any phone number for him. He felt strange about doing it, but pressed the numerals 4-1-1 anyway. He gave his request to an operator, and a computer voice gave the number of the consulate of the Union of Soviet Socialist Republics.

The weather had continued to worsen as they pushed south into the Sea of Japan. From the *Dnieper*'s attack periscope, William Carrigan took in the black line of low-lying storm clouds that covered the southern horizon. Of course, from their current depth, sixty-five feet beneath the choppy water's surface, even a passing typhoon would hardly be noticeable. But in the event that they were forced to surface, any storm would be a problem.

So far, their progress had remained excellent. Angling the scope due west, he increased its magnification, and could just make out the distant shoreline. This landfall belonged to Cape Gamova. To the immediate south of this rocky promontory was the narrow entrance to the Strait of Posjet. Carrigan's gut instinctively tightened as he remembered the last time he'd peered out to this headland. He shook his head in wonder at the strange hand that fate had dealt him.

Had he really changed that much in the past four decades? Except for the additional wrinkles and gray hairs, Carrigan still believed that he attacked each day with the same old gusto. Working constantly with a group of competent young men and women around helped him to share in their exuberance and energy. He genuinely enjoyed their presence, the way

313

he relished the time spent with the young sailors these past couple of weeks. Little did they realize that he was continuing to learn from them, even as he taught them the ropes aboard the *Dnieper*.

He imagined that his old shipmates felt likewise. Except for the daily progress sessions, he continued to see little of these veterans. This was especially true of Stan Lukowski, who was said to be sleeping and even taking his meals in the engine room. Proud of their diligence, he stepped back from the periscope well and scanned the adjoining control room. First to meet his gaze was Randall Spencer. The young Captain had been standing beside the navigation table. He looked uncharacteristically tense and worried. Carrigan nodded in awareness of his concern and Spencer crossed the compartment to join him.

"We've got a honey of a storm moving in off the coast," said Carrigan. "We might want to consider delaying our entrance into Posjet until it passes."

Spencer looked down at his watch. "Will that really be necessary? If it's all the same with you, I'm not going to rest until we get inside that bay."

"I know what you mean," returned the veteran. "We've come a hell of a long way to hold back now, but Mother Nature just might give us no other option. And, of course, there's that suspected minefield to consider. It was at this point that I slowed up the *Abalone*. We waited here almost twenty-four hours for that Jap tanker to show itself and lead us safely through both the field and that sub net."

"Unfortunately, we don't have any spare time to waste," the young officer reminded him. "If you don't mind, I'm going to have another look through that chart bin. The *Dnieper* had to be carrying some sort of schematic of these waters."

Carrigan nodded. "Be my guest, Captain. Meanwhile, I'll just keep an eye on events topside. Perhaps this weather will be calling home some of the Soviet Navy's best soon. If so, we'll follow them all the way to their front door."

As Carrigan returned to the periscope, he saw that conditions had continued to deteriorate. He was forced to raise the lens higher than he would have liked, to keep it free from the ever-rising swells. He was in the process of scanning the advancing shoreline when a familiar voice spoke up behind him.

"See anyone familiar up there, Skipper?"

Carrigan didn't have to look around to know that this question came from his XO. "That's a negative, Mr. Donner. I'm afraid that our group of Tojo's finest is long retired by now."

"If not, they're probably the owners of the automobile factories that are presently putting our workers on the unemployment rolls," said Donner.

Carrigan smiled at this. "Sometimes I wonder who won that war after all."

"I hear you, Skipper. By the way, I hear we've got some weather topside. Is it going to keep us from penetrating the strait as planned?"

Carrigan backed away from the periscope. "Have a look for yourself, Pete."

While Donner snuggled up to the lens coupling, Carrigan reached into his pants pocket and pulled out his pipe. He thoughtfully chewed on its bit while the veteran XO reached for the periscope's magnification knob.

"That storm's a nasty one all right, Skipper. If you ask me, we'd better hold up out here until it blows itself out."

"If we only had that luxury," said Carrigan somberly. "Time is a commodity that we have precious little left of. Yet, even without that storm, we're not going anywhere until we know the exact position of that suspected minefield."

No sooner were these words out of his mouth than an excited voice shouted out from the compartment's rear.

"I found it!" exclaimed Spencer. "For security's sake they've left out the adjoining landmasses, but someone penciled in the location in the upper corner. I'll bet my pension that these red x's indicate the position of those mines."

Carrigan hastily scanned the chart. "You sure better hope so, my friend. Otherwise, that retirement is going to be upon you a hell of a lot sooner than you had anticipated."

The storm blew in suddenly from the west. Since the net keeper's hut had windows only on its eastern wall, the tempest was upon Pavel Yagoda quickly and without warning. It initially struck with a gust of howling wind. Then the black storm clouds roiled overhead, to be followed by a near-solid sheet of pouring rain. Fortunately he had repaired the roof only last fall, and he survived this deluge without a single leak. There was a roaring fire in the hearth and plenty of hot tea and vodka to further take off the chill.

Seated in his favorite rocker, before the massive picture window that lined the hut's eastern wall, the seventy-one-year-old net keeper looked out to the surging seas beyond Cape Gamova. Barely visible through the veil of falling precipitation, the swells were huge and topped with frothing white caps. As an ex-Navy man who had seen his share of action, Pavel would take his current vantage point over being at sea in the storm any day of the week. Why, just looking at the smashing waves was enough to get one seasick!

The white-haired old-timer took a sip of his drink and smacked his lips appreciatively. Warm and comfortable, he passed the time remembering other storms such as this one, when he wasn't as fortunate to have solid land beneath him.

Once, in the opening days of the Great War, he had been assigned to a destroyer group with a mission to escort a convoy of merchantmen down the coast of Norway. As it turned out, the Germans were the least of their problems, for they faced storm after angry storm. They were battered by swells up to thirty feet high, but their real concern was the ice that coated their decks. Its great weight constantly threatened to capsize them. To knock it loose, the Captain had ordered the conscripts to tie lifelines around their waists and have a go at the ice with fire axes. Pavel had been one of those poor sailors sent on the dangerous, bitingly cold mission. Somehow he had survived, yet there were many of his comrades who hadn't been so lucky.

The mere thought of those adventurous days

brought goosebumps to his skin. Another sip of hot tea, spiked with a dash of fiery vodka, served to bring new warmth to his brittle bones and he sighed contentedly. He had lived through the worst that both Mother Nature and man could throw at him. And through it all, Pavel Yagoda had remained a loyal citizen, still doing his part to keep the Rodina free.

The old-timer looked back out to the raging sea, and remembered those days immediately after the war's conclusion, when he had briefly served aboard a captured German U-boat. They had been on a trial run in the Barents Sea, and still weren't rated to take the sub under. Several hours away from Murmansk, a vicious fall storm swept down from the Arctic. Designed without a stabilizing keel, the surfaced sub was tossed around like a child's toy. Pavel was trapped within the sealed contents of this vessel, which stunk of rotten food and diesel oil. He learned what it was like to vomit your very guts out, while your shipmates did the same beside you. Why, even the Captain joined in, splattering the back of the Zampolit's greatcoat with the partially digested remains of his morning meal. They had talked about that afternoon for months afterwards!

Pavel's current duty was dull in comparison to those action-filled days of his youth. Lately he had been going to sea only a few times each year, and even then it was only for a half-day's outing at the most. As net keeper, his responsibility was to insure that the automatic net-opener did its job properly. This high-tech device was in vast contrast to their previous methods of keeping unauthorized vessels out of the Posjet channel. Less than two years ago, they had operated the net the old-fashioned way, by pulling it open and shut with a specially adapted trawler. Today, they let a robot do all the work.

He certainly had to admit that he had seen great changes in his seventy-one years. Since the Great War, the world seemed to have altered its very character. Most of these innovations took place in the field of electronics. Only last summer he'd been invited to tour one of the Rodina's newest warships, which was visiting the adjoining naval base. Why, the vessel didn't even have a single gun on it! Supersonic missiles were the instruments that modern wars would be fought with. And guiding these deadly weapons to their targets were some of the most complex electronic systems he had ever laid eyes on. Of course manning these consoles was a new breed of highly trained sailors, who were more like computer technicians than the ignorant conscripts of old.

Pavel had emerged from that tour humbled and impressed. He'd returned to his hut with a greater understanding of the importance of his current duty. There could be no doubting that the Imperialists would just love to get one of their attack subs into Posjet Bay without the Rodina's knowledge. Not only could they initiate a complete reconaissance of this highly sensitive area. If they wished to initiate hostilities, they could even take out several top-of-the-line warships and submarines like sitting ducks.

Though his monotonous duty was somewhat boring, and often got on his nerves, he'd learned to pass hours at a time just by contemplating the sea before him. Much to his surprise, he'd learned that the waters had a personality all their own. This afternoon the seas were angry and full of wind-whipped fury. Yet only several hours earlier at dawn, the rising sun had illuminated a scene of pure tranquility. At that time no smashing white caps had stretched to the horizon. In their place had been a smooth sheet of unbroken water that looked more like solid glass than the liquid it really was.

At night this sea took on an identity altogether different. Nothing could be as inspiring as watching a full moon rise up over the surging bay. Once such a majestic event had actually changed the very core of Pavel's perception, and for the briefest of magical moments he had had a crystal-clear understanding of his place in the vast universe. Though such a thing could sound silly to others, the old-timer was positive that the experience had been very real. He would cherish it always.

A splattering of hailstones sharply echoed off the hut's corrugated tin roof, and Pavel anxiously stirred. Peering out into a noon sky that was almost as black as that of the night, he concentrated his gaze on the rolling swells. The wind gusted wildly, and for a second he could have sworn that he had seen a dark, elongated object break the agitated surface of the strait, approximately five hundred meters from the closed face of the net. When the swells temporarily passed and he again sighted this alien form at the bottom of a deep trough, he knew that his eyes weren't playing tricks on him. Without a second's hesitation, he reached for the binoculars that were kept draped over the rocker's left arm.

His hands were steady and he had no trouble picking out the bobbing outline of a submarine's conning tower. Pavel could just make out the rest of its upper deck before a massive wave buried the vessel in a whitish coat of frothing seawater. From what little he saw of the superstructure, he could positively identify it as one of their Whiskey-class boats. He knew this for certain, for he had served on just such a sub a mere two decades ago.

The old-timer sat forward excitedly when a pair of oil-skinned figures emerged on the sail's exposed bridge. Ducking from the fury of the waves that extended well above them, they were still able to utilize a hand-held signal lamp to relay a message in international Morse code.

The series of dots, dashes, and spaces that they so urgently conveyed told a story of tragic proportions. Not only did the poor submarine have an inoperable radio and an overheated diesel engine, but there was sickness on board to boot. Without giving their valiant plea a second thought, Pavel hurriedly stood up to hit the switch that would open the net and allow these brave sailors the haven of quieter waters.

CHAPTER FOURTEEN

William Carrigan couldn't believe how easy it had been to convince the keeper to open the net. He had to admit that, though the storm was extremely uncomfortable for the crew, its presence had made their ploy that much more believable. It would have taken an awfully hard individual to refuse their urgent request for assistance.

Once they entered the relatively sheltered waters of the strait, the relief was almost instantaneous. The waters were still choppy, yet the swells were of a far gentler nature. This allowed most of the *Dnieper*'s complement to recover from the seasickness that had possessed them during their brief trip topside.

Taking advantage of the poor visibility that had arrived along with the storm, they were able to remain on the surface for almost their entire transit through the strait. Navigation in this narrow channel could have been a problem, and there was no substitute for several good pairs of eyes to see them into the bay safely.

Finally Carrigan ordered them back down to periscope depth. Randall Spencer took his turn at the scope, efficiently marking the bearings that would lead them further toward their ultimate goal. This allowed Carrigan to position himself beside the diving console. There Helmut Keller perched anxiously, his strong hands ready to instantly retrim the boat if it should be needed.

Forty-three years before, the *Abalone* had chanced upon a pocket of fresh water in this very same portion of the bay. Deposited there by one of the numerous river estuaries that emptied themselves nearby, this unexpected current had a far lighter density than they were prepared for. As a result, the *Abalone* had become many tons overweight in a matter of seconds. Stan Lukowski had been at the trim controls at that time, and it was his cool expertise alone that had pulled them out of what easily could have been a fatal dive. Miraculously, he'd done so without causing them to breach. Such an unwanted maneuver would have been equally as fatal, for a Japanese patrol boat had been passing above them at that very same time and surely would have spotted them.

Four decades later, the tension was just as thick. Carrigan realized that they would all too soon be passing by Posjet's small naval base. This would put them only a few precious miles from the drop-off point that they desired. It was teamwork that had gotten them this far, and it would be this same united effort that would bring their mission success. Carrigan looked up and quickly checked the gauges of the helm. He took in their present course, speed, and depth, and noticed how somber the seated helmsmen seemed. He turned his glance back to the diving console and the supple hands of the muscular German.

"What do you mean, what was my mother's maiden name? I tell you that I'm a Soviet naval officer, and that my command may have very well been hijacked by the Americans!"

Red-faced with frustrated anger, Ivan Koslov felt his blood boil. Here he had gone and risked his very life to get to San Francisco, only to find that his countrymen at the Soviet consulate wouldn't even believe his story. They only looked at him the way a schoolteacher would look at a child caught in the midst of a bizarre lie.

From the very beginning, they had treated him with close-minded skepticism. Why, the KGB goon who had been sent to the hotel to pick him up would hardly even stare him in the eye! It was as if they thought he was a CIA plant or something!

To save further aggravation, Koslov told his inquisitors that he had nothing left to say until the Consul himself was there to take his disposition. But the honorable Igor Pavlovich Turiakin was presently hosting a soiree in the counsulate's ballroom and wouldn't be available until sometime later.

Koslov could hardly believe it when the consulate's beanpole of a political officer had the nerve to order him locked up in a cellar holding cell. Finding himself without the energy to fight this decision, the *Dnieper*'s Zampolit followed his thick-necked escorts without complaint.

The basement was cold and smelled of raw sewage. As he lay on the narrow, sheetless cot, he could just hear the bass line of what sounded like a disco tune in the distance. He could only surmise that this noise was coming from the cocktail party that he had been told of. Koslov grimaced at this thought. He could just imagine the wide-eyed Consul gayly making the rounds of his Western guests. Certainly every type of delicacy known to the Rodina was being served to this understanding, decadent crowd. And here he was, a hero of the people, locked away in this stinking hellhole, without even a stale crust of bread or a cup of water.

Koslov's stomach growled in protest as he remembered that all he'd had to eat that day was a piece of ripe melon. One of the cantaloupes he'd been unloading had slipped from his grasp and broken open on the van's rear bumper. Until that time, he'd eaten nothing since his simple hobo feast in the drafty boxcar. Just because he was now a hero, did that mean that he had to go and starve himself? And now for his own countrymen to treat him so disrespectfully! Was his selfless effort even worth his great personal sacrifice? Why, he was putting his damn life on the line! Didn't these bureaucratic morons realize this?

Such maddening thoughts only served to raise his blood pressure even higher. Wet drops of sweat dripped down his jowls, and even his shirt was completely matted with perspiration. Hearing the distant disco music only served to frustrate him even further, and in a vain attempt to block this music out he rolled over on his side and covered his open ear with a foul-smelling pillow. It was in this awkward position that he eventually drifted off to sleep.

Koslov was abruptly awakened by the loud squeal of a rusted metal door hinge. He pushed away the stinking pillow that still covered the side of his head, and stiffly sat up. Standing before him was a tall, immaculately dressed gentleman whose mere bearing suggested power and authority. When he spoke, his words were delivered crisply and distinctly.

"So you are the naval officer that my staff tells me of. Please pardon your initial reception, but as you well know, we must be extremely careful here. But if your incredible story indeed holds true, welcome back to the Rodina, comrade!"

Vladivostok Naval Command was located in a new, multi-storied building that overlooked the wharf area. Inside this complex all phases of the base's operations were handled. This included logistics and personnel. Chronically overworked and understaffed, many of the hundreds of professional bureaucrats who presently were on duty there were busy coordinating two diversely different events. One of these was a pure military operation, the final testing of the Posjet laser battle station. The other involved the visit of the country's highest official. Of course, there was also the Pacific Command's normal day-to-day business to contend with.

Senior Lieutenant Alexi Barykino had been the ranking investigative officer present when the top-priority, scrambled satellite transmission arrived from their consulate in San Francisco. An eighteen-year Navy veteran, Barykino specialized in security. In fact, one of the primary reasons that he was assigned to this shift was to help monitor the presence of General Secretary Viktor Chernavin.

It had already been a most trying day. Yet now that Chernavin was finally aboard the frigate *Ivan Komarov*, he could relax, knowing that for the time being their esteemed leader was safe.

The thirty-nine-year-old officer was looking forward to a long-delayed dinner break when the call from faroff California was received in Vladivostok. Naturally, it somehow found its way to his cluttered desk.

The consulate's initial request was to confirm whether or not a certain Zampolit by the name of Ivan Koslov was a current member of the Soviet Navy. This query seemed simple enough, and Barykino utilized his desktop computer terminal to search the Navy's personnel files. Whisking through over 500,000 individual names, the screen showed some three dozen I. Koslovs. Yet only one of those listed was a qualified political officer. This Ukrainian was currently assigned to the Whiskey-class attack sub *Dnieper*.

Barykino relayed this information, and in return received a somewhat fantastic report which said that this same Ivan Koslov was currently in San Francisco. To make matters even more confusing, the Zampolit was swearing that the *Dnieper* had run aground in the enemy's Strait of Juan de Fuca over two weeks before, and had been subsequently captured by the Americans. Because of a malfunctioning radio, the crew had been unable to inform Command of their misfortune, and it was only because of the Zampolit's ability to escape captivity that this tragic incident could at long last be reported.

During his time spent with Intelligence, Barykino had certainly heard his share of tall tales, but this one had to be the craziest yet. He bade the consulate goodbye with a promise to get back to them in due course, and hung up the receiver laughing.

This was just what he needed to make his day complete, he thought as he checked his watch. Deliberating whether or not he should file this report in his wastebasket, he pushed his chair away from his desk and rose to go down to the cafeteria before it closed.

He was fortunate to get one of the last meals served. The borscht was watery and the stew meatless, yet at least he now had something solid in his previously empty belly. After sharing a cup of tea with an attractive secretary from one of the accounting offices, Barykino somewhat leisurely made his way back to the desk he had been stuck behind for the past twelve and a half hours. There, sitting on the very top of his memo-laden blotter, was the strange dispatch from San Francisco.

As a veteran bureaucrat, he knew that this message would have to be dealt with eventually. He wasn't about to begin a more involved investigation at this late hour, but a little preliminary work would undoubtedly clear it off of his desk permanently.

Barykino accessed the computer to find out more about the Whiskey-class vessel *Dnieper*. He needed the latest security code to enter the naval operations files. After a bit of cross-checking, he found that this same sub was home-ported right in Vladivostok. Any additional information as to its current whereabouts was available on a need-to-know basis only.

With this channel shut down, Barykino tried a different tack. This time he asked the computer for a detailed description of all Soviet sub activity in the Pacific for the last two weeks. Beyond the standard security code, he had to enter both his name and serial number for this request to be processed. Since the resulting document was well over one hundred pages long, he asked for a scan which would pick out any mention of a vessel named *Dnieper*. The monitor beeped and displayed but a single entry.

Originating precisely ten days ago from the log of the Akula-class attack sub *Baikal*, the dispatch recorded monitoring the *Dnieper* as it entered the open ocean off the Strait of Juan de Fuca, presumably on its voyage back home. At the mere mention of Juan de Fuca, Barykino's attention sharpened. Quickly he reread the communique sent from San Francisco. Strangely enough, this fellow who said that he was the *Dnieper*'s Zampolit had also mentioned this same body of water. Yet he had made a definite point of emphasizing that their sub had ran aground well over two weeks ago — and the crew had been taken prisoner. If this was indeed the case, and Ivan Koslov was in fact telling the truth, then who had been at the helm of this Whiskey-class submarine a mere ten days ago? A tenseness gathered in the senior lieutenant's gut as his intuition flashed a warning sign. With his curiosity now fully aroused, he turned to continue the investigation with a new degree of seriousness.

Peter Lowell first began having second thoughts about volunteering to help out his boss soon after meeting Lieutenant Vince Paterson and the rest of the members of SEAL team Alpha. With names sounding more like characters from a Grade-B adventure movie, they seemed to be just the type of all-brawn, no-brains guys that he always had trouble relating to. Yet, much to his surprise, he soon found out otherwise.

Lowell immediately hit it off with Ed Sanger, the commando whose handle was Wizard. As the team's electronics expert, and its only Annapolis graduate, he had much in common with the whiz-kid from Carrigan Industries. In a way, Sanger reminded Peter of his first roommate at Caltech. It had been *his* initial idea to rig the Super Bowl scoreboard. The Wizard seemed to have the same sort of conniving mind and quick intelligence. Peter admired these traits, yet never forgot that Sanger was also a trained killer.

For the first couple of days, he had been busy getting himself familiar with the submarine. He was surprised to learn that several of the old-timers that were present on the vessel had been William Carrigan's shipmates during World War II. His boss had never said much about his exploits during the war, and Peter got to know a little more about this fascinating man that he respected so much.

He sat in on several of the training sessions that

were constantly taking place there, and they reminded him of being back in college once again. One of his favorite instructors was Peter Donner, William Carrigan's XO. The gray-haired professor had a way getting one intricately involved with the subject matter being discussed. With the help of a sharp sense of humor and a thorough knowledge of the area, the veteran made the physics of submarining sound so basic and simple. With his help, Lowell soon had a better understanding of just what systems could be monitored from the boat's control room.

Back in the *Dnieper*'s engine room, two other personable veterans gave him a quick lesson in diesel-electric propulsion. Both Stan Lukowski and Helmut Keller did their best to explain the sub's unique power-plant design. All the while, the grease-stained chiefs were constantly barking out orders to their men, who were in the midst of a hurried engine overhaul.

After getting an elementary lesson in torpedo fire-control systems from their weapons officer, Mac Brady, Lowell allowed himself to be dragged outdoors by the members of the SEAL team. It was a typical wet, windy Washington State afternoon as the team boarded a small patrol boat and cruised up the choppy waters of Puget Sound. Peter got another chance to view the immense Trident submarine that he had seen earlier, and soon found himself far away from any sign of humanity. They anchored approximately a half-mile off the rugged, tree-lined shore, and Lowell was instructed to join the team in the boat's cabin. There he was ordered to change into a set of camouflaged fatigues. Dressed exactly like his teammates now, he took in a simple briefing.

Minutes later, they were up on the wet, wind-swept deck. A black, rubber liferaft was inflated and thrown overboard. One by one, they climbed over the side and entered this fragile-looking craft. Peter rather unceremoniously slipped off the last rung of the ladder and fell into the raft on his side. Only the quick reflexes and strong arms of his waiting companions kept him from plunging into the angry waters around them.

Each man was given a collapsible, lightweight metallic paddle, and they began their way toward shore. Peter quickly learned how to utilize his oar most efficiently. Even with five men rowing, it took them over an hour to finally reach land. By this time they were thoroughly soaked. Upon reaching the narrow, rock-strewn beach, they quickly climbed out of the raft and scrambled into the surrounding tree line.

Peter had been instructed to stay on the heels of Ed Sanger. Yet, as they proceeded to hurry inland, it was all that he could do to keep up with Wizard's incredible pace. Ever thankful that he still took at least three days out of every week to ride his ten-speed, Lowell huffed and puffed and somehow kept up with his escort. This jogging went on for a good two miles, until they came upon some sort of concrete bunker set in the forest. As they approached this structure, the woods suddenly filled with the deafening blast of automactic weapons fire. It was only as he dove to the ground for shelter that Peter realized they were being sprayed with live ammo.

This exercise was repeated the following afternoon. Twenty-four hours before they were scheduled to set sail for the Soviet Union, they even did it at night. Though his bruised body ached constantly, somehow the Caltech grad persevered.

The moment that they finally put to sea was somewhat anticlimatic. For some reason Peter had been expecting to hear brass bands playing, sending them off to war. Much to his dismay, the sub pen was merely flooded and, with a minimum of on-lookers, they plunged into the waiting waters of Puget Sound under their own power.

Peter was berthed with the rest of the SEAL team in the forward torpedo room. He would never forget the moment he realized that his narrow mattress was set squarely on top of a rack of torpedoes. So much for a sound night's sleep!

For the first couple of days he had trouble with seasickness. The "puss pads" that William Carrigan had shared with him helped, but the drug they dispensed made him dizzy and groggy. The tight confines of the sub itself, and the constant smell of oil and diesel fuel, only added to his queasiness.

It took him a while, but he finally got his sea legs. For the past couple of days, he had even gotten his appetite back. Since the SEALs had little to do during the crossing but work on their equipment and do their best to exercise, chow time was something to look forward to. Surprisingly enough, the meals were quite tasty. Why, on the evening that they crossed the International Date Line, they were even served lobster tails and filet mignons. Peter wondered if the cook had found such delectables buried in the original Soviet larder.

For the last couple of days he'd noticed that the crew's usually calm demeanor was giving way to a feeling of general uneasiness. This had all come to a head earlier today, when the orders to surface had come from the control room. There must have been a major storm brewing topside, for it was all Peter could do to remain standing when they finally completed their ascent. At the complete mercy of these swells, the *Dnieper* was tossed to and fro. Peter cursed himself for having just consumed a complete meal, and he was all too soon emptying his stomach of its contents. It didn't make him feel any better to find several members of the SEAL team in the same distress.

Fortunately, their visit topside was a brief one. Yet, now that they were below the sea's surface once again, a new urgency possessed the crew. When Lieutenant Paterson ordered Alpha team to begin the final preparation of their gear, Peter knew that the time had come for them to do their thing. Though he was still a bit numbed by nausea, he didn't even find himself really nervous. Of course, he still had trouble grasping the reality of what they were about to attempt. Battle was something that he had only seen take place in the movies, and even that was carefully staged so that the good guys always were sure to win.

Peter had just finished dressing himself in his fatigues when William Carrigan ducked into the torpedo room. Looking distinguished even in his blue coveralls, the industrialist approached the corner of the compartment where the team had assembled.

"Gentlemen, I thought that you'd like to know that we've just picked up the prearranged signal from our Soviet contact on shore. We're currently maneuvering as close in to this beacon as we dare."

Vince Paterson absorbed this revelation and turned to address the strike team. "This is it, men. Mount up!"

While the SEALs began lifting the waterproof satchels in which their weapons were stored, Carrigan walked over to address the lone civilian among them. "How are you doing, Mr. Lowell? Are you going to make it?"

Peter forced a nervous smile. "It's not often that a guy like me gets a chance for a genuine adventure, Mr. C. I'd better take advantage of it while the opportunity's present."

Carrigan grinned and patted him on the arm with a fatherly touch. "You'll do fine, son. Just keep that big head of yours down, and do what Lieutenant Paterson tells you. We're relying on you to find the spots where our explosives will do the most damage. I don't have to remind you to take out that data-processing room."

Lowell mocked a salute. "Don't worry, Mr. C. I know just the places where we can hurt them the most."

"I'm sure you do, son. Hit them a good one for me!"

Carrigan stepped aside as the SEALs made their way toward the emergency hatch, cut into the torpedo room's forward ceiling. All too soon the *Dnieper* would surface, and the commandos would scramble out this hatch, deploy their raft, and be off for the shoreline. Meanwhile, the sub would return to the protective depths to await their return.

As he watched this group of young men initiate their last-minute preparations, Carrigan couldn't help but flash back forty-three years in time. Though their enemy had been vastly different, the squad of Army Rangers had faced an uncannily similar objective. Strangely enough, they had also brought along a single civilian expert.

The mere thought of his beloved Lydia caused a heaviness to gather in his stomach, for he would take to his grave his last sight of his soul mate as she slipped off into the black night. Of course, neither Lydia nor any member of the Ranger squad had ever made it back to the *Abalone*. Carrigan could only pray to God that today, forty-three years later, all involved would survive to see yet another day.

One-hundred twenty-five kilometers to the northeast of Posjet Bay, the night found Senior Lieutenant Alexi Barykino well into his investigation. Though his duty shift had long since ended, eighteen years of naval service had given the officer the instinct to know when he was on to something important. What had started out as a probable joke was rapidly turning into a possible crisis of the first degree. Yet he had still failed to find enough concrete evidence to disturb the admiral with his suspicions.

It had been the Akula-class vessel's report that had spurred him into action. Since more accurate data was unavailable to him, he had to take it for granted that the Zampolit, Ivan Koslov, was indeed telling the truth. If this fact held, then it had to be an American crew at the helm of the *Dnieper* ten days ago. Fantastic as this seemed, Barykino tried to weigh all the angles.

There was always the possibility that the *Baikal* had mistakenly identified another sub as being the *Dnieper*. Perhaps there could have been another Whiskey-class boat in the sector, one with a security clearance that kept it out of the normal operations documents. Couldn't this be the contact that the *Rodina's* newest attack vessel had chanced upon? Or maybe it was merely an American submarine, with a signature that somehow matched the *Dnieper's*. After all, Juan de Fuca was an active transit channel for a good deal of Yankee naval traffic. Yet, as attractive as these possibilities seemed, Barykino's instincts still urged action.

In order to get the hard facts that he still needed, the thirty-nine-year-old officer was relying upon his computer for help. After a variety of file searches had proved futile, he decided to proceed as if the *Dnieper* had indeed left American waters ten days ago. Regardless of the nationality of the sailors who manned this vessel, Alexi charted an imaginary course, from Juan de Fuca back to its home port. It was as he drew this route up on a computer-enhanced map of the Pacific, that his eyes went to the strait of water separating Sakhalin and the Japanese island of Hokkaido. If the *Dnieper* was indeed headed back to Vladivostok, the sub would have to pass through this vital chokepoint. Because the waters there were littered with hydrophones that recorded all traffic, proof of this passage would surely be in their possession.

Hurriedly, he addressed his keyboard. When the *Dnieper* failed to be on the list of vessels that were recently identified as having penetrated La Perouse Strait he queried for any unidentified submarine traffic that had been monitored there in the last forty-eight hours. Much to his amazement, it was from a report filed in the very building that he currently sat in that his answer came.

The dispatch had originated at Sakhalin's Aniva Port Command. As he suspected, it concerned a signature footprint recently picked up by their hydrophones. Two facts immediately caught his eye. The first was that this contact had been identified as a yet-unknown Whiskey-class vessel that had been penetrating La Perouse Strait from the east. Even more shocking was the date on which this submarine had supposedly passed. For it was exactly ten days after the *Baikal* had recorded monitoring the *Dnieper* as it left Juan de Fuca. Such a time span would allow the *Dnieper* an ample opportunity to cross the Pacific. Yet one disturbing question still remained. If it was the *Dnieper*, what nationality was its crew?

To get a proper answer, Barykino picked up his telephone and dialed the office of Admiral Tasejevo, the commander of the Pacific fleet. Though he was well aware that the admiral was currently down at Posjet with both the General Secretary and the Defense Minister, one of his aides could surely access the information that he needed. He had

338

several good acquaintances in this office. Unfortunately, none of them was currently on duty. Barykino was thus forced to speak with a dull-toned captain third-rank, who sounded as if he had been roused from a catnap.

To make matters as simple as possible, Barykino decided upon the direct approach. After identifying himself, his rank, and the office he served in, he asked the captain for the status of the attack submarine *Dnieper*.

Irritated at having been disturbed by a lowly senior lieutenant, the stubborn aide retorted that such information was privileged. If Barykino needed it so badly, he would have to go through normal channels like everyone else.

Having no time for games, the lieutenant found himself losing his temper. His face was flushed and his voice rose excitedly as he urged the aide to help him. He pleaded that the security of the Rodina could possibly be threatened. He then decided to play his trump card. Since the captain wouldn't help him, he said, he would just have to call Admiral Tasejevo directly.

The aide paused. Fearing that this crazy senior lieutenant would indeed dare disturb the admiral's peace of mind, he decided that it was better for all concerned to cooperate. He addressed his computer keyboard and found that the *Dnieper* was presently in the midst of an ultra-sensitive assignment. Since even he didn't have the authority to find out exactly where duty had called the sub, he could only tell the senior lieutenant that it was definitely still at its patrol station, somewhere near America's Pacific

Northwest, and wasn't due back in port for at least three weeks.

This was all that Barykino needed to know. Thanking the aide for his assistance, he hung up the receiver and stared out at the map of the Pacific that still graced his terminal's screen. His line of sight focused in on Vladivostok, then followed the coastline southward. At the very edge of Soviet territory, near their border with North Korea, his glance halted on an insignificant looking geographical feature: the Bay of Posjet.

While straining to clear his mind, Barykino shivered with a sudden wave of inspiration. Why couldn't Posjet be the ultimate goal of this submarine? Well aware of both the super-sensitive laser facility that lay on the banks of this bay and the high-ranking dignitaries that were currently assembled there, Barykino imagined what havoc the enemy could wreak in those waters. With this sobering thought in mind, he addressed his keyboard in an effort to learn exactly what defenses Posjet had available to hold off an attack by a submarine. Once this was determined, he gambled on a single phone call. Though he could very well be on the trail of a threat that didn't even exist, he requested immediate transport to the Strait of Posjet.

CHAPTER FIFTEEN

The full brunt of the storm had hit Lev and Tanya just as they made their way onto the crest where the wooden lean-to was situated. The rains fell so heavily that they could barely see the village of Posjet down below, or even the bay that it bordered. Since the going in such an icy downpour would be extremely slow and dangerous, Lev decided to take shelter in the dilapidated structure. The roof and walls leaked, but at least the chilling gusts were somewhat blocked.

Lev's guess was that this tempest would vent itself quickly. Tanya hoped that this would indeed be the case, for otherwise the remainder of their hike would be a wet, precarious one. It was imperative that they reached the rendezvous point by sunset. Since the bay was still at least a two-hour hike away, they couldn't tarry there long.

The wind howled and shook the lean-to's flimsy walls. Tanya reached into her backpack and pulled out the thermos. After pouring two cups of hot tea, one of which she handed to her uncle, she sipped the steaming fluid and felt its warmth radiate through her shivering body. She briefly closed her eyes and meditated on the long road that had brought her to this desolate overlook.

The weeks just passed had been extremely traumatic ones for Tanya. During this time the Movement had asked much from her, and she had yet to turn them down. The events had come to a head less than two days ago, when Grigori Kisnev revealed to her the exact date of the Premier's arrival. The senior lieutenant's untimely death at the hands of that gang of hooligans had almost kept her from getting this all-important news back to Tavricanka.

If she hadn't heard the two militia detectives questioning the concierge, she would have surely been brought in for questioning herself. Like a thief on the run, she had sprinted down the fire escape and made it to the station just as her bus was loading. This time her trip southward had had no delays.

Uncle Lev had been working in the shop when she arrived and shared the news with him. His eyes sparkled as he rushed off to inform his contact that General Secretary Chernavin would be arriving in Vladivostok presently. The furrier returned later that evening with an unusually solemn face. Over a glass of cherry brandy, he told her of the operation that had already been put into motion.

It would be the Movement's responsibility to make available an operative familiar with the Posjet region. This agent had less than twenty-four hours to make his way to a prearranged rendezvous point on the shoreline beside the Bay of Posjet, to the immediate south of the village. There, beginning at sunset and continuing every five minutes thereafter, he would aim a red-lensed flashlight out into the waters, for exactly ten seconds each time. If all went as planned, this signal would call in a group of specially trained commandos, who were presently being conveyed into the bay by submarine. Once these troops were on land, the operative would then lead them to the security fence that surrounded the laser battle station. This barrier would be penetrated and the laser facility subsequently destroyed.

Though it all sounded easy enough, her uncle warned her that this mission would be fraught with danger. Not only was this site one of the most heavily guarded in the entire Rodina. The General Secretary's presence there would put these troops into an even greater state of alert.

Well aware that Lev's fears were based on truth, Tanya asked him who this "lucky" volunteer from the Movement would be. Her uncle shrugged his shoulders and said that, as far as he was concerned, there was only one man for the mission — himself.

Tanya was quick to argue otherwise. Since the entire operation depended upon getting that operative down to the bay in the first place, sending only a single person would be a grave mistake. Anything from a twisted ankle to a misplaced animal trap could keep this individual from making his appointment. Thus Tanya advised that, for safety's sake, the Movement had to supply at least two persons to make this trip. Without waiting for his rebuttal, she volunteered herself as the second individual.

As she expected, her uncle wouldn't hear of such a thing. She had done enough for the Movement already, he argued. Risking her life for such an operation was too much more for them to ask.

It took another hour of spirited arguing, but the furrier finally gave in. He did so only after Tanya brought up her mother. Pleading that Lara would be the first to volunteer her own services if she were still alive today, Tanya begged him to allow her the honor of finally avenging Lara's tragic death. There were tears in his eyes when he nodded his head and agreed to take his niece along. His one condition was that when they eventually reached the laser facility's security fence, she had to promise to stay well hidden in the woods. This sounded fair enough to Tanya, who refilled their glasses and offered a toast to the success of their mission.

Sleep proved virtually impossible, and both of them were up and dressed well before the dawn. They efficiently assembled their gear and were soon off southward again in Lev's trustworthy truck.

As on their last trip down the peninsula, a military roadblock sent them back into the woods and off onto the footpath. The sky was cloudy, yet the trail was still dry so that they were able to make excellent progress. It wasn't until they started up the steep, rocky cliff that led to the lean-to that the rains began.

Tanya's recollection of this tangled web of events passed like a dream, and she returned to reality only when her uncle abruptly spoke out.

"Didn't I tell you that this storm would soon vent itself? My lumbago wasn't aching enough for this

344

one to be a real tempest."

Sure enough, she noticed that the heavy patter of raindrops could no longer be heard splattering on the sides of their shelter. Though the wind still gusted, she poked her head outside and scanned the southern horizon. The squall line still veiled Posjet and the bay beyond, yet it was evident that the front was moving its way quickly to the southeast. The clouds above were noticeably less ominous, and contained but a mere trace of drizzle.

"Well, my brave niece, shall we get on with it?"

Lev's simple query was all that was needed to get Tanya to crawl out of the lean-to and stretch on the muddy hilltop. Her uncle followed and pointed to the village now visible far below.

"We must be extremely cautious from here on out. Not only is the footing slippery, but we can look forward to encountering Army patrols as we continue getting nearer to the bay. Are you certain that you still want to go through with this, little one?"

She didn't give the question the dignity of an answer. Tanya silently turned to begin her way down the narrow trail that led from the crest.

The night was black, with only a few patches of clear sky visible, as the raft holding SEAL team Alpha headed toward the shoreline. Seated in its stern, Lieutenant Vince Paterson judged their progress. They had been afloat for a good quarter of an hour now. Behind them, the *Dnieper* had long since descended to safer waters.

A storm front had only recently passed, and the

resulting swells did everything in their power to hold them back. Yet the commandos handled their paddles like the experts that they were and, ever so gradually, a narrow, rock-strewn beach took form in the distance. Continuing to guide them forward was a brief shaft of dim red light that came from shore every five minutes.

The strike team leader stirred anxiously. For all his thousands of hours of practice, this would be Paterson's first real taste of actual combat. He found himself a bit nervous, and was doing his best to not convey this emotion to his men.

So far, each member of his squad had seemed to be taking his call to duty all in stride. This included the civilian, Peter Lowell. Though Paterson wasn't exactly thrilled with the idea of taking this neophyte into battle, the scientist's knowledge would make things much easier once they penetrated the installation itself. At that time each passing second would be invaluable, and with Lowell's assistance, they could place their charges without any wasted effort. Not the most physically coordinated of persons, Lowell was presently doing his best to help out with his oar.

Digging into the icy water with a paddle himself, Paterson looked up when the red light beckoned once again. He checked his luminescent wristwatch, noted the passage of yet another five minutes, and increased the pace of his stroke. The light flashed one more time before they finally hit land.

Indian was the first to jump out of the raft. Waist deep in the water, their point man guided the raft onto a relatively smooth portion of the rocky beach.

The rest of the men quickly abandoned the craft at this point. While Gator and Indian picked up the raft to hide it in the tree line, Wizard, Peter Lowell, and Paterson shouldered their sealed equipment satchels and took off to find cover. They did so behind a shelf of shoulder-high granite.

With a surgeon's precision and a gambler's speed, they assembled their weapons. Both Paterson and Wizard readied identical submachine guns, while Indian put the finishing touches on his Baretta combat shotgun, and Gator clipped the nightscope onto his specially designed M16 Colt Commando. They were in the process of mounting their explosives satchels on their backs, when Indian signaled that someone was approaching. Paterson pulled Peter Lowell down alongside him, behind the granite ledge, while the rest of the men took their own cover. The lieutenant's heart was madly pounding in his chest as he peered up over the jagged shelf and spied a familiar-looking, dim red light peering out of the adjoining forest. It was with great relief that he whistled the all-clear sign.

Caution ruled their every movement as the SEALs assembled in the cramped clearing. They stared into the darkness as the sounds of crackling underbrush announced the continued approach of their as yet unidentified guests. A full minute later, two individuals broke from the tree line.

Paterson looked on as the first figure became visible. He was a dark, heavy-set, bearded bear of a man, who wore a loose-fitting coat of fur. On his heels followed a considerably slighter figure, whom the SEAL leader was surprised to find was a woman—and a damn attractive one at that. She also wore fur, and sported short blond hair and big, dark eyes.

Quite unexpectedly, the lead figure greeted them in perfect English. "Dr. Livingstone, I presume?"

Exactly 157 feet beneath the surface of Posjet Bay, the attack sub *Dnieper* lay on the muddy bottom, its engineering systems shut down in a state of ultra-quiet. In the vessel's wardroom, two solemn figures sipped their coffees. Both William Carrigan and Randall Spencer knew that they had succeeded in carrying out their portion of the mission. Now it was up to the SEAL team to complete it.

After checking his watch for the dozenth time that hour, Spencer let out a nervous sigh. "I'll tell you, the waiting is the hardest part. I wonder if they've linked up with those operatives as yet."

Well aware of the reasons for the young officer's apprehensions, Carrigan did his best to relieve them. "Easy now, Captain. I'm afraid there's nothing left for us to do but continue to let fate take its course. From what I've seen of that strike team, if anybody can pull this thing out, those boys are the ones who can do it."

Taking heart from the veteran's coolness, Spencer shrugged his shoulders. "I guess you're right. Worrying isn't going to get them to that facility any quicker. What was it like forty-three years ago?"

Carrigan grinned. "To tell you the truth, I was as nervous as the first-time bridegroom. Of course, we were fighting a real war then. When you're up against an enemy who attacked first, you've really got no choice but to put your life on the line almost daily."

"This cold war crap really can get a bit aggravating," commented Spencer. "At least you guys knew where you stood. Today, we're not sure how far to let the Soviets push us. I can't begin to tell you how often I've been forced to hold back while the Soviets went to every extreme to provoke us into action. Why we've even had those SOBs attempt to send one of their attack subs right into San Diego Harbor. I mean, is such a flagrant move an act of war or not?"

"That's the scary part," reflected Carrigan. "Because the American people better wake up to the fact that basic Marxist ideology insists that the capitalist West will seek to destroy the Soviet State in the end. Thus they keep their entire country keyed up for this eventual conflict, and earmark over a third of all public expenditures for the military. This laser facility of theirs is only the tip of the iceberg. Even if we do succeed in taking it out, unless we come to terms with them with an across-the-board, verifiable arms freeze, it's just going to be a matter of time before they deploy an even more potent weapons system."

Spencer shook his head. "Sometimes I only wish that we could go ahead and fight this war and get it over with. My men constantly express this same frustration, and many times we find ourselves discussing what it would have been like to serve back in the forties. You've had a taste of the real stuff, Commander. Tell me, is today's mission really that different?"

Carrigan thought a moment before answering. "Not really. Except for a formal declaration of war by the Congress, we're still out here protecting our country's interests. Of course, four decades ago, our enemy was a substantially different one."

"What did the Japanese possibly have here that warranted Command sending you into this bay forty-three years ago?" asked Spencer. "After all, they had to know the great risks of such a mission. And at the time the war was almost over."

Again Carrigan briefly hesitated before replying. "You don't know the half of it, lad. If it wasn't for the *Abalone* and that squad of Rangers, the war's course could have very possibly taken a major change of direction. In a way, fate had chosen my crew for that operation long before Command had any inkling of the type of installation the bay sheltered at that time.

"It all started in the Atlantic theater of all places. The Krauts had just thrown in the towel, and because of a malfunctioning radio, the *Abalone* didn't even know that V-E Day had dawned. When a German U-boat sailed before our scope, I was set to send them on their final dive when Chief Lukowski finally got the receiver going. We learned of the surrender and proceeded to escort the Kraut boat back to the States.

"That U-boat sure was carrying some interesting cargo. It was on its way to Japan when they got word of the war's conclusion. The Krauts were transferring a dozen metal cylinders of what we later learned was enriched uranium. We also found two dead Japanese scientists. They'd committed hari-

350

kiri. There was also an extremely cooperative young German sailor by the name of Helmut Keller.

"Not long afterward, the *Abalone* was transferred to the Pacific. Little did we realize it at the time, but our mission into this bay began on the very afternoon we pulled in that U-boat.

"The Japanese called their weapons project Genzai Bakudan. We would soon call this same kind of instrument simply the atomic bomb. You see, we were not the only power on the elusive trail to unlocking the power of the atom. The Germans began work on the bomb in the 1930s, and the Japanese followed soon afterwards.

"Attracted by the natural isolation of this bay and the abundant hydroelectric power sources available here, the Japanese chose this spot to finalize work on their own atomic weapon. They hoped to utilize it in a last-ditch attempt to halt the impending US invasion of their homeland. Our Rangers put a quick end to any such dream, and there can be no doubt that their sacrifice was well worth it.

"Today, we are up against a weapons system that could very well prove to be just as important as the A-bomb. With luck we located the Soviet laser battle station on the banks of the same bay where the Japanese weapons lab once stood. I can only pray that we are as successful now as we were forty-three years ago. Otherwise our great losses during the war may all too soon be for nothing."

Randall took in this incredible narrative. It made him conscious of what the world would have been like if the *Abalone* had failed four decades ago. He couldn't help but wonder if someday they'd look back to today's mission in the same way. He looked again at his watch, and visualized the SEAL team's progress as they continued on toward their all-important goal.

The only vehicle that Alexi Barykino found available for the trip down to Posjet was a Yakolev-36 Forger B aircraft. Though he had originally requested a helicopter, the senior lieutenant had to make do with the dual-seat trainer. All of Command's choppers were presently being utilized. This was his first flight in a Yak-36, and he was impressed with the plane's VTOL (vertical take-off and landing) capabilities. It certainly would allow him to get down to the bay much quicker than a helicopter would.

They zipped southward down the coast at a speed well over 700 miles per hour. The pilot was a grim-faced young man who had greeted him with a crisp salute and was satisfied to keep the conversation at a minimum. This was fine with Barykino, who used this time to prepare for the upcoming confrontation.

It was cramped and noisy in the fighter's back seat. In the dull luminescent glow of the plane's digital control panel, Barykino looked down at the chart that lay on his lap. His first destination would be the structure at the strait's entrance. The hut was circled on his chart in red. Its inhabitant might well prove his theory one way or the other.

The Yak-36 vibrated in a pocket of turbulence left over from a storm front that had only recently passed. Alexi reached up to steady himself as the screech of the Forger's turbojet engine rose significantly. This was followed by the intercom's sudden activation.

"Lieutenant, I believe I have our goal in sight. This landing could be dangerous. Are you certain that you don't want to use Posjet's airfield instead?"

Barykino wasted no time speaking into the chin-mounted transmitter. "There is no time for that now, comrade. I must get down to that hut with all due haste."

Resigned to carry out the request of his superior, the pilot responded, "Very well, sir. I am initiating our descent presently."

The roar of the engines rose even louder as the Forger's dual-lift thrusters were activated. Braking in midair, the plane then began settling down to earth with the grace of an eagle returning to its nest. They hit the earth with a noticeable jolt, and only then did the engines lose their maddening whine.

Once the plexiglas canopy was lifted, Barykino began the somewhat awkward task of climbing down the footholds that were recessed into the plane's fuselage. After ordering the pilot to wait for him, he turned to approach the small stone hut that lay less than a quarter of a kilometer away.

The night was moonless and Alexi angled the flashlight that he had wisely brought along to illuminate the narrow pathway. As he neared his goal, he could hear the sound of crashing seawater in the distance.

Barykino finally reached the hut's front door, and firmly knocked on its scarred, wooden surface. Failing at first to get a response, he pounded even harder. Just when he feared that its occupant was out for the evening, an old man's voice came from inside.

"Hold on! I'm moving these tired old bones as quickly as they'll allow me."

A full thirty seconds later, the door creaked open. Greeting the lieutenant was a wizened, beard-stubbled old-timer whose red-flannel pajamas showed that he had been called from bed. He eyed the uniform of the man who had awakened him and asked cautiously, "And how can I help you, lieutenant?"

Alexi had learned that the old man's name was Pavel Yagoda. A decorated veteran of the Great War, this man was serving the Rodina even now in the closing years of his life. The Intelligence officer entered the hut and, after declining a cup of tea, got down to business.

"Comrade Yagoda, as keeper of the Posjet net station, you have knowledge of all the vessels that pass through this strait. I am inquiring about a certain Whiskey-class submarine that could have entered the channel sometime this afternoon."

"Oh, you mean the one with the mechanical difficulties," said Pavel thoughtfully. "If I remember correctly, their signal said something about an inoperable radio, an overheating engine, and sickness on board. Why, they arrived here during the very worst of today's storm, and with the size of those swells, it was somewhat of a miracle that I even spotted them. Those brave sailors sure must have had one hell of a case of seasickness. Though personally, I've sailed through seas even higher. Why, once when I was assigned to convoy duty in Norway, we were forced to sail through a full-fledged hurricane. Why, I could have sworn that I was going to vomit out my very insides!"

Before the veteran could continue on, Barykino said, "We appreciate your sacrifice, Comrade Yagoda, but there is one urgent question that I still have for you. Did you allow this submarine entrance into the bay?"

Pavel's creased forehead narrowed. "Why, of course I did, lieutenant. Why, it was the least that I could do for those poor, brave souls."

The old man's response turned Barykino's stomach. With yet another aspect of his incredible theory verified, he excused himself and sprinted out of the hut into the cool, moist blackness.

In the comfortable sitting room of a large house located less than a dozen kilometers from the net keeper's hut, General Secretary Viktor Chernavin accepted a hearty toast from his host. Admiral Tasejevo had been more than gracious. Not only did he open up his very home to the Secretary. He had just treated Chernavin to a sumptuous feast that included Kobe beef and fresh shellfish flown up all the way from the South China Sea. Joining them was Marshal Alexi Kudikov. The virile Defense Minister was in unusually high spirits, and had punctuated the evening with many a bawdy tale taken from his years of military service. In fact, he had just finished telling the story of the time he personally took on the entire staff of a Vietnamese whorehouse when one of the admiral's aides arrived with an urgent dispatch. The white-haired naval officer excused the messenger before addressing his esteemed guests.

"Comrades, this evening calls for additional celebration. For I have just been informed by my technicians that the final obstacle has been cleared for tomorrow morning's test. If all continues on schedule, the dawn skies above Posjet will fill with the streaking light of three separate MIRV'd ICBM warheads launched from our base at Tyuratam. With our very eyes we shall witness history as these warheads are engaged by the laser and destroyed."

"This glorious update gives us but another reason to raise our glasses in toast," said Chernavin. He made certain that all present had a full glass of champagne before continuing. "To our beloved Motherland! May her brave citizens sleep soundly knowing that their great sacrifices shall not be in vain."

As each of the three took a sip of their drinks, Marshal Kudikov rose to offer the next toast. "And to the great foresight of our illustrious General Secretary, who has taken it upon himself to authorize the operation whose success will change the very course of history!"

Knowing full well what the Defense Minister was referring to, the General Secretary met this toast with a polite nod. After emptying his glass, Chernavin walked over to take a seat before the blazing fireplace. With his gaze locked on the burning embers, he allowed himself a moment of silent introspection.

Through all the excitement of the past few days, Chernavin had found one thought constantly at the back of his mind. It had become especially evident when he was in the midst of his tour of inspection at the nearby naval facility at Vladivostock. As he examined the rows of gray warships and black-hulled submarines that lined the wharves there, he realized that these same vessels would spearhead their surprise attack on the US. His short cruise down to Posjet aboard the *Ivan Komarov* gave him an even better chance to meet the sort of men who would be called upon to launch the first strategic warheads. He found that it was one thing to ponder such an attack from the isolated confines of his dacha at Voronkl. It was something altogether different to actually see the hardware and shake hands with the men they would be relying on for success.

Up to the moment he'd landed in Vladivostok, the attack plan had been nothing but an impersonal series of charts, tables, and reports. The second he'd entered the base and set his eyes on much of the reality behind the data, the operation had taken on a new perspective. For many of these men would never return from their missions, while others would survive only to find their families incinerated by America's vain attempt to counterattack. Would these brave sailors approve of his difficult decision then?

Chernavin sighed and focused his gaze further into the sizzling embers. For better or for worse, he had made his decision. Though some historians might judge him harshly, others would understand that he had dared to take a chance for real greatness. Risk was part of any dare, and few could question the utter sincerity of his motives. With capitalism no longer present to constantly hold them back, the Rodina would at long last accomplish the goals that her original founders had envisioned. The entire world would thus benefit.

The logs hissed and crackled, and Chernavin took strength in the fact that he was only applying the lesson that the wolf had taught man from the beginning of recorded time. Ultimate survival was only for the fit and the pitiless. A successful hunter knew this instinctively, and thus insured the continuation of its species.

CHAPTER SIXTEEN

It took them less than thirty minutes to get to the fence that surrounded the laser facility. Along the way, they'd encountered but a single patrol. Indian was quick to hear their approach and beckoned the others to take cover. This group of sentries was comprised of a squad of young conscripts from Soviet Georgia. Only recently transferred from this southern province, they made the mistake of vocally expressing their dissatisfaction with the cold. It was this chatter that gave them away. Soon afterward, Alpha team reached the security perimeter.

One of the local trappers from Tavricanka had told Lev Litvov about the drainage tunnel. Cut beneath the fence to reroute a brook that meandered through the southern portion of the base, the pre-fabricated concrete tunnel could be penetrated during times of low water by a man on his hands and knees. Though this stream was most likely running full after the recent storm, Lev had no alternatives. It was rumored that the fence was electrified and implanted with sensors.

While the Americans checked out this possible entryway, the furrier took his niece aside to enforce her portion of the bargain. "Now, this will be as far as you'll be going, little one. Wait for us near these bushes. We won't be gone long."

There was a heaviness in Tanya's chest as she looked up into the kind face of her guardian. "Oh, uncle, are you certain that you won't be needing me?"

"Absolutely not!" responded Lev firmly. "You've had a chance to check out the men who will be accompanying me. Don't worry, little one. I will be in excellent hands."

Suddenly remembering one other thing, the furrier reached into his breast pocket and extracted a hand-sized leather wallet. "I almost forgot one small item that I wanted you to hold for me while I'm gone, little one. Keep it near your heart and it will bring me peace wherever I go."

Tanya reached out for this object and was about to open it when her uncle stopped her. "Please, not now, little one. At least wait for my return. Now, I'd better get back to the others. Take care of yourself, my precious."

This goodbye was delivered with such emotion that Tanya couldn't stop crying. She hugged the massive furrier and whispered adoringly in his ear, "May God be with you, Uncle Lev. Please make it back safely."

He kissed his niece firmly on each cheek and swallowed her with his gaze, before turning and walking off quickly. Tanya cautiously followed him, and emerged at the clearing beside the fence just as the commando leader was in the process of briefing his men.

"It's going to be a little wet, but we should be able to make it. Now, what do you say about crashing this party?"

The others grunted anxiously. Yet one sandy-haired young soldier, who somehow didn't seem to fit in with the others, turned toward Tanya and asked, "What about the girl?"

Lev was quick to respond. "My niece will be staying out here. Inside, she will only get in the way."

Seemingly satisfied with this answer, the young man took a long last look at Tanya while the others began moving.

"For Christ's sake, Lowell. Are you coming or not?" said a hushed voice from the group.

With this, the scholarly-looking commando politely nodded and turned to rejoin his companions.

Tanya watched them as they climbed down a fairly steep bank and entered the stream bed. The water was well over their calves as they ducked down and disappeared into the blackness.

It was suddenly very quiet, and for the first time that evening Tanya felt fear. An owl mournfully hooted in the distance, while a cool breeze gusted through the limbs of the ancient pines that surrounded her. Feeling scared and alone, Tanya nervously fingered the leather wallet that her uncle had given her. Remembering his request, she slipped it into the breast pocket of her sweater without daring to open it.

Meanwhile, as Tanya slipped into a thick clump of bushes to begin her anxious wait, Peter Lowell did his best to keep up with the others. The tunnel that they were currently crawling through was little more than a sewage pipe. Forced to proceed on his hands and knees, Peter found that the numbingly cold water covered most of his legs, arms and torso. Only his back and head remained dry. The big Russian that he was following had trouble making it through the tight confines easily and, though the tunnel didn't extend for a great distance, Lowell was forced to endure the wet, uncomfortable conditions longer than he would have liked to.

The air seemed much colder when they eventually crawled out of the cramped passageway. Waiting for them on the banks of the brook were the men of Alpha team. Wizard signaled them to take cover. When a dog growled close by, it took both Lev and Peter only seconds to flop belly-first into the thick mud that lined this portion of the stream.

It seemed to take an eternity for the sentry dog and its handlers to move on. Indian softly whistled the all-clear, and the men gathered behind a newly fallen tree trunk. Lev and Peter were so covered with mud that they were hardly recognizable, except for the Russian's great girth. While the SEALs readjusted their backpacks and inserted dry ammo magazines into their weapons, Vince Paterson pointed into that section of forest that lay immediately before them.

"That portion of woods seems to be less frequently traveled. Will that get us close enough to our objective, my friend?"

The furrier replied while peeling the caked mud from his beard. "The trapper who scouted these woods for us said that the main installation lies to the northeast, a good kilometer from the stream. Since the direction in which you point lies due north, it should serve us well."

"Then, if there aren't any party poopers, let's do it, gentlemen. Indian, to the point. Gator will follow, with Wizard and Lowell behind. I'll take up the slack along with our muddy host here. Keep an eye peeled for sensors and keep off those triggers unless it's absolutely do or die. Do you read me?"

No response to Paterson's directive was needed as the men snapped into action. With memories of their brief excursions into the woods of Washington State fresh in his mind, Peter Lowell fell in on the electronics specialist's heels. His fatigues were soon dry and the very haste of their advance brought new warmth to Lowell's previously chilled bones.

With a minimum of double-tracking, they continued to the north. Except for several portions that were covered with a thorn-encrusted, knee-high shrub, the forest floor was generally free from debris. Twice they had to halt to let patrols pass. Each time the sentries who made up these patrols walked by carelessly. Their loud chatter was ceaseless. Much to Alpha team's good fortune, none of the patrols had dogs.

Lowell had managed to get accustomed to their pace, and proceeded without hardly even losing his breath. He found his night vision sharpening, and got a certain thrill just knowing that he was actually hiking the woods of the Soviet Far East. With thoughts of his sedentary existence back in the States a world away, he stirred when a soft bird whistle came from the forest before him. Able to pick out Indian's signals by now, the scientist followed his escort to a stand of thick pine trees. Clearly visible ahead was a bright spot of light, piercing the darkness like something alien. It was their point man who explained what lay beyond.

"I believe we've hit pay dirt, lieutenant. There's a complex up there with all sorts of buildings in it. The only problem is that the place is just crawling with unfriendlies."

Paterson took in Indian's assessment and somberly shook his head. "Nobody said that this would be easy. We can always set up a diversion while Gator and Wizard lay down the charges. Yet that still leaves us without knowing which structures house the really vital gear. Somehow we have to get our Mr. Lowell in so that he can earn his keep."

No sooner were these words said when the sound of distant voices sent them diving for cover. Two sentries were soon visible walking on the other side of the tree line. One of these individuals was tall and heavy-set, whereas his companion was slightly built in comparison. As it turned out, the idea popped into Vince Paterson's head at about the same time that it dawned on Lev Litvov. Without bothering to share his inspiration with Peter Lowell, Paterson sent out two of his men to do their thing.

With barely a peep of protest, both sentries went down with cleanly broken necks. Carrying their inert bodies back into the woods, both Gator and Indian dumped the corpses rather unceremoniously at their leader's feet. This was Peter Lowell's first close-up look at a dead man and he had little time for squeamishness as Paterson addressed him.

"Well, Mr. Lowell, does the little one here appear to be your coat size?"

A quarter of an hour later, the Caltech grad found himself walking into the well-lit complex dressed in the uniform of a Soviet Army corporal. Ambling commandingly at his side was "Sergeant" Lev Litvov. Peter valiantly tried to keep the fear from his eyes, yet inwardly he was a nervous wreck. Keeping his glance averted whenever possible, Lowell relied upon his confident escort to make good their daring ploy.

Lev returned the greetings of a passing three-man patrol and led Peter down a narrow, asphalt-paved street. One-story aluminum-paneled structures lined both sides of this thoroughfare. The muted hum of machinery came from nearby. This buzzing whir became even louder when the door to one of the buildings they were passing slid open and a pair of white-smocked technicians exited. Before the door automatically shut itself, Lowell was able to get a quick view of the assortment of equipment that lay inside. Most of it was extremely familiar.

It reminded him of a similar building that graced the grounds of the Lawrence Livermore Laboratory, and the young scientist quickly identified the Soviet facility's generator station. This was confirmed when they passed a snaking mass of thick cables that led from this structure to an adjoining one. There two armed guards stood before a reinforced entranceway. In order not to raise their suspicions, Lev increased the pace of their stride, yet not before Peter was able to spot a dome-like form set into this building's roof. He knew that this had to be where the laser itself was stored.

In quick succession they passed by the installation's phased-array radar site—where the targets were tracked, another power plant, and finally the all-important data-processing station. Only after he was certain that he had each vital location memorized did Lowell signal his escort that he had seen enough. They turned to retrace their steps just as a low-flying jet aircraft roared loudly overhead.

From the back seat of the Yak-36 fighter, Senior Lieutenant Alexi Barykino peered downward at the passing conglomeration of buildings visible below. Even from his present height, it appeared that their security was tight. Dozens of patrols could be seen walking the narrow streets, while the compound itself was completely surrounded by a well-lit buffer zone. Yet, even with this in mind, he couldn't help but feel apprehensive.

The net keeper's revelation had only made his bewildering theory that much more plausible. He could thus only assume that if this phantom submarine was indeed the *Dnieper*, its purpose was to somehow destroy the facility that he currently flew above. Most likely the Imperialists would make such an attempt by landing one of their infamous Special Forces teams. Yet how they planned to penetrate the Soviet ground defenses was still a puzzle to him.

But his job was to take nothing for granted and to follow every possibility through, no matter how absurd it might seem. Though he could very well be worried over nothing, Barykino had to see this thing out to the end. After all, his investigative instincts had never let him down before.

The senior lieutenant looked down at his watch, then looked forward as the pitch of the Forger's engines rose. He exhaled in relief upon spotting the airfield below.

The plane landed near the control tower and Barykino rushed from the cockpit, as soon as the canopy was raised. Waiting for him on the ground was a short, mustached colonel, whose bored glance showed his indifference. The lieutenant saluted.

"Thank you for meeting me here, colonel. It is imperative that you inform your sentries assigned to the laser facility that a group of American commandos could very well be on their way into the compound, even as we speak."

Little moved by this emotional disclosure, the colonel commented calmly, "Easy now, lieutenant. Our security details always operate with just such a possibility in mind. Now why don't you take a moment to explain just what has led you to such an incredible supposition."

Ever aware that each passing second could lead the enemy that much closer to their goal, Barykino strained to answer his host politely. "Of course, colonel. But would you mind if I did so while we continued on to the base itself? I won't be able to rest until I see that complex with my own eyes."

Shrugging his shoulders, the colonel waved his driver to pick them up. They piled into the Zil sedan. As they turned towards the laser facility the lieutenant began his tale, beginning with the initial phone call from their consulate in San Francisco.

He finished explaining what he had learned at the net keeper's hut as they pulled up before the structure housing security. Before exiting, the colonel thoughtfully looked at his guest and spoke firmly.

"This is all very fascinating, lieutenant, but you still lack any concrete evidence. Not only would it be virtually impossible for an American crew to sail one of our subs across the Pacific on such short notice. It would be equally as difficult to penetrate this facility. I appreciate your effort. To ease your needless concerns, I shall give you the services of one of my crack squads of sentries. They will be happy to make the rounds with you."

Relieved that the colonel had not dismissed him altogether, Barykino's tone lightened. "Thank you, sir. Let's just hope that my ramblings are indeed foolishness. Before I initiate these rounds, can I assume that General Secretary Chernavin is safe and sound?"

At this the colonel grinned. "My, aren't you the worrying type! With a mind like yours, you should transfer to the KGB, comrade. Now, get on with your urgent inspection. The safety of the General Secretary will never be compromised!"

Knowing that he had already asked too much, Barykino humbly backed down. For a lowly naval officer to twice question the security arrangements was flirting with trouble. Quite happy to have the services of the squad of sentries, the lieutenant again thanked his host, and then went off to meet with them at the compound's armory.

As promised, the four-man team was waiting for him by an open four-wheeled vehicle. Three of them had Kalashnikovs strapped to their backs, while their leader carried one of the new AKS-74 assault rifles. They greeted him politely and invited him to take a seat in the forward passenger position so that their tour of inspection could begin.

With a minimum of conversation, they traveled up and down the compound's narrow roadways. The streets were laid out in a general east-west pattern, cutting through the four dozen or so structures that comprised the facility itself. They passed many other patrols, and Barykino could see that the situation indeed appeared to be well under control.

But as they drove down the wide stretch of open space that lay between the structures themselves and the woods beyond, a series of small explosions sounded behind them. This was followed by a rapid, staccato burst of small-arms fire. Barykino's gut instantly soured as he reached out for the automatic pistol in his holster. With a grinding screech, the driver reversed their direction, and the vehicle sped off to see what this disruption was all about.

A hushed tenseness possessed the *Dnieper*'s control room as Randall Spencer issued the orders sending the vessel to its periscope depth. Helmut Keller's steady hands were on the ballast controls. With a series of precise movements he vented several tons of seawater from the ballast tanks. Substantially lightened, the sub lifted off the muddy bottom of the bay and began to ascend.

William Carrigan stood beside the periscope well, with one eye on the depth gauge and the other on the clock. If all went as planned, the charges that the SEALs had left behind would be detonating any moment now. This would hopefully give them just enough time to get back to the *Dnieper* before the dawn broke.

Carrigan knew that any number of things could keep the commandos from succeeding. Surely the odds were far from in their favor. Not really having any idea what would greet him when the periscope broke the water's surface, he could only continue to pray for the best.

Acting as the current diving officer, Peter Donner called out each ten-foot increment of their rising depth. It seemed to take the XO an eternity before they reached the seventy-foot level. Carrigan waited for another five feet to click off the depth gauge before ordering, "Up periscope!"

The veteran snuggled up to the lens coupling and turned the scope due north. This allowed him to scan the shores of their objective as soon as the lens broke free from the waters of Posjet Bay. He found himself unprepared for the amazing sight that soon greeted him.

Like a scene out of Dante's *Inferno*, the entire shoreline seemed to be engulfed in flames. Reflected off the surrounding seas, this conflagration rose high into the night sky. Smoke billowed upward in abundance, and Carrigan could see that the fire was continuing to spread among the surrounding trees. His heart was pounding proudly in his chest, and only when a voice called from behind him did he realize that he had not yet shared this sighting with the others.

"Well, Commander, what's out there?" questioned Randall Spencer expectantly.

Somehow managing to hold back his discovery, Carrigan backed away and beckoned Spencer to have a look for himself. The young officer did so and excitedly screamed out, "My God, they've done it!"

Carrigan grinned widely as a chorus of cheers broke from all those present. Peter Donner had to remind them that a state of ultra-quiet still existed, yet this didn't stop the sailors from celebrating in their own way. High-fives and smiles were exchanged, and even the usually sedate Helmut Keller got into the act. The rest of the crew were notified, and the *Dnieper*'s entire complement gloried in their victory.

Looking back to the wall-mounted clock, Carrigan calculated the time left until dawn. Conscious that their triumph wouldn't be complete until the men that were responsible for this fire were safely back on board, he walked over to navigation to take one last look at the rendezvous point. There he was joined by Lieutenant Monihan. Together they checked, then double-checked the prearranged coordinates. Only when he was absolutely certain of their accuracy did the veteran order the *Dnieper* forward, powered by the silent surge of her electric motors.

The minutes left until dawn seemed to pass all too quickly. A familiar tenseness returned to the control room as the men anticipated the arrival of SEAL team Alpha. This anxiety was most apparent at the periscope as well. There, for the past half-hour, Randall Spencer had completely scanned the surrounding waters every five minutes. With his back bent to keep the lens of the scope as close to the bay's surface as possible, the young officer tirelessly peered out onto the smooth waters, seeking any sign of his countrymen. Carrigan noted his effort and approached with an offer of relief. Though Spencer initially refused, a mug of coffee proved to be enough of an incentive to convince the young, dedicated officer to take a breather.

Carrigan took his place at the scope and turned his line of sight to the shoreline. The flames still blazed with an uncontrollable fury. With the gradual coming of dawn, the volume of smoke was only that much more apparent. Certain that they had dealt the facility a fatal blow, Carrigan turned his attentions back to the bay's surface. He searched in vain for any sign of the red flashlight that would indicate the team's approach. Failing to spot this signal, he resumed his scan, haunted by the similar vision of empty seas that had been with him for the last four decades. For somewhere in the blackness along with the SEALs were a squad of Army Rangers and his beautiful Lydia. He prayed that Strike Team Alpha wouldn't share their fate. Suddenly the sonar called out in warning, "We've got a surface contact, bearing zero-six-zero! Range is twelve thousand yards and closing. It sounds like some sort of patrol craft."

Cursing at this report, Carrigan stared into the lens coupling with renewed intensity. Now that his greatest fears had come to pass, he faced the question he'd kept at the back of his mind, refusing to let it surface. Would he be forced to abandon his countrymen today as he had forty-three years ago?

Once again the voice of the sonar operator shouted out in warning, "We've got another surface contact, bearing two-eight-zero, sir! Range is thirteen thousand yards, but this one's coming in with a bone in her teeth!"

Carrigan's pulse quickened as he hurriedly calculated the little time they had left. Feeling hopelessly impotent, he was just about to relay the orders sending the *Dnieper* back into the silent depths when a flickering pin-prick of red light broke from the nearby waters. Rubbing his weary eyes to make certain he wasn't seeing things, Carrigan not only saw the red light, but the bare outline of a raft as well. He shouted immediately.

"We've got them! Emergency ascent! Get that deck party topside the moment we break water. We're going to have just enough time to retrieve them before pulling the plug, so move it!"

The sound of venting ballast surged in response, and the *Dnieper* angled up toward the surface. Still able to utilize the scope, Carrigan switched it to maximum power. In the gathering light of dawn, he took in the raft's paddling occupants. Much to his relief, Peter Lowell was visible, perched precariously on the raft's stern. Yet try as he could, Carrigan could spot only a single blond-haired passenger, with fair skin and a slight figure that could only belong to a woman.

Viktor Chernavin had only just lain down to get some rest in preparation for the morning's activities when the first explosion literally knocked him from his bed. Stumbling to his feet, he managed to get to the window just as his two security guards came bursting into his room. Relieved to find the General Secretary uninjured, they joined him at the window, and took in a scene of fiery devastation.

The residence they currently occupied was less than a kilometer away from the compound holding the laser facility. Yet even at this distance, they could still feel the heat from the great flames that flickered high into the night sky. When a series of secondary explosions rocked the installation, his bodyguards convinced him that his exposed position was just too dangerous at the moment. Taking their advice, he hastily slipped on some clothes and followed his men out to a waiting car. This put him on the opposite side from the compound. But Chernavin merely had to look to the horizon to see the ghostly light produced by the rising flames.

As the Secretary prepared to enter the black sedan, two familiar figures darted toward him from the house. He recognized them as being his Defense Minister and the Commander of the Pacific fleet. Marshal Alexi Kudikov appeared uncharacteristically confused, and wore only part of his uniform. Beside him, the silver-haired admiral, who was still dressed in red-satin pajamas, looked equally as rattled. Chernavin delayed entering the car in order to greet them.

"Good heavens, comrades, what in the world is occurring out there?"

As if to emphasize this question, another explosion sounded in the distance. This was followed by the faraway, howling whine of sirens from various emergency vehicles.

Clearing his throat, and doing his best to tuck in his shirt, Marshal Kudikov offered an answer. "It must be some sort of technical problem. Surely our men will have it under control shortly."

Another explosion roared, and this time it was the admiral who meekly added, "The Marshal is right. When dealing with high-tech equipment, such things can happen. Most likely it's only a generator that somehow shorted out and then caused a fire. We will have it out in no time, and perhaps then our test can proceed as scheduled."

"I doubt that, comrades!" said a deep voice from the blackness.

All eyes turned to the side of the residence, where a uniformed figure was suddenly visible, steadily approaching them. With his face blackened with soot and his naval greatcoat torn, this individual continued on as the Secretary's guards ran to intercept him with their pistols drawn. Chernavin sensed that this man meant them no harm, and called his men off just as they reached his side. Seeing this, the figure solemnly nodded.

"Thank you, Comrade General Secretary. Senior Lieutenant Alexi Barykino at your service, sir."

Instantly trusting this officer's sincerity, Chernavin waved him forward. "Now perhaps you can tell us all something about this disaster that has yet escaped us?"

The senior lieutenant couldn't help but smile at

this. "I certainly can, sir. I will start out by emphasizing that this holocaust was definitely not caused by a mere accident. This disaster was carefully planned and carried out by operatives from the United States of America!"

Several secondary explosions roared in the background, yet Viktor Chernavin focused his attention entirely on the naval officer's dark gaze. Again sensing his legitimacy, the General Secretary took him aside and quickly learned the shocking story of the *Dnieper*'s tragic hijacking. Only when Alexi Barykino was completely finished with his incredible narrative, did Chernavin beckon his aides to join them.

While the Senior Lieutenant repeated his story, Chernavin slowly walked away. Standing on the sloped, gravel driveway, with his gaze locked on the still-blazing horizon, he vainly attempted to make some sort of logical sense out of this inconceivable story that sounded more like pure fiction than fact.

The one thing that couldn't be doubted was the senior lieutenant's utter belief in his own theory. The young man seemed bright and in complete control of his wits. As he followed the trail all the way from Vladivostok, Barykino had been prompted totally by his own initiative. This was the type of service that Chernavin most respected. Surmising that the naval officer could have indeed stumbled onto a clandestine mission of fantastic proportions, the General Secretary knew that it still wasn't too late for the Soviet Union to gain the advantage. For, though they might have lost the services of the laser battle station, an even greater propaganda coup awaited them if they could capture this American crew red-handed. Then the world would only have to see these pirates, and the pictures of the destruction they caused, to know that the peace-loving peoples of the Soviet Union had once more been the innocent victims of bloodthirsty Imperialism. The public outcry would be deafening, and the Rodina would win a major victory without having to fire a single shot. Relishing this thought, Chernavin turned to delegate the challenging task of capturing the ones responsible into the capable hands of Senior Lieutenant Alexi Barykino.

CHAPTER SEVENTEEN

After concluding a sixty-day patrol off the enemy's coastline, the crew of the Akula-class attack sub *Baikal* looked forward to entering their own territorial waters once again. There would be a quick ceremonial stop at the naval base at Posjet, before returning to their home port of Vladivostok for a much-needed refitting.

The Captain knew the waters they were currently sailing through well, for he had been at the helm of the *Baikal* when she underwent her preliminary sea trials right here in the northwestern portion of the Sea of Japan. Those had been exciting days, and he would never forget how thrilled he was about the boat's performance. This same excitement still returned every time he took his place in the vessel's attack center. With its digital consoles and flashing computer terminals, the *Baikal* appeared more like some sort of space ship than an object bound to earth. With this comparison in mind, the seasoned senior officer approached the communications station.

From this console the coded stream of data would be transmitted that would automatically trigger Posjet's sub net. Only then could they enter the channel and relax, knowing that they were at long last back in the Rodina.

The signal indicating an incoming transmission arrived in the net keeper's hut with a distinct electronic buzz. This had already been a morning the memory of which Pavel Yagoda would take to his grave. First there had been the frantic arrival of that senior lieutenant from Naval Intelligence. Not sure what the young man was getting so flustered about, Pavel could only guess that it concerned that poor Whiskey-class submarine that he had let in earlier. The old-timer had only just returned to his bed when the first explosions sounded in the distance.

The top-secret installation at Posjet was rumored to hold some type of newfangled secret weapon, and it was subject to frequent tests. Yet the sharp, bass tones that met Pavel's ears were strangely familiar. They reminded him of the sound of raw explosives. He jumped from his mattress with the impression that a real battle was taking place close by. This was startlingly confirmed when he opened his front door and found much of the western horizon engulfed in faraway flames. It was not long afterward that the receiver began buzzing.

Fearing that an actual war had broken out, Pavel made his way quickly to the monitor to confirm the legitimacy of this code before allowing the net to open. If an enemy had indeed attacked, he would have to take extra care to personally check out all incoming vessels. He put the automatic opener on manual override, and did his best to double-check this incoming data with his computer's memory banks. His hands were stiff with arthritis, and his progress was thus slow, yet with a painstaking effort he persevered. Only after verifying this code as indeed belonging to the Akula-class vessel *Baikal* did he trigger the switch which would swing the net open.

The old-timer was satisfied that he had done his duty well. Still puzzled though by the explosions that had rocked the opposite end of the bay, he decided to put a call into Command in an effort to learn their source. He had just put on his tea kettle and was in the process of walking over to the telephone when it began ringing. The wizened veteran picked it up on the third ring.

Addressing him on the other end of the line was the firm voice of Senior Lieutenant Alexi Barykino. The young officer, whom he had encountered only hours before, issued a series of frantic directives. He emphasized that under no conditions was Pavel to allow the net to be opened unless he was under Barykino's direct orders to do so.

Somewhat hesitantly, the net keeper remarked that he had only just opened the channel to allow an Akula-class submarine to enter. The senior lieutenant cursed, and pleaded with the old-timer to close it again as soon as this vessel was clear. Vowing that he would do just that, Pavel hung up the phone and made his way back to the computer terminal. He allowed himself a breath of relief only after finding that the net had already resealed itself.

By the time he had disconnected the automatic program, so that the net could only be operated by his own command, Pavel's water was boiling. Satisfied that he had already done a day's work and then some, he made himself a cup of extra strong, black tea. As he sipped this steaming brew he remembered that he had forgotten to ask the senior lieutenant what all those explosions had been all about.

Chief sonarman Toni Mariani had been a member of the *Stingray*'s crew for a little more than two months when the orders arrived transferring them to the *Dnieper*. Before this time, he had been a sonar operator aboard one of the newest Spruance-class destroyers. This was a career that the slight, curly-haired twenty-one-year-old had aimed for since he was a youngster. As he grew up in the Williamsburg section of Brooklyn, the idea of escaping the confines of the crowded city, to sail the adventurous high seas, had greatly appealed to him. It had called him so that, the very day he graduated from high school, he had enlisted in the Navy.

During his entrance examinations he learned that he had abnormally sensitive hearing. He had always prided himself as being a music lover, and seemed always to be the one to complain if the stereo had a cracked speaker. Now he knew why he could pick out minuscule distortions and his buddies could not.

To take advantage of this God-given gift, he accepted a position in sonar school. This decision allowed him to take his first trip to San Diego, and he gloried in the California sunshine. This was especially appreciated since it was winter back in Brooklyn, with the usual icy winds and drifts of dirty snow.

He graduated in the top tenth of his class. This gave him practically the first choice of open duty slots. When he learned that a new Spruance destroyer needed the services of an additional "sound man," he immediately applied. Much to his surprise, he got the position.

Two years in Hawaii passed like a dream come true. The islands cultivated a pace of their own, and during every leave he was quick to go native. Why, he even had an Oriental lover, whose curvaceous figure and sensuous, caring ways drove him absolutely crazy.

Harsh naval reality brought him down to earth on the morning that he received the orders sending him back to San Diego. Though he certainly would miss Hawaii, and the high-tech environs of the Spruance's CIC, he found himself sort of looking forward to his new assignment aboard the USS *Stingray*.

Toni was soon to learn that submariners were a breed apart. This was especially true of the *Stingray*'s handpicked crew. As one of the last of her type, the diesel-electric vessel was a living reminder of the pre-nuclear age. Powered by good old-fashioned fossil fuels, her auxiliary equipment was top notch. This included the sub's sonar gear. Using this system for both offensive and defensive purposes, the crew depended upon sonar for their very survival. Toni was proud of this fact, and worked even harder to be the best at his craft that he could.

He was just getting the feel of the *Stingray*'s sensor arrays when the reassignment sent them to the *Dnieper*. The youngster had to admit that he was at first intimidated with the idea of sailing inside a Russian submarine. Not only was the equipment alien, but there was something spooky about taking off in one of the enemy's own vessels. Peter Donner soon taught him otherwise.

The veteran XO took extra time with him to explain the exact nature of their upcoming mission. With the additional help of both Chief Keller and Captain Spencer, Toni got a better understanding of just how the Soviet sonar gear differed from their own. Once the consoles were relabeled into English, he learned that the two systems were in many ways similar. This was especially the case with the *Dnieper*'s passive hydrophone array.

It was this series of hull-mounted, ultra-sensitive microphones that Toni was presently monitoring. His shift had already been a long one, yet he dared not move an inch from the console. The Captain had made it quite clear that their very lives could be in his hands these next few minutes. Stimulated by a mug of strong, black coffee, he carefully scanned the waters before them. It was at this exact moment that he picked up both the sound of another advancing submarine and the distinctive grating squeal of the closing sub net. Hurriedly, he turned to inform the Captain.

Spencer was immediately at his side. Trusting Toni explicitly, he ordered their forward speed to be cut to a mere crawl. The sonarman knew this was so that the vessel that was about to pass them on their port side would be unable to detect their presence. Since it was extremely unlikely that this sub would resort to active sonar right here within the protective confines of its own channel, cutting the *Dnieper*'s sound signature was as good as making her invisible.

Toni listened intently to the surging cavitational hiss of this boat's propellers. Finding it rather hard to believe their current circumstances, he anxiously sat forward. He pressed the headphones tightly to his ears, closed his eyes, and took a moment to contemplate the extent of their travels so far.

The trip across the Pacific had been stimulating enough. Without the expert assistance of the veterans aboard, it would have been practically impossible. To Toni, the ten-day time period merely gave him that much longer to become familiar with his station. When they pulled into Posjet themselves, he felt confident and ready for action.

So far, it seemed that everything was working out perfectly. They had penetrated the bay and the commandos they landed there had apparently succeeded in carrying out their mission. Though four brave men never returned, at least the *Dnieper* now had a decent chance of escaping without detection.

The one obstacle that they currently faced was the closed sub net that lay approximately ten thousand feet from their bow. If they had arrived at this point only a few minutes earlier, they could have merely slipped through when the barrier opened to let the sub that was currently passing them go through. With this entry now closed to them, Toni could only pray that the officers gathered behind him at the navigation table would figure out a way to get them to open waters.

"Well, gentlemen, I'm certainly open to any suggestions."

Taking in William Carrigan's grave words were Captain Spencer, Peter Donner, and Stephen Monihan. None of the officers was quick with a response as each of them bent over the chart to further study their current position.

"How did you get out of this damn bay forty-three years ago?" queried Spencer matter-of-factly.

Carrigan answered with a sigh, "We were lucky. When our explosives blew, the Jap crew maintaining the net thought that they were being invaded and ran straight for the hills. As fate would have it, they left the channel wide open."

"Lucky's not the word for it," reflected the young Captain.

Standing beside Spencer, Peter Donner suddenly reached out with his right index finger and traced the line of small x's that indicated the position of the net as it stretched across the channel's mouth. "You know, Skipper, it looks like the deeper water on our starboard extends all the way to that cliff the net is supposedly anchored into. What if we were to smack a couple of torpedoes into that precipice? There's always the chance that the resulting concussion will dislodge the net, and then we're out of here."

Contemplating this idea, Carrigan couldn't help but grin. Seeing that Randall Spencer was doing likewise, the veteran officer responded.

"XO, I think that you're wasting your talents at Norton Academy. You'd still make a damn fine tactician. What do you think, Captain?"

Spencer responded while returning his gaze back to the chart. "I'd say that, right now, we really don't have much choice in the matter. If no one else has a better alternative, let's go for it. But to hit just the right angle to make it work, we're going to need a hell of a fine torpedo shot."

"And I happen to know just the guy to call on for that miracle," offered Carrigan, who met his XO's glance with a wink. "Mr. Donner, I'll give you the honor of briefing Chief Brady on just what we're going to need."

The Kamov Ka-25 Hormone helicopter was a squat, ugly-looking vehicle, yet Alexi Barykino was glad to have its services. It had picked him up soon after his chance meeting with the General Secretary and his staff was concluded.

Designed especially for anti-submarine operations, the chopper was presently hovering above the waters of Posjet Bay, with its chin-mounted surface-search radar and dunking sonar units activated. Since he had gotten the word to the old net keeper to keep the channel sealed, the *Dnieper* would have absolutely no way of escaping them. He relished the moment when the American crew would eventually be forced to surface, at least to charge their batteries. Sooner or later, he would hand those barbarians over to the General Secretary. Of that fact he was certain.

Rubbing his hands together expectantly, he

scanned the horizon. The sun was rapidly rising in the clear blue sky, and it appeared that at least he could count on the weather to cooperate. The flames that had scarred the northern shoreline had finally subsided. Yet thick, black smoke still billowed upwards, a tragic reminder of the night's dastardly raid.

Barykino's stomach knotted as he considered how very close he had come to disrupting the Americans' plans. He was thankful that he had been around to at least inform the Secretary of the ones responsible, and he swore with his life that this time he'd carry out his duty until the very end.

How strange it had been standing there on the gravel driveway, with three of the Rodina's most powerful men gathered before him. Viktor Chernavin had taken him instantly into his trust. As he commanded the Defense Minister and Admiral Tasejevo to offer Barykino any assistance that he might desire, the senior lieutenant had glowed with a feeling of real power. Having previously only seen these illustrious figures far away on a viewing platform or on television, he shivered in awareness of his situation. Now it was solely up to him not to let this illustrious trio down.

The chopper was in the process of dropping a series of sonobuoys in a rough pattern, extending from the harbor area to the sub net, when their sonar operator called out excitedly.

"I've got something, sir! I can't say for certain, but it sounds like a pair of live torpedoes."

This strange report was followed by two sharp detonations. The copilot shouted:

"Over there against the far cliff, on the south side of the channel! There seems to be some sort of landslide."

Following his pointed finger, Barykino caught sight of this phenomenou just as a massive stone wall went crashing down into the surrounding waters of the strait. His face flushed with the realization that this would just about be where the other end of the net would be anchored.

"I've got engine noise!" cried the sensor operator. "They're churning the water something fierce, and headed right toward the southern mouth of the channel!"

Smashing his fist into his thigh, Barykino called out to the pilot. "After them, comrade! We cannot allow these bastards to escape so easily."

The Hormone's dual Glushenkov turboshafts roared in response, and Barykino had to hold onto the bottom of the bench he had been seated on to keep from tumbling over. As the helicopter soared forward, he realized that, if the Americans made it into the open seas, capturing them alive would be extremely difficult. With no other options before him, he decided that now was the time to call out the reinforcements.

CHAPTER EIGHTEEN

At 250 feet beneath the surface, the *Dnieper*'s twin screws bit into the cool waters of the Sea of Japan. Still technically in Soviet-controlled territory, the sub raced eastward at its top submerged speed of twenty-one knots.

Inside the vessel's hull, the forty-eight members of its crew worked together with an unselfish, coordinated effort. Few outsiders would have believed that these men had had barely three weeks training in operating this particular class of submarine. More like seasoned veterans, they manned their stations oblivious to fatigue, and seemingly impervious to their current predicament. With one unified goal in mind, they focused their labor solely on attaining the safety of the open seas.

Unknown to the crew of the *Dnieper* was the fact that the Soviet Krivak-class frigate *Ivan Komarov* had been given the task of tracking them down. Scrambled from its berth in Posjet Bay in a matter of minutes, the sleek, gray warship was already streaming through the strait, its four powerful gas turbines punching out a good thirty-two knots of speed.

One of the most heavily armed ships of its type afloat, the *Ivan Komarov* was designed with antisubmarine warfare in mind. To handle this task, it incorporated both hull-mounted and variable-depth sonars. This latter device could be towed from the frigate's stern, and directed into the silent depths where their quarry would most likely be found. Once spotted, the sub could then be dispatched with a variety of weapons, which ranged from torpedoes to depth bombs.

Confident that they had more than enough tools to track the pirated Whiskey-class vessel down, Captain Igor Slatkin sat in his command chair located on the ship's upper bridge. The grizzled, thirty-year naval veteran scanned the advancing seas, all the while explaining his vessel's capabilities to his special guest.

Senior Lieutenant Alexi Barykino had boarded the frigate seconds before the final line was cast off. A personal call from Admiral Tasejevo himself had prepared Captain Slatkin for the Naval Intelligence officer's arrival. With no time to spare, the senior lieutenant had climbed to the bridge as the ship surged from its berth.

Now that Barykino knew exactly what the *Ivan Komarov* was designed to do, he couldn't help but share the Captain's optimism. With their superior speed and sensors, the job of hunting down the *Dnieper* was all but a normal day's work for the

390

two-hundred-and-twenty-man crew.

Barykino took additional strength from knowing that they were no longer confined to merely capturing the outlaw sub. Only a few minutes earlier, as they rounded the cape and entered the Sea of Japan, a call had arrived from Viktor Chernavin. The General Secretary had asked to personally talk with Barykino, and had informed him that, if they couldn't cripple the *Dnieper*, they were to destroy it with no questions asked. They could always rely on naval salvage experts to bring up from the depths the evidence that would shock an entire planet. Barykino had signed off by swearing that he would do everything within his power to avenge the loss of the laser installation. After he heard the Secretary's plea to do just that, the line had gone dead, and Barykino had returned his gaze to the vast sea now before them.

He was just beginning to believe that they faced a seemingly impossible task when the intercom activated. He found himself holding his breath as the calm voice of a lieutenant was heard from the frigate's attack center. His report was brief and to the point. Not only had they located their quarry, but, even as he spoke, the proper firing coordinates were being fed into their weapons systems.

A broad grin creased the Captain's face as he turned toward his guest and commented, "Now you know why they call my ship the wolf of the sea. If it's blood that you want, you've come to the right vessel. Let's hit them with a salvo of depth bombs to put the so-called fear of God in them."

Slatkin was actually laughing as he reached over

to the intercom and informed the fire-control officer of his decision.

Peter Lowell had been in the sub's cramped head, busily trying to scrub the caked mud from his hands and face, when the first blasts rocked the *Dnieper*. They were loud, bass, crackling affairs that shook their hull and caused dried flakes of paint to fall from the ceiling. Hanging onto the metal washbasin to keep his balance, the Caltech grad realized the precariousness of his position.

Men had died so that he and the girl named Tanya could make it to this supposedly safe haven. Though Lieutenant Paterson, his Sioux point man, and the big Russian had never returned to the rendezvous point after making good the diversionary efforts, his group had managed to make it out of the compound and into the woods. With the bulk of the plastic charges set on timed fuses, they couldn't afford to wait any longer for the others.

The Louisianan known as Gator proved to be a crack shot as he gunned down an entire patrol they had stumbled upon while sprinting for the outer security perimeter. But a mine soon afterwards took him down. With no time to mourn, they made it to the stream bed and crawled down its slippery bank. Wizard had just ordered Peter to proceed him into the drainage tunnel when a burst of bullets struck the Annapolis grad full in the back. Even then, he managed to turn around and hold off the approaching Russians while the civilian made good his escape.

Outside the fence, Peter linked up with the girl. As they began sprinting for the shoreline the first charges detonated at the facility. By the grace of God, they eventually made it to the raft and, with the horizon painted in flames, into the hold of the *Dnieper*. After all that, to die in the depths of the sea seemed like the ultimate travesty.

Not known for his bravado, Peter nevertheless derived inspiration from the manner in which the men of SEAL team Alpha met their deaths. Noble, proud, and brave to the end, they gave their lives unselfishly, for a purpose. The scientist could only learn from their example and, like them, prepare himself to meet his Maker with dignity.

When another series of deafening blasts rang out, he decided that it was time to try to get to the control room. At least he'd have a better idea of just what they were up against up there.

The deck beneath him was quivering as he ducked into the wardroom. He passed the Captain's cabin where Tanya lay inside. Thankful that they had talked her into taking a mild sedative, he continued down the narrow passageway as the lights suddenly flickered, then failed altogether. Fear overtook him and he groped madly about in the darkness. Cold metal pipes met his blind grasp and one of these seemed to be coated with water. He could only imagine the horrible way they would die if the hull split open. Then he jumped when the auxiliary lighting system took over. Peter sighed in relief, and practically ran the rest of the way into the control room.

He found the scene waiting for him there no

393

better. With the deck littered with fallen debris, a group of soaked men could be seen perched above the helm, in the process of attempting to halt a jet of water spurting from a cracked nozzle. Anxiously watching their progress were William Carrigan, Peter Donner, and Captain Spencer.

There was another thunderous explosion, which sent Lowell reeling into the periscope well. Taking the brunt of this collision with his right shoulder, the young scientist's body trembled in fear and pain. As the rumbling aftershocks faded, a soothing, familiar voice spoke up for all present to hear.

"Right now, panic is still our worst enemy," cautioned William Carrigan firmly. "Don't forget that there are several of us here that have been through such a depth-charge attack before. You'd be amazed at the amount of punishment one of these little ladies can take. So stay alert, and keep at your stations. And if God is still with us, we'll see our way out of this mess yet."

This advice provided only temporary relief. Almost at once the seaman assigned to the sound-powered telephone somberly added, "Sir, we have leakage in both the engine room and the torpedo compartment!"

Peter watched Carrigan take this news with a grimace. His boss looked upward and seemed to be imploring the heavens for divine intervention, when the room filled with the spinning hiss of their pursuer's propellers and the distinctive metallic tone of their active sonar.

"Sonar contact dead ahead of us, Captain!"

The weapons officer's spirited observation caused

Alexi Barykino and Igor Slatkin to hurriedly divert their glances to the waters directly in front of the *Ivan Komarov*'s knife-like bow. Though no vessel was visible there, both men knew that a mere hundred or so meters of water lay between themselves and their quarry.

With assured confidence, the frigate's Captain addressed his guest. "Well, lieutenant, since our little depth-bomb greeting failed to convince the Imperialists to surface, shall we quit playing around and finish them off once and for all?"

Realizing that the crew of the *Dnieper* had had their fair chance of surrendering, Barykino nodded. "You may go ahead and do whatever you feel is necessary to immediately stop them, Captain."

Slatkin grinned and turned to pick up the intercom. "Comrade weapons officer, you may initiate the targeting of our forward SS-N-14 battery. And for the sake of the Rodina, make your aim true!"

The mood inside the *Dnieper*'s control room was a tense one, as its three senior officers gathered behind the sonar console. Though the depth-charging had temporarily halted, their sensors hinted that the enemy was still dangerously close.

Only minutes ago the sound of the frigate's propellers had abruptly halted. This was most likely to allow their sonar an undisturbed scan of the waters below. Since the *Dnieper* didn't dare trigger its own active sonar to pin the warship down, they were relying solely on the boat's passive system to give them any hint of the enemy's location.

Seated at the sonar console was senior technician Toni Mariani. Well aware of the trio of concerned officers who stood behind him, he readjusted his headphones and turned up the passive array's volume gain another full notch. He scanned the seas directly before them, and a sudden burst of throaty noise sounded. Quickly triangulating its source, he turned to inform the Captain.

"Sir, I believe I've reestablished contact! Bearing is dead ahead, with a range of thirty-five hundred yards."

Carrigan was the first to respond. "That's them, all right. Chances are they're just itching to initiate their final attack. If they hit us with a bevy of homing torpedoes, there's no way we can escape at this angle."

"I don't know about that, Skipper," interrupted Peter Donner. "Do you remember old Red Coe and the *Skipjack*? If you ask me, this would be the perfect time for a down-the-throat shot."

Absorbing this idea, Carrigan responded thoughtfully, "Damn it, Peter, you just might be on to something. Get on the horn and let Mac know that we're going to be needing another miracle from him and his boys."

Not certain what they were talking about, Randall Spencer spoke up. "You don't really think that we have a chance in hell to take that frigate out?"

"You better hope that the odds are better than that, Captain," retorted Carrigan. "If Lieutenant Commander Red Coe could do it back in '42, there's no reason that we can't pull it off today. So if you want to at least go down fighting, let's go calculate us a decent gyro angle."

The young officer could only shrug his shoulders, and follow the veteran over to the periscope well.

Senior Lieutenant Alexi Barykino stood on the frigate's exposed bridge, scanning the advancing waters with a pair of powerful binoculars. From the hushed conversation going on behind him, he knew that they were only seconds away from releasing their battery of SS-N-14 homing torpedoes. Once these potent weapons hit the water, the *Dnieper* would be doomed.

Though he certainly would have preferred to take the Americans alive, this was the next-best thing. At the very least the ones responsible would not escape unpunished.

Barykino stirred, anxious for the attack to begin. Once the first debris floated to the surface, he could finally initiate that call to Viktor Chernavin. Certainly there would be a promotion in store for him. Why, he could even very well find himself transferred to the General Staff in Moscow.

Gloating with this thought, the Naval Intelligence officer almost missed the strange pair of tight, spiraling tracks suddenly visible in the clear water several hundred meters from the *Ivan Komarov*'s bow. Pure horror registered in his consciousness upon identifying this alien wake as belonging to a torpedo! His throat instinctively constricted, and it seemed to take forever to call out in warning. Yet he could have saved his last breath, for a second later, the prow of the frigate buckled under the force of a pair of resounding explosions. This was followed by a single, deafening blast as the warship's forward ammunition magazine ignited. As a result, not a single member of the frigate's two-hundred-and-twenty-man crew survived.

At a distance of 1,500 yards, the sound of the warship breaking up could be clearly heard by all those on board the *Dnieper*. This was especially the case with Toni Mariani, whose sensitive hydrophones picked up not only the noise of renting steel, but also the pitiful screams of those unfortunate Soviet sailors still trapped inside the doomed vessel.

Though all present in the control room felt relief, there was no outward show of emotion. They would hold off their celebration until reaching the open waters of the Pacific. With this immediate destination in mind, they proceeded to the northeast with every knot of available speed that their straining engines could muster.

CHAPTER NINETEEN

The sun had risen high over the waters of the bay. It was turning out to be a pleasant, spotlessly clear winter's morning, with just a teasing hint of spring in the air. From his vantage point in the command center of Posjet's naval base, Viktor Chernavin stood on an exposed balcony, staring out at the calm waters, with a face etched with stunned disbelief. Numb to the effects of the sun, he shivered with a chilling dread produced by both frustrated anger and the fear of total failure.

Not only had he just learned that the laser battle station was a complete loss, with over 40 men dead and 100 wounded. Minutes ago the *Ivan Komarov* had been blown apart as well. Preliminary reports showed few signs of the 220 brave sailors who'd once manned this warship. Included among the missing was Senior Lieutenant Alexi Barykino.

Chernavin sighed heavily at the irony of it all. Only hours before, how very confident he had been. This feeling of self-assurance had been equally shared by the members of his staff. They had already taken it for granted that the laser facility would pass its final and most demanding test. Looking way beyond, they were already planning what the planet would be like once their preemptive nuclear strike had eliminated the power of capitalism once and for all.

As it looked now, the Rodina wouldn't be able to come up with any concrete evidence linking the raid on the laser installation with the Americans. Such proof was of vital importance if they were to salvage some sort of propaganda victory from this tragic turn of events.

Angrily pounding his fist into the balcony's wooden railing, Chernavin cursed his impotence. Here he was, the leader of the world's most powerful nation, and he still couldn't even track down a single, thirty-year-old, diesel-electric submarine. With the billions of rubles the Navy annually drained from the budget, surely such a minor task was not too much to ask for. With his blood pressure rising to dangerously high levels, the General Secretary had decided to vent his anger on his staff when both Marshal Kudikov and Admiral Tasejevo ducked outside to join him.

Quick to note their leader's sour mood, the Defense Minister wasted no time. "All is not yet lost, Comrade General Secretary. We believe we have an excellent idea just where the malefactors are headed. To intercept them, Admiral Tasejevo here has already called in every available submarine in the area. Leading this armada into battle is the Rodina's latest attack vessel, the *Baikal*. Thus we shall yet have the heads of the monsters responsible for this debacle."

Temporarily placated by this revelation, Chernavin nodded. "Very well, marshal. But you must be absolutely certain to keep on top of this operation every second. I want constant updates!"

"Of course, sir," returned the Defense Minister with a click of his heels.

Afraid that he might still lose his temper, Chernavin abruptly turned away from the two officers. He walked back to the railing, and did his best to calm himself by taking in a series of deep, full breaths. It was only then that he noticed that the air was warm and sweet with the scent of the surrounding pine forest.

Diverting his gaze to the solid wall of trees that hugged the shoreline, Chernavin found it hard to believe that only a few precious weeks ago, his mood had been vastly different. How very happy he had been at that time, innocently wandering the birch forest that surrounded his beloved dacha at Voronkl. Could he ever forget how thrilled he had been when he chanced upon the carcass of that freshly killed deer and, seconds later, actually encountered the predator that had taken the buck down?

The great mystery that the wolf had communicated to him at that moment had given him the inner strength to make the most difficult decision of his long, arduous life. Yet today, this most primal of natural laws had somehow worked against him. Lulled into over-confident complacency, the Rodina had been beaten to the punch by an adversary that now demanded new respect. For at long last the United States of America had awakened and dared to take the initiative.

Without their laser battle station to protect them, the Rodina would be forced to cancel any upcoming plans for a preemptive strike. To do otherwise would be national suicide. Locked in their stalemate of arms again, the two superpowers would continue to waste their resources, with each side's military strength growing to the point of ridiculousness.

The mere thought of such a world depressed Chernavin, who had been so close to cutting the Motherland free. Yet if the fates still willed it, they still had one last chance to sway the world's opinion to their side. If the *Dnieper* could be stopped, the entire planet would soon know that the so-called peace-loving peoples of the United States were nothing but bloodthirsty wolves masked in sheep's clothing.

Having been in the Navy for the last twenty-three years, the captain of the Akula class attack sub *Baikal* had long ago learned never to question the fickle ways of Command. Too many times he had received orders that were completely absurd. Yet each time he challenged them, the results had been the same—a black mark on his permanent service record and strict orders to carry out his directives just as initially instructed.

In the Soviet Navy, any initiative on the part of its officers was not the least bit desired. One went about blindly obeying one's superiors, or risked spending a lifetime locked away in a Siberian Gulag. The Captain knew that such horror stories were true, and had long since lost any desire on his part to buck the system. Yet he had to admit that this morning's puzzling emergency orders had driven him to the very limit of his patience.

They had arrived in Posjet anxious to get on with the ceremonial rubbish that Command had in mind, and then be off to Vladivostok. Sixty days at sea was enough to ask of any man. This was particularly true when the very nature of their duty hadn't sent them to the surface at all in two months.

The *Baikal* had just ascended and was in the process of approaching the small naval base that hugged the bay when they first spotted the smoke. It poured from the woods to the south of the base, as though a major fire had only recently taken place there. Anxious to learn the exact nature of this blaze, the captain began initiating the final berthing procedures, only to have new orders arrive from Command.

Without any explanation offered, the *Baikal* was directed to return to the Sea of Japan with all due haste. There they were to head towards the northern transit lane and, using every means available, track down and destroy the Whiskey class-vessel *Dnieper*.

When the Captain asked for a clarification of the last portion of this directive, it was repeated from the lips of Admiral Tasejevo himself. Without further ado, the Captain copied the receipt of the signal, and sent his men scurrying to their action stations.

With the throttle wide open, the *Baikal* surged back out of the bay and through the straits that protected it. Powered by a pair of massive nuclear reactors, by the time they turned northwards and hit open waters they were doing a good forty knots.

While pacing the spacious deck of the attack center, the Captain informed the sonar operators of the vessel they sought. Both men nodded and addressed their computer keyboards with a frenzy of hand movement. Before sharing the exact nature of their assignment with his senior lieutenant, the Captain did his best to come up with some rational reason behind Command's shocking request. For how often did he get the orders to sink his fellow countrymen?

He squeezed his eyes shut and did his best to remember just what he knew about the *Dnieper*'s current complement. The only officer that he really was familiar with was its captain, Dmitri Zinyagin. The two had known each other for the past five years, and had shared many a drink together at the Red Pelican. If he remembered correctly, only last fall Dmitri had griped to him about his Zampolit. Political officers were people every Soviet line commander had to learn to live with, and he had urged Zinyagin to be patient. Perhaps the two had finally gone after one another. But was this a reason to hunt them down like the enemy?

Could there have been a mutiny? He remembered their last encounter with the *Dnieper*, several weeks before. Their sonar had picked up the Whiskey-class vessel as it cruised out of the water of Juan de Fuca. Because they were leaving their patrol station a good fourteen days earlier than expected, the Captain had thought that they must have encountered some sort of technical difficulties that were sending them homeward. Since contacting them on the radio was forbidden, he had only been able to log the incident and silently wish his comrades a safe voyage.

Perhaps that was when the mutiny took place. That could explain why they had left before scheduled. Hoping to find Posjet a safe haven, the mutineers must have quickly worn out their welcome. And now the *Baikal* had been called in to eliminate them. Yet did this warrant putting a torpedo into their side?

Soviet justice was swift and final. Since the *Baikal* was merely an arm of this sword, he would do as ordered. Surely Command had to be well aware of the facts involved. He just wished that they would have been a little more open with him. Suddenly the senior sonar operator called to him calmly.

"Sir, our sensors have made contact with the *Dnieper*, on bearing zero-four-zero. Range is approximately sixty kilometers, yet we're quickly closing the gap."

The captain knew that this just about put the *Dnieper* within the range of their SS-N-16, an extremely potent ASW system that incorporated a homing torpedo slung beneath an air-launched missile. He knew he'd have to instruct the senior lieutenant to program the distinctive acoustic signature of their bogey into the torpedo's search system. The

Captain crossed the deck to approach him at the fire-control station.

As he scanned the waters directly behind the *Dnieper*, Toni Mariani picked up the swirling wash of an oncoming submarine. Though it was still a good distance away, the sonar operator could tell from this signature that the vessel was putting out an incredible amount of forward speed. Before informing the Captain, he hastily performed a 360-degree search of the seas around them, to be certain that this contact was the only one that they would have to contend with. Sure enough, their forward hydrophones had also triggered. Yet this signature was substantially fainter, reminding the alert technician of the footprint left by a slower-moving, diesel-electric submarine. After getting a preliminary bearing on both these bogeys, he turned to relay the information.

"Sonar has two underwater contacts to report!"

This revelation caused three officers to immediately gather behind the seated New Yorker. Captain Spencer, William Carrigan, and Peter Donner all looked on with concern as Mariani continued.

"We seem to be sandwiched in between them, sir. The clearest signal is coming from that contact approaching in our wake. Even though it's at the maximum range, this one's coming in with a bone in its teeth and has to be a nuke running at full power. Bogey number two lies directly ahead of us on bearing two-two-zero. Its signature is less distinct, and most probably belongs to another diesel boat."

"So it's the old squeeze play," reflected Donner thoughtfully.

Randall Spencer looked to William Carrigan. "Well, what do you think, Commander? Should we attempt engaging them?"

Carrigan shook his head. "If that sub in our baffles is indeed a nuke, chances are that she'll be carrying weapons with a far greater attack range than our own. I'm afraid that this time offense just isn't going to work for us."

Stimulated by this thought, the veteran XO responded, "Skipper, do you remember that time in the Bay of Biscay when the Abalone was caught between that pair of U-boats? When you pulled the plug and put us on the bottom, those two kraut subs almost rammed into each other trying to figure out where in the hell we had disappeared to."

Carrigan remembered the incident well, and was quick to see what his XO was getting at. "Mr. Donner, I believe you just gave us a new lease on life. Let's take the *Dnieper* down, deep and fast. Then we'll shut her up the best we can. If we hold our sound integrity, there's still a decent chance that those Russkies will pass us right on by."

Randall Spencer had no objections to this plan, and turned to help carry it out.

The Whiskey-class attack submarine *Pravda* was on the last leg of its final journey. Due to be put into inactive reserve status after thirty-four years of faithful service, the *Pravda* had been on its way to Vladivostok when it got the call to hunt down the *Dnieper*. Taking it for granted that a mutiny had occurred aboard their sister ship, the *Pravda*'s attack staff had gathered in the control room to plan their pursuit.

The boat's Captain had just turned sixty the day before and, like his present command, would be forced to retire from the sea at the conclusion of this patrol. Thus he took this unexpected call to duty as a fitting way to end a career that had spanned four decades. Though he hated to go out attacking one of the Rodina's own submarines, Command must have its reasons. Loyal to the very end, he merely looked at their prey as the enemy.

His face beamed with satisfaction when their sonar operator reported a contact approaching them from the southwest. When it was learned that this vessel's signature exactly matched that of the *Dnieper*'s, he grinned and informed his weapons officer to prepare a pair of homing torpedoes. Designed to be drawn in by the target's acoustic footprint, the torpedoes were launched with a jolting swoosh of compressed air.

All appeared to be going smoothly, until their sonar operator suddenly bent forward to turn up the gain of his hydrophone's volume regulator. Scratching his beard, he turned to address the Captain.

"I don't understand it, sir. They were there right before us only seconds ago. Now there's absolutely nothing!"

Guessing that the mutineers most probably had

headed for the depths to button up in a state of ultra-quiet, the veteran commander was about to order the *Pravda* to follow them down when the sonar technician shouted out, with a tone edged with panic, "I'm picking up a surface disturbance above us, sir! It sounds like some sort of encapsulated torpedo. There's the sound of an active propeller which appears to be homing in on us!"

Cursing in anger, the Captain ordered the *Pravda* into a tight emergency dive. The sub's battered hull-plates groaned in protest, yet she managed to respond to each command that the helm asked of her. The *Pravda* was even beginning to outdistance the weapon when the torpedo surged forward with a sudden burst of speed. This was followed by a reverberating explosion, as its warhead exploded inside the *Pravda*'s engine room. Cracked in half like a split water pipe, the sub drifted down into the black depths, on a final dive into oblivion.

"We got her!" cried the *Baikal*'s excited sonar operator.

Strangely enough, their success caused no shouts of joyous celebration from the crew. Conscious that their SS-N-16 had most likely snuffed out the lives of their own countrymen, the men of the *Baikal* solemnly went about their business.

Noting their seriousness, the Captain felt a bit saddened himself. No matter how misdirected the mutineers might have been, taking their lives in this manner seemed a bit extreme. Couldn't Command have negotiated with them? For, even if they had indeed surrendered to the Americans, all the Imperialists would be getting was a thirty-year-old vessel and a crew of malcontents. Surely there were no state secrets locked within the *Dnieper*'s rusted hull. Yet an example was needed, and fate had provided the *Baikal* to carry out the sentence.

"Sir, there's something over here that I'd like you to listen to."

This unusual request from the senior sonar technician interrupted the Captain's thoughts. He quickly crossed the compartment and clipped on a pair of auxilliary headphones. It took him several seconds to get accustomed to the natural hiss of the sea as amplified by their bow hydrophones. To better aid his concentration, he closed his eyes and focused his attention solely on his hearing. Two distinctly different sounds soon met his ears. The fainter of these signatures seemed to emanate from another submarine. Vibrating up from the waters below them, he picked out the near-silent whirl that would be left in the wake of an escaping diesel-electric boat. Yet his stomach soured upon identifying the louder of the two footprints, for it could only belong to a pair of rapidly approaching acoustic homing torpedoes.

As the Captain frantically relayed a series of emergency escape maneuvers, a single thought crossed his mind. If their SS-N-16 hadn't just taken out the *Dnieper*, then what had it smacked into?

Deep beneath the waters of the Sea of Japan, Toni

Mariani perched before the sonar console, monitoring the Akula-class vessel's desperate dive for cover. The Soviet manned submarine had attempted maneuvers of the most desperate sort, yet still the homing torpedoes remained on their tail. Most happy that their situations weren't reversed, Mariani grimaced when a pair of muffled explosions veiled the sound of this pursuit. As this rumbling detonation faded, a distinctive sound that was getting to be a bit too familiar filtered through the *Dnieper*'s hydrophones. The tearing of steel and the collapse of internal bulkheads indicated that the Akula had shared a fate very similar to that of the Whiskey-class sub that had exploded only a few minutes earlier.

Though they were in the process of hunting the *Dnieper* down, the Soviets who had just lost their lives were still fellow submariners. A bit saddened that it had come down to this, Mariani pushed back his headphones and turned to grimly address the trio of officers who stood behind him.

"They didn't make it."

The technician's curt observation brought a relieved sigh from Peter Donner. "And to think that those two subs bought it without us having to fire a shot."

Randall Spencer wiped off the glistening band of sweat that had gathered on his forehead. "I don't know about you, gentlemen, but I think a little prayer is in order. Then I'll see about charting us the quickest route out of this infernal sea."

Nodding in compliance, William Carrigan lowered

411

his eyes along with his fellow senior officers. His chest was heavy as he thanked the Lord for not only allowing them to succeed, but also for providing the renewed services of such men as Peter Donner, Mac Brady, Stan Lukowski, and Helmut Keller. With equal intensity, he prayed for those departed souls who weren't so fortunate. This included the brave men of SEAL team Alpha.

It was later that afternoon, as the *Dnieper* continued on towards the open waters of the Pacific, that William Carrigan received a visit from the young woman who had arrived alongside Peter Lowell. He was seated in his cabin at the time, busy working on his log, when she entered with a polite knock. This was his first close-up view of the girl, and he couldn't help but be impressed with her innocent beauty and near-perfect English.

"Commander Carrigan, I hope you'll pardon this interruption. I'm Tanya Markova and I wanted to thank you for all that you did back there."

"Nonsense," replied Carrigan as he rose to pull down the "hot-seat" for her. "I'm the one who should be thanking you. Without your help and that of your people, this whole operation wouldn't have been possible."

These words seemed to cause a sad glow to mask her brow. A tear rolled down her cheek and she bravely struggled for control.

"I can imagine how you must feel," observed Carrigan compassionately. "Is this your first time

412

out of the Soviet Union?"

She nodded and Carrigan sat forward, cautious about choosing his words carefully. "Well, you can rest easily knowing that you have a new home if you so desire. I'm certain that the United States of America would be proud to have a fine young woman like yourself as a citizen. Did you leave any family back home?"

Tanya looked up and caught his trusting gaze. "Not really. The only relative that I really cared for was killed back at Posjet."

The mere thought of her uncle caused Tanya to suddenly remember the leather packet that he had given her, right before he left to penetrate the laser facility. Fumbling into the breast pocket of her sweater to make certain it was still there, she gratefully pulled out the hand-sized wallet.

"What have you got there?" asked her dignified host, who had stuck a strange-looking pipe into the corner of his mouth.

She grasped onto the packet as if it were a priceless relic, and bravely answered, "You know, I really don't know what it contains. My uncle gave it to me immediately before he left with your commandos. With all the excitement of our escape and all, I completely forgot that I had it."

"Well, what's stopping you from going on and opening it?" Carrigan urged.

Her uncle had made it a point to make her promise not to peek inside until he returned. Since he would never be doing so, she followed the American's suggestion and dared to open it up.

Inside was a protective plastic folder that held a set of clipped photographs. Her face broke in a fond smile as she flipped through them taking in the jolly furrier, herself as a child, and several views of her dear mother. But as she came to the last photo of the set, her expression turned to puzzlement. This was easily the oldest picture of the series, and showed a strangely familiar young man and woman seated at what the Polynesians would call a luau. Though it was yellow with age, she could see that the woman's blonde features were much like her mother's — or her own, for that matter. It was only as she turned the photograph over and read its caption that she gasped in wonder. It read simply: "Lydia and Commander William Carrigan; Honolulu, Hawaii — July 1945."

Shocked into speechlessness, Tanya turned the picture over and studied the face of the young officer seated at the table. She looked up and shivered in awareness, for an older version of this same man was presently sitting right before her! Tanya's hand was shaking as she handed the photograph to her host.

Carrigan had been aware of the girl's strange behavior as she studied this snapshot, and all too soon found out what was the cause of her astonishment. He gazed at the picture and remembered the exact moment it had been taken, as if it had happened only yesterday. Flushed with astonishment, he managed a single question.

"Who is this woman to you?"

Tanya looked into his eyes as if viewing a ghost.

414

"Why she's my grandmother!"

Instantly aware of the miracle that had brought them together, Carrigan reached out to take Tanya into his arms. The tears were already rolling down his cheeks as he held her close, his heartbeat pulsating madly. For, although his beloved Lydia had never returned to him, the young girl who could very well be his granddaughter had!

The Wingman Series
By Mack Maloney